Psychic Surv
Books O1

BLAKEMORT

THIRTEEN

ROSAMUND

ALSO BY SHANI STRUTHERS

EVE: A PSYCHIC SURVEYS PREQUEL

PSYCHIC SURVEYS BOOK ONE:
THE HAUNTING OF HIGHDOWN HALL

PSYCHIC SURVEYS BOOK TWO:
RISE TO ME

PSYCHIC SURVEYS BOOK THREE:
44 GILMORE STREET

PSYCHIC SURVEYS BOOK FOUR:
OLD CROSS COTTAGE

PSYCHIC SURVEYS BOOK FIVE:
DESCENSION

THIS HAUNTED WORLD BOOK ONE:
THE VENETIAN

THIS HAUNTED WORLD BOOK TWO:
THE ELEVENTH FLOOR

JESSA*MINE*
(JESSAMINE SERIES BOOK ONE)

COMRAICH
(JESSAMINE SERIES BOOK TWO)

Psychic Surveys Companion Novels
Books One, Two And Three

BLAKEMORT

THIRTEEN

ROSAMUND

SHANI STRUTHERS

Psychic Surveys Companion Novels Books One, Two & Three:
Blakemort, Thirteen, Rosamund
Copyright © Shani Struthers 2019

The right of Shani Struthers to be identified as the Author of the work has been asserted by her in accordance with the Copyright, Designs and Patents Act 1988. All rights reserved in all media. No part of this publication may be reproduced, stored in a retrieval system, or transmitted in any form or by any means, electronic, mechanical, recording, photocopying, the Internet or otherwise, without the prior written consent of the copyright holder, nor be otherwise circulated in any form of binding or cover other than that in which it is published and without a similar condition being imposed on the subsequent purchaser.

Storyland Press
www.storylandpress.com

ISBN: 978-1-7943-3913-2

All characters and events featured in this publication are purely fictitious and any resemblance to any person, place, organisation/company, living or dead, is entirely coincidental.

For Misty Struthers, no more waiting.

As much as I love writing, building a relationship with readers is even more exciting! I occasionally send newsletters with details on new releases, special offers and other bits of news relating to the Psychic Surveys series as well as all my other books. If you'd like to subscribe, sign up here!

www.shanistruthers.com

Psychic Surveys Companion Novel
Book One

BLAKEMORT

Prologue

THIS is not really a story about me. It's about the house I lived in as a child. A house that couldn't be called a home – that should *never* have been a home. And yet we lived there for years, my family and I. But we weren't the only ones. There were others that resided alongside us. Unseen but lurking; sometimes in dark corners in the dead of night, sometimes in bright daylight, just out of sight, but present nonetheless, watching, waiting. I used to wonder what they waited for. Did they want me to acknowledge them? Shout at the top of my voice that I knew they were there, that I was aware of them? I remember the first time I did. I was alone in my room, a child of seven – nearly eight, in that way that 'nearly' is so important to the young. I was happy; one of the few times I was in that place. The sun was streaming in through the window despite it being mid-winter and I was playing with my dolls – Barbie (of course) and her many friends (most of whom were Barbie dolls too and therefore identical), driving them around in a pink plastic jeep that I considered the very height of chic. They went under the legs of my desk, fixed grins in place, round the perimeter of my wardrobe, whizzing under the bed to emerge the other side, finally stopping outside their tall pink townhouse – part of the Malibu collection. I was engrossed in my game, a bona fide member of the Barbie gang, when I realised the atmosphere had changed. The sun wasn't as bright anymore. The room wasn't as warm. It was cold and growing colder. I started to shiver, pulled the cardigan I was wearing tightly around me. But it was no use. This wasn't the kind of 'cold' that wool could guard against. This could penetrate fabric and skin, burying itself deep into bones and chilling the marrow. It's the kind that lingers in the memory long after it's gone, that once you've experienced it, you can never forget. It's *preternatural*.

I breathed outwards, certain I'd see plumes of mist appearing in front of me. There was nothing but still I began to shake, my teeth chattering in my head, the sound hurting my brain like a woodpecker in the forest gone crazy.

"You're here again aren't you? I can sense you."

At least one of them: the boy.

"I can feel you. I… I've always been able to do that, ever since I can remember. Who are you?"

Swallowing hard I turned my head from side to side, slowly, a fraction at a time, not wanting to frighten them as much as they were frightening me. I had no one to talk to about this ability of mine. I'd tried to talk to Mum once, to tell her what I'd just told the ghosts – that I could sense them. She hadn't been cross with me, on the contrary. 'Corinna, darling, what an imagination you have!' She was laughing and so I had laughed. Perhaps it was my imagination; usually your mum is right about everything. But I knew. Inside I knew. The world has many layers and there's so much that we can't see. That *I* can't see. But once upon a time I could hear…

Corinna…

It was my name being called – no, not called – *whispered*.

Corinna…

As I stood, the dolls in my hands fell to the floor. They'd seemed so alive minutes before, but now they were dead, like whatever else was in the room.

My breathing was ragged and I tried to calm it, but I was a child, a scared and bewildered child. I didn't yet know the techniques involved in maintaining composure when dealing with the paranormal. That house always had an atmosphere. We moved into it when I was five and, apparently, I'd cried solidly for the first week. I was inconsolable, Mum said, but gradually I grew used to the way it was. And there were moments of peace, when whatever was there retreated into the shadows and left us alone, left me alone. But this wasn't one of them. They were the bold ones, not me. Quickly, I closed my eyes and refused to look, my hands rigid by my side. The boy – if that's who it was – was standing in front of me, staring with fathomless eyes. *Ask again what they want.* That's what I should have done. What I *wished* I'd done. Instead, I started screaming, primal fear taking over – fear of the unknown.

The ghost, the spirit, or whatever you want to call it, responded to that scream. Whether from fear or rage I don't know – it could have been both. A thud forced me to open my eyes. The dolls lying at my feet had been snatched up and thrown across the room. *My poor dolls,* I remember thinking. *My poor, poor dolls!* The bed started to shake too, banging from side to side, making an almighty racket that hurt my ears, and the wardrobe door flew open as if a howling wind had got behind it. But none of it could compare to what happened next. I felt pressure around my neck and hot breath on my face. Even now I don't know how that's possible, how a spirit's breath can be *hot*. Spectral hands began to tighten. So easily they lifted me off my feet.

Stop it! Stop it!

I couldn't speak, but I could think.

Please stop it!

And then rather than hear its reply, I saw it scribed in my mind: *I'll never stop. Never. None of us will.*

I was thrown back, hitting the wall as hard as my dolls had.

The door to my room burst open too.

"Corinna, what's all this noise?"

Mum rushed to my side.

"What are you doing down there, sweetheart? And your dolls, one of their head's been split open. Did you do that?" She looked so confused. "*Why* did you do it?"

Not me. Not me.

I wanted so much to speak, to explain, but shock had rendered me mute.

It was them… him. The boy, I'm sure of it, so full of spite.

This is his story really; his, the house's and the other spirits that the house 'owned'. Because it wouldn't let him go, it wouldn't let any of them go. As the boy retreated, still angry with me for screaming, for making such a fuss, and as the sun dared to shine again, albeit tentatively, I suspected something else: it trapped the living too.

Part One
The First Christmas

Chapter One

THERE are many haunted houses in the world. I know that now. But when I was a child I thought I was the only one to experience such horror, so I kept my mouth shut. No child wants to stand out, not for something as weird as that. We took the house because the rent was cheap. It was also grand. I remember my mother saying that: my *single* mother. She'd split from my dad. It was just my older brother, Mum, and I who moved there.

"Wow, kids! What do you think? It's grand isn't it? Much more than we're used to."

She tossed her hair as she spoke – red like mine – and tried to look happy. I say 'tried' because I knew she was sad inside. I was sensitive to emotions too and the divorce between my parents had been hard on her. He'd fallen in love with another woman, or that's what she told us.

When I asked why, she shrugged and said, 'I don't know, it's what people do I guess. They meet someone else and… they fall in love.' There were tears in her eyes but she didn't let them fall. She just kept on smiling, trying to make an effort, to shield us as much as she could. I couldn't understand it though. How could Dad have done such a thing? Mum – Helena – was beautiful with her red hair, her green eyes, and her laughing mouth. She was the most beautiful thing I'd ever seen. We saw Dad regularly after the divorce; he'd take us out every other weekend, usually on the Saturday. My brother was closer to him than I was. He longed for his visits, used to pace up and down the floor, impatient for Dad to arrive. Me? I preferred being with Mum. The 'escape' from Blakemort was nice though; I couldn't deny that, having an entire day's break from it.

I suppose I'd better start describing the house. First of all, it was bigger than an ordinary house, much bigger. It was also very run down, decrepit even – a crumbling mess. The rent was cheap because it belonged to an artist friend of Mum's called Carol, who'd gone to live and work abroad. They'd only recently got back in touch, talking to each other on the phone every now and again and, hearing of Mum's predicament, she'd quickly made the offer. Mum was a graphic designer and worked from home. She earned good money but Dad contributed too, never missing a payment until I, the youngest child, turned eighteen. As Mum said, 'Falling in love with someone else doesn't make you a bad person.' It didn't. But I still hated the fact he'd hurt her. I also hated that we'd moved because of him – to house-sit effectively, to look after a property that didn't *want* to be looked after. But my family was oblivious to that as we approached, they continued walking, straight into its clutches.

Everything was wrong about Blakemort. It was old. Parts of it dated back to the seventeenth century, apparently. Other parts had been added to it over the years, and not sympathetically. It was a higgledy-piggledy house; a hotchpotch – both such amusing terms. But, as I told you, I wasn't amused that day, I was crying.

"Cry baby, cry baby!" Ethan, my brother, sang, his voice cruel rather than melodic.

"Come on, darling," Mum intervened. "It'll be all right."

If only.

Located a few miles from where we'd lived in Ringmer, Sussex – although to me it might as well have been on another planet – in the village of Whitesmith, the house stood very much on its own, as if it wasn't part of the village at all, but was shunned by it. Much of the grounds were overgrown and there were brambles with sharp thorns everywhere. The house we'd lived in previously – the house my parents' had had to sell – was a modern house, semi-detached with light airy rooms. This house was white, but the paint was patchy, peeling off in so many places – a 'dirty' white you could say. It had a large chimney jutting skywards and a silvered oak door studded with wrought iron furnishings, which looked as if it would creak when you opened it. It was off centre too, that's what struck me. The ivy that grew around it not as green as it should be, but withered looking, as if its life force was being leeched. There was no plaque with Blakemort etched on it. Nowhere did I ever see its name written in black and white. It was just what we'd been told it was called. I've often wondered about that, amongst a host of other things. But then again, I suppose it needed no announcement. Such arrogance suited it.

We didn't go in straight away – a subconscious action perhaps on Mum's part, trying to delay the inevitable. Instead, she led us round to the back of the house, down a side path where more brambles and weeds encroached, making the route difficult. Mum did her best to clear the way, stamping with her feet and creating a trail of sorts. Sullenly, I followed in her wake, my thumb jammed in my mouth to stop myself from crying – a tactic that didn't work. If it was unwelcoming from the front, at the back it was forbidding. There was a rounded bay with three windows on the first floor, the frames of which looked rotten. On the ground floor of the bay were two windows and in-between them – again off centre – a glass-panelled door whose splintered surround was painted black. There and then I resolved never to use that door. I had an instinct it led to places as rotten as its frame. There was another set of windows to the right and then a chimneybreast. Further right of the chimneybreast was what I now know to be an add-on: a building that came towards me – the long part of an L. And above, in the roof, were the eaves windows – three of them. Again they seemed to be less than uniformly placed, blackened glass hiding an even blacker interior. Staring at them, I wanted so badly to turn and run, to return to the house that we'd left, to the life that had left us, but all I could do was cry.

"Oh, come on." Mum swept me into her arms. "It could do with some fresh paint I admit, perhaps a few window frames replaced but Carol said it's really quite comfortable inside. And it's big, so big. When it's raining it doesn't matter. There'll be plenty of room for you and Ethan to play. You can even scooter inside!"

None of which consoled me.

"Just leave her, Mum, she's stupid."

"Ethan! That's enough. I've told you before, don't be rude to your sister."

"I wouldn't if she wasn't so stupid."

Back then my brother was always mean to me. When we moved, he was eight to my five and he was surly, even more so than in later teenage years. Of course I now realise that it was mainly due to the separation of our parents. Unlike Mum and me he had dark hair – just like Dad's – and similar features too. We were like clones of our parents, right down to the bickering.

I clung even tighter.

"Don't want to go in there."

"We have to," Mum cajoled.

"No!"

"Come on—"

"Bad place."

"It's not bad, it's just… in need of a bit of love, that's all."

Love? Like it would know what to do with love!

"Bad place," I repeated. "Don't want it!"

"Darling, we have no choice."

Mum's voice was sweet but sadness had crept in; a resignation. Miserable, I started sucking my thumb again. I knew we had no choice.

It began to drizzle so we returned to the front. The removal van was due to arrive soon but we'd brought some stuff in the Volvo Mum used to drive, a few small boxes containing essentials, and she suggested we start ferrying them into the house.

"We can explore too, before they get here. Won't that be fun? A real adventure."

She tried so hard to keep positive.

As we walked, I looked over her shoulder. A part of me said not to, to bury my face instead. I always knew, you see, when a spirit was close by. I'm a 'sensitive'. That's the term for someone like me – who can sense a spirit, but can't always see them. But that day I did see someone, standing in the garden beyond, through the trees and the hedges, most of them winter bare. It was just a fleeting glimpse, one that most people would dismiss, but not me. It was a man, not a child, although, as you know by now, there are children here. He was tall and dressed in dark clothing – as unwelcoming as the house. He had a sneer on his face, I was sure of it, and an expression in his eyes I don't want to think about – even now.

Tears – yet more of them – rolled down my cheeks. As Mum opened the car boot the rain became heavier, as if the weather was mourning alongside me.

The date was December 2nd 1999. December was always a bad month in that house – when most things happened, when the *worst* thing happened. But that would be in years to come. We lived there until 2003. We couldn't stay for 2004. Even Mum agreed with that, no matter how low the rent. Even so, I had years to endure; years that are burnt into my memory. I'm twenty-two now (no 'almost' about it) and I've told this story to no one, not even my closest friends, Ruby, Theo and Ness. They know nothing about Blakemort, let alone my experiences there and how receptive I was during that time. But now… now I have to say something, on paper at least. There's an urge to get it straight in my head – all that happened.

It's fair to say that when you have a psychic ability, demons can haunt you. They're attracted to you *because* of that ability and it's hard to persuade them to let go, in some cases nigh on impossible. In many ways, that house is my demon. Although I left it just before I was ten, like so many others, I'm still there. I keep laughing, keep smiling, following the advice of my mother, but it's becoming harder.

That house… that damned house. Will it ever stop haunting me?

Chapter Two

DESPITE Carol having departed only two weeks before, the house had a musty smell to it. Whilst not a stench, it was obtrusive, growing stronger as you climbed upwards. But first, the downstairs – Mum said, 'Let's explore' and so we did.

From the car I'd retrieved a bag of teddies that I usually slept with – three of them in total, each one the equivalent of a comfort blanket. I clutched that bag to my chest, needing all the comfort I could get. Mum inserted the key Carol had sent her into the front door, wiggled it slightly, and pushed it open – rather than a creak, it seemed to groan. Immediately inside was a lobby, meant for muddy boots and hanging coats. Beyond that was the hall, which seemed vast to me, like a cavern, although you must remember that at the time I was small. It was also empty – just a wooden chair placed forlornly in one corner and a side table on which sat an earthenware jug, a few sprigs of crumbling dried lavender placed within it. A chandelier hung from the beamed ceiling – not a twinkly one made from glass, this was blackened iron, hard and unyielding. The walls were panelled in a dark hardwood and beneath me, the floorboards were dark too, almost black. I took it all in, whilst trying to stop from shaking. Mum was right about one thing: you could scooter in there easily enough.

"Come on, there's a parlour to our left," Mum enthused.

"A parlour, what's that?" asked Ethan.

"A kind of reception room," Mum answered, "where you greet guests."

"Are we going to have guests?"

"I hope so, Ethan. We're a little out in the sticks, but you never know."

There was a pair of heavy green silk curtains at the window in the parlour, which rustled slightly as we entered and another empty sideboard. A painting on the wall of rolling hills caught in the moonlight should have been pleasant but instead it was eerie, and also slightly crooked. Mum noticed too and went to straighten it but when we left the room, I looked back – it was crooked again. To the right of the lobby was a similar sized room – 'the morning room' Mum announced, giggling.

More wooden beams weighed heavily over us in the drawing room but at least it had a decent amount of furniture, including two big squashy sofas, their red material more of a faded pink and an even more washed-out rug lying in-between them. The dining room was also furnished with a long refectory table, gnarled in several places, and six chairs. To the back of the house was the music room. This was the room with the bay windows and *that* door, the one with the black surround.

Ethan started complaining because it had no instruments in it.

"Where are the guitars?"

"Guitars?" Mum answered good-naturedly enough. "It would have had a piano in it, Ethan, not guitars. Maybe we ought to get one, it'd be fun to have singsongs in here wouldn't it, like they did in the old days. Can you imagine…?"

As she said it, her voice trailed off. I noticed she wasn't laughing, giggling, or smiling – she actually seemed uneasy. Could it be that like me she realised the music room was not meant for lingering in, for having a 'singsong'? It was a gathering place certainly, but not for the likes of us.

Almost pushing my brother and me out of there, we entered the kitchen instead – located in the long stem of the L. Not small and cosy, it was large, industrial even, with orange, brown, and cream lino covering the floor in a busy pattern that hurt your eyes. The cupboards consisted of yet more dark wood and the cream worktop had significantly yellowed in places. Looking around, Mum had her 'happy' face back on.

"Isn't it wonderful?" she declared. "Look how many windows there are! On sunny days it'll be a joy to have breakfast in here."

Ethan muttered something vaguely supportive, whilst I clutched my teddies harder. I couldn't forget the music room and how all eyes – no matter that they were unseen – had been trained on me, sensing the one that could sense them. As for the windows in the kitchen, they looked out onto the garden – not a sight I wanted to see again, especially if that man was still present. I imagined him drifting closer on silent feet, peering in through the glass, the look in his eyes intensifying. I yelped.

"What is it, darling, are you all right?"

Before I could answer, my brother pushed past me and

almost knocked me off my feet. Mum steadied me then followed after him, calling for me to follow. It was time to venture upstairs. Back in the hall, we started climbing, Mum and Ethan clinging to the bannister. I couldn't because of my teddies, but I didn't want to touch it anyway or think about who'd run their hands up and down it previously.

As I've said, the musty smell was stronger upstairs. Even now, after so many years away, I can smell it. In the lonely reaches of the night when sleep plays hard to get, it drifts towards me, finds its way in, and settles alongside the coldness.

There were five bedrooms in total on the first floor, and my brother darted in and out of each one, wanting to lay claim to the best, although Mum just laughed and told him she was the one entitled to the best. Surprisingly, most of the bedrooms were actually quite small, not grand at all, with beds in only three of them and random items of furniture stored in the other two. Apparently Carol had lived there on her own, as she wasn't married and had no children. Being alone in that house is a thought I find abhorrent – to be the only living person. As we edged towards the room above the music room – the master bedroom – I continued to drag my feet.

Don't want that room! Don't want that room!

I didn't want to go anywhere near it. The atmosphere was heavier on the approach, like wading through treacle.

"This is my room!" Mum declared and I wilted. Sometimes I would wake in the night and when I did, I'd creep in with her and Dad – lately with just her of course – but I wouldn't be able to do that anymore. The floor between rooms was no barrier to what was downstairs – they'd drift upwards easily enough and tower over me whilst I slept; so many of them, far too many. Oh, the tears! They were drowning me.

Mum noticed me loitering in the doorway.

"Come on, come in!"

I stood perfectly still.

"Come on," she said again.

Ethan, who was at the window, turned his head and sneered – I imagined the look on his face to be the same as that of the man in the garden.

I was about to shake my head and tell her no, when I felt a hand at the base of my spine. I tensed, knew to brace myself but it was no use. The hand drew back and then slammed into me with such force that I flew forwards, landing heavily on my knees, the threadbare carpet offering no cushion at all and my bag flying.

"Oh, darling, did you trip?" Mum was beside me in an instant.

"I was pushed!" I wailed.

"Don't be silly, Ethan's nowhere near you."

"Not by Ethan!"

Mum set me on my feet again and gathered my teddies. "Perhaps you tripped over those laces of yours, are they undone?"

She asked the question but didn't bother to check, she just hugged me to her. Behind me, I could hear a faint trace of laughter.

"Let's choose your room!" Mum suggested. It was a mercy to be led away from hers, albeit a small one. "Which one of those that we've seen do you like?"

Ethan had already chosen the one nearest to Mum's but that was all right, I didn't want it anyway. I think Mum was surprised when I chose the furthest.

"I'm not sure," she said, looking around. It was also small, perhaps the smallest of the five. A frown marred her pretty features, "I think you should be closer to me."

"I want this one!"

"But—"

"Please." There was no mistaking the desperation in my voice.

She looked at me, scrutinised me even. After a moment she bent down so that we were eye-level. Placing her hands on my cheeks, her thumbs drying my tears, she said, "We'll be happy here, I promise. I'll do my level best to ensure that we are."

I didn't know what the word 'ensure' meant then or what 'level best' was but I got the gist regardless – she was saying we'd be okay, that I wasn't to be upset. But she was wrong, so very wrong. And my room, whilst not as bad as hers, was still alive. All the rooms were, as was the house itself.

It lived alongside the dead.

Chapter Three

WE didn't have time to go to the attic as the removal van pulled up, the driver honking the horn to indicate his arrival.

"Never mind," said Mum, "Carol said not to bother anyway, it's only used for storage, it's not habitable or anything. Perhaps we shouldn't go poking around in her belongings anyway. It doesn't seem right somehow."

Remembering how black the eaves windows had appeared from the back of the house, how secretive, I was glad as I was honestly not sure how much more I could bear.

Mum was occupied with directing the men to put what furniture where. Ethan had grabbed his scooter and was getting in everyone's way as they trudged to and fro, Mum shouting at him on several occasions to stop what he was doing and help – not that he did of course. I tried to keep close to Mum but she got irritated with me too and sat me on one of the sofas in the drawing room, telling me in her stern voice to stay put. I drew my legs up and huddled into the corner, doing my utmost not to notice that there was a depression in the cushion to the right of me. Instead I buried my face in my teddies, breathed in their familiar smell, and closed my eyes.

How long I sat like that I don't know but there came a cry from one of the removal men followed by a rush of expletives – or 'bad words' as I used to call them back then. I opened my eyes and listened as Mum's voice added to the mix, asking the man over and over again if he was all right and apologising profusely. I'd been told to stay put but I couldn't. A naturally inquisitive child, I had to go and see what was happening. The man – Mum called him Greg – was lying in a heap at the bottom of the staircase, clutching his ankle.

"Who left that bloody toy on the stair? It wasn't there when I went up!"

It was one of my dolls.

"Oh, dear, oh, dear," Mum was bending down, trying to tend to his ankle, but he wouldn't let her touch it. "It must have fallen out of one of the boxes." She then corrected herself. "I don't see how though, they're all sealed with parcel tape."

"Your kid must have dropped it!"

Mum bristled. "My kid, as you call her, is in the drawing room."

"Your other kid then!"

"It's a doll. My other 'kid' doesn't play with dolls."

"No, he's on the bleedin' scooter, getting in our way!"

Another man appeared on the scene and interrupted. "Come on, Greg, get over it, you've not broken anything. We've got to get on, we've got another job to get to."

The other man helped Greg up whilst Mum stood by, her lips clamped together to prevent her from saying anything more. When they moved away she darted forward and grabbed the doll, holding it in her hands and staring at it, clearly confused as to how it got there. It was Annie – a rag doll, and I'd seen Mum pack her away, stored for the journey right at the bottom of one of those boxes. As I stared I thought I could hear laughter again, an echo of it, but it held no humour, quite the opposite.

I remained standing in the doorway. Mum was distracted so she didn't notice me anyway but I felt safer there, away from that sofa and whoever it was sitting beside me. When everything was in and placed in the right rooms, Mum settled the bill with the removal men. They almost snatched the money out of her hand, hurrying from the house as fast as they could, Greg the only one to look back over his shoulder, his complexion much greyer than when he'd entered the house.

Later that evening, Mum cooked dinner for us and then complained when I wouldn't eat, but only half-heartedly, being too exhausted to insist otherwise. Instead, she cleared the plates and suggested we all get ready for bed, asking me and Ethan if we'd like to sleep in with her – 'a first night treat', she described it. 'All of us together.' Ethan promptly said no and disappeared to his own room and I just started crying again. The thought of being alone in any room in that house was awful but worse still was being in her room, even if she was sleeping right beside me.

Having helped me to wash and change into my pyjamas she took me to my room, not quite believing that I too had refused her. I never had before. I begged her to stay with me until I fell asleep and she agreed – lying beside me and stroking my hair. I think she was humming a tune as well, a Christmas hymn. For some reason it annoyed me, but only vaguely. Like her I was too tired to care that much.

Even so, oblivion took a long while to come simply because I was trying to force it, but the next thing I remember was waking with bright sunlight filtering in through the flimsy curtains that fluttered at the window despite none being open. I'd made it to morning! A tiny glimmer of hope began to build as I sat and looked around. The only things in my room were the things that were supposed to be there: my dolls, my dolls' house, my teddies, my clothes, a chest of drawers, a wardrobe, a desk, the bed and me. I was so grateful for that fact I started smiling – a big grin spreading across my face. Of course, being older and wiser, I know that it takes an enormous amount of energy for spirits to do what they'd done the day we moved in – manifest in the garden, push me in the back, make a doll materialise from out of nowhere, whisper and laugh. Inbetween they'd need to rest, recuperate. That's regarding the spirits. Regarding the house, it was a different beast entirely. It was constant, ever watchful. It watched me as I grinned in relief and so my grin quickly faded. That house – it *despised* us. So vividly that word formed in my mind.

"Mum," I asked a few hours later as we were unpacking stuff from boxes, trying to find a space for everything, with only Mum venturing into the music room to position a vase here or an occasional table there, "what does despise mean?"

She stopped unwrapping what was in her hands – another vase I think – and looked at me with something akin to horror. "Despise? That's a horrible word, where did you learn that?" Before I could answer, her nostrils started flaring and her lips pursed. "It's Ethan isn't it? Honestly, that boy, wait 'til I get hold of him."

She placed the vase back on the floor, stood up, and

started shouting his name. Immediately I jumped up and tugged at her skirt.

"It's not him, Mum. I just… know it."

She turned her head sideways to look at me. "How do you just know it?"

I shrugged.

She seemed to consider my words and then knelt again, resumed what she'd been doing. "Like I said, it's a horrible word, mean and nasty."

"But what does it mean?" I asked again, refusing to give up.

"It's… well, it's the opposite of love."

"Hate?"

Mum didn't answer; she just nodded her head.

Having had confirmation, I realised it was no real surprise. I'd gathered as much.

* * *

There are so many incidents similar to those I've described that happened at the house; toys that went missing, only to turn up somewhere else, snippets of voices talking that weren't ours, glimpses of those that hovered near. There was a lot of bad luck too. The vase Mum had placed in the music room was one of her favourites, yet one morning she came down to find it lying on the floor, smashed to pieces. Little things also counted, food got burnt easily, the heating behaved erratically – it was either too high, roasting us, or refusing to come on at all. The hot water would run cold, despite the immersion being switched on hours beforehand. Mum grew more and more frustrated, kept muttering that 'no wonder the rent was cheap, nothing bloody works' but not once did she acknowledge any reason for it other than a mechanical one – and how could I tell her differently? I didn't have the words to explain at that age, and secondly, she'd never have believed me – she didn't *want* to believe.

Yes, there were many things but I can only tell so much. In fact, some things I've forgotten, they only come to mind when I strain to recall. It's amazing how blasé you become, how you adapt. But, of course, there's stuff you can't forget, that's too big to forget, and I'll focus on that. I've already said that the worst times in that house were around Christmas. Such a joyful time of year normally, a time when children grow so excited and we were no exception. That first Christmas, the last of the millennium, only twenty-three days from the day we moved in was one we were looking forward to, despite what had happened to us as a family. Deep down all I wanted was my old life back in the house in Ringmer with Mum and Dad, but I longed for more dolls too, more furniture for my dolls' house, a brand new bike. Ethan wanted a skateboard; he felt he was getting too old for a scooter. He also wanted Dad to join us and asked him to do just that. He didn't but someone else did, another 'inhabitant' that stepped forward from the shadows and picked on me as a conduit.

Chapter Four

BEFORE our first Christmas at Blakemort, I should mention the attic. Like two of the bedrooms, Mum said that Carol used the room on the third floor solely for storage and not to bother going up there, that it was most probably locked. Ethan being Ethan, however, was bored one afternoon and, when Mum was working – she'd set up office in the morning room – he grabbed my hand and dragged me up the stairs.

"Where are we going?" I asked.

"To the attic."

"No, I don't want to!" I protested, happy to take Mum's advice.

"You're such a wuss."

"I am not!"

"You are!"

"No!"

"Then come and explore with me. Don't you ever wonder what's above us when you lie in bed at night? Can't you hear the noises sometimes, like footsteps running up and down, the scratching too, as if something's trapped and wants to get out?"

I ground to a halt on the landing, forcing him to stop. "You can hear those things too?"

My brother's eyes locked onto mine and, for a moment, as we gazed at each other, the four walls that enclosed us fell away. I remember it so well, how hopeful I was, and then he laughed – a sound with as much cruelty in it as the ghost laugh.

"God, you're gullible!"

"Gulli... what?"

"Stupid, you're stupid." When I didn't react he rolled his eyes, grabbed my hand again and continued to drag me. "Just come on," he said.

There's the main staircase in Blakemort and then there's the staircase to the attic. It doesn't carry on from the main one as you'd expect, there's the long, long landing, and then it turns and goes upwards again. Not wide either, it's much narrower. The walls either side of it are covered in a floral wallpaper that has browned with age and is peeling in some corners, as if the house doesn't like such a cheerful pattern and wants it gone. It's strange really because whenever I think of that staircase now, I think of it as hidden, but it wasn't, it was just... tucked away.

Up the second set of stairs, Ethan pushed me in front of him – blocking any attempt to turn and run. *It's okay. It's okay. It's okay.* I repeated those words as I climbed, trying to convince myself. Certainly it didn't feel any worse than downstairs, but even so, I didn't want to go up there. I'd discovered enough about Blakemort.

Close up we could see that the door wasn't locked as Mum had suggested, that it was very slightly ajar. Ethan joined me on the step just outside it, a frown on his face.

"Have you been up here before?" he asked.

I shook my head. "Why?"

"'Cos it's open, that's why."

Open but not welcoming. Nothing about the house was welcoming.

"Go on then," he said, "go inside."

He pushed me again, right into the door and it gaped further. It was so dark in there, as black as the coal we used for shovelling into the fire.

"There must be a light," Ethan said, his hand groping the walls either side of him and finding a pull rather than a switch, which he tugged at.

When it came on, the light was yellow, sickly somehow, failing to illuminate all areas of such a vast space. Plenty of darkness remained. Another smell accompanied the usual musty one, one I couldn't describe at the time but now know to be decay. The room was packed. It couldn't just be with things belonging to Carol, but perhaps Carol's family too, or other owners – items forgotten about or not wanted and left to… rot. There were old chairs, some stacked on top of each other, their mesh frames unravelling, a long refectory table similar to the one in the dining room that we never used, just as gnarled, and a couple of prams, old-fashioned, like no prams I'd ever seen before – used for babies or dolls, I don't know which. A clothes rail too, metal hangers swaying lightly on it, and piles of clothes to the side, as if they'd been torn off. Dark and dreary, I couldn't imagine them being worn again, they were solely the refuge of house spiders. Against the wall, paintings half-covered by a sheet had their backs to us and boxes formed several misshapen towers.

Ethan was agog. "It's full of treasure!"

Never would I have said that, not in a million years.

Walking over to one of the towers, he started prodding. "What's in here do you reckon?"

Why was he asking me? How would I know?

Struggling slightly, he took down the top-most box and placed it in front of him, immediately opening the cardboard flaps and rummaging inside. Whilst he was busy, I took the opportunity to look around – staring at what I couldn't see. I got a sense of children again, some even younger than me, plus adults that cowered, not bold at all. I was amazed. Was it possible that ghosts hide? That they get frightened too?

"Ugh, look!" Ethan pulled what looked like an emaciated fox from the box – my mouth fell open in horror. "How flea bitten is this?"

"Don't touch it!" I yelled. "It might bite you."

"Bite me? How can it bite me? It's dead!" He took the ghastly item and draped it around his shoulders. I can tell you what it is now; it was one of those fur stoles that ladies used to drape across their shoulders, complete with face, legs, and tail – a fashion item of the 1930s. Shocking, absolutely shocking. I honestly think it was at that moment that I decided to become a vegetarian. Funnily enough, of all the things that happened at that house, I find that memory one of the queasiest.

Ethan seemed to revel in my horror but even he appeared slightly disgusted when he finally took it off his shoulders and discarded it to lie forlornly on the floor. He returned his attention to the box. "What else is in here?" he asked again.

I crept closer – curiosity not responsible for such an action, but simply the need to be close to someone living and breathing, even if it was my brother.

He dug further, pulling out smooth oval glass weights but with insects inside them, trapped for eternity. I swallowed – again in horror. There was a rabbit foot hanging from a fob – lucky for some I guess – as well as a framed picture with row after row of butterflies pinned to cardboard, their colours remaining iridescent long after their demise. Rather than appalled, Ethan was fascinated, his dark eyes growing wider and wider. Then his face crumpled. "Oh, I thought there'd be more groovy stuff." He picked up a handful of something. "These are just photos," he said, unimpressed.

The photos joined the fox fur on the floor. Whilst he made sure there wasn't anything else macabre enough in the box to satisfy a little boy's strange desires, I bent down and picked up one of the photos. It was black and white, very old. In fact I wondered if it would crumble to dust in my hands. When it didn't, I examined it carefully. There was a woman dressed in a high-collared black dress sitting upright, her eyes closed, her expression solemn. Two children leant in either side of her, one in a white dress and the other in a frilly white shirt – a boy and a girl, similar ages to Ethan and me. Their eyes were closed too. Why had somebody photographed them sleeping? I picked up another photo – this one of a child much younger, lying on a fur rug, her eyes closed and her hands joined together as if in prayer. Dolls surrounded her, all wearing bonnets and fancy dresses, as far removed from Barbie as you could get. The strange thing about the dolls was they also had their eyes closed. In yet another, two men were sitting, one with his arm around the other – his brother perhaps? He had his eyes open at least but the other man's eyes were closed and he was slumped. Every photo I looked at, the scenario was similar.

They're dead.

As though it had caught fire I dropped the photograph. "What?"

Ethan ignored me. He'd walked over to a rocking chair and was sitting in it, swaying back and forth.

"What did you say?"

That box is full of the dead.

Was it Ethan talking? I couldn't quite make it out. I took a step or two forwards, to peer closer at him. Like the people in the photos, he had his eyes closed.

You're dead too.

I began shaking, violently shaking.

"Ethan!"

Or at least you will be.

"Ethan!"

Soon.

"ETHAN!"

His eyes sprang open; I was so relieved to see it.

"I want to go," I declared, feeling sick to my stomach.

"Go? But we've only just got here, there's lots to see yet."

"We shouldn't be here," I replied. Not meaning just the attic, but the house itself.

There was a wild fluttering above me. I was so surprised to encounter something living aside from us that I screamed and fell back, landing amongst the photos.

Ethan howled with laughter. "You idiot, it's a bat, or an owl. Oh, bloody hell," he said, enjoying immensely that he was out of earshot of Mum and could therefore swear to his heart's content. "How bloody brilliant if it was a bat!"

He scrambled towards me and looked up too but

whatever had made the noise was quiet now. His eyes spying one of the glass weights he'd handled before, he picked it up, intending to throw it, to disturb what was there.

"DON'T!" I screamed again, and then more pitifully. "Please don't."

He paused, considered my words, and then mercifully relented. "Come on," he said, "it's hot in here. Besides, I'm bored. *You're* boring. I'm going to play in my bedroom. There's only crap here anyway."

He stepped over me – literally stepped over me – made his way to the door and banged it shut behind him. No longer open, or even ajar, it confined me within – imprisoned me. What was overhead immediately started fluttering again and in dark corners I could sense writhing. Who was it that had whispered? A boy – the same age as Ethan or thereabouts and even worse than him, if such a thing were possible. My arms were on the floor behind me, supporting my weight but I sat up straight and drew them inwards, trying to curl into a ball instead, to make myself tiny, tinier still, invisible. I had to get up, get out of there, but I couldn't move. I swallowed, my eyes darting to the left and to the right. *Who are you? Who's here?*

Something swooped – the bat, the owl, whatever creature it was, black feathers in my face and a smell so bitter it blinded me further. I screamed but worse than that I wet myself, my arms flailing in an attempt to keep the damned thing away. Even in my terror I felt shame that I couldn't control my bladder – that urine was pouring from me – all over the photos, staining them, destroying them. I wanted them destroyed!

"Get away! Get away! Get away!"

Surely my screaming would alert Ethan and he'd come rushing back.

"Get away!"

I pushed myself upwards. If no one would save me, I had to save myself.

The thing that was beating about my head retreated – vanished, as if it had never been. Gone. Just like that. Somehow that was even more frightening – its sudden disappearance. Looking back, I'm not even sure it was real. In fact, right now, at this moment, sitting here writing, I'd bet money it wasn't. It was simply an *illusion*, some kind of magic trick. Certainly, it never appeared again. But alone as I was, or more accurately not alone, I didn't have time to contemplate it. My chest rising and falling, sobs starting to engulf me, snot pouring from my nose, my legs hot and sticky, I could only contemplate escape – but damn my feet, they wouldn't work!

"Mum! Mum! Mum!" I'd call for her instead but if Ethan couldn't hear me from one floor down, Mum wouldn't be able to from the kitchen, or the morning room or the drawing room, or wherever it was she happened to be. I had to change tack.

"He didn't mean it. When he said there's only crap in here, he didn't mean you."

Was that a growl or someone sniggering?

"I don't think you're crap!"

Another noise: definitely a growl.

"I just want to… help."

It was as good a word as any.

"Honestly, that's all I want to do, help."

I was completely defenceless, a little girl against so many. I braced myself, shut my eyes, prepared for something to swoop again or to come racing forwards from the shadows, to launch another attack. Instead, something took my hand – *someone,* with fingers not seen but felt, closing around mine. They didn't pull, or tug, they simply held onto me. I strained to see an outline of the body attached but I couldn't.

That someone cajoled me and got me moving at last, towards the door. They must have opened it because I didn't and yet it swung from its catch. Accompanying me down the narrow stairway, all the way to my bedroom, we passed Ethan's room, the sound of kappowing coming from inside as he forced his soldiers to pit their wits against each other in a seemingly endless battle. It pushed my bedroom door open too. As I've mentioned, I had a desk in my room, just a small one, somewhere where I could sit and draw if I wanted to. But there was a sheet of paper on it now and a pen, not items I'd placed there. Whatever had hold of my hand, it wanted me to write.

Chapter Five

I was five, nearly six, and in terms of writing I could just about manage my own name, Mum, Dad, Cat, Hat, Mat, but very little more. In fact, regarding my own name, a lot of the time I spelt it *Crin* – it was so much easier. I do the same thing now, sign stuff *Crin*, and even encourage people to call me that too. Some do, some don't; Mum steadfastly refuses. What had hold of my hand released it and pulled the chair back, rattling it slightly as though growing impatient.

How I wanted the comfort of my mother but in that moment there was no comfort to be had. Instead, I saw no choice but to do as it wanted. I sat, reached out, picked up the pen, and let my hand hover over the blank sheet.

"I can't," was all I said, trying to explain, but it was no use.

No longer my hand but that of the other, it started gliding over the page, haphazardly at first – I think it was as new to this as I was – making unintelligible marks, lines, zigzags, and circles even. Gradually more control was exercised and marks resembling words began to appear.

"I can't understand," I repeated. What else could I say? But my hand kept writing.

Tears filled my eyes. I wished I could read better, that I could understand what was going on.

"Who are you?" I asked. He or she – I didn't even know that much – seemed gentler than the others I'd encountered, less vicious. I even wondered if we might be friends. Ah, I was such an innocent! The being couldn't answer me, not in a way I'd understand, only through writing – a way that made no sense to me at all.

Frustration rose. "Talk to me instead!"

Normally a shy child, reserved, I was sometimes prone to the odd tantrum. I broke the hold it had over me, stood up, and threw the pen down. I didn't want to write anymore, what was the use of it? Growing angrier still, I leant forward with the intention of picking up the paper and of tearing it to shreds, and that's when this benign being became less so. It shoved me hard, sending me flying back to land at the side of my bed. In an equally fighting mood I scrambled to my feet and dived forwards again, determined to destroy what it had created. But I couldn't move! It was as if a wall had sprung up in front of me. I brought my fists up and beat at the air, yelling still.

What a sight I must have looked, my hair wild, my clothes awry and stinking of urine! Just as I sometimes did with Ethan I continued to retaliate, remembering that memorable time I'd shut his fingers in the doorjamb. He'd been taunting me about something, calling me names again – stupid, dumb, idiot – the usual. It was in my bedroom in our old house, just before we moved. When he turned to leave, he trailed his fingers along the width of the door, into the hollow – I noticed, seized my chance, kicked out and slammed it shut, his hand in the wrong place at the wrong time. The cry he emitted was so satisfying… for about a minute. And then it burst open, Mum standing on the other side – a look of abject horror on her face.

"What's happened? What the hell's happened? Oh, Ethan, are you okay, darling? What did you do?"

"SHE did it!" Ethan continued to scream, pointing at me. "She slammed the door on my hand deliberately!"

"Corinna?" Mum looked as if she didn't believe a word – not her small daughter, surely? She wasn't capable. But children are far more capable than they look.

Ethan was making such a song and dance about it, clutching his hand to his chest, and shouting the house down. There was even a spot of blood, staining the carpet beneath his feet, the crimson a stark contrast to the oatmeal. I stood there, hoping Mum wouldn't believe such a thing of me. But my silence was damning.

"Corinna, was it you?" she said whilst hugging her other injured child to her.

Should I lie – say no?

"Corinna?"

It was bad to lie wasn't it?

"CORINNA!"

"Yes," I blurted out. I couldn't lie. I shouldn't.

If only I had.

I was confined to my room for the rest of the day – a beautiful day, full of sunshine, we'd been promised a trip to the beach but that was cancelled, as I had to learn that 'violence will not be tolerated in this house.' But violence was tolerated at Blakemort, all the time. Because no one believed it was being administered.

The wall – for want of a better description – forced me

all the way onto the bed, lowering itself, coming closer, closer still. I held my hands out to fend it off but they were forced back too. It was bearing down, the feeling similar to being buried alive, or at least how I imagine that to be, as suffocating. Panic flooded through me; fear too, wiping away any boldness that might have surfaced, obliterating it entirely. I couldn't breathe. I was going to be crushed. Surely I was going to be crushed!

I won't tear the paper up. I won't.

Still the weight was on me.

Promise. I promise.

Was this it? Was I going to die? Upstairs, in the attic, that's what I'd been told was going to happen, but so soon?

Please listen to me!

I *was* going to die. This thing was going to kill me. My chest seemed to cave as air was forced from my lungs. Everything was going black, my sight failing too.

"Ethan, Corinna, come down and see who's here!"

I heard the words but they were so far away.

"Come on, we have a visitor!"

We had a visitor? Well, I had a visitor too – an unwelcome one.

"Ethan! There you are. What have you done to your hair? It's all over the place. Get it combed. Where's your sister? Fine then, if you won't tell me, I'll go and find her myself. She must be in her bedroom. Oh, this is so exciting!"

Just before consciousness deserted me, Mum burst into the room.

She took one look at me and hurried over.

"Darling, this is no time for a nap. Come on, Aunt Julia's here!"

* * *

"Ethan! Corinna! Come and give me the biggest hug."

Aunt Julia was different to Mum, even though they were sisters. Mum, whilst not petite was of medium stature, but Julia was tall. Amazonian I think you'd call it, with blonde hair that was straight rather than red and wavy. She had a sprinkling of freckles on her nose but no more than that and this wonderful warmth to her that I always responded to. Running, I leapt into her arms. If she noticed that I smelt peculiar, that I was damp, she didn't say, didn't even so much as wrinkle her nose, she just hugged me close, and to this day, I'm grateful that she did. That she realised how much I needed hugging in that moment. What had happened, the battle that had been fought upstairs, it was over – for now. But I hadn't won it. Oh, no. That piece of paper – I wouldn't tear it up, I'd keep it. I *had* to keep it.

"Oh, sweetheart, how lovely to see you."

With one hand Aunt Julia was stroking my hair. Ethan hovered close by, clearly waiting his turn but I didn't care, he could wait. He'd left me in the attic, had shut me in and I hated him for it – *despised* him.

Finally, I was released and Ethan saw his chance, stepped forward, and elbowed me aside. I might be making this up in retrospect but I think my lip curled and I snarled at him, actually snarled. But like I say, I could be making that up. I'm sure if Mum had caught me snarling, she'd have smacked my legs. Talking of which, Mum finally noticed there was an odour.

"Darling, have you… you know…?"

Shame returned with a vengeance.

"I… I…" But how could I explain? How could I possibly explain?

Mum's face fell. "Oh, dear," she said, reaching for my hand, but I didn't reach back. I didn't want anyone to hold my hand again.

"Come on," she prompted, wrinkling her nose.

Aunt Julia looked over Ethan's shoulder. "What's the matter, Hel?"

Mum gestured towards me. "She needs a bit of a wash."

"A wash?" Aunt Julia turned towards me too, my face burning as she did. There was laughter again, coming from the direction of the music room – no one to hear it but me. She let Ethan go. "I'll take her upstairs if you like, run a bath and whilst I'm at it, she can show me around." Focusing on me, she added, "Would you like that, sweetie? You and me together exploring this big old house?"

As much as I relished time alone with Aunt Julia, no I didn't want to go exploring. I wanted to run, as fast and as far away as I possibly could.

Pushing Ethan gently away from her, ignoring his disgruntled look, she held out her hand. I was happy to take hers at least. As I did, the laughter died down.

Aunt Julia was Mum's younger sister and the reason they looked so different was because they had different dads – neither of them took after their mother, my Nan, who had died when I was a toddler. I sometimes wonder if the fact she came from a broken home meant Mum accepted the break-up of her own family so readily. But what do I know? Nothing really on that score, because Mum never talked about it, not then and not now. She just… accepted it. Still, I couldn't help but wish she'd tried harder with Dad. If she had, we wouldn't have had to leave our house. We wouldn't have ended up at Blakemort – all that had happened would simply *cease* to have happened. That's what I thought anyway. Now I wince. Why do we always think it's the woman who should try harder? Why not the man? They get away with so much.

Aunt Julia wasn't married and neither did she have kids. That's why she loved us so much, I think. She doted on Ethan and me, if I'm truthful me especially. Stepping aside, she let me lead the way and so I did, again seeing no option but to carry out the wishes of others. Mum asked Ethan to come and help her in the kitchen, but he was disgruntled about that too – reckoned he'd drawn the short straw. If only he knew.

I didn't want to climb those stairs again and face what was there. But was downstairs any better? Earlier, when Mum had dashed into my room, whatever was holding me down had disappeared as quickly as that which had swooped in the attic – another magic trick. I was able to sit up again and breathe, although not hide the shock and bewilderment on my face. Little matter, as Mum didn't notice anyway.

I showed my aunt around, hesitating at Mum's bedroom again but she went in anyway, declared it 'nice', nothing more, nothing less, left it, and headed for the bathroom instead. The bathroom was a cold room – even submerged in hot water you'd shiver. Whenever I had to use it, I tried to do so as quickly as possible, never lingering. Aunt Julia ran the taps and I half expected dark matter to gush out but it was only ever water – albeit water that had a slight tinge to it. 'It's because of the piping,' Mum had already explained to me. 'It must be as ancient as Blakemort itself', but somehow I never bought that. Despite scrubbing at myself with soap and a flannel, it was impossible to feel clean in that house.

After I'd been bathed and wrapped in a towel, and with Mum and Ethan still busy downstairs preparing dinner, we walked to my room.

"I'm dying to see it," Aunt Julia declared, her choice of words not the greatest under the circumstances.

On entering, she said it was 'lovely' but it was just a room with cream walls, the paint patchy in places and fluttering curtains at the window. It was far from lovely.

"Let's get you some clean clothes," she continued, walking over to the wardrobe.

In the centre of the room I stood still, steadfastly refusing to look at the piece of paper on my desk, to acknowledge it. There remained a trace of boldness in me despite what had happened. But it began fluttering too, capturing the attention of my aunt. Instead of opening the wardrobe doors, she turned her head towards the desk.

"What's this?" she said, beginning to change direction.

"No, don't…" I began, but too late.

She had reached the desk, picked up the piece of paper, and read the words I wasn't able to. Her eyes widening as she managed to decipher the scrawls, she grew stormy when usually she reminds me of a bright summer's day.

"Corinna?" she questioned, waving it in front of me.

I did what I always did in awkward situations at that age – I burst out crying.

Immediately she was all concern.

"Oh, it's okay, it's all right, sweetie," she said, clutching the piece of paper but hurrying over to me. "I know it's not you that's responsible. You can't write yet, surely." Her lips pursed, much the same way as Mum's did. "And even if you could, you wouldn't write this." She paused again and tried to make sense of it. "It must be Ethan," she declared. "That flaming Ethan! This is taking teasing to a whole new level."

Abruptly releasing me, she marched out of my room and back downstairs. That was the day before Christmas Eve. On Christmas Day, she left.

Chapter Six

ON the way down, I tried to tell Aunt Julia it wasn't Ethan responsible. As angry as I was with him it wasn't fair that he should be blamed for something he didn't do. She wasn't listening. Perhaps that was just as well. After all, who was I going to say did it – a ghost? I could imagine the look on her face if I did.

With me behind her, now running to keep up, she barged into the kitchen, waving the offending piece of paper in front of her. Mum, who was stirring something, or rather had her hand over Ethan's hand, making him stir it, looked sideways at us.

"What's the matter, Ju–?"

She didn't get much further as Aunt Julia erupted.

"This! This is what's the matter, Helena. She's a five-year-old girl for God's sake. What the hell is Ethan doing writing this sort of stuff and leaving it in her room? I don't even care if she can't read it yet, it's not right. It's... weird."

"Ethan?" Still Mum was thunderstruck.

"Yes, Ethan!"

Before I could interrupt to try and save Ethan again,

Aunt Julia slammed the sheet of paper onto the yellowed worktop and said, "Take a look, go on… see for yourself why I'm so upset."

Wiping her hands on her apron, Mum did as she was asked, her expression growing even more bewildered as her eyes scanned what was laid out beneath her.

"What? I don't understand. Ethan?" She shook her head as if to try and shake from memory what she'd seen. "Why'd you write this?"

"Write what?"

"THIS!"

Mum shouting made both my brother and me jump.

"I didn't write anything!" he yelled back.

"Don't lie."

"I'm not."

"He didn't!" My voice was small compared to theirs and easily lost.

"This is…" Mum screwed up her nose. "Horrible!"

"I've done nothing wrong," Ethan continued to protest. And then, still indignant, he pushed past Mum and started to read aloud. "House, Dead, Hate, Hurt, Kill, You, You, You."

As Mum said, horrible words – a horrible sentiment – but there was a strange relief in hearing them at last.

"I know they argue, Hel, but honestly, this is beyond the pale."

Tears were springing to Ethan's eyes. "I didn't write it!"

"Of course you did!" Aunt Julia responded.

"Hang on," Mum turned on her sister. "Ethan's my child, let me deal with him."

But Aunt Julia was just as fiery as Mum. "I think you'd better, Helena, this is bullying of the worst kind. I can't think why you haven't nipped it in the bud before."

"Don't tell me how to bring up my children."

"I'm trying to help."

"Coming in here and shouting the odds. You think that's helping?"

Mum squared up to Aunt Julia, the two of them standing face to face, the difference between them even more pertinent – Aunt Julia, a warrior woman, Mum, a red dragon and capable of breathing fire.

"He's my son, Ju, and if he wrote those words, I'll deal with him, not you."

Ethan was crying in earnest now and I have to say, I couldn't blame him.

"I just want to help," Aunt Julia insisted. "Things have obviously got a bit much for you lately."

"I'm on top of my game, thanks."

"It's hard being a single parent, I get that—"

"I don't need telling."

"Then let me help."

"YOU'RE NOT HELPING!"

Mum's voice seemed to cause a mini-earthquake as pots and pans began to rattle, and the drawers too. The smell of burning filled the air, and that's what finally distracted Mum. "Oh, God, the chilli!"

No longer in a fighting stance, she rushed over to it, but it was ruined apparently, sticking to the pan. "But I turned the flame down," she was muttering. "Didn't I?"

The kitchen implements stilled. No one seemed to have noticed what had happened to them but me, but then Mum and Aunt Julia were focused only on each other, and Ethan, he'd been staring at them in terrified awe. Once again, the spirits had played to the gallery – the gallery with only me standing in it. Mum was furious.

"Look what you've done with your wild accusations, you've ruined dinner."

"I wasn't the one who left the heat up high."

"Nor did I!" Mum screeched before once again turning to Ethan. "Did you turn the flame up? It was you, wasn't it? Who else could it be?" She was accusing him as readily as Aunt Julia had. Poor Ethan. Hot tears seemed to sizzle on his cheeks as he ran from the room. I had to dart out of his way or he'd have mowed me down. He ran up the stairs crying over his shoulder as he went. "I hate you, I hate all of you."

That house, so easily it inspired that emotion.

Mum kept blinking her eyelids, trying not to cry. Even Aunt Julia looked shocked. "I'm sorry, Hel, I shouldn't have come in here shouting the odds as you say. I should have talked to you privately."

"Damn right you should," Mum mumbled, doing her best to resurrect dinner.

"It's just… Look at that paper, look at it. Those words seem *carved* onto it. If it was Ethan, and I don't know who else it could be, he's really troubled. You know, what with the divorce and everything…"

"Don't you think we all are?" Tears fell from Mum's eyes now, a torrent of them, like a dam bursting. "Like you said, it's hard, Ju, bloody hard!"

"Oh, I know, I know." Aunt Julia bridged the gap between them and tried to hug her. At first Mum was having none of it.

"You don't know. How can you? You've no bloody idea."

"Hel, come on."

"No!"

But Aunt Julia was bigger than Mum and more determined. Against her wishes, Mum was enveloped in her sister's arms and, after a moment, she stopped resisting, needing that hug as much as I had earlier.

I looked on, hoping that was it. That we could just get on and prepare for Christmas. That someone would take that sheet of paper and destroy it. No one did.

* * *

Christmas Eve is almost as good as Christmas Day isn't it? I think it's the anticipation, there's so much to look forward to, so much to hope for. After the argument, we ate burnt chilli with soggy rice and then we went to bed, all of us exhausted. Aunt Julia was staying in my room on a mattress on the floor. It was her idea, but after what had happened I was so pleased she was beside me. She'd sort of made up with Ethan, apologised to him, told him to speak to her if he had any 'issues' but Ethan had that look in his eyes – that 'unforgiving' look. It didn't seem to worry Aunt Julia but it did me. I tried to speak to him too, to tell him I'd never said it was him who wrote on that paper, but he just brushed me off, too lost in his own fury. As for that paper, at breakfast the next morning – on the hotly anticipated Christmas Eve – it was gone. When Mum temporarily left the kitchen, I opened some drawers, searching for it, and sure enough it had been stuffed into one of them, shoved down the side – out of sight, out of mind, but not my mind. I couldn't forget it.

Mum came bustling back in, Aunt Julia and Ethan

trailing in separately behind her. For breakfast she whipped up scrambled eggs and we crowded round the table to eat it. At first the atmosphere was sullen but gradually it lifted and Aunt Julia, determined to atone for yesterday, offered to take us shopping. She wasn't flashy, Aunt Julia, but she was stylish with close fitting clothes, and perfect hair and make-up. Mum, on the other hand, liked loose skirts and blouses, just a hint of lipstick and lots of bangles on her arms. It's a look I loved, reminding me of something exotic, a gypsy woman, and one I adopted when I grew older, although I added a bit of an Emo twist. I think with our Titian curls, we dress to suit our hair! But I digress. As I said Aunt Julia wasn't flashy, but she had a good job in finance, and a flat in London, she could afford to spoil us a bit. In some ways she was everything Mum wasn't, but I'd never seen resentment between them, never witnessed an argument before – only ever in that house.

And there was more to come.

Chapter Seven

LEAVING Blakemort, we all piled into Mum's Volvo and headed into Brighton. First on the list was a visit to Santa, who was holding court in the shopping mall. Ethan refused to go in but I was beside myself, the wait in the queue nothing less than excruciating. I almost wet myself again, but this time with pure excitement. I must add here that Ethan and I knew most of our Christmas presents came from Mum and Dad, they encouraged us to believe in the magic of Santa but not that he spent a fortune on every child! Rather it was visiting him in his grotto that was of the utmost importance, the sheer thrill of it. Not that Ethan thought so, hence his refusal. It was so different to how he was last year, when he'd been as eager as me, if not more so.

Afterwards, we headed to Browns Restaurant for a burger and a milkshake – another treat. It was there that I opened the gift Santa had given me – Mum had told me to wait until we were sitting down, to savour the moment, rather than rip into it. As the waitress brought our drinks over, I retrieved the gift from her handbag, my fingers trembling as I peeled back layers of cheerful wrapping paper, resplendent with reindeers and striped candy canes. What I saw caused me to tremble for different reasons. It was a notepad and pen, an innocent enough gift; some might even say a welcome one, but not me, not after what had happened. Everyone around the table stared at it for a few seconds before I threw it from me.

"Don't want it!" I declared.

Mum didn't react initially. She continued to stare and then she placed her glass down and picked it up instead. "It's just a notepad and pen," she mumbled before tucking it into her bag, out of sight, out of mind again.

The gift soured lunch. Even far from it, the house was having an effect. We did a bit more shopping afterwards, waited for night to fall so we could admire the lights the Council had strung up in the city centre, which weren't that impressive to be honest, and then we trundled home to have cheese and biscuits for dinner – something of a family tradition on Christmas Eve. I think I shook all the way back to Blakemort, Mum taking it easy on that long dark country road that led to the house, the trees towering over us to form a tunnel. Even in daylight the sun had a hard time trying to filter through. As we travelled, I glanced at Ethan. He was biting his nails, a dreadful habit of his, right down to the quick.

Pulling into the gravel driveway, a crunch beneath our feet as we exited the car, the house reminded me of a spider, waiting to strike. It's strange with Blakemort. It didn't want you there but it didn't want you gone either – it fed on you.

Keeping my eyes on the ground, we walked to the front door, all of us taking our time, no one in a rush to get inside. Mum was going to light a fire in the drawing room, where we'd erected a Christmas tree a few days before, and had already stacked up logs beside the coal bucket. They were neat no more. As we entered that room, single file, Mum groaned. "Who the hell did that?"

The logs were scattered everywhere, some of them charred, as if they'd been burnt already.

"What a mess. What a bloody mess!"

I don't think I've ever heard Mum swear so much as when she was in that house.

"They probably just took a tumble," Aunt Julia replied. "Let's get it cleared up and the fire sorted. It's freezing in here."

Which was strange as it was a mild December and certainly not freezing outside.

"Brrr," Aunt Julia made a show of hugging herself. "Doesn't your heating work?"

"It does, when it wants to," answered Mum irritably. "Which is hardly ever."

I looked at the Christmas tree, half expecting to see it dashed to the floor too, but it was intact. Incredible really come to think about it, as it was such an obvious target. But that tree, once adorned, was never felled, not in all the years I lived there. The ghosts, the spirits, the entities, they were more original than that.

Mum and Aunt Julia coaxed the fire into life whilst we went upstairs to change into our pyjamas. Mum never put the presents under the tree until late on Christmas Eve; she knew we'd never be able to leave them alone otherwise, continually prodding and poking at them. Usually, she hid them in her bedroom. They were certainly safe there, from me anyway, but Ethan wanted to go in.

"Come on, they'll be under her bed or in the wardrobe

or something."

"No. Mum will get cross."

"Mum knows we go in and look, we always do."

"No," I said again.

Ethan screwed up his face. "What's wrong with you, you used to be fun."

"I don't like Mum's room."

'Why not? It's fine."

"It's not."

For a moment Ethan was quiet and then he moved forwards and grabbed my arm. "What's wrong with it, tell me." And then slightly more agitated, "What's wrong with this house, Corinna?"

So he knew, like me he knew.

"It's—"

There was a huge crash, coming from the direction of one of the spare rooms – the one next to mine.

Ethan's eyes widened. "What was that?"

Before I could answer Mum called up the stairs, asking the same question. Hearing no response, she started climbing, Aunt Julia behind her.

"It wasn't me," Ethan said, when she reached the landing. "It came from in there."

The door to that particular room was shut and had been since the day we'd arrived, only briefly had we all taken a look in there. It was one of the storage rooms.

"Oh, for goodness' sake." Mum was still irritable. "I never said it was you, did I?"

Without hesitation she opened the door. I stood rigid, expecting a figure of some sort to come rushing at us. It's funny isn't it, how a figure as familiar as a human being can be so damned terrifying. No such thing happened, but there was another mess to be cleaned up. A mirror – large with an ornate surround, French apparently and an antique – had crashed to the ground and glass lay in smithereens.

"I don't bloody believe it," Mum declared. "I just don't."

"Point me in the direction of the dust pan and brush and I'll do it later," said Aunt Julia. "Right now, we need to eat, the kids must be starving."

We were. The burger we'd consumed had been hours ago.

Without changing our clothes, we all went down to the living room, the fire was roaring but not lending much warmth. It was still cold. Mum cursed again then left us and went into the kitchen. When she returned her face was like thunder.

"What's wrong?" asked Aunt Julia.

"It's the cheese," she replied. "I only bought it yesterday, but already it's gone mouldy. And before you say it, no I'm not talking about the blue, I'm talking about the cheddar, the Brie, the manchego, everything. It's all sodding gone off!"

* * *

Ethan got his skateboard and I got my bike. Dad had also sent lavish presents. '… trying to make up for his absence,' I heard Mum say to Julia, '… for the damage that he's done.' We must have thought so too, because somehow his gifts seemed to elicit no joy, only sadness, no matter how shiny and new they were.

After all the gifts had been opened, Mum and Aunt Julia

went off to prepare Christmas lunch – roast turkey with all the trimmings. Ethan and I remained in the living room, but not for long.

"Bring your bike and let's go to the music room," Ethan suggested. "It's a great place to skateboard."

My heart sank but how long could I keep saying no to him? Besides it'd be all right, wouldn't it? Everything's all right at Christmas.

As I followed him towards it, I was sure I could hear whispering, but it was very faint. Ethan was right, the music room was perfect for hammering up and down, the expanse of floor space too tantalising to ignore. We could have gone outside I suppose but it was raining again – which was such a disappointment as we'd prayed so hard for snow – and neither one of us fancied getting wet. Ethan started practicing immediately and I did too, not hard really as my bike had stabilisers.

"Take them off," Ethan called over his shoulders. "Practice properly."

I ignored him and continued to peddle.

There was laughter from the kitchen – good laughter – the sound of Mum and Aunt Julia getting on again. I smiled to hear it.

"Take the stabilisers off," Ethan called again.

I rolled my eyes at him.

"Go on, don't be such a chicken."

"I'm not a chicken," I protested at last.

"You are, you're a chicken," he retaliated, but it wasn't with his usual venom, he sounded cheerful. "Chicken, chicken, chicken."

"I'm not," I said again, but cheerful too. The day wasn't turning out so bad.

I gripped the handles harder, peddling fast, really getting the hang of my lovely new bike with its pink and white frame and white leather handles. Mum had spared no expense; this was the bike I'd set my heart on. Peddling faster, faster still, I was on my fourth or fifth run, approaching the door that led into the garden. I had to brake, or I'd be in danger of going through it. I wasn't overly panicked though; there was still some distance left. Beside me, Ethan was keeping apace. My hands closed around the brakes and I squeezed. Nothing happened. Frowning, I squeezed again… and again. Why weren't they working? They'd been just fine before. Even so, I continued hurtling forwards. We were both going to go through the door! I took my feet off the pedals – that would work surely? But they continued spinning.

"Mum! Mum!" I yelled, panic setting in, unlike Ethan, who was laughing, enjoying the thrill.

"MUM!"

"Chicken, chicken, chicken!" Ethan was at it again.

The glass door – the one I hated so much, loomed closer, ever closer. I had a sudden vision, of my face cracked and bleeding, shards of glass sticking out like some hideous mountain range. And my eyes! Oh, my eyes. They'd been ripped to shreds. The vision caused me to scream, startling myself but also Ethan, who lurched towards me, knocking me off my bike just a fraction or so before we reached the door. It sent me flying into the wall instead, only my bike continuing onwards, bang smack into the frail pane and shattering it completely.

"Oh, good God! What now?"

It was Mum, at the entrance to the music room, wild-eyed, Aunt Julia the same.

A blast of air enveloped me, icy in its embrace. Ethan, who was on top of me, pushed himself off, one fist striking out as he did, cursing me for having screamed, for toppling us both.

"Don't you dare hit her!" It was my champion, Aunt Julia. She grabbed him and hauled him to his feet. "Don't you bloody dare, you brat!"

"JULIA!" Mum yelled.

Aunt Julia whirled towards her. "You've lost control, Helena, completely."

I was wailing, Ethan was wailing. The ghosts, they started laughing again.

Mum snatched Ethan to her whilst Aunt Julia knelt down to see to me.

"Is she okay?" Mum asked, her voice as brittle as the glass.

"She's fine," Aunt Julia muttered. 'No cuts or bruises that I can see."

"Good. But I'm afraid I can't have you staying here any longer, Julia, I'd like you to pack your bags and leave. Children, go into the kitchen now. Dinner's almost ready."

Part Two
The Second and Third Christmas

Chapter Eight

OUR first Christmas was over and it had been a disaster. Aunt Julia did as Mum asked and readied herself to leave, giving only me a kiss goodbye. I was inconsolable but Mum was not in a soothing mood. Instead she tried to patch the broken pane with cardboard and whilst she did dinner was ruined. None of us had an appetite anyway.

We didn't want to play any more with our bike or skateboard either – like the presents Dad had got us, they'd lost their shine.

On the twenty-seventh we went to Dad's and then, a few days later, it was the New Year celebrations, Mum allowing us to stay up and count down the minutes on the TV as one century yielded to another. A momentous occasion – screams and cheers poured into the room courtesy of that tiny box. Yet to me, it seemed anything but. Rather, I clung to what was gone and could see nothing to look forward to. Time was a strange thing in that house. It passed, as it always did, but slowly, so very slowly. It only ever went fast when we were outside the house, at school perhaps, or out shopping, or with Dad on a Saturday. Then it seemed to be on a spool, winding us swiftly back towards it, whereupon it would move at a grudging pace again.

The days, the weeks and the months passed. Lots more happened, but as I've said, for the purpose of this retelling I want to focus on the main events – principally Christmas. Even so, throughout the year things went wrong. The pane in the music room door had to be replaced, costing Mum money she could ill afford. The heating continued to play up, either not coming on at all or going into overdrive. One time I touched the radiator, even though I'd been told not to and it burnt my hand. I couldn't believe it; it was like touching flames leaving a sore red patch that took its time to heal. Light bulbs overhead kept fizzing and popping. Mum said they cost a small fortune to replace. The milkman used to leave two pints a day but too often the milk was sour, so Mum finally cancelled the order. Strangely enough though, the milk she bought from the supermarket soured just as easily – she never could work it out. But I could. Nothing could thrive in that house – food, plants, even us. As a family we failed to thrive and Mum lost work. She was good at what she did, previously in demand but clients got fed up with her failing to call them back. "But I never got your message," she'd protest. "Are you sure you left one?" Of course they had, but nothing was ever recorded, the answer machine wiped clean as soon as the last sentence was uttered. With less money coming in, we couldn't buy as much food and I swear we began to look ill, the three of us

– our pallor grey. I'd been quite plump before we moved to that house, a good covering of puppy fat on my bones, but by the time we left my ribs jutted out. As I said, the hauntings continued, the scraping noises above in the attic where I hadn't dared venture again, the low, cruel, laughter, the sensation of being followed wherever I went, the eyes that were always on me. And the flies. I haven't yet mentioned the flies. They were incessant. No matter what Mum did, what sprays and repellents she bought, or how many times she swatted at them, there were always flies in that house – swarming over everything. The writing too, that wasn't a one-off incident. Whoever had guided me had more to say.

Having turned six, it was imperative I learnt to read as soon as possible so I could understand what was being scribed. We think the young don't know much. We assume their common sense is fairly limited, but when I reflect, I was mature beyond my years. What was happening forced me to grow up fast. I had a sense that if I learned what was being said, it would empower me in some way. Mum couldn't believe how eager I was to have extra-curricular lessons with her – she was stunned in fact. 'You've had a long day at school, darling,' she'd say, 'why don't you just relax instead, go and watch the TV.' I'd shake my head and insist, 'I have to learn, Mummy, I have to.' She'd give in then, spend hours with me at the kitchen table, going over and over again simple storybook words until they lodged in my mind – until those strangely mysterious scrawls known as letters began to make sense; until something clicked. I could read! It was like I'd performed a magic trick of my own. I overtook Ethan who hated reading and wouldn't dream of picking up a book of his own accord. 'It's boring,' he'd say. Not for me it wasn't. It was a lifeline.

It was coming round to Christmas again, our second in the house and the first of the new millennium. No Aunt Julia to visit this time as she and Mum were still angry with each other – a fact Mum seemed slightly dazed by as if she couldn't quite believe their feud had lasted for so long. As Mum had had us last year, Dad was supposed to have us this year, just for the day. We'd have Christmas Eve at home at least and then Boxing Day, but still I was upset.

"What are you going to do, Mum?" I asked. "Whilst we're at Dad's?"

"I'll be fine, darling, I'll watch TV and stuff myself with far too many mince pies."

"But I want to be with you."

"I know, but it's only one day and besides, we'll make Boxing Day our Christmas Day, so really you're very lucky – you'll have two Christmases!"

I didn't feel lucky.

Christmas Eve came and went – uneventfully – and on Christmas morning we were up early, washed, dressed and waiting for Dad. He never showed. We waited and waited until eventually the phone in Mum's office started ringing. She rushed to answer it.

"Oh, I see, the car won't start. Well, I could drive them to you. No? Why not? It's too late? It's not too late, it's not even noon. Paul, have you been drinking, is that what this is all about? You have haven't you? You've been drinking. Started the celebrations a bit early haven't you? Don't tell me not to raise my voice. I'll shout if I bloody well want to. You have no say in what I do. You gave up any entitlement when you walked out on me, on the kids, when you let us all down. And don't tell me not to start on that again. You've been partying all night with that girlfriend of yours and now you're so hung-over you can't even get out of bed. Talk about a mid-life crisis, you're pathetic, do you know that, a pathetic specimen of a man! And no you can't have them on Boxing Day instead. We've got plans for Boxing Day. Believe me, if I had my way you wouldn't have them at all. You don't deserve them."

I'd been standing in the hallway with my brother, listening. In my stomach a peculiar mix of emotions churned but chief amongst them was relief, I'd hated the thought of her spending Christmas Day in that house alone. Ethan, however, was a different story. Not just his face, his entire body crumpled – honestly I've never seen him look so distraught, either before or after. That's another thing that haunts me – Ethan in that moment. No boy should have his heart broken. Tears began to form in the corner of his eyes, a few of them escaping, racing down his cheeks to fall on the floor. I laid my hand on his arm and tried to comfort him but of course it was useless.

"Get off me," he yelled. Turning on his heel he ran to the staircase and raced up it.

"But Ethan what about our presents?" We could open Mum's at least.

"I don't want any presents!"

That stunned me. How could a child not want presents?

Mum eventually came out of the morning room. Her eyes were red and sore, as if she'd been crying too. Seeing me, she forced herself to brighten.

"Change of plan, love," she said. "You're staying here

today, Daddy's not feeling well." She looked from left to right. "Where's your brother?"

"He's upstairs, he's crying."

"Crying? Oh, is he? I'll, erm… I'll go and see him."

"But what about our presents?" I whined again.

She only glanced at me as she walked past. "Your presents will have to wait."

* * *

We did open gifts later that day, when Mum was finally able to coax Ethan downstairs. Again it was a sombre affair. There was no tearing the paper off with eager hands, desperate to see what was inside, and no breathless excitement. In fact, Ethan had to be persuaded to open some of his – he just couldn't be bothered. One present that managed to incite a degree of enthusiasm, in me at least, was a tall rectangle, such a familiar shape. My smile faded, however, when I saw that the Barbie doll inside it was the wrong one. I had to try really hard to hide my disappointment, particularly as I'd taken pains to write on my Christmas wish list the Argos catalogue number of the one I wanted. How could Mum have got it so wrong? She'd also forgotten to buy batteries for the games we'd received so they couldn't be played with until the shops opened again – they just sat there, useless bits of plastic with no life in them. Dinner was okay but the gravy had congealed, making me feel a bit sick, and afterwards Ethan returned to his room and holed himself in there. Mum tried to entice me to a game of cards, sitting in front of a roaring log fire but her heart wasn't in it. We played a couple of rounds of snap but then she got bored, stood up, and decamped to the kitchen to start the cleaning up.

I stared into the fire for a while, enjoying the vibrant colours when I thought I saw something else in it, something that wasn't so pretty. I blinked a couple of times and peered closer. There was definitely a shape – a face, long and thin, as black as soot but with eyes that were red and its mouth kept twisting and turning, stuck in some kind of perpetual scream. At the same time as the vision I was aware of a depression on the sofa next to me. It was in the exact same spot as the first time I'd sat there, on the day we arrived. I jumped up in fright, knocking over an occasional table that had the cards on it and they scattered everywhere. Above me the light flickered ominously. My arm drew outwards and I watched in fascination as it seemed to lift of its own volition and then a hand slipped in mine. I knew what it wanted – for me to start writing. Could I disobey? Flee to the kitchen instead? I was too scared to try.

Slowly, I walked forwards, one foot in front of the other, reached the staircase and began to climb. In my bedroom, a pen and paper were laid out on the desk as they'd been laid out before. Sitting down, I picked up the pen and started to write.

Long time ago. Long time. Many of us. Many. Many. Evil. Death. House built on death. Ground soaked in death. Bad place. Bad bad place. You can't leave. Never. Every brick. The land. Lost. Some hide. Some follow. Evil. Evil. Evil.

The words became a scrawl, became unintelligible. Soon my hand was my own again, I was able to flex my fingers and make them obey my will. I tried to read what I could. There were some words that I struggled with, but I got the gist. Believe me, I got the gist. I knew too that Mum couldn't see this, or Ethan. They were both sad enough already. I didn't want to make them sadder. I dragged my chair over to the wardrobe. Standing on it, the paper clutched in my hand, I placed it on top with the other sheet of paper I'd retrieved from the kitchen drawer. I kept them safe.

Chapter Nine

THE third Christmas we spent in that house, Aunt Julia came back. By then I'd written plenty more. I still had trouble reading some of it and had since ceased trying – as long as I wrote, the thing that forced me didn't attack – that was incentive enough. Aged seven (nearly eight), I was surviving alongside the dead, turning my face away from those that stared outwards from dark corners, acting deaf when there were knocks on walls in the dead of night or footsteps running up and down the landing that belonged to neither Ethan nor me. As for the flies, I kept batting at them, praying they wouldn't land on me whilst I was sleeping and lay a multitude of eggs.

I was beyond happy to hear that Aunt Julia was coming – that she and Mum had put an end to their stupid argument. Mum was pleased too. Despite her worries over money – which seemed to have aged her since we'd been here, with lines that I'd never noticed before now apparent on her face – she seemed lighter, and took to humming. One song in particular, or rather one hymn; the one that she had hummed the first Christmas we were here: *Silent Night*. I preferred more jolly festive tunes. This one was too melancholy. She hummed it constantly and again it annoyed me. It annoyed the house too. I could feel its fury surge when she started but how could I tell her to stop? First, I didn't want to spoil what little happiness she possessed nowadays; and secondly, to explain that the house hated that song – *despised* it – would make her angry too. There was no point in adding to the mix.

Aunt Julia was arriving the same day as before, the day before Christmas Eve, or Christmas Eve Eve as Ethan and I used to call it in an attempt to string the holiday out, to make it another magical day. It certainly would be with Aunt Julia on the way. I couldn't wait to see her and hoped she hadn't forgotten me in the time she'd been away, but of course she hadn't. She rang the doorbell and I made sure I was there to open it, my aunt looking delighted to see me, scooping me up in her arms.

"Oh, I've missed you." She breathed the words into my ear. I didn't need to look at her face to know she was crying.

When at last she put me down, Mum stepped forward and she and Aunt Julia stared at each other. They were tense moments and I wondered whether they might change their minds about such a grand reunion. A huge sigh of relief escaped me as they hugged each other instead, both of them sobbing and saying how sorry they were, that they didn't know what they'd been thinking. Ethan hung back – lurking in the shadows as so many did. Mum started to coax him forwards but Aunt Julia said it was okay, to leave it to her. She had a bag slung over her shoulder and she reached into it and brought out a big pack of jelly beans, the really expensive ones that we're rarely allowed to have and, even better, the ones that contained all the vile flavours: smelly socks, rotten egg, canned dog food, the works. Each nasty flavour is matched with 10 look-alike tasty flavours and you have to take potluck when you pick one – believe me, you don't want to get one of the 'bogus beans', they really do taste disgusting. We'd only played the jellybean game once before and it had been a lot of fun. As she wriggled the box enticingly at him, I looked on enviously and then all envy disappeared as he broke into a huge grin – that was like a present in itself, seeing Ethan happy.

He came racing over, took the box, and then gave Aunt Julia the hug that she wanted. Things were good; we'd made them good, despite everything. Christmas 2001 was going to be our best ever. Dad and Mum had made up too, albeit tentatively and he was taking us out for the morning on Christmas Eve. But it was Christmas Eve Eve as I've said and we were eager to get Aunt Julia – who was staying until the day after Boxing Day – all settled in. She wasn't staying in my room this time; Mum wanted her in with her. "Let's share, like we used to when we were kids." Accusingly, she added, "God knows, my children don't want to anymore."

I felt like stamping my foot and crying, demanding Aunt Julia in with me again, but somehow I knew it would do no good, they only had eyes for each other. It was years later that I learnt Mum and Aunt Julia had never argued before, not even as kids. Up until Blakemort they'd always got on.

Because Aunt Julia was coming, Mum had bought an extra big Christmas tree and we'd made loads of decorations to hang from its branches. Proudly we showed them off and she made the appropriate gestures, oohing and ahhing at everything. We'd also hung up tinsel and paper chains, and popped leaves and pinecones that we'd glittered ourselves on every surface available, even the music room, which was still largely empty. It was just a big old room with glittered pinecones on the mantelpiece and a brand new windowpane. Mum had draped tinsel over the picture in the parlour too, the one that was always crooked, but every morning when we went downstairs, it would be in a heap on the floor, as if it had slid off. Eventually, we just left it there, stepping over it, with Mum citing 'subsidence' as the cause. Thankfully there were very few pictures elsewhere in the house, although there were faded patches where pictures had once hung. I remembered those in the attic; the ones turned towards the wall and a shiver ran through me.

We helped Aunt Julia unpack the small suitcase she'd brought with her, trying to ignore a much larger bag, the one with our presents in she said and therefore strictly off peeking limits. Afterwards we went downstairs for supper – Mum had made spaghetti carbonara, a family favourite, perfectly cooked because she didn't take her eyes off the saucepans for a minute. She poured wine for both her and her sister and Coca-Cola for us as we happily settled round the table to catch up on news, the children included in the conversation as much at the adults. We laughed, me perhaps more than the others, keen to replace cruel laughter with the real thing – I regarded any time we did that as a small triumph. The dinner eaten, we retired to the drawing room to sit in front of the fire to chat and play cards, me keeping my gaze carefully averted from the flames all the while, lest I see faces in them again.

The night continued to pass in a peaceful manner. No

one forced me to write anything and only one fly buzzed close to my head, and even that disappeared after a while. The following day we went out with Dad and he spoiled us rotten, taking us to McDonald's (don't shoot me but it was a real favourite back then) and to an ice-cream parlour for chocolate sundaes. On the return drive to Blakemort, his presents for us bulged tantalisingly in the boot of the car, any trepidation I had at returning home outweighed by the sheer excitement of what was in them.

Dad carried the presents into the house and Mum offered to help him. They were civil to each other, even kissed each other on the cheek in greeting but Mum wasn't as relaxed as she normally was. She held herself a little taller, the smile on her face not quite reaching her eyes. Dad had been to the house before to pick us up but never lingered. This time, because Aunt Julia was there, he hung around a bit longer. Dad always liked Aunt Julia; said she was a laugh. She was civil to him too, but as she spoke her words were slightly clipped.

"My, what a lot of presents you've got them," she remarked.

"Well, they're worth it," Dad replied, ruffling Ethan's hair, who was looking up adoringly at him. "Where shall I put them, underneath the Christmas tree?"

"Might as well." It was Mum who answered. "It's late enough in the day now."

"Looks lovely in here," he said, noting the log fire. Even so, he shivered as if he was cold not warm. "Very grand isn't it?"

"I suppose, we're used to it now, it's just home."

"And Carol, have you heard from her?"

Mum looked genuinely perplexed, "No, I haven't

actually. Not for a while. But, as long as the rent's paid on time she's happy, I suppose."

"I hope she's well," Dad continued.

"Yeah, me too. Erm…" Mum looked at Aunt Julia as she addressed Dad as if she needed her approval, "would you like to stay for hot chocolate? I was just about to make the kids some."

That was news to me – welcome news!

Dad hesitated too, and also glanced at Aunt Julia for approval, he must have been so nervous! "Erm… yeah, yeah, okay, that'd be lovely."

I couldn't believe my luck, we were all going to sit round the kitchen table together, Mum, Dad, Aunt Julia, Ethan and me, having hot chocolate. Could it get any better?

Mum piled the whipped cream on our drinks, the marshmallows and the sprinkles; it was like a taste of heaven. Dad deliberately gave himself a cream moustache and we all giggled to see it. Mum's smile relaxed. She seemed happy in his company and he in hers – so happy that it was hard to believe they weren't together anymore. But I refused to think about such sad things, I was simply going to pretend they were. I was getting good at that: make-believing all was well.

When Dad got up to leave even he looked sad about it. He said goodbye to us kids and then Mum walked him to the door.

"Have a good Christmas," I heard her say.

"I will, and you. It's nice that Julia's come to stay."

"It is, we feel very lucky."

"Ethan was upset by the rift between you—"

"Yes, well, that's all over now," Mum interrupted.

"We're starting afresh." And then as if she couldn't resist, "Something you know all about."

There was a pause, in which I held my breath.

"I miss the kids," Dad returned, and his voice sounded like Ethan's, lost. "I miss you. Do you think—"

"No, Paul, I don't."

"No, no, of course not. Sorry, I… I didn't mean to offend you. Look, I'd better get going, Carrie will wonder where I am."

"I'm sure."

"She's nice you know. If you met her you'd like her. If the kids were allowed—"

"They're not, I'm warning you, Paul, I don't want them meeting her."

"No, okay, she makes herself scarce when they come over. Don't worry about it."

"I'm not worried, I'm just saying."

"I know, I know." Another pause. "You're always just saying."

"What's that supposed to mean?" Mum's voice had risen slightly.

"Nothing, nothing at all. Happy Christmas, Hel."

"Happy Christmas, Paul."

The door closed, not only shutting Dad out but some of the magic too.

Chapter Ten

IT'S amazing how resilient children are, how we can bounce right back. Ethan had overheard the conversation too but before he could react, Aunt Julia grabbed us both by the waist, and yelled 'It's Christmas!' in true Slade style. How could we not react positively to such enthusiasm? We whooped and we cheered and when Mum returned, she smiled to see it, the haunted look on her face quickly dissolving.

"More hot chocolate?" Aunt Julia teased.

"No, Ju, absolutely not!" Mum countered. "Not unless you want them up all night vomiting into a bucket. Come on, it's getting late, let's go upstairs, get bath time underway and then we'll pile into Ethan's room for Christmas stories."

Christmas stories? Brilliant! We'd had them last year, but they'd been so half-hearted, as everything about last Christmas was. This year they were sure to be better. I hoped for lots and lots, with Mum and Julia taking it in turns to read them.

We settled into Ethan's room, picking our way through all the Lego on the floor – huge amounts of it, used to build tanks, cars, towers, spaceships, and castles. As Mum opened *Christmas at the Carters* we snuggled up to the adults, listening to the soothing lull of their voices. All was quiet except for that – gloriously quiet. Content, I found myself growing drowsy and fought to stay awake, not wanting to miss a moment of the story but my eyelids felt like they had weights attached.

As I drifted, I became aware of another voice alongside Mum's – faint at first, barely a whisper. I couldn't work out what it was saying, and I wasn't overly concerned, as it didn't sound threatening at all. Rather it was benign – quite benign – repeating one word over and over. Eventually, I opened my eyes to find myself in darkness. How strange. When you open your eyes the darkness fades. What was going on? Mum's voice faded too as the whispering became more insistent.

"Who's there?" I asked, my own voice an echo. "What are you saying?" I caught movement to one side and turned my head, but could see nothing. "Where's Mum?"

There was only laughter – *hissing* laughter.

"I want Mum!"

More movement, but this time it was on my other side.

Gone.

"Mum's not gone."

Dead.

"Mum's not dead!"

You.

"I'm not dead either."

Dead.

All of you.

Dead.

Dead.

Dead.

I opened my mouth to scream but no sound came out. I took a breath, tried to speak at least.

"Don't like you, don't want you."

I was so frightened I thought I was going to wet myself again. That would have been the worst thing ever – showing them how afraid I was.

"Leave me alone. Go away."

Dead.
You're dead.
All of you.

There were definitely shapes in the darkness and the more I stared the clearer they became. We were in a room – a long room and there was a mantelpiece in it – I couldn't see much more than that because of the figures but there might have been furniture too, an old piano to one side. There were so many figures, all heights and all ages, some just kids, like me, some much older, older than Mum and Dad even, ancient they looked, their clothes like no clothes I'd ever seen before. Rags. Just rags. I stared and I stared. I couldn't tear my gaze away, but oh, how I wished I could. There were so many of them, and their eyes… There was such hatred in them, as if they wanted to reach out and tear me apart. As if that would *please* them. I was going to wet myself. I knew it. They were edging closer, ever closer.

"Who are you?" It was my voice that was a whisper now. "*What* are you?"

Dead.
Dead.
Dead.

Yes, *they* were the dead, and this room, the music room,

was the gathering place.

Tears sprung to my eyes. There was nothing I could do, and nowhere I could go. There didn't appear to be a door behind me anymore, it was at the far end, between two sets of windows, and there were faces against that too, pressed up against the glass. Amongst those inside was a boy, his face in shadow but spiteful nonetheless, the boy that I would scream at later in the year and who would throw me against the wall and watch me slide down it. He caught me staring and opened his mouth wide, wider still. Everyone copied him, in his thrall. What were they going to do, deafen me with screams? I waited, braced myself. There was no screaming. There were flies. Millions and millions of them I swear, pouring out of their mouths and heading towards me like a big black cloud, writhing, poisonous, wanting to consume me whole, to feast on my flesh, my blood, my bones, my *soul*.

I closed my eyes, steeled myself further and then a hand gripped mine and pulled me backwards. I fell and continued falling, all the way into wakefulness.

* * *

"Sweetheart, it's all right. It's a dream, just a dream, that's all."

Aunt Julia meant well, but it wasn't a dream she'd woken me from, it was a nightmare, a living nightmare. My sobs were uncontrollable, but thankfully my pyjama bottoms were dry – I can just imagine the fuss Ethan would have made if I'd wet myself on his bed. Mum declared me 'over-excited', said it had been a long day, but

I cried some more and begged for another story, desperate for her company still. All the while Ethan rolled his eyes as if dismayed at how pathetic his sister was. Mum finished with *The Night Before Christmas,* which was another family favourite. I loved it but the opening paragraph, *'Twas the night before Christmas, when all through the house, not a creature was stirring, not even a mouse'* didn't sit well. Blakemort wasn't silent. It was stirring. It was Christmas after all, and the house hated it. I begged to sleep in Ethan's room that night and much to my surprise he didn't protest; in fact, he said it'd be okay, albeit begrudgingly. Aunt Julia smiled indulgently at his 'graciousness' and that at least seemed to please him.

"On the floor though, not in my bed. I'm not having her next to me."

On the floor was fine, we could always drag my mattress in.

Ah, that third Christmas, so quickly it deteriorated.

Miraculously, and despite my fears, a peaceful night did ensue. Mum was right about something: I was exhausted, and I slept with no further dreaming. Up early, I rushed to the window hoping for deep swathes of snow. I'd never experienced a white Christmas before, and it looked like I wasn't going to that year either, as the sun shone brightly. I closed the curtains again, crept over to Ethan, and shook him awake. The morning was spent opening our presents, which included all the things on my list, Barbie's house, Barbie's car; the works. My earlier disappointment was forgotten. I was thrilled. Mum had even made sure to get a stock of batteries in this time – lights could flash, horns could blare, it was perfect, just perfect.

Later Mum cooked dinner whilst Aunt Julia swatted

flies.

"You need to get pest control in here," she commented.

"We already have," Mum replied. "Twice."

After dinner – which was delicious – Ethan suggested we set up our toys in the music room. Mum's 'no' and my 'no' were simultaneous.

"Just stay out of the music room," she ordered. "Come into the drawing room instead, where we can keep an eye on you."

Mum got the fire going, complaining of the cold again and she and Aunt Julia sat close to it, finishing the last of their wine.

After a while, still eager to please Aunt Julia, I think, and to remain in her good books, Ethan offered to make the adults a cup of tea.

Aunt Julia was surprised. "Are you sure he's okay to use the kettle, Hel?"

"Of course, Ju, it's one of his duties to keep his Mum fuelled with tea. He's ten you know, nearly eleven, not a baby."

Aunt Julia didn't look convinced.

Ethan sprang to his feet. "Do you have sugar, Aunt Julia?"

"Yes, I do, just the one thanks. But, honestly, I don't mind making—"

"Ju," Mum interrupted, "let him do it, he wants to."

Aunt Julia sat back in her chair and smiled. "That'll be lovely, Ethan. Go easy on the milk in mine though, I just have a dash."

Mum leaned across to say something to Aunt Julia and she laughed. She then stood up, straightened the skirt she was wearing and said she was popping upstairs to the bathroom. There was a toilet downstairs but we never used that one. It was ancient with one of those peculiar chain flushes that caused the water to erupt in a spectacular explosion before swirling away. Enough to put anyone off!

In her absence, Aunt Julia came to sit with me on the floor, picking up one of my dolls, remarking on how pretty she was, and toying with her hair.

When the scream came it took a moment to register.

"What the bloody hell?" Aunt Julia forced aside surprise and scrabbled to her feet. And then, her complexion grew paler. "Ethan!"

I stood too and we rushed forwards, out of the drawing room and in the direction of the kitchen. In the hallway, we heard another scream, this one coming from upstairs. Aunt Julia and I looked at each other in complete and utter bewilderment. Which way should we go? Who should we see to first? A tumbling behind us caught our attention – Mum flying down the stairs, her arms flailing and her red curls forming some kind of billowing curtain around her head.

"What the bloody hell?" Aunt Julia repeated.

I could only stare as realisation dawned. The house had been quiet in the past few days, but in its own way it was like a battery too, storing its energy, needing it to recharge so it could lash out again – and this time in the most violent of ways.

Chapter Eleven

I ran to Mum but Aunt Julia ran to Ethan in the kitchen – both of them were still yelling, the sound punctuated with sobs and, in Mum's case, a few choice expletives.

"Mummy!" I was yelling just as loud, terrified by the pain that was so clearly etched on her face.

"My leg," she said in-between gasps, "my bloody leg."

It wasn't bloody but it was lying at a strange angle, twisted like her mouth.

"Ethan," she continued, her breathing laboured. "What's happened to Ethan?"

"I don't know," I replied pitifully.

"I must go to him…" She made to rise and then screamed again, unable to move at all. "Oh, shit, my leg. What the hell have I done to it?"

Tears were pouring down her face and mine – we were both so helpless.

"Go and see what's happening to Ethan." When I failed to move she urged me on. "Go on, Corinna. See if he's all right."

Reluctantly I stood and crossed the hall to the kitchen. Ethan was howling, Aunt Julia running his arm under cold water, the shock on her face reflecting my own.

"There you are," she said on sight of me. "What about Mum, how is she?"

"She… she can't move. Her leg looks funny."

"Funny?" Aunt Julia queried before adding, "Oh, Christ, oh, bloody hell, I can't believe this."

"She wants to know what's happened to Ethan."

"Ethan burnt himself using the kettle," she shook her head and looked again at his arm. "It's pretty bad."

"There was a face at the window," Ethan blurted out. "I was about to pour water in the cups when I saw this person looking in – a man, a nasty man. He was scowling at me and pointing." My brother was shaking violently as he recalled. "It was like… he *blamed* me or something. I was so scared my hand slipped."

I was stunned. Ethan had seen the man in the garden – actually seen him? The same one that I'd caught a glimpse of the day we moved in? The nightmare I'd had also came to mind. Just how many of them were out there, in the grounds surrounding the house, waiting to gain entry? It was crowded outside as well as in.

Aunt Julia turned the tap off. "I don't know if I'm doing the right thing running cold water on a burn, whether it should be cool not cold, and that water, for some reason, it's freezing. I just… I don't know." She looked towards the kitchen doorway, in the direction of the stairwell. "We need an ambulance. Here, stay with Ethan, Corinna, I'm going to see your Mum, she'll agree with me I'm sure. We need help."

We swapped stations, me looking up at my brother, his face blotchy, and his arm absolutely livid. I gulped to see it, feeling sorry for him.

"Where'd you see the man?" I asked.

He inclined his head towards the window that looked over the garden. "There. He was standing right there."

"What was he like?"

He gulped too. "He was… old."

Old? Yes, I suppose a lot of them were old – older than we can imagine.

"He's not there anymore, he's gone," I said, trying to console him. But it was a lie. As soon as I said it, I knew it was a lie. He *was* there. He was always there; a blackened soul with a mouth that swarmed flies. *Hurry up, Aunt Julia. Hurry up.* What if the man appeared again and made me pour boiling water over my arm too?

Aunt Julia rushed back in, her cheeks suffused with colour and her eyes wide. "The ambulance is on its way. Your mum's broken her leg. What with that and poor Ethan's arm, I think we're going to be at the hospital for quite a while. Come on, Ethan, out of the kitchen, let's go and wait with Mum." Briefly she glanced towards the kitchen window. "We need to stick together."

* * *

The ambulance seemed to take an age to arrive and meanwhile all four of us sat on the stairs, Aunt Julia with her arm around Mum, who looked drained, her skin ashen. I sat with Ethan on the step above, so close our arms were touching, both of us needing that comfort. The house was silent but it wouldn't fool me again. I wouldn't kid myself that the ghosts had gone away. They weren't going anywhere. It seemed to grow dark in that hall. The light was fading outside, certainly, but there should still be some pouring in through the windows from the music room, the drawing room, the parlour, and the kitchen too, but it was as if it was afraid to encroach. I started trembling again – we all were, Mum and Ethan through shock whereas Aunt Julia said she felt cold, and it was. It was very cold, but that had nothing to do with why I was shaking. No longer still, I caught movement again, a figure dashing across the hallway. I wanted to cry – so badly I wanted to cry – but what I didn't want was to add to the already considerable distress, so I bit down on my lip, so hard I'm sure I tasted the metallic tang of blood in my mouth. Despite the darkness, neither Aunt Julia nor I moved to switch the light on. We all simply sat there and let it engulf us. When I think about that moment, I liken us to four orphans caught in a storm, huddled together, at the mercy of the elements – or the elementals… an altogether more sinister force.

At last there was the sound of a siren in the distance. Aunt Julia jumped to her feet, her hand clutching her chest and breathing heavily, as though she'd been running in a race. "About time," she said as she rushed to open the door.

"Hello, love, sorry about the wait. Where are the patients?" the first paramedic asked.

"Follow me," Aunt Julia replied, explaining what had happened en route.

Mum and Ethan were whisked off to hospital in Eastbourne and Aunt Julia and I followed in Mum's car, Aunt Julia complaining she hadn't driven for a while and was a bit nervous behind the wheel, but she did okay as far as I can remember. Despite my concern, I was so relieved to be away from that house, to have escaped. We had to wait such a long time to be seen but I didn't mind, the longer the better as far as I was concerned. Mum had indeed broken her leg and they were going to keep her in, Ethan too. Which meant it would just be Aunt Julia and I returning to the house. That's when I had an almighty tantrum. Right there and then, in the hospital corridor, the lighting stark above my head. I couldn't go back to Blakemort. I wouldn't!

Aunt Julia, usually so patient, was having none of it.

"We have to go back, Corinna! Stop this at once."

"No, no, no," I sobbed.

"We can't stay on the ward, they don't allow visitors overnight."

"I want Mummy!"

"Mummy's gone to have her leg fixed. But don't worry I'm here and I'll look after you. I'm sure she'll be out tomorrow… or the next day."

"I WANT MUMMY!"

"YOU CAN'T HAVE MUMMY. NOT TONIGHT!"

A nurse passed by and asked if we were all right. Aunt Julia did her best to explain but she was on the verge of tears too.

"Look, I'm not promising anything but there might be a room free on the ward where her brother is. It's for parents to stay overnight but well… you're close family, so it will be all right I'm sure. Let me go and check."

Mercifully, there *was* a room free. Aunt Julia calmed and so did I. "We've got no overnight clothes," she said, "but what does it matter? I think the main thing we need is sleep, just sleep. It'll all seem so much better in the morning."

I prayed for her words to be true, but of course they weren't. In the morning we'd have to go home, face it all over again. But that night at least there was respite.

Chapter Twelve

BOTH Mum and Ethan were released from hospital the next day and we drove home, Aunt Julia at the wheel again as Mum sat very gingerly in the front seat with her leg in plaster and Ethan sat in the back with me, admiring his bandaged hand and arm.

"That was quite a tumble you took," Aunt Julia was saying.

"Yeah, yeah, it was," agreed Mum.

"What happened exactly?"

"I… well…" Mum shook her head as if to clear an unwanted memory. "To be honest, Ju, it's all a bit of a blur."

"I'm sure it is. Where pain's concerned, the mind shuts down to protect itself."

I listened with interest to that and even slightly agreed. Perhaps that's how I'd been able to last so long in that house, because my mind had simply shut down – most of the time anyway. And if that were the case, maybe, just maybe, that's why the house had hit out at Mum and Ethan, because it wanted me to take notice, and so it would force the issue. Then again, what happened to them could be purely accidental, no evil force behind it at all. I tried so hard to convince myself of that.

Arriving home, Mum asked Aunt Julia to help her upstairs to her bedroom, as what had happened had taken its toll and she wanted to rest. Besides, she said, the painkillers she had to take were the kind that made you drowsy and right now, she could barely keep her eyes open. All of us went upstairs in the end, still feeling the need to be together, even if subconsciously, and the three of them went to her bedroom, whilst I peeled off towards mine. Making a point of leaving my door wide open, maintaining contact that way, I crossed over to my bed, sat down, and looked around. Earlier in the year I had confronted one of the spirits. It's the story I first wrote about, concerning the boy. I made a huge fuss on sensing him and got thrown against the wall for my trouble. I felt like crying out again – screaming and yelling at the silent watchers but that memory deterred me. Even so, I wanted to know why there were so many ghosts and what they wanted from us. The only answers were in the writing I was forced to do but they weren't answers as such – they were just a collection of random words, some repeated over and over again. I don't think I need to reiterate which ones at this stage. As for what else was written I needed more help in deciphering it. I was simply too young to make sense of it on my own. But who could I ask? Who could I possibly trust to ask?

There was a scraping noise above me, that strange fluttering, and at my window a fly was constantly hurling himself against it – on a death mission too. Ignoring it all, I curled up on my bed in a foetal position, like Mum, wanting only to sleep, although there seemed to be little solace in that anymore with dreams so often turning to nightmares. I could feel myself well up but I don't remember tears falling. What I remember next is Aunt Julia's voice waking me for lunch. "… and then you and Ethan can go into the garden to play for a bit, it's cold but it's not raining and well, frankly, I think the fresh air will do you both good. The heating's gone crazy again; it's stuffy in here. Not healthy, not healthy at all."

If only she knew how unhealthy it was.

I sat up just before she left the room. "Can't we come to live with you, Aunt Julia?"

She paused for a moment, her back towards me and then turned, a smile on her face but it didn't sit easy. "Darling, my flat's tiny, there isn't the room."

"We could sleep on the floor."

Aunt Julia shook her head. "It's not possible."

"But that man that Ethan saw—"

"He's gone now, he was probably just a passer-by. He'd got lost or something."

"Then why didn't he knock on the door? That's what someone lost would do, wouldn't they? Why'd he stand and stare in through the window? Why'd he point?"

"Darling, I… I don't know."

Because he wasn't a passer-by, that's why. Surely she realised that too – being located in the middle of nowhere there was really nothing to pass by.

Wanting to keep her with me, I asked another question. "Do you like it here?"

"Here?"

"In this house."

"I suppose so." Again a pause, before she asked, "Don't you?"

"I hate it."

There I'd said it – taken another chance. Now the house knew. It *knew*.

"You won't be here forever."

Wouldn't we? It felt like forever already.

"Things will change, you'll see. Stuff never stays the same."

The smile slipped from her face entirely and I was surprised to sense a glimmer of sadness within her. I realised then how little I knew about her life. Was she happy in London? Did she have a boyfriend? Would she ever get married?

"Why haven't you got children?" I asked.

Chasing the sadness away, she burst out laughing. "My, oh my, you are full of questions today!"

I shrugged my shoulders. "But why? You'd make a good mummy."

She crossed the room and came to sit by me, one arm snaking around my shoulders, pulling me close. "That's sweet of you to say so, darling. Maybe I will have children one day. I hope so. I'm just waiting to meet the right man."

That confused me.

"Is Daddy the right man for Mummy?"

She bit her lip. "He was."

"I wish they'd get back together. I lie in bed at night, wishing just that." And I did, night after night, praying; always praying.

"Oh, honey, I wish I could make it better."

"If we came to live with you it would be."

She shook her head. "You belong here."

My heart missed a beat when she said that.

* * *

After lunch, Aunt Julia was still insisting we go into the garden. Funnily enough, we'd never really explored it fully. Aside from my own reasons, it was a bit of a jungle out there, brambles and weeds spreading everywhere. Mum was never into gardening, and we certainly couldn't afford to pay anyone for its upkeep, so the brambles simply took over, their thorny spines as much of a barrier as anything unnatural.

Mum had been given lunch upstairs in her bedroom and was apparently sleeping again. Neither Ethan nor I wanted to go outside. Ethan said he felt 'too ill'.

"I know your arm is sore, Ethan—"

"And my hand!"

"And your hand," Aunt Julia conceded, "but luckily the burns were largely superficial. You're hurting but you're not ill, not in that sense. Now come on, outside, the pair of you. I'll come with you if you like. God knows I'd love some fresh air too."

There was clearly no way out of it, not unless I threw another tantrum again and frankly, I didn't have the energy. Our chairs scraping against the lino as we stood up, we followed after her, first to the lobby to get our coats and wellies on, and then out of the front door to traipse down the side path that led into the garden.

It was cold outside but Aunt Julia was right, the air was fresh – it made me realise how stale it was indoors and we breathed in big gulps of it. We stood with our backs to the music room and our faces to the bramble patch where I'd first glimpsed that figure. Because Ethan had seen him too, it made him real. What if he suddenly appeared on the path before us? I'd be terrified but at the same time relieved. If everyone could see him and realise what he was, a ghost, they'd have to believe everything I had to tell them. The more I thought about it, the more I wanted him to appear. I found myself silently begging. *Please. Please. Please.* But of course Blakemort panders to no one.

"Over here," Aunt Julia said. "There looks to be some kind of path. Come on."

Again we followed, childish curiosity winning out. Was there a path? Even Ethan looked mildly interested. She was right, there was, brick paved – a continuation of the one from the side of the house really but it had been obscured not just by brambles, but moss and lichen too, making it slippery underfoot. Aunt Julia screamed, almost fell, clinging onto some brambles to stop herself, only her leather gloves saved her hand from being ripped to pieces.

I stopped. "We shouldn't go any further. It's dangerous."

"Nonsense," she replied, "it's an adventure. Just be careful that's all."

Ethan turned to sneer at me. "Or stay here if you're too scared to follow."

Scared? I had every right to be! Even so, I'd show him and I'd be careful, as Aunt Julia had instructed. We all had to be careful.

The brambles formed a kind of hedge, effectively cutting off what lay beyond. Not that it was particularly impressive, it was just more thicket, some of it downright impenetrable in places, a shield almost. I was beginning to get bored of fighting our way through it, and tired, and cold. I hated it out there as much as I hated it indoors. I grew increasingly whiney, wanting to see Mum, for her to be helped downstairs to the drawing room so I could curl up beside her, my head in her lap. I was on the verge of turning, leaving them to their senseless exploring, I'd brave the return journey on my own, when Aunt Julia gasped.

"Look," she said, shoving her hair from her eyes, "over there, in the distance. There's some kind of enclosure."

We both looked to where she was pointing. I wasn't sure what an enclosure was but I saw a gate and a picket fence either side of it with quite a few slats missing. Behind it was a bank of trees, forested land that looked as dense as the thicket had earlier. We drew closer, our feet squelching in the mud. Inside the fence was a small circle of land, tall grass obscuring what lay there. Almost.

I'll never forget the feeling that hit me as I continued to stare, trying to make out what was being hidden and then realising, *abruptly* realising. It was horror. Pure horror. Worse than any I'd felt before. There were crosses rising up between the grasses. And strange crosses at that, not made of stone. Again they were slats of wood, crisscrossed, crudely so. We kids could have done better should we ever want to be engaged in such a macabre task. They seemed homemade. They *were* homemade. Fashioned in the home behind us? The more I looked, the more crosses I saw. There were just so many of them. It was a graveyard we'd stumbled on but not a resting place. I could sense there was no rest there.

"Oh, my God," Aunt Julia breathed. "What the hell?"

She didn't move; she seemed almost cast in stone but not Ethan. He pushed open the gate and darted inside, looking around in awe.

"Are there names on the crosses?" Aunt Julia called.

Ethan knelt down. "Erm… yeah, but just carved onto the wood. There are no dates or anything, not like you get in a proper cemetery."

'A proper cemetery.' Those words still resonate with me. This wasn't a proper cemetery. There was nothing sacrosanct about this ground.

Ethan started laughing and immediately my skin began to crawl. "How cool is this?" he was saying. "We've got a graveyard in our garden. How many kids have got a graveyard in their garden? Wait 'til I tell my friends at school."

"Ethan, I'm not sure—" Aunt Julia began but Ethan wasn't listening.

"Joseph Bastard, Edward Bastard, Jonathan Bastard, Emily Bastard, Sarah Bastard, Bastard, Bastard, Bastard – they've all got swear words for surnames!"

"No, that can't be," Aunt Julia replied. At last she went in, had to check for herself. She knelt down too, brushing aside wisps of grass so she could read. "You're right," she said, after a moment. "Every one of them has 'Bastard' after their first name, but why? What a strange thing to do."

"'Cos they're evil!" Ethan laughed. "They're bastards!"

Aunt Julia flinched. "Stop saying that word."

"But it's true. Bastard! Bastard! Bastard!" God, he was enjoying himself was Ethan, not only swearing but taunting too.

Aunt Julia stood and placed her hands on her hips. She looked furious. "Stop it, Ethan! Stop it, do you hear? I'm serious, stop saying that."

"Why? It's not a swear word," Ethan insisted, not cowered at all. "It's a surname. I can say it as much as I like!"

He continued to chant, squaring up to Aunt Julia as Mum had squared up to her during her first Christmas here. I could tell she was growing more and more angry.

"Ethan!" I called, a warning in my voice but when did he ever listen to me? I'll tell you when. Never. Nonetheless

I called his name again, trying to get him to turn towards me, for the spell he was under to be broken. Because that's what it seemed like, that he was under a spell.

Another shock lay in wait. Aunt Julia's hand came out and slapped him hard across the face. That silenced him. It silenced us all. Aunt Julia was dumbstruck, as if she couldn't quite believe what she'd done.

Eventually her expression changed. She reached out and grabbed hold of Ethan's good arm. He was struggling but her hold was firm, you might even say desperate. "I'm sorry, I'm so sorry," she kept saying. "Honestly, Ethan, I don't know what came over me." He stopped struggling but only because he knew it was no use. He was no match for Aunt Julia. Her hands still on him, she knelt beside him, stared into his eyes, both an appeal and a warning in them. "Your mum's been through a lot lately, let's not, erm… tell her about this. Let's… keep it between ourselves. I'm sorry, Ethan, you know how sorry I am. I love you. Honestly I do, and it won't happen again. I promise. That… that game you want, that new racing game you've been after, for your computer, if you're a good boy from now on, I'll buy it for you. Yes, I will, honestly, it's yours, all yours. Just don't tell Mum about what happened, or about this graveyard either." She glanced only briefly at it as she said that. "It's not as if it's in your garden, not really. It's on the land behind. There's really no need to tell her. She's got a lot on her plate, your poor mum. The last thing she needs is more worry."

I'd crept closer and could see Ethan's face – at the promise of a new racing game, he'd become sly instead of defiant. Aunt Julia knew she'd won.

She stood up, briefly hugged Ethan, and then turned to

me. "Did you hear that, sweetie, we're not going to mention anything to your Mum about any of this. After all, we don't want any more bad stuff to happen do we?"

Of course we didn't, or at least *I* didn't.

"Corinna…" she prompted, "you have to promise you won't say a word."

"I promise." My voice trembled as I said it.

"Oh, good, that's good. And promises shouldn't be broken." Her smile seemed unnaturally wide. "I've got an idea, let's see how Mum is, whether she's awake yet. Perhaps she's up for a game of cards. That'll be fun, won't it, a game of cards, or Scrabble. I know how much you love Scrabble. Especially you, Corinna."

The pair of them left the circle with the crosses in it and Aunt Julia reached for my hand, pulling me towards the house, all of us complicit in keeping a secret this time.

Chapter Thirteen

SO that was our third Christmas. Finding the graveyard, the names on the crosses, Aunt Julia slapping Ethan – actually slapping him – which was just as shocking as Mum breaking her leg and Ethan burning himself. I never thought my aunt capable of such an action and inside I was reeling from it. Ethan, however, continued to look smug. I had a feeling Aunt Julia would be spoiling him a lot in the future. As promised, neither of us said anything to Mum about what we found, but perhaps we should have – perhaps that was a mistake. In a house like Blakemort, honesty is protection. I realise that now. If you keep secrets, you're playing into its hands.

Once in the house Ethan started looking at the Argos catalogue, no doubt earmarking all the goodies he could make Aunt Julia buy him. I wanted to go to Mum, but not upstairs, not in her bedroom, so I asked my aunt to bring her down.

"Of course," Aunt Julia replied, "I'll go and fetch her right now." It seems I had the power to make her do whatever I wanted as well. But she needn't have worried so much about me. If Mum found out what she'd done, the feud would start up again and God knows how long it would continue this time. I didn't want that either.

Mum came downstairs, the fire was lit, dinner was prepared, and we all sat on the sofas eating it – Mum's leg resting on a cushioned chair. It was soon bedtime and we were told to go and get our pyjamas on. "You're a big girl now," Mum said, looking at me, "you can wash and dress yourself. And don't skimp either. Two minutes you brush your teeth for, no less. And brush your hair too, you look like a wild child."

I got to the sink in the bathroom first but Ethan jostled me out of the way, reaching for his toothbrush. I stood slightly behind him, cross about that, about everything. When he finished I took my turn but he didn't leave the bathroom, instead he stood there and stared at me. I frowned and continued brushing, two minutes as Mum had said, wishing we had our old egg timer so I could get it exact. Still Ethan was staring.

I cut the brushing short.

"What is it, what's wrong?" I asked, confused by his sudden interest.

"I was just wondering."

"Wondering what?"

"About your name."

"My name?"

"Yeah. What it would sound like."

"Sound like?" I questioned. "Ethan, I don't know what you mean."

His lip curled as he sneered at me.

"Corinna Bastard," he said before turning and stalking off.

* * *

Crying again, I rushed downstairs. Mum hushed and soothed me, asked what was wrong, but I couldn't tell her, especially with Aunt Julia in the room, so I just said my brother was being mean again.

Mum's face fell. She looked as upset as I was. "I'll speak to him tomorrow and tell him not to be such a tease."

Tease? How easily one word can belittle such actions! He was turning out to be as cruel as the ghost boy. Talking of whom, I wondered what Bastard he was? He must be one of them. Joseph, Jonathan, Edward, one of the names that Ethan hadn't read out perhaps? I cried harder, only stopping to sip at the hot chocolate that Aunt Julia had rushed off to make me especially, trying to take comfort in its silky warm taste. It was sour though, the milk having turned again probably.

Pushing the hot chocolate aside, I refused to go back upstairs, and said I wanted to sleep on Mum's lap whilst they talked. Mum relented, not wanting to upset me further. But I didn't really sleep, I dozed, and whilst dozing I listened.

"You really don't mind staying a few more days, Ju?"

"Of course not, I'm not going to leave you in the state you're in."

"But your job—"

"Can take a back seat. Look, you need to rest, especially in the first week or so, to give that leg a chance to mend."

"Yeah, I suppose so, but it's six weeks of this I've got to look forward to."

"I can't stay that long."

Mum laughed. "Oh, I know, Ju, I wasn't suggesting. I'll get used to it, improvise; come down the stairs on my bum, that sort of thing. People have had to put up with far worse. Besides, Paul will help with the kids, I'm sure. If his girlfriend lets him."

"What a pain though. What a bloody pain."

"Literally."

They both laughed at that.

"How's the work going, Ju? You enjoying your new job?"

That was news to me. I didn't know my aunt had a new job.

"It's okay. Finance is finance isn't it, wherever you are, but at least it pays well."

Mum sighed, her hand on my hair, intermittently stroking it. "I could do with a job that pays well at the moment."

"Funny times aren't they? Hard times for some."

"Right now it's hard times all the time."

"Do you… regret, you know…?"

"Not giving Paul a second chance?"

There was silence in which Aunt Julia must have nodded.

"No." Mum's voice was firm. "I couldn't, you know… What he did, that level of betrayal, I never thought, never imagined… It just killed what was between us stone dead, for me anyway." There was another pause. "I feel bad for the kids though."

"Don't. You're doing great with them."

"I'm not so sure about that, they're not getting on great, not at all. They're always fighting, and Ethan, he's just so… miserable sometimes, depressed even."

"Ever since the break-up?"

"Yeah, and moving to Blakemort, the whole package I think. Corinna hates it here too, she never says so but I know it."

"She's said it to me."

I imagined Mum raising an eyebrow. "Oh, really, when?"

Aunt Julia told her.

"Do *you* like it here?" Aunt Julia asked Mum the exact same question I'd asked her and like Aunt Julia, she hesitated before replying

"I like that the rent's cheap," she replied at last. "That helps a great deal. I wish I could afford to rent somewhere closer to the kids' school, well… to everything really. To civilisation. We're a bit cut off here but I can't, it's as simple as that. We hardly made anything on our house, especially when it's divided between two people."

"Paul's bought though."

"Paul's bought with his girlfriend. Besides, he earns more than me." Mum shifted a bit. "Maybe this year will be better and work will pick up, so I can add to my savings."

"I hope so."

Mum must have frowned because Aunt Julia asked her what was wrong.

"Oh, nothing, nothing."

"Hel, come on, I'm your sister. You can't fool me."

"It's just… the little one hating this house, refusing to come into my bedroom, being so unsettled. You know she cries all the time, it's upsetting."

I was indignant at that – I did not cry all the time, not anymore! Did I?

"It's a big house," Aunt Julia offered, "especially when you're little – and to kids that can be scary."

"Scary? Yeah, and that man at the window, the one that

shocked Ethan, that's scary too."

"Hel," – There was a wary note in Aunt Julia's voice – "have you remembered what happened when you fell? Were you panicking because you heard Ethan scream?"

"Every mum panics when they hear their kid scream."

"Yeah, I understand that but did you trip or something?"

Mum stopped stroking my hair and her whole body tensed.

"Trip? I don't know."

"What do you mean you don't know?"

I tensed too, just as much as Mum.

"Because I don't think I did trip."

"Oh?"

"It felt like I was pushed."

Part Three
The Fourth Christmas

Chapter Fourteen

"I don't understand it, I just don't understand it!"

I looked up from where I was sitting on the sofa, a book balanced in one hand. "What's the matter, Mum?"

"It's this mould. It's everywhere, absolutely everywhere. As soon as I clean it, it comes racing back. It's going to take over the whole house at this rate!"

Mum was over in the far corner, on her hands and knees, a bucket of water by her side, water that had turned black with filth. "I'm fed up of it, I really am. This house… this bloody house… what with the heating, the electrics, and the flies. God, the flies!"

"Why don't we move?" I asked the question, still hoping for a favourable answer.

"We can't, not yet. I've already explained that."

She had but not to me, to Aunt Julia, all those months ago. I could recall their conversation word for word, how she thought she'd been pushed down the stairs, that time she'd broken her leg. But then, in the next breath she'd denied it: "Ignore me. I'm getting confused. All those painkillers are addling my brain." And with that any hope I had of confiding in her faded – she didn't want to believe that something malevolent might be responsible. No one does. Who can blame them?

Mum stood up, she looked so cross I wondered if she might stamp her foot like I used to when I was younger. She didn't. She just took the bucket of water and carried it through to the kitchen, ready to change it for fresh. Weary but determined.

It was November, and we were on the run-up to Christmas again, our fourth Christmas and by now, instead of looking forward to it, *longing* for it, I was dreading it. Any childish enthusiasm successfully extinguished. Even Ethan was less bothered, not that we saw that much of Ethan anyway. After school he'd lock himself in his room, playing with yet another computer game Aunt Julia had sent him. Mum was baffled. "I can't believe how much you're spoiling him," she remarked once. They were speaking on the telephone so what my aunt's excuse was, I don't know.

Aunt Julia was planning on visiting again at Christmas even though she was now seeing someone. "It's tradition," Mum said, or at least it had become tradition since Mum had split with Dad – a show of sisterly support at a time when no one should be alone. She'd been down in the summer too, but only overnight and Mum had gone to see her on one of the rare occasions we actually stayed over at Dad's. That was one good thing about Christmas at least, Aunt Julia being here. Despite what had happened I missed her and anyway, I'd come to the conclusion that Ethan deserved that smack. I didn't blame her one bit.

It was a rainy weekend, hence Mum was cleaning – "Making a start on getting the house halfway decent for Christmas," she said. Ethan had gone out with Dad but I'd opted to stay at home with Mum, she seemed so agitated lately and again I was worried for her. It hadn't been the best of years – Mum's leg had mended but she'd not been well for a lot of it, as she'd had several colds and a cough that lingered. Ethan had been ill too, developing a mysterious rash on his stomach, like he'd been pricked with a thousand tiny needles. The doctor had said it was nothing to worry about but I began to wonder about those marks, and just who was responsible for them. I'd been okay, by and large, the odd sniffle, but Mum and Ethan were always poorly, and Ethan had missed quite a chunk of school.

Not me though. I never missed school – I had too much to learn. The book I was reading was a chapter book, aimed at much older children. I was eight (going on nine) but I could read really well and write too – of an 'excellent standard' according to my pleased teachers. I spent so much time practising both I was advanced beyond my years. With Mum busy and Ethan absent, I decided to go upstairs to my room, to look at the stash of papers I kept hidden.

Automatic writing – that's what the practice is called – I know that well enough now, a psychic ability whereby either your subconscious or something supernatural takes control to produce written matter. It can happen in either a trance or a waking state – with me it was mostly in a waking state. Skeptics claim it's *only* the subconscious mind in action and in many cases I think they're right. But there was no way my mind could conjure up any of this and from such a young age too. Besides, I could feel the hand that took hold of mine; could sense their insistence, and also lately their desperation. But of what? Of being discovered? By who exactly?

Dragging my chair over to the wardrobe, I climbed on it, ignoring how wobbly it was and the threat of it buckling beneath me. Quickly retrieving the box with the stash in it I took it over to my bed. Beforehand, I had pulled the curtains – I don't know why I did this, it just made it more private somehow as if what was outside couldn't peek in. Silly I know. I was on the second floor, but then again, there's a school of thought that suggests spirits can hover. Sillier still, there were plenty in the house itself, but somehow it just seemed safer being cocooned, so I went with those feelings, as children often do. Lifting the lid of the box, I stared at the contents, which were in a bit of a jumble I have to admit and I was momentarily cross with myself for not keeping them in the order they'd been written. But then I shrugged. What the heck. A lot of the stuff repeated itself anyway. But, and this was only very recently, the writing was becoming more sophisticated. It was as though whoever was using me as a conduit was growing with me. Either that or making better use of my enhanced skills. I started sifting through. There was always much use of the word *Death* and *Evil,* as if the writer was trying to drum it home but it didn't have to try so hard. Remembering what was above me, in the attic; in the makeshift cemetery we'd discovered; in the music room, and those that hid just out of sight, I knew well enough what was here. *Bad place.* That was repeated a lot too, often 'bad' in capital letters with an exclamation mark after it: *BAD! BAD! BAD!* I knew that too but what could I do about it?

On some pieces of paper there was nonsense scrawled, letters haphazard and shaky, as if whoever possessed me was quaking with fear. I would feel fear too, great swathes of it washing over me – emotions by proxy. And on another sheet there'd just been crosses, of all shapes and sizes. This was before we'd discovered the cemetery. I now think this was the spirit's way of telling me about it. I handled another piece of paper; one I'd read a hundred times over. *Some hide. Some don't.* Who were the ones hiding and why? Only once had I asked that question out loud and my hand had replied with one simple instruction: *Don't.*

I breathed a sigh of exasperation. As I've said before, the writing was becoming a bit more sophisticated in that different words were at last being used, not variations of the same ones. *Long ago* had been employed many times but now there was the use of the word *History* and *Key.* There were other additions too – *Danger. Leave. Go.* But most recently was the use of the word *Quick. Must be quick.* Sometimes I got the impression those words referred to me, to us as a family, and sometimes to the writer itself – they had to be quick because they feared retribution.

All this was just surmising though. I didn't know anything for sure and, at a time when I should still be playing with Barbie dolls (I didn't do that so much after that incident with the boy) I was trying to figure out the mystery of my surroundings instead; something I resented. Part of me wanted to take the box downstairs and throw it in the fire and whenever that thought popped up, I'd hear a voice in my head chanting *Do it! Do it! Do it!* And that's why I didn't because I attributed that voice to the boy who'd stepped forward. The spite in it was all too familiar.

Another thought occurred. When I'd tried to destroy the first piece of paper, rip it up, something had stopped me, a force so strong I'd likened it to a wall, bending me backwards over the bed, crushing me, warning me. But was it a warning for the greater good? Don't destroy this paper because you need it; if you want to survive you have to understand. I inhaled. Felt proud of myself for coming to that conclusion, for realising something: that there were two forces at war in Blakemort – a second one that, like me, was given to moments of boldness, who didn't just take all the house had to throw at them, who came out of hiding sometimes and fought back.

I also thought of Mum and Ethan – all that had happened to them, and wondered if they were easy targets. Those who don't believe, who won't even countenance such things, sometimes the reason for that is fear. It was hard to believe in Ethan's case because he was always so bolshie, but Mum only ever wanted to think about good things, so she'd bury her head in the sand when it came to the bad, and not confront such issues. Run away from them or, in Dad's case, let them run from her. It's not a criticism, I love my mother, but sometimes you have to meet the problems head on. Or so I reckoned – optimism returning as I began to feel braver too, like the characters I'd read about in so many books, all of whom overcame adversity by refusing to be cowed. There was a mystery surrounding me – the mystery of Blakemort – and I congratulated myself even further when I put two words together from my unseen scribe and made sudden sense of them. *History* is the *key*. I had to find out the history of the house if I was going to prove as valiant as those in fiction.

Chapter Fifteen

I rushed downstairs. Mum had gone back into the living room and was still scrubbing, still muttering. I heard her say, "How did it come to this? How did it ever come to this?"

Because you didn't stay and fight for Dad, or send that girlfriend of his packing.

With my newfound sense of knowledge I was sure she could have seen her off – won the fight. I hadn't met Carrie yet but who could compare to Mum? Despite my adoration of her, rage surged as I watched her on her hands and knees. I tried to fight it. I shouldn't be angry with her, I shouldn't! She was suffering, but then so were we. Why couldn't she have forgiven Dad? Was it really so difficult? Would I be as unforgiving when I grew up? Would I be the same as her, stubborn to a fault?

The rage in me grew fiercer as my gaze was drawn towards the fireplace. There were only blackened embers in it, but to the side was an iron poker hanging from a stand. I couldn't stop staring at it; it was as though my head was caught in a vice. All too vividly I imagined walking over to that poker and picking it up, loving the cold, hard feel of it in my hand, the sheer weight. My fingers tightened. What? It seemed I had it my hand already! I was also standing behind Mum, her back to me as she continually washed the wall, continually muttered. If she started to hum that tune… Oh, God, if she started to do that… My hand hovering for only a few moments, I hit out. There was such strength in my arm; such will. Blood spurted everywhere, like some sort of festive decoration, splattering not only walls, covering the mould, but me too – decorating me. It was on my lips and my tongue ran across them, enjoying the taste, wanting more, to gulp from the fountain that sprayed upwards, to quench a sudden, perhaps insatiable desire. Mum was on the floor, her head broken this time, not her leg; an injury she was never going to recover from.

"Oh, there you are, darling, I was wondering where you'd got to."

I was confused. Mum was speaking, but how? She was dead wasn't she? I blinked and shook my head so violently that Mum stopped what she was doing and came over to me. I hadn't moved at all. I was in the same spot!

"What's wrong? Don't do that, sweetie, you'll addle your brain."

My body was shaking too. That vision had been so real! I really thought I'd committed such a vile crime – or rather that I'd been made to – that poor Mum had been battered to death! Coming from the distance of the music room I could hear laughter, such dire amusement in it and, rather than frighten me, it strengthened my resolve. I stopped shaking my head, held back the tears, refused to give those who watched that satisfaction. Instead I looked my bemused mum straight in the eye.

"I forgot to tell you, we're doing a history project at school. We've got to pick a house and learn about the history of it." I shrugged, my manner convincingly casual, at least I hoped so. "Blakemort's old, can you help me find out all about it?"

* * *

Ethan arrived home after dinner, hugging Dad goodbye in the car and rushing in. He only said a brief hello to us but he looked furtive as if he had something to hide. Mum reckoned so too because she stared after him as he took the stairs two at a time.

"Did you enjoy your day?" she called but he didn't reply. "Oh, well," she continued, "let's presume he did."

Dad hadn't come in but then I'd seen him that morning anyway, so I wasn't really fussed. I had other things on my mind.

"Mum, when shall we make a start on my history project?"

"Your history project?" The absent-minded nature of her reply indicated she'd forgotten I'd asked.

"Yes, I mentioned it earlier."

"That's right, hmm, yes, well… I'm not sure how we really go about it to be honest. I could email Carol to see what she knows. Other than that, I imagine we go to our local record office; there must be something about Blakemort there, some house deeds, or a registry of who's lived here through the years. We could even try the Internet and see what we find on there. When does the project have to be in for?"

"Soon," I said, remembering the word *quick* and how many times it had been written.

"Let's go to my office and try the Internet first."

The Internet then wasn't quite what it is today but, as Mum said, it was worth trying. Firing up her computer, Mum typed 'Blakemort, Whitesmith' into the search bar. At first nothing happened as the computer 'thought' about it, I always used to imagine little cells like whorls spinning away inside its 'mind' when it did that. We both waited patiently – it seemed to be taking an age – Mum occasionally shivering, as it was cold, and getting colder, the temperature plummeting.

"Come on, come on," she was saying. I think she was eager to return to the fire, to warm up or try, at least.

At last the screen changed and pages upon pages of information came up but nothing to do with Blakemort. When Mum tried to click on one of the links, all it said was 'page unavailable'.

"Try again," I urged, wondering if it was another game being played – the spirits somehow manipulating our search, or rather hindering it. She made a mistake though and typed in 'Blackmort' instead. The first few links referred to company names but there, at the bottom was a link to '*The Black Death: The Greatest Catastrophe Ever*.'

"Look, Mum," I said, pointing. We'd been taught about the Black Death in school; that it had taken place during the Middle Ages and rats had been a main carrier of the disease. It had been both fascinating and awful to learn about, with drawings of people whose skin were covered in boils. So many people had died from it, more than I could comprehend, and I was saddened to think of children losing parents, and parents losing children, all the loved ones that had perished because they'd fallen ill. "Do you think that happened here too?"

Mum looked at me. "Here? Do you mean in Sussex?"

I nodded. I suppose that is what I meant. I tended to think of the Black Death as having happened mainly in London but rats got everywhere, we'd even had one in the house recently. Mum had heard a rustling in the kitchen, gone to investigate and disturbed one the 'size of a small cat' she'd said. She chased after it with a broom but it got away – disappeared to where it had come from. Of the spirits that lingered, some of them could easily have died from the plague. This was an old house, an ancient house, housing ancient souls perhaps.

Mum typed in Black Death, Sussex and called up a page. '*In the early 1330s an outbreak of the bubonic plague started in China. In October 1347, Italian merchant ships carried the plague to Italy, and then to Europe. By August 1348, the plague reached England, where it was known as the Black Death, because of black pustules forming on the skin.*' On and on she read, some of what she was saying making sense, some of it too advanced for me and which I had to reread later, as an adult, to make sense of it. '*Also in the small towns of Rye and Winchelsea are areas known as Deadman's Lane believed to be where the plague victims were buried. Other villages too, in and around Sussex, were badly affected.*' There was also a grid on this page with the title 'Villages Referenced', Mum scrolled down and sure enough Whitesmith was mentioned. There had been victims here, plenty of them. We learnt that entire Sussex villages had been either destroyed or abandoned because of the plague, villages that were mentioned in the Domesday Book but were now no more. The narrator listed them –

Upper Burnham, Old Parham, Cadlow – to name but a few. Mum read from the list and then came to an abrupt halt.

"What's the matter?" I asked.

"Upper Burnham sounds familiar."

I shrugged. "Why?"

"I… I don't know, it just does. Maybe it's similar to another village I know of. Old Parham for example, there's a village elsewhere in Sussex simply called Parham, one that's thriving I'm glad to say. In fact, it has a beautiful house open to the public, Parham House and Gardens. We visited it once but you were tiny, you wouldn't remember." She paused. "The lost villages of Sussex, it sounds so sad doesn't it?"

The way she said it, she sounded lost too. I had another question for her.

"Mum, what does the word 'mort' mean?"

"Mort?"

"It's French isn't it?" How I knew that at such a young age I'll never know, perhaps once again it had been referred to in school.

"Yes," she replied. "Yes of course it is." Again she paused. "It means death."

* * *

We stopped our search soon after, Mum said that 'morbid affairs' were side-tracking us. There was nothing specifically about our house anyway, not on the Internet, so, after promising me a trip to the local record office, she declared it bedtime.

"And like I said, I'll email Carol. She might be able to tell us something more."

On our way upstairs, Mum peeked into Ethan's room and was surprised to find him already asleep. Then she went to get ready for bed herself, whilst I brushed my teeth and got changed into pyjamas.

I'd gone to my room, got into bed and was waiting for Mum to come and say goodnight to me as she always did.

I'd pushed the door to, but it began to open, sliding against the carpet slowly, very slowly. I was puzzled. What was Mum doing? Why didn't she just come in?

"Mum?" I called.

Still the door was opening and then, with a sudden bang, it slammed against my wall, the force so intense it caused it to rebound.

I stared in amazement, wondering what had just happened. For a few seconds it remained shut and then it creaked and started to open again, just as slowly.

I held my breath, waiting for a repeat performance.

Mum appeared in the doorway, a line running deep across the bridge of her nose.

"I've remembered something," she said.

Relieved at seeing her it took a moment to ask what she'd remembered.

"That village name, the one that sounded familiar – Upper Burnham – it was Carol who mentioned it to me." She crossed the room to sit on my bed. "It'll make an interesting snippet for your project actually, come to think of it. This house is on the edge of the village of Whitesmith. But actually, Carol said, before boundaries moved, it was classified as being in another village."

Another village? I frowned, trying to make sense of what

she meant.

Mum noticed my puzzled reaction and laughed. "Yes, Blakemort originally stood in the village of Upper Burnham, so it must have been the only house that survived the plague, that wasn't abandoned, or razed to the ground."

"Razed to the ground? What does that mean?"

"It means that the majority of houses were burnt. Fire was seen as cleansing, as a means of purification, and that's what they had to do, purify the ground that had become tainted."

I was horrified. "Did they burn people too?"

"No, no, no," she shook her head, smiled again, "not whilst they were alive, of course not. But if they died from the plague then yes, I'm sure bodies were burnt, or cremated as we call it, they had to be. It was all about containing the disease you see, and stopping it from spreading." She retracted her hand and sat up straight, looking pleased with herself and expecting me to look pleased too, I think. "It's a great starting point for your project isn't it? How many children can say that, eh?"

"Say what?" I asked warily.

"That they live in a lost village."

Chapter Sixteen

THE next day was Sunday so there was no going off to the record office until the following Saturday at least. I was half relieved and half disappointed. I really didn't want to know anything else about the house, I simply wanted to leave it, but because I couldn't I had no choice but to try and find out more. I lived in a lost village – a thought that prevented me from sleeping, wondering at the significance of it.

My head was still full of it the next day as I rose from bed and made my way to the kitchen for breakfast. Ethan and Mum were already there, sitting opposite each other, Mum clutching a mug of tea in her hands and shaking slightly. I looked closer. She was definitely shaking. Her eyes were red too and something glistened on her cheek – tears. I turned towards Ethan. He was solemn, but more than that, defensive, his arms folded tightly across his chest.

I sat too. There were several cereal packets in front of me, and a pint of milk that was no doubt curdled. I gulped. Should I speak first or wait for Mum to tell me what was going on? She didn't. It was Ethan.

"Dad's getting married," he burst out.

I was incredulous. Dad was getting married? Just like that? But of course it wasn't just like that, was it? He and Mum had been divorced for a long time now, almost half my lifetime. When would I get used to that fact?

"Mum?" I said, feeling anxious because she looked so hurt. In that moment I honestly thought I'd never see her smile again. "Is Dad really getting married?"

She didn't even look at me as she replied. "Yes, Corinna, he is *really* getting married." She placed her mug down and leant towards me. "And do you know what's great? What's so damned great?"

I was surprised, was there anything great about this? I opened my mouth to reply, to ask 'what' but she started speaking again.

"They're having a Christmas wedding. They're getting married on Christmas Day!"

My mouth fell open. Dad was getting married. And it was to take place on Christmas Day?

"To his girlfriend?" I asked, not knowing what else to say.

"Of course to his bloody girlfriend!"

The one I'd never met.

It was as if Ethan had read my mind. "I've met her," he replied, his voice stuffed with defiant pride.

"When?" I asked, even more stunned. Mum had been so adamant we weren't to meet her. She didn't care how serious it was between Carrie and my dad. But now I suppose it was about as serious as it could get.

"When do you think, stupid? Yesterday."

The day I'd chosen not to go. I looked at Mum.

"I don't believe it," she said, shaking her head, this news

another grim revelation. "I don't bloody believe it." As she stood, the chair behind her went flying, crashing to the ground. "Why didn't you tell me last night you'd met her?" she screamed.

"Because I didn't feel like it," he yelled back.

"You didn't feel like it? But you had no problem bouncing in here this morning to tell me he was getting married! Did Dad ask you to tell me, to do his dirty work?"

"He didn't say not to, he said he was going to call you today."

"And break the news, break the oh-so-wonderful news." Mum walked over to the sink, seemed to have to hold onto it for support before turning round again. "Where did you go with your father and his girlfriend yesterday, Ethan?"

"Her name's Carrie," Ethan pointed out.

"I know what her sodding name is! Tell me where you went."

"We didn't go anywhere. Dad had to pop back to his flat, we went inside, and she was there. She introduced herself and made me a milkshake. She's nice."

"She's nice because she made you a milkshake? That's all it takes. And now suddenly you can't get enough of her? She's the queen of fucking everything!"

I gasped. Mum swore, I've already mentioned that, but she'd never dropped the F-bomb before, never in front of us anyway.

"What about all the stuff I do for you?" she continued to challenge. "You never say I'm nice do you? You can barely even grunt thank you at me."

Ethan stood too. "You're just jealous 'cos Dad loves her and not you anymore."

"Don't you dare talk to me like that!"

"I will! You're stupid, just as stupid as Corinna. That's why he doesn't love you. And Carrie's nice. She's younger too and prettier."

I couldn't believe what I was hearing. Or seeing. Mum had grabbed a metal ladle and was heading towards Ethan with it. "You horrid, ungrateful little boy."

Ethan stood his ground but only for a second and then he started backing away, but slowly, the two of them involved in some sort of twisted dance. "I don't want to live with you anymore, I want to live with Dad and Carrie. I've told him that too."

Mum's eyes were so wide I thought they were going to pop.

"You…" she scrabbled for a word, seemed to struggle to find one and then it was as though she hit the jackpot, "…bastard!"

I gasped again, as did Ethan, and then he turned and ran, out of the kitchen and into the music room. *The door, he's going to open the door to the garden!*

I got up and ran too. Mum behind me.

"Don't open it!" I cried as he turned the key that had sat in the lock for years. It was rusted. Surely it was rusted. It wouldn't turn, it'd be jammed shut. But wouldn't you know it, it opened easily, far too easily, without any resistance whatsoever

As he ran in the direction of the cemetery, he left the door wide open, winter cold blasting us as more of the unseen poured in.

Chapter Seventeen

MUM was distraught, I was distraught, both of us for different reasons.

Mum also had her hand clamped over her mouth as if she couldn't quite believe the words she had uttered, the insults she'd hurled and at her own son.

"Oh, God," she kept saying. "Where do you think he's going?"

I could have told her where but I was focused on something else. Not a swarm of flies this time but a swarm of people, begging for access for so long and now being granted it. I fancied there'd be a never-ending supply of all those who had ever lived and perished in the lost village, who'd come into contact with this house and been trapped by it; some willingly, some unwillingly. After all, like attracts like, that's the belief I adhere to. In which case, evil attracts evil, fear the fearful, and horror the horrified. As my senses became overwhelmed I was caught in a vice again, my breath being extracted from me, slowly, painfully. I could neither inhale nor exhale and my vision was beginning to blur. I had to breathe. I had to! I tried so hard but it was useless. Panic gripped hard and I started shaking, more violently than I'd ever done before. I lost my balance, toppled over, with paroxysms rendering me unable to do anything but be at their mercy as they ripped through me from head to toe.

"CORINNA!" Mum screamed and fell to her knees, her hands on my shoulders, trying to calm me but the force of my spasms shook her too. She looked behind her, screamed again, but not at me – at Ethan. "COME BACK," she was saying. "HELP!"

I started to feel sick, as though I was in a washing machine on full spin. I was going to be sick, bile rising upwards and scorching my throat. If I did I might die. And that's what the house wanted wasn't it? More death.

Help me!

I was screaming it in my head.

Please someone help me! Ethan! Mum! Or the one that helped me before.

The one who'd grabbed my hand and pulled me out of that terrible nightmare.

You have to help me, please!

Rather than being sick I was choking, my tongue too big for my mouth and getting bigger, swelling up, becoming thick, impossibly thick.

I thought I could hear chanting from far off but coming closer – unintelligible words but with a rhythm to them, a diabolical rhythm.

My eyesight faded further as blackness encroached. It's strange but I could see more in this heavy-lidded darkness than when my eyes were wide open. Shapes again, human shapes, were twisting and turning, their mouths open and chanting.

Mum was still screaming for Ethan but either he

couldn't hear her or he was ignoring her. In-between she was sobbing and adding her own chant to the mix, "OhmyGod, ohmyGod, ohmyGod."

Was this it? I was going to die? At aged eight my life was over. It was an appalling thought but what concerned me more was what lay in wait on the other side; figures such as the ones I imagined, whose eyes burned into the heart of me, trying to penetrate my soul, corrupt it and make it like theirs.

Legion! That was the word they were chanting! Legion. What did it mean? I'd never heard it before.

And then another voice filtered through. "Turn over, on your side."

A man's voice, but not Dad's, not anyone I knew.

"Turn over," Mum repeated the man's words, "on your side. Come on, Corinna," she cajoled, "you have to turn on your side."

Hands were helping me to roll over, not one but two pairs. As soon as I was in that position my breathing eased, only slightly at first, almost teasingly and then at last I was able to gulp, swallowing greedily. Air filled my lungs and the darkness receded. My eyelids were so heavy but I managed to open them, to turn my head slightly, to look upwards. The man towering over me was strangely tall – long, like he'd been stretched. He had on some kind of overcoat, which was dark and scratchy looking, and a white shirt with a high collar. The hat on his head was also tall, almost comical – a top hat I suppose you'd call it – but his expression was deadly serious.

"Breathe," he was saying. "Breathe."

Again Mum echoed him. "Breathe. Breathe."

I was and I continued to do so.

"That's it, that's good. Breathe."

He was crouching, I realised, but then he stood up, filling my entire vision.

"You're going to be fine," he said and Mum said the same.

Then he backed away, step by step. I tried to lift my head to stare after him but I couldn't. It was too much effort. I tried to call out but I couldn't do that either. With a suddenness that was startling, my stomach heaved, its contents rushing upwards as my body convulsed and vomit spewed from me in a torrent.

"Oh, God." It was Mum again, the stranger nowhere to be seen. "Oh, thank God, Ethan! There you are! Go into my office and call an ambulance. Don't just stand there, do it now. Quick!"

Yes, Ethan, quick! That's what I was always being told, that we had to be quick.

I think I blacked out again because I don't remember much thereafter. I only fully came to in the ambulance as I was being whisked to hospital, faces looming over me again, but kindly faces, not a man this time, but two women, dressed in clothes that were familiar at least – paramedic uniforms.

Mum was beside me too, and Ethan, Mum holding my hand and squeezing it gently every few seconds, trying to reassure me, to tell me that she was there.

I started to speak but faltered, my throat was still on fire.

"Don't, darling, it's okay," Mum pleaded. "We can talk later."

But I had to know. It was imperative.

"Who was that man?" I croaked, not even recognising my own voice.

"What man?"

"Helped me. Strange man."

Mum looked at the paramedics, her face a mask of worry.

I tried again. "Mum, who was he? The man in the music room."

She bit down on her lip. I thought I saw a faint trace of red against the white of her teeth.

"You were dreaming, darling. No, not dreaming, hallucinating maybe."

"No."

"You were." She glanced again at the paramedics. "There was no man, sweetie, there was just you and me, and then Ethan. Only us three."

* * *

After twenty-four hours I got a clean bill of health and was able to return home. They couldn't find anything wrong with me and declared it an anomaly, a one-off. Mum looked shattered but she did her utmost to make me smile on the way home, saying we were going to make a start on decorating the house for Christmas and that Aunt Julia was coming down earlier than anticipated because we were going to have Christmas sooner due to the fact we'd be at Dad's wedding on Christmas Day.

"Are you coming to the wedding?" I asked her.

She laughed, too high-pitched to be genuine. "No, Julia and I are spending the day together. We'll be fine."

Ethan was in the back of the car, not saying a word, his head hanging low. I wondered if he and Mum had made up. Certainly she included him in the conversation but he wasn't exactly replying with anything approaching enthusiasm – just a grunt here and there in typical Ethan style. I had a few days off school and stuck close to Mum during that time. She even indulged me by sleeping in my bedroom as I still refused to sleep in hers, and I'd lie awake and listen to her gentle snoring, all the while trying to calculate how many there were in the house besides us and where they'd fled to, the dead that had poured in through the music room door. What dark corners did they favour? How many watched at any one time? And the man who had tended to me, who was he? Not evil. He didn't look evil. Not Legion. Whatever Legion was. Was he the same person who made me write? I didn't think so. I was a sensitive and somehow I sensed that. I had so much to find out about Blakemort and it seemed such a daunting prospect for a little girl. I was tired, so tired, and Mum was tired too, exhausted. And Ethan, well… he was just Ethan.

Lying there, listening to the various sounds I'd grown used to, I felt helpless again. Whatever was at Blakemort had the power to hurt us, *physically* hurt us. That had already been demonstrated. There were forces working with us but most were against. The house itself was against us. And I'd do well not to forget that. Or let my guard down in the future and think things were going well, that they were magical. All three of us had left the house in an ambulance at varying stages since we'd moved in – the next time we might be heading straight for the morgue.

Chapter Eighteen

LEGION – I looked it up in the dictionary. It meant a vast number of people or things – a crowd, a mass, a multitude – endless. Such a definition did not inspire confidence; rather it enforced what I already knew – that there were so many here. With Mum gone from my room – she was downstairs in her office working – I sat at my desk, a clean sheet of paper in front of me, my pen poised. I daren't speak out loud, but in my mind I whispered.

Are you part of Legion?

My hand stayed where it was, no ghostly guide directing me.

If not, who are you?

Still nothing.

I'm frightened.

A confidence I would only share with my guide.

Very frightened.

Frustrated too by the enduring silence.

Are you frightened?

Slowly my hand began to move.

Quick, be quick. Legion. Bad. Evil. Possess. Be quick. Careful. Be careful.

I looked at the paper, read the words easily enough. *What is Legion?*

Death. Always. Ancient. Craft. Target. House. Alive.

My hand started to shake from side to side as the writing became more frantic.

Can't fight. Quick. Be quick. Can't win. Quick. Quick. Quick.

The pen flew out of my hand, smashed into the wall, and then flew back at me, aiming straight for my eye. I screamed, threw myself sideways off the chair, landing heavily on my left arm. It's a wonder I didn't break it. The sheet of paper crumpled into a tight ball, as if an invisible hand was squeezing it, then it burst into a ball of flame that only petered out when what was at its centre was incinerated. Blackened ash dropped onto the table. Terrified, I glanced upwards, to the top of my wardrobe and then wished I hadn't. Whoever it was that was with me seemed to follow the line of my eye. "Don't!" I yelled, jumping up and rushing at the wardrobe too. "Please."

But you can't plead with Legion.

The box was pushed off the top of the wardrobe, only narrowly missing me; the lid ripped off and the contents scattered. I started picking up what I could but I was pushed as I was pushed on my first day here, as Mum was pushed, straight into the wall whilst every sheet was torn into a thousand tiny pieces before my eyes, a flurry of white, the only snowstorm I'd ever seen, and covering the carpet beneath me.

A scream sounded – far away but close – as though it had travelled down a long, long tunnel, and it was filled with agony. I closed my eyes, knew what it meant.

The one that guided my hand hadn't been quick enough.

* * *

I tried to clean the mess as best I could but I didn't make a very good job of it. Tiny pieces of paper clung to the pile of the carpet, refusing to give, determined to serve as a reminder. If Mum came in and saw them, I'd have to make up some tale about what had happened, say it was me who tore it all up and take the blame. Whatever I came up with, it was the least of my problems. My problem was simply trying to survive, and not only that but to ensure my family survived alongside me.

Aunt Julia arrived a few days later. I wondered if visiting Blakemort meant she was in danger too, but I could hardly throw a tantrum and insist she stay away. I'd grown out of tantrums, or at least I was trying to. Besides which, I craved the comfort of her company. Only coming into contact with the house periodically, she seemed the antithesis of us – life infused her, whereas ours was being drained day by day.

Mum was the one who opened the door to her this time and she literally fell into her arms, relief evident in her as well.

"Oh, Julia, I'm so glad you're here, that someone's here."

She said it as if we weren't – her own children, her flesh and blood.

Aunt Julia's face was pinched with fury. "He's a selfish bastard. Fancy getting married at Christmas."

"It's what she wanted apparently," Mum replied, her voice low too. "What she'd always dreamt of, a Christmas wedding."

"I don't care. He's got kids. It's just… selfish," she repeated.

Mum looked over her shoulder at us. "We'd better not do this now."

She'd remembered us after all.

After we'd said hello too, we went through to the kitchen. Mum said she had wine on the go, and offered Aunt Julia a glass, which she accepted. Ethan hung around begrudgingly. He'd heard the initial conversation between them and looked sullen about it. In a way I didn't blame him. A Christmas Day wedding seemed romantic to me too. I even thought I might like to do the same when I was grown up. I had visions of travelling to the church in a horse-drawn carriage through a winter white landscape, my dress a perfect meringue, my hair a mass of ringlets – a Barbie hangover if ever there was one. Even so, I could see how upset Mum was. She'd hardly eaten a thing since finding out and the weight was dropping off her. Her arms and legs were also red and sore; the rash similar to the one Ethan had developed a couple of years back. She kept scratching at her skin, making it bleed.

The fit that I'd had preoccupied Mum for a few days but then I heard her on the phone to Dad. She was having it out with him for introducing Carrie to Ethan without her consent.

"An accident?" she was saying. "A bloody convenient accident. Yes, I know they're going to have to meet her, especially now you're getting married." A pause. "Christmas Day… no, it's not just another day, Paul, it's… it's far from another day. I want them back in the evening. Are you going to drop them home? I don't see why I should have to pick them up. I've got Julia here, we'll be *trying* to enjoy ourselves."

All her words were either laced with sarcasm or sadness.

As Christmas was coming round fast, it was deemed that I meet Carrie too, spend a day with her and Dad. Ethan came along, desperate to be out of the house I think, away from Mum and Aunt Julia taking it in turns to get riled up about the forthcoming event. Dad picked us up – without Carrie – and then we met her in a restaurant in Brighton. I didn't know what I'd been expecting, from the way Ethan had spoken of her, someone young and glamorous, exotic even but she was fairly ordinary, of average height, with hair that was neither blonde nor brown but somewhere in-between and blue eyes. If anything, Mum was far more exotic, much prettier, or at least she had been up until recently, but now she was so thin, so pale, she looked like a ghost herself; this realisation startled me. I had to swallow hard, remind myself I was away from the house and to make the most of it, and that I was meeting my Dad's new girlfriend, his soon-to-be wife, 'our new step-mother' as Ethan had whispered to me one night, although that was something I'd resolved never to call her. She held out her hand and I took it, surprised by her firm grasp. It reminded me of how Mum's used to be: confident. Such a contrast to how it was now. Despite my misgivings, lunch was enjoyable – we had calamari to start with, a favourite of mine and Ethan's, margarita pizza, and a huge slab of chocolate cake. We then went for a wander in Brighton's Lanes, a network of tiny cobbled streets, home predominantly to antique shops, before tucking into an ice-cream sundae on the pier. Dad seemed relaxed, happy, and so did Carrie. They were discreet in front of us but occasionally I spied their hands brushing together, their fingers clasping.

By the time we were delivered home, I was going into a sugar-induced coma. I slept most of the way, waking as Dad's tires hit the gravel drive of home. That word – home – it conjures up such comforts, especially at Christmas. It makes you think of roaring log fires, ones without screaming faces appearing in them, of the smell of baking, cinnamon, and allspice, not the stench of something rotten, of mould that can't be eradicated. It's a sanctuary, a haven from the rest of the world, not a snare, a trap, waiting to add you to its already extensive collection.

We got out of the car and Dad kissed Ethan goodbye and told him to run along. He put a hand on my arm, indicating for me to hang back. I looked up at him, at my Dad, the man who'd left us for another woman, who was moving on and leaving us behind. Sadness overwhelmed me and it hurt, it actually hurt.

I suppose it doesn't take a psychic to be able to sense emotion.

"I'll always love you, you know," Dad whispered, his hand remaining where it was. "Carrie… she'll be an addition to our family not a replacement. Someone you can grow to love and who will grow to love you. She's really very nice you know."

I did know. I'd just spent the day with her, but even so, she wasn't Mum.

"She won't drive a wedge between us." Dad continued. "Now that you've met her, that Mum's okay with that, it'll be different. We'll all get along."

Mum okay with us meeting Carrie? Hardly. She simply had no choice in the matter.

"Corinna?"

I kicked at a few bits of gravel. "I suppose," was all the reply I could muster.

"You do like her don't you?"

"Uh-huh."

He looked towards the house. "Do you like living here?"

That was a change of direction. He'd never asked me that question before. What could I say? How could I answer? What if the house was listening?

"It's all right." Still I was mumbling.

"Ethan seems to like it but it's a colossal old place isn't it, and I know your mum has trouble with the heating."

She did, amongst other things.

"What if… what if I helped Mum out a bit and got you a place closer to Lewes, to me and Carrie?"

That got my attention. "We could move?"

Dad held up his hands but he was smiling, glad to have fired a spark of excitement in me. "Obviously I'll have to speak to Mum, but we could work something out, I'm sure. Work's okay for me at the moment, although I know Mum's struggling a bit. If I can make things easier, it'd be good. And you're my kids. I want you closer. Lewes is nice and you go to school there anyway, it'd be handy in many ways."

I can't tell you the relief that surged through me at his words – it might have been night, but it was as though the sun had started to shine, promising a bright, new future, one in which we could be happy again. Oh, to see Mum happy, her red hair abundant instead of lank, her green eyes sparkling. I threw myself at his legs.

"Oh, Dad, that'd be great, really great. Do you promise?"

"I promise, but don't tell Mum, not just yet, let me broach the subject."

He was laughing heartily now, whilst wrapping his arms around me. I think it was the first proper hug we'd had in a long time.

Eventually I extracted myself from him and stared defiantly at the house. *Yes, we're going to leave you. We're getting out.* Dad looked too and as we did I noticed movement at one of the upstairs windows, not Mum's bedroom, that didn't overlook the front; it was in one of the spare rooms. Was that Mum? It looked like it, even though, in the darkness, everything about her was dark too, no red glint of hair, instead she was monochrome. It was Mum! I was certain of it. What was she doing, spying on us? I shrugged. I suppose it didn't matter, we had great news, and hopefully Dad would share it with her soon. I thought of lifting my hand to wave, started to but then I stopped. There was someone else in the room, standing right behind her. Aunt Julia? No, this woman didn't have sleek hair; she had short hair, shaggy like a dog's. There was no one in the house with short, shaggy hair, unless we had a visitor? As my hand reached out to hold Dad's, to find comfort in him beside me, I realised that of course we had a visitor, but not one that was living. No living visitor would be doing what she was doing: standing so close behind Mum with her hands both sides of her face and screaming.

Chapter Nineteen

CHRISTMAS Day arrived – the day of the wedding. Usually such buzz and excitement accompanies a wedding, as it's a celebration of love with two people committing to each other for the rest of their lives. Or at least they say 'I do' with that intention on the day. Of course there was no such buzz in our house – far from it. Ethan was the only one even remotely excited, as he jumped from bed early that morning and pulled me from mine, dragging me downstairs to open our presents. I always expected to see our gifts violated on Christmas morning, packages ripped into, their contents mutilated, but as I've said before, the spirits weren't that obvious.

There weren't as many presents as in previous years. Mum had warned us there wouldn't be. "You're getting bigger now, both of you, and what you want tends to cost more. Besides, you know money's tight, we'll just have to make do."

Aunt Julia had actually bought the bulk of presents, and I noticed there were several more for Ethan than there were for me. I glanced at Ethan who was looking greedily at his stash. Was it because Aunt Julia was still afraid he'd tell

Mum what happened in the cemetery that day? He wasn't her favourite; I knew that, even though she'd never actually voiced those words. I was. So why was she spoiling him? I didn't know what the term was at the time but I do now – emotional blackmail. Is that what he was guilty of? Even now, I don't know if that's the case but I suspect it was. Ethan can be very manipulative when he wants to be.

The fact that Ethan's pile of presents was bigger than mine, was another reason for discord. I couldn't help but feel resentment.

Ethan strode over to the Christmas tree, its branches already brittle. He sank onto his knees, selected a present, and started to open it.

"Don't," I said. "Wait for Mum and Aunt Julia."

He shook his head. "It's not my fault if they're still asleep."

"Ethan," I continued to insist. "Mum will be cross."

"So? Mum's always cross."

"That's not fair, she's… just sad at the moment."

"She's always cross, she's always sad and she's always stupid, just like you."

"Shut up! She's not."

"Yes, she is and when Dad marries Carrie I'm going to live with them, get away from you both."

"Ethan!" I couldn't believe he'd be so mean.

His eyes on what he'd unwrapped, he whooped in delight. "Yeah! It's that new game I wanted – *Titan Run*."

"You can't leave us," I said, not caring about yet another new game. "We're a family."

"We're part of Dad's family too."

"But Mum's not well, can't you see that? Don't you care?"

He looked at me then and I swear it wasn't his eyes looking back at me. There was a look in them I'd never seen before and that made me recoil as it had such hatred in it, such loathing. "No, I don't, not anymore."

I stood there, stunned, knowing more than ever that we had to get away – the three of us, together. This house… it was infecting him.

There was movement behind me, a sleepy-looking Mum and Aunt Julia entered the drawing room.

"I went to your rooms to wake you," Mum said, it was something she always did. "Why'd you come down first, why didn't you wake me?" Glancing at Ethan, noting the open package, she sighed. "Oh, Ethan, why did you do that? You shouldn't start without us." She asked the questions but not once did she wait or even seem to expect an answer, instead she went over to the sofa, sat on it, and stared blankly ahead. Aunt Julia offered to make hot chocolate for everyone but our lack of enthusiasm meant she didn't bother. She came and sat too.

"I suppose we'd better hurry," said Mum, her voice as detached as her gaze. "Dad's picking you up at eleven and you've got to get showered and dressed."

I opened what presents I had, taking it in turns with Ethan, me running out before him and Mum and Aunt Julia looking embarrassed about it. But by then I'd ceased caring. After we'd opened our presents, it was the turn of Mum and Aunt Julia. Dad had taken us shopping for Mum's presents and we'd bought her posh bubble bath, matching shower gel and perfume, which she smiled at but then put aside, seeming to forget about them. Aunt Julia, as well as spoiling Ethan, had spoilt Mum, with lots of expensive make-up, hair products, and a silk top in a gorgeous shade of emerald – a colour Mum used to wear a lot when she was married to Dad. Again Mum thanked her but her lacklustre manner matched mine entirely. Only Ethan loved what he got but I couldn't be glad about that, not when it was ill gained.

We had a light breakfast, no one was particularly hungry, and then we traipsed upstairs to get washed and dressed. Aunt Julia helped me to get ready, plaiting my hair into two neat braids, adjusting the sash to my fancy new dress, and making sure my shoes were pristine. Dad wasn't having a big wedding in a church or anything, Carrie had opted for a humanist ceremony, which sounded odd to me: I didn't know what on earth a humanist was back then. Held in the grounds of her parents' house, they'd invited very few people besides us, but Dad had helped us choose new outfits, and bought them as well, wanting us to do him proud.

It was ten past eleven when we heard knocking on the door.

Mum went to answer it. "You're late," she began but stopped when she saw Dad's face.

"Late? Late? I'm hardly going to be late picking up my children on the day of my wedding am I? I've been out there for an age banging on this bloody door!"

"Rubbish," Mum retaliated. "We'd have heard you if you had."

"Don't tell me it's rubbish, I've been banging, shouting, the lot. God help me, I was about to kick the damn door down! What's wrong with you? I know I got here early, but I thought you'd have them waiting by eleven at least."

"Waiting? Like good little children you mean, to be trooped off to see their daddy marry another woman? Oh, excuse me for not pandering to your every whim."

"It's hardly pandering—"

"Yes it is. It's exactly that. You want everyone to pander to you. It's pathetic. *You're* pathetic. Poor Carrie, I pity her, I really do. What she's letting herself in for!"

"Let's not do this now—"

Still Mum wouldn't let him speak.

"Because I refused to pander to you, you went and got someone who did, didn't you? A doll, that's all you want, someone to fetch and carry for you, to be at your beck and call. I wish I could warn her. I should have thought of warning her before. I can't think why I didn't. And kids, do you plan on having more kids? Forgetting about the ones you've already got, replacing them like you replaced me."

"Helena!" It wasn't Dad who'd shouted at her; he seemed shocked by her outburst, dumbstruck. It was Aunt Julia, stepping forward and tugging on Mum's arm. "Stop. You have to stop." With her head she motioned back at us.

As though fury had released its stronghold, Mum came to. She turned to glance our way and then looked at Dad. She was so pale, so small, so bewildered. Borrowing a leaf out of my book, she burst into tears.

"I'm sorry," she said, "so sorry. I don't know what came over me."

I thought Dad was going to continue shouting but he didn't. Aunt Julia still had hold of Mum's arm and Dad reached out too.

"Look, I'm sorry, okay, for everything. I wish…" he stopped what he was saying and shook his head. "There's no point in wishing, what's done is done. I can't turn back the clock. I can't change what happened. But I want you to know that I am sorry, truly sorry. I've got regrets, plenty of them. As for kids, I've already explained this to Corinna and to Ethan too, I've no intention of replacing anyone."

Except Mum, as she'd pointed out. He'd already done that.

Dad looked at his watch. "I'm going to be late…"

"Kids, come on," it was Aunt Julia, herding us along.

Ethan sidestepped Dad and I did too, but rather than wait by his car, I stopped and turned back. Dad hadn't moved, and his hand remained on Mum's arm. Aunt Julia had stepped aside too, giving them the space to be alone. Mum was still crying and I think Dad was equally as upset. He pulled her towards him and gave her a kiss on the forehead, his lips lingering. Mum allowing them to. It was such an intimate gesture – the gesture of lovers – or lovers that had once been. Aunt Julia had tears in her eyes on seeing it and those that had gathered in mine fell.

This was a family affair. Some might say it had nothing to do with the house at all. But I disagree. Dad had moved on and was forging a new life but there was no way Mum could, not whilst we were at Blakemort. It wouldn't allow for life, let alone *new* life. I thought of Dad's words again and his offer to get us out of the house as if he sensed it was half the reason for Mum's decline.

Quick. Be quick.

Yes, we had to be, and not spend another year, another Christmas here.

But as you know, there was another Christmas to come.

Part Four
The Last Christmas

Chapter Twenty

PRIDE got in the way of escape.

"No way, absolutely no way. Just who does he think he is?"

I half suspected Mum wouldn't acccpt any financial help from Dad. When he spoke to her about what was on his mind, she slammed him for it, screeching – literally screeching – on the phone that she didn't need his help. She was wrong; we did, but I was nine (nearly ten) and kids don't get in the way of adult affairs. The only thing I said after the phone call – we were in the kitchen and she was slamming pots and pans and banging cupboard doors – was that it would be nice to move, words I'd uttered several times before. She just glared at me.

"Yes, it would be, wouldn't it, Corinna, but on my terms, not his!"

I could have howled with frustration at that point but I

remained mute, trying to contain my feelings as much as possible.

"Mum, that history project—"

"What history project?"

"You remember I told you, the one where we have to find out about an old house."

"That was ages ago."

"I know but—"

"Get Ethan to help you. God knows I've got enough to deal with. Another client's just cancelled on me, never got the concept drawings I sent apparently, even though I emailed *and* posted them, recorded delivery too. It was a major client. I was kind of relying on them. I'm going to have to spend precious time drumming up a bit of new business to compensate, so really any schoolwork you've got, it's Ethan or bust."

I sighed. As if Ethan would help me.

The first few months of that year – 2003 – I remember as being very dark, as the three of us detached even further from one another. That's the only way I can think of to describe it: detached. Mum was constantly holed up in her office, Ethan stayed in his bedroom, and I was either in my bedroom or in the drawing room, reading and writing or colouring in. There were no safe rooms in the house, not at all, but there were rooms I deemed less threatening, and those two were it. Stuff had happened in them certainly but in some way it seemed to be more tempered. There was no more writing, even though I sat at my desk, ready, willing, and able. But whoever had guided my hand and who had been caught that day, was still in hiding. Either that or they'd been destroyed. Nonetheless, I kept that pen and paper handy, just in case.

The black mould that Mum tried so hard to scrub away was spreading, affecting not just the drawing room, the parlour and the morning room but also our bedrooms. It was like the walls were diseased. The flies were increasing too, especially during summer, so many dead and living bodies littering windowsills; the dead ones the result of Mum and Ethan's handiwork. I couldn't bring myself to kill them despite the fact I couldn't bear them. The latent vegetarian in me coming to the fore again, I think.

The heating took to clicking on in summer too, despite Mum fiddling with the dials, turning it off even – it just kept bursting into life, old pipes relentlessly cranking up, clattering away, even screeching sometimes, as Mum had screeched.

"I must get in touch with Carol," Mum would mutter. "This house is a joke."

And I think she did but she never received any replies – something that infuriated her more. 'Why pass on an email address, if you never check the damn thing?"

Mum had taken up smoking. Apparently she used to smoke before having kids but had given it up when she got pregnant with Ethan. She was puffing her way through packet after packet, for a time I don't think I saw her without a cigarette in her hand. And that cough she had – it was getting worse. Her face becoming gaunt, skeletal even, as she snacked on cigarettes instead of food. She looked old – my young, vibrant and ever-smiling mother. She didn't smell the same, she smelt of cigarettes of course but something else too – despair? It has a smell, I swear, it's sour, it lodges in your throat, the inside of your nose, your memory, and it stays there.

But even though she was depressed, there was still a

spark of the old Mum.

"If we're going to have to stay in this house," she determined, "for a while longer at least, let's make it look… more cheerful."

And we tried; we really did. Mum hauled me, and when she could persuade him, Ethan, around second hand furniture shops and antique fairs such as Ardingly, full of precious junk. We'd head out in the Volvo with Mum actually looking enthusiastic. "We're going to find a bargain today, kids. We're going to make Blakemort a palace!"

It would never be a palace, but even so, we managed to find some nice pieces of furniture and lugged them home, as well as several pictures to hang on walls, some in watercolours, others in oils. I kept steering her towards brighter paintings although she kept veering towards the dull of grey and black.

Mum was quite handy with DIY, I suppose she had to be without a man about the house and when home she busied herself positioning what we'd bought, dragging chairs over to stand on whilst she hammered nails into the walls.

"Damn," she said once, having missed the wall and hit her thumb. We ran it under cold water and she took a break whilst the pain subsided. What horrified me was that she was beginning to fill the music room with furniture and paintings, 'making it look cosy'. A vast room it could never be that, but, of course, that's not the only reason. It was already overcrowded – with the unseen. Every stick of furniture ever placed in that room sat awkwardly. In fact, every stick of furniture placed in that room never stayed in place. A wooden chair, a chaise longue, a sideboard, they were all moved back and forth, a few inches here and a few inches there, just enough to make them look out of place, untidy. Mum used to accuse us kids of moving the furniture, and when we denied it, she wouldn't be told otherwise. "Just leave off," she'd say, whilst lighting another cigarette. She'd also get annoyed that the pictures, like the one in the parlour, never hung straight but after a while she ceased caring. I suppose there's only so much you can bother about in the end.

The months passed and winter gave way to spring, to brighter, sunnier days. We did our utmost to live as a normal family and to a degree we managed it – as far as a disconnected family can. Although I'd told myself not to let my guard down I couldn't help but grow desensitised to what was going on, able to ignore figures dashing to and fro out of the corner of my eye, the sounds that I've described, the fear even. Every so often I was able to close a lid on it. Perhaps that was my mistake. I feel now that the house liked a challenge, and that it suffered boredom too, but there was patience in that boredom, time in which to devise new ways to torment. And, oh, who it tormented! I honestly think of that house as something sentient. It sits and it broods, it calculates and considers. I've told you before that there are ancient parts to the house, but what was there before? Another building? There could have been, sitting on lost ground, wretched ground, a ground caught between two worlds.

And into that world, Mum at last invited others.

Chapter Twenty-One

"I don't want a friend home for tea," I protested. In truth, I was horrified by the thought of it; for their sake, not mine.

"Don't be silly, darling, it'd be lovely to have a friend round. They could even sleep the night if it's on a Friday, you could have a pyjama party. Now won't that be fun?"

Of course, Mum had suggested before that we bring friends home for tea, and certainly there'd been visits to friends' houses after school but we lived quite a distance from Lewes, and everyone we knew lived either there or in Brighton. It just wasn't convenient for people to return visit. Something I'd been relieved about as I got to know the house better – never insisting otherwise. Mum had said, when we first moved in, that she hoped we had plenty of visitors but to be honest, besides Aunt Julia we never did. Mum used to have a wide circle of friends when we lived in Ringmer and I often wondered what had happened to them, and who had stopped bothering with whom? Of course, as a single mum it was difficult for her to go out without us, but she wore a disappointed look very quickly after we'd moved there, as if she couldn't quite believe how easily she'd been dropped. Gradually, I think she stopped any effort to make social arrangements; she grew despondent instead, even spending Saturdays whilst we were with Dad alone. But right then, at that minute, she seemed desperate to rectify the isolation in our lives, on my behalf at least. Not only was she talking about a sleepover but also throwing a birthday party for me, which was ridiculous as my birthday had already been and gone.

"Nothing wrong with having a belated event," she declared.

"I don't want it."

"Why ever not? All girls your age want a party. It's a chance to dress up, to be the centre of attention. We can hold it in the music room."

The mere thought!

"I don't want one and it's my birthday not yours."

"There's no need to be so ungrateful."

"What about Ethan?" I suggested, desperate to deflect interest. His was coming up soon.

"I've already asked and he was horrified. Just wants to stay in his room that one, playing those computer games of his. Honestly, teenage boys, it's not healthy."

Nor was this house I wanted to yell but I didn't, I just kept shaking my head, refusing to entertain the idea.

Mum paused, clearly disappointed. "Well, have a friend over then. You must have a friend over."

In the end I asked Lucy. She was the closest thing I had to a best friend. She said yes and a date was arranged. Even now I cringe to recall what happened.

It was Friday, as Mum had suggested and it was just before we broke up for the summer. Mum had picked us up from school and we'd gone into Lewes for tea afterwards, Mum perhaps worried about dishing up burnt offerings again. Lucy was in my class at school, not as shy as me, but confident with light brown hair that fell past her shoulders and a sprinkling of freckles on her nose. She was as comfortable in Mum's company as she was in mine, which impressed me. As a child I was always shy with adults I didn't know well. In the Italian restaurant just off the High Street I felt proud as she nattered away to Mum, telling her about what we were doing in school, our teacher, the forthcoming summer holidays and what she was going to do during them, holiday primarily, in France, with her parents and two younger sisters.

Mum seemed happy too. Away from the house she had some colour in her cheeks.

"Talking of school work," she said, looking from Lucy to me, "I never asked; what mark did you get for your history project?"

Lucy screwed up her nose. "What history project?"

"Erm…" I tried to interrupt but Mum was talking again.

"You had to research the history of an ancient house remember? We were going to do Blakemort, I was going to help you, but then…" she shrugged, added almost absentmindedly, "things got in the way as things often do."

"We didn't have a history project," Lucy replied.

Mum looked confused as inside I wilted. "What?"

Lucy repeated herself and Mum looked at me. "Then why did you say you did? I don't understand."

"I… erm… I wanted to find out more about the house."

"You could have just said that. Why make up something about a school project?"

"I don't know."

"You don't have to tell lies, you know," Mum added and I flinched.

"I didn't mean to lie."

"You did."

"I thought you'd take me more seriously if I said it was a school project, that's all."

"After this I don't know if I'll take you seriously again. If there's one thing I can't stand in life, it's liars."

"I'm not a liar!" I couldn't believe it. Why was she acting like this, making a point of it, going on and on? Where was the easy-going, laughing Mum I adored?

Still her eyes bored into mine. "You know what, Corinna, get over it will you? It's a house, just a bloody house. We'll live in it until Carol returns, if she ever does bother to return that is, and then we'll move. That's the only thing you need to know."

I was stunned, she'd sworn in front of my friend! Not that she seemed to realise or even care. She turned slightly, looked out of the window, but I could still see the expression on her face, it was stony. In more ways than one she was changing.

With tea over and the atmosphere strained, we drove back to Blakemort – even Lucy, ever-confident Lucy, looked a bit nervous and that was before we'd drawn up. I know I said I'd only concentrate on Christmas but what happened over the next twenty-four hours had a significant impact. It helped me to understand how dangerous the house really was, how clever, how insidious. It was a summer's day, as I've said, although approaching the house down that dark, dark lane you'd never believe it. We got home late afternoon, with the sun low in the sky. On seeing the house, Lucy perked up – was wowed by it in fact.

"You live in a mansion!" she exclaimed.

"I've told you, it's just a house," Mum corrected, her tone still offhand.

Our feet crunching against the gravel, Mum muttered about the 'bloody weeds' that were surrounding us in a circle at the front and growing ever higher. "I must do something about them," she continued. But she hadn't so far and I doubted she ever would. She just seemed to *hope* they'd go away.

Inside the house, Lucy grew even more wide-eyed. "Wow!" she kept saying, and then, "Where's your brother?" I was surprised she'd asked, that she was interested.

"He's out with Dad, but he'll be coming home soon."

"Oh, good, I like Ethan, he's fun."

Fun? Ethan? I'd never have put those two words together. Before I could protest, Lucy announced she was going to explore and was off, just like that, tearing through the house. I stood and stared. I'm not sure what I'd been expecting really, her to recoil, to be like me, to sense the wrongness of it all? But she didn't. She ran happily across the hallway, her feet clacking against floorboards this time, straight into the music room.

That's when I started running.

"Not that way—"

It was too late. She'd opened the door, gone into the garden and was waiting for me to follow.

* * *

Time seemed static as I stood in front of the music room door. Behind me, Mum had gone to the kitchen or to her office, it was always as if the house had devoured her, as if she was no more. In contrast, Lucy was in front, framed by weeds, tall plants and trees, her mouth open and one finger beckoning. "Come on," she said. "Hurry."

The last time it was open, so many had come rushing through, but all was still in that moment. I couldn't sense anything untoward, just the slightest of breezes drifting towards me, but warm, rather than that awful bone-chilling cold. I took a step forward. It would be all right, of course it would. It was just a door, a simple door.

Laughter? Was that laughter? It was, coming from Lucy. For some reason, my hesitation was amusing her. "Scaredy-cat," she was calling.

"I'm not!" I protested, determined to show her.

Forcing myself not to think anymore, not to *feel*, I continued moving, getting closer and closer. Under the lintel, time slowed even more. It was as if I'd entered a tunnel, some kind of portal, one with no summer's day waiting at the end of it, no hope at all of emergence. My feet moved faster as my breath came in short sharp gasps. I wondered whether to close my eyes, just in case someone appeared but somehow I knew that would do no good. Because that someone, that *something*, was inside me, actually inside me… maybe even the house itself. I'd swallowed it as earlier it had swallowed my mother – become a part of it, as much as the bricks, the plaster, and the lath. It had wormed its way into my bloodstream, been digested. What a thought! What a horrid, horrid thought! And not possible, surely it wasn't possible. I belonged to the house, and all because I'd passed through the music room door? Magic at work again, a black magic, darker than pitch. I was not a part of Blakemort!

I slammed against something. What was it? A wall? I heard a cry as Lucy went flying; her brown hair like a pair of eagle wings either side of her.

She landed heavily on her bottom, no longer laughing but stunned instead, beginning to cry.

"Ouch, you idiot, you stupid, stupid idiot! Why'd you do that for?"

Because I was trying to escape!

I thought it but didn't say it. Words had never seemed so futile.

Chapter Twenty-Two

ONCE I'd apologised and fussed over Lucy, she seemed to recover. She picked herself up, dusted herself down and then ran again, finding the little path that led to the cemetery, although how she did I'll never know, it was more overgrown than ever. Stamping on the brambles determinedly, she didn't appear to notice whenever one swiped at her skin and scratched it; she simply continued to drive forwards, as relentless as Aunt Julia had been. Talking of whom, I hadn't been there since the day she'd slapped Ethan, but I had to follow Lucy, I had no choice. Not only was fear lying in the pit of my stomach but resignation too.

It wasn't long before I caught sight of the picket fence. Lucy turned to me, excitement enlivening eyes that were as brown as her hair.

"This house," she said, "these woods that you back onto, they're amazing. And that, over there, is it what I think it is? A graveyard?"

"We can't go in," I said. "The surnames of everyone, it's a rude word."

"A rude word?"

"A swear word."

"What, like fuck you mean?"

I winced to hear it. We all swear, I know that, but somehow on the lips of a child, such words seem shocking.

I shook my head. "No, not that word, it's…" I swallowed. "Bastard."

"What?"

"Bastard." Repeating that word brought back the memory of Ethan standing behind me in the bathroom, staring at me, calling me Corinna Bastard.

Lucy was initially quiet and then she broke into a grin. "Cool," she said, darting forwards again.

She kicked at the gate, which swung open, readily, almost greedily. In the circle, she bent down to start reading. "Joseph Bastard, Edward Bastard…" Names I'd heard already. "And these crosses, they've got something else on them too."

"What?" I called. "Dates?" That was strange, Ethan said there weren't any.

"No, not dates, nothing like that. They're symbols, a circle with a sort of star in the middle. Don't be a baby, come and see."

Come and see? Perhaps I should. As an adult, working as a freelance psychic consultant for Ruby Davis' company, Psychic Surveys, we specialise in domestic spiritual clearance – we visit houses that are supposedly haunted and, if they are, we use psychic connection to try and persuade the grounded spirit to go to the light, or 'home' if you want to call it that; a *proper* home. Theo, another member of the Psychic Surveys team, whom I'm probably the closest to – she's like a second mother to me – has a saying: 'Knowledge is armour'. What she means is, the more you know about a situation, the better prepared you are to deal with it. At that moment, looking at my friend kneeling amongst the crosses, I knew those words to be true long before I'd heard them. I couldn't remain ignorant.

My feet like lead, I forced them to move, placing one in front of the other, my hand reaching out and pushing the gate open. It was bad in there, bad, bad, bad. As bad as it was in the attic, in the music room, in Mum's room. There were so many souls, and I got the impression that, like the woman who'd stood behind Mum screaming, they were doing the same – for all eternity. It was yet another vision that repelled me. I almost turned and walked out, but Lucy was calling me again, insisting I look.

I knelt too, in front of one of the crosses. She was right; a jagged circle was carved into each one, with some kind of a star in the middle of it. I had no idea what it was back then but somehow it seemed familiar – as if I *should* know.

Lucy reached out and touched the symbol, tracing her finger around it.

"It's spooky isn't it?" she said, not in a horrified manner, rather she was… entranced. "Have you noticed something else too?" she asked.

I shook my head. Hadn't we noticed enough?

"The crosses are strange, they're not like normal crosses are they?"

I hated having to look at them but I stared harder, wondering what she meant.

"The crisscross bit," she elaborated, 'it's quite far down. It should be higher than that." She sat back on her heels. "I don't know… it's as if they're upside down."

Upside down? She was right! That's exactly what they

were – wrong, all wrong.

I stood up, one hand flying to my chest in fright. "We need to get out of here."

Lucy looked at me, confused. "Why?"

"We just do."

Without waiting for her to comment further, I started walking towards the gate and then it occurred to me: the graveyard itself was contained within a circle, and the crosses, where they'd been planted, did they form a star shape too? Outside the picket fence, I glanced back thinking I could see a rough outline of a star inside but the tall grass obscured everything, or distorted it, whichever was more apt. I returned my gaze in the direction of Blakemort. Was it possible I could see the graveyard from inside the house, from on high perhaps, the eaves windows? That would mean venturing into the attic again and I couldn't, I just couldn't.

Lucy grabbed hold of my sleeve. "Let's go back to the house, explore inside."

I'd never seen her like this before, so excited. She was a bright girl; in fact I envied how clever she was at times, how effortlessly she grasped facts of a mathematical nature at school, whilst I struggled with the basics. She was enthusiastic certainly, with a zest for life, yet in that moment, she looked… manic.

As we returned to the house, I stopped her from going through the music room door again, by insisting we walk round the side instead so we could go in the front way. We had to knock loudly several times to get Mum's attention.

"Sorry," she said finally answering, a distracted look in her eyes, "I didn't hear you." Just like she hadn't heard Dad on the morning of his wedding. "Are you hungry?"

she continued, but we weren't, we'd already eaten a big meal. Just as well, because she wandered back into her office without waiting for us to reply.

Fulfilling her wishes, I showed Lucy the rest of the downstairs, her eyes still wide, only once wrinkling her nose with distaste when she saw the black mould fanning outwards on the walls in the drawing room.

"What's that?" she asked.

"Damp," I told her.

"Nasty."

It was, but it was also the least of our problems.

Climbing the stairs, her fingers trailed along the bannister. "I wish my house was like this," she said, almost breathily.

You don't. Again I didn't voice that thought.

Upstairs, I wanted to take her straight to my bedroom, but she insisted on peeking in all of them, lingering mainly in Ethan's, which she declared 'cool'. We stood just in the doorway and I didn't think it was cool at all. It was unbelievably messy, with his clothes on the floor where he'd dropped them, his bed unmade. But worst of all was the smell. I couldn't quite place it, but it was pungent, offensive even. Not that wide-eyed Lucy seemed to notice, she was so in awe of him. Why hadn't Mum been in to clean Ethan's room, or at least ordered him to? Come to think of it, she hadn't been in to tidy mine recently. I tried to think of the last time and realised I couldn't.

I wanted to escape Ethan's room, the whole unsavoury feel of it. "Come on," I urged.

Lucy seemed happy enough to follow me and then she caught a glimpse of another stairway, the one that hid itself away.

"What's this?" she said, going towards it.

As I'd done when she'd hurtled towards the music room door, I yelled, "Don't!"

Again she ignored me. Standing at the bottom of those narrow stairs, she stared upwards. "It's the stairs to the attic!"

I groaned. Why, oh why, did this house fascinate her? I'm sorry to say I began doubting myself in that moment. Believing that perhaps I was just too imaginative a child. There was nothing wrong with Blakemort, absolutely nothing. It was normal. I wasn't. I was *abnormal*. And then I shook my head. The graveyard... I didn't make that up. That was real enough.

"Let's go on up," she said, her foot already on the lowest tread.

"Let's just go to my bedroom, we can play with Barbie—"

She sniggered. "I don't play with Barbie anymore. No one does, stupid."

Oh, that word! Ethan used it all the time and now Lucy.

I strode forward and pushed past her. "Okay, okay, come on then, let's go. Let's do what you want to do and explore the attic, the boring old attic."

But it hadn't been boring before. I only hoped it would be this time. And, as kids do, I searched for a positive. At the very least I might catch a glimpse of the graveyard – to see if it really did resemble the shape on the crosses. As I've said, I hadn't been up there since that first year having carefully avoided it, whereas Ethan just didn't seem bothered by it. Mum never suggested it either, but why would she? People don't hang about in such places. But some things do. Some prefer them.

As it had been before, the door was slightly ajar. Pushing it open, I did as Ethan had and groped for the light pull, half expecting something to grab my hand and drag me in. I tugged and light of sorts relieved the gloom.

"It's packed full of stuff!" said Lucy.

It was. Dead stuff.

She walked over to the box that Ethan had delved into and gingerly looked inside. "Be good if we had a torch," she said, "it's hard to see stuff properly."

"Come over here," I said steering her away from it, from any photos that lay spoiled at her feet, that I'd urinated on in terror. "There's loads of clothes over here, just lying around."

Despite myself I was intrigued. Could they be dressing up clothes? They certainly looked like it. There were masks as well as cloaks, black in colour, and shifts, bundles and bundles of them. One mask in particular caught my attention, its nose was in the shape of a beak and, like everything else in that house, it smelt rank, but this time in an earthy sort of way, herbal almost, like the oregano Mum used in her bolognaise but a hundred times worse; nothing appetising about it at all. Whilst Lucy held a cloak up, I shifted over to one of the windows in an attempt to spot the graveyard.

"What do you think?" Lucy said, having draped herself in the garment.

"Hmm, cool," I said, not looking.

"I'll put one of the masks on too," she added.

"Yeah, sure, it'll be funny."

Where was it? Over to the left a bit, perhaps a bit more to the right, through that clump of trees that stood like sentinels. There it was! Tiny now but the picket fence gave it depth at least. I squinted, peered harder. Yes, the crosses did form some sort of shape but still the grass obscured them, it could be a star, it could well be a star. If only I could have magnified the whole thing just to be sure. Readjusting my eyesight, I blinked several times, looked to the left slightly, and that's when I saw what was engraved on the wood of the windowsill: more of those symbols – the circle and the cross – other marks too, letters, but none that I recognised. It was an alphabet of another kind. I reached up to trace them as Lucy had traced them outside, felt the roughness of the carving, wondered if splinters might lodge in my fingertips and then I screamed as something flew at me, my hand striking out instead.

"Lucy!" I said, hardly believing what I'd done. I hadn't realised it was her; I thought it was the fluttering thing that had attacked me before. Certainly, all I'd seen was something black in the corner of my eye but that had been the cloak she wore, the whiteness of her face covered by something black too, a mask. I rushed towards her. "I'm sorry, I didn't mean—"

"That's the second time you've hit me!"

"I didn't mean to, and besides, the first time I bumped into you, I didn't hit you."

I was in danger of gabbling so I shut up, reached out a hand, but she slapped it away.

"Don't touch me. Don't you dare touch me!"

"Lucy, I'm sorry." I was desperate for her to calm down. Anger in that house only incited more. "Let me help you."

"No!"

She got herself up, struggling slightly, before standing right in front of me. In the black cloak and the black mask she looked almost inhuman; a shape, a shadow, or something that belonged to the shadows, that should never see the daylight.

"You're stupid that's what you are, and violent. Wait 'til I tell my Mum what you've done, when I tell *your* Mum, that we were playing, that you attacked me."

Again I was stunned. How could she say such words to me, threaten me like that? I hadn't hit her, not deliberately and we weren't playing, we were exploring, something I didn't want to do, which she *made* me do. Anger rose in me too.

"Don't you dare tell my mum," I warned.

"I will, and you'll be in trouble, big trouble."

I took a step forwards. "You'd better not, I'm warning you."

"Or you'll do what? You're stupid, you can't do anything."

"Stop calling me stupid."

"I won't, because that's what you are. Stupid, stupid, stupid!"

"Stop it!"

"Stupid, stupid, stupid!" She repeated it on a loop, each word a blow too.

I was breathing so hard, my chest rising up and down as fury began to blind me. Often it's described as a red mist and I think that's accurate enough. Certainly it seemed to obscure my vision. In front of me all was hazy, the black of her and the black of the others blending, the excitement, the *hatred* in the air palpable. My hands bunched into fists as the others formed a circle around us – always a circle – as they closed us in and trapped us. Couldn't she sense them too? Was she really oblivious? She must have been, and stupid too, despite hurling that word at me.

Go on. Kill her!

It was a voice in my ear. I turned my head abruptly but there was no one there.

Kill her!

The voice in my other ear now, but again disembodied.

KILL HER!

It was screaming, the sound a knife blade, as sharp, and as piercing.

Or we'll kill you!

One hand rising, I drew it back. It was down to her or me. Only one of us would survive. The cloak and the mask helped, as it didn't look like Lucy. It didn't look like anyone. Faceless and formless, she was easier to kill… to kill… to kill…

I gasped. What was I thinking? She was supposed to be my friend, my best friend.

Lucy had a change of heart too. She stopped chanting, took off her mask, her expression as confused as mine I'm sure.

"Corinna, I'm—"

As if my fist had a will of its own, it drew back and then forwards, sending Lucy flying for the third time.

Chapter Twenty-Three

NEEDLESS to say, Lucy didn't stay that night, she ran from the attic, tripping over the black cloak on several occasions and nearly falling again, screaming for my mother. I ran after her, shaking violently, every now and then glancing at my right hand, as if it didn't belong to me – and it hadn't, not during the moment it came into contact with Lucy's face. It wasn't my fault, it wasn't! Not that Lucy would believe me, or Mum, or Lucy's Mum. She was horrified when she came racing over to pick Lucy up and Mum bore the full brunt of her anger instead of me – ordering me in the drawing room and closing the door. Left me in there to listen, to them, and to the laughter that echoed around. Had the boy, that spiteful boy, that *evil* boy, grabbed hold of my fist? Was he the one responsible? There were just so many of them it was impossible to tell.

The following week there were only three days left at school before term was finally over and Mum kept me home, insisting it was the best thing to do, that the fuss over what had happened would die down if I stayed away. Ethan had been furious that he'd had to go in when I didn't, had looked at me as if I'd choreographed the whole thing, but there was one thing he didn't do: he didn't call me stupid.

We didn't go away that year, there was no way we could afford to, and eventually summer gave way to autumn and the start of a new school year. Lucy hadn't forgotten my supposed treatment of her and made sure several others turned their backs on me too. I spent so many playtimes on my own, and no one ever visited the house again, nor was I invited to their houses, not anymore. It was just the routine of school, home and going out with Dad on a Saturday. That's what the house had done – it had isolated us. How I longed for Aunt Julia's visits at least.

"She is coming for Christmas, isn't she?" I checked with Mum one afternoon when we were in the kitchen. Mum was attempting to make scones, but she'd already burnt the first batch. "Mum," I said again, having to prompt her, as she kept a strict eye on the timing of the second.

"Hmm, yes, yes, I think so. If we're still here that is."

I could hardly believe my ears. "What do you mean if we're still here?"

Finally she looked at me. "Well, I'm not sure I can face another winter, you know? Freezing one minute, boiling the next. And it's too far out. I want to be closer to life."

Closer to life? Me too! I wanted nothing more.

Barely able to contain my excitement, I started jumping up and down. "When can we move? When? When? When?"

Mum laughed and as she did I was struck by how lovely it was to see a genuine smile light up her face, it had been a long time since I'd seen that, too long. Retrieving the scones from the oven, that batch only slightly better than the first, despite her diligence, Mum affectionately told me to calm down. "We can't just move in an instant, it doesn't work like that. I've got to give Carol notice. It's only polite. Then we have to start looking. Well, I say start, but to be honest I've been looking already."

"I thought we couldn't afford to move," I said, worried again.

Mum averted her gaze at this and I had to prompt her again for an answer.

"I've accepted help from your dad," she confided, before giving a defiant shrug. "I don't see why not. I look after his children so it's for your benefit as well as mine." She looked around her. "I just don't think it's good for us being here that's all."

My heart skipped a beat. She'd noticed! I wasn't alone. My relief was incredible. It seemed to flood right through me. *But don't let the house know.* Quickly the words formed in my mind. *Keep your plans as secret as possible.* But have you tried keeping things from the walls that surround you, the very air that you breathe? It's impossible. That was something I didn't want to think about. All I wanted to do was to soak up what she'd told me and to dream of a future without Blakemort in it.

Mum called Ethan and we sat at the kitchen table with a pot of tea, the not-so-burnt scones and the jam and the cream. This was our dinner, and, in that moment, as far as I was concerned, it was the dinner of kings and queens! Covering one half of my scone with butter, I reached for the jam and piled that on too, but as my knife dipped into the clotted cream, I saw it congeal before my eyes.

Mum noticed too. "What the heck? I bought that cream yesterday, checked the sell by date specially and it was fine. God, I don't know, it's just…" She shook her head, started agitating at her lip. "The sooner Carol replies to my emails the better."

After tea, I followed Ethan upstairs. Mum had said she'd told him earlier about her plans, although it wasn't within my earshot, and I wanted to gauge his reaction. Ethan stopped just shy of opening his door and turned to me. He was nearly thirteen now and I suppose I could understand the effect he'd had on Lucy earlier in the year. His face was nice enough; he had big eyes, and thick dark hair. He'd also grown recently, he was head and shoulders above me, and his arms were strong, despite doing nothing but sitting in front of his computer, playing endless games. What marred his looks slightly was a rash of spots along his jawline. They reminded me of the rash he'd once had – tiny dents and holes, as if someone had stuck pins into him.

"It's great news, isn't it, Ethan, about moving?" I kept my voice deliberately low.

Ethan looked far from impressed. "Not really, I like it here."

"Like what exactly?" I was curious to know.

"It's big, big enough so I don't have to bump into you anyway."

I ignored his comment and carried on, "We might go to live in Lewes, or in Brighton, Mum hasn't decided yet." Wherever it was I longed for a small house, terraced too, with shops close by, cars and people – ordinary people.

"Whatever…" He really wasn't giving much away. "I'll believe it when I see it."

He turned his back on me and went to open his bedroom door.

"What do you mean you'll believe it when you see it? Don't you believe Mum?"

He shrugged.

"Ethan?"

"Mum's different isn't she? She's not the same anymore."

Nor are you! I wanted to shout.

"It's this house," I said at last, hardly daring to believe my own bravery. "It's because of the house."

He turned his head to look me in the eye. I held his gaze, refusing to be intimidated. *Go on say it. Call me stupid. I dare you.*

He didn't, he just sneered some more and then entered his den, leaving me alone on the landing with the house bristling around me.

* * *

It was later in the month of October that I went into Ethan's room, not on Halloween, although Halloween would have certainly suited the occasion. I don't know where he'd gone – probably to a friend's or something – and I was on my way to the bathroom when a familiar smell assailed me, drifting out of his room, vaporous almost and filling the air. What was going on behind closed doors? If Mum wasn't curious, I was. I decided to take a peek. He'd never know.

Despite Mum being downstairs, I tiptoed across. Silly really, there was no reason not to walk boldly over. My breathing slightly ragged, I pushed open the door. That smell… it far surpassed that of his trainers and, believe me, they were bad enough. My eyes started watering, and I almost choked. How come Mum hadn't noticed this? His bedroom was right next to hers.

I slipped inside, not closing the door entirely behind me, but leaving it open just a crack. The curtains were closed on an already darkening night; I suspected those curtains were never opened, that Ethan always shut the light out. Groping for the light switch, I finally found it; the light was the same sickly yellow as in the attic, leaving so much gloom. His room was as untidy as I'd expected it to be, clothes and shoes everywhere, computer games strewn across the surface of his desk, which already vied for space with a computer and a small TV. He had shelves on the walls too, books, *Star Wars* figures and packs of Top Trumps adorning them. Long gone was the Lego, taken to some charity shop for someone else to play with. Tentatively, I made my way over to the desk and opened various drawers, which were stuffed full with socks, underwear, t-shirts, more computer games, and a homework book. Selecting the latter, I flicked through it, although it didn't contain much, but then Ethan wasn't keen on homework and would do anything he could to get out of it. Mum used to make him, but I guess she didn't anymore.

So all was normal. What wasn't? I scanned shelves again, the floor, then went over to the curtains, to move them aside so I could check the windowsill. Puzzled, I stopped to think. If he had something to hide, something rotten, where would it be? My eyes rested on the wardrobe in the far corner. Of course! After all, that's where I'd hidden something too.

I took a deep breath and walked over, the light flickering above me as I moved. A warning? It certainly felt like one. Standing in front of the wardrobe, it was a solid piece of furniture, already in situ when we arrived, the dark wood giving it an old-fashioned appearance. It had a thin piece of mirror running down the middle of it, tarnished slightly with brown spots – reminding me of the kind you sometimes see on the back of old people's hands. I caught sight of my reflection, something I was wary of doing. I always hated looking at myself in mirrors in that house, wondering if when I turned away, my reflection would still be staring outwards.

I reached out a hand, as did my mirror image, turned the handle, and heard the click as it yielded. The smell as good as flew at me. Gagging, I lifted both hands to my face in a bid to protect myself. And then my hands dropped as my mouth fell open. There were no clothes in the wardrobe, none at all. But it was far from empty.

Ethan had been in the attic! Clearly he'd been there on several occasions. What was up there: the insects forever trapped in glass weights, the pinned butterflies, a few of the photographs – the dead things basically – he'd looted them. Not only were they in his wardrobe, he'd added to them a collection of his own: flies. There were so many flies, lying in heaps, their bodies rotting. There were the carcasses of larger insects too – beetles, centipedes and spiders. He must have spent ages rummaging in the garden for them. And something else, something I had to force myself to look at – a field mouse, a tiny little field mouse, staked, as the butterflies were staked, one half of it putrefying. I could hardly tear my gaze away, not because I was fascinated but because I was trying to tell myself that Ethan didn't do this, that he didn't know it was there and that someone else was responsible. Ethan might be a pain, he might be nasty to me, but he was still my brother and I loved him. I didn't want him to be capable of this. I was about to turn, get out, when I saw something in the wardrobe move. What was it? What could possibly live amongst so many dead? And if it was alive, could I help it? Release it from my brother and his tyranny? I leaned forward slightly. Yes, there was something in there, beneath layers of flies, struggling to get out. Dare I find a stick… something I could use to poke around a bit? There was no way I was touching anything with my hands. I looked behind me; the best thing I could find was a pen. It was no good. I needed something longer. What else, what else? A ruler! That'd do – at least it meant I didn't have to put my hand inside the wardrobe, I could just hold it at the tip. I didn't want to do it, I really didn't, but I happen to believe all creatures are sacred, that we should help anything in peril. Even so, I hoped it wasn't a spider, I'd never killed one, but the big ones frightened me.

I started moving the ruler, shifting the vile contents, trying to ignore the aroma of death and decay. Where was it, the thing I'd seen moving? Had I imagined it, with my mind playing tricks on me? But no, I'd seen rippling and heaving, there was something there. Reaching further in, it was as if the ruler started moving of its own accord, left to right, only slightly at first, imperceptibly, but then with more force.

Let it go. Turn and run.

Those were my instructions to myself and I was about to obey them when it seemed as if something crawled up the ruler – yes, crawled – and closed itself around my hand instead. I screamed, started pulling back in earnest now.

"Let go of me! Let go of me!"

What was it that had me in its clasp? Nothing that was remotely human. It was insectile, many legged, and it wanted to impale me too.

"No!" I continued to scream. "No! No! No!"

As much as it pulled, I pulled too, my other hand flat against the wardrobe, in an attempt to give myself extra leverage. I was failing, drastically. This thing was much stronger than me, I was going to fall into the wardrobe, be shut in, and left to fester.

"Help! Someone help me!"

But Mum was downstairs, she'd never be able to hear me – the house would make sure of it.

"Help!" My voice was hoarse; soon I wouldn't be able to scream at all. "Help!"

My call was answered but cruelly. I was thrown back, hitting my head against one of the drawers on Ethan's desk and the wardrobe door slammed shut. But the horrors weren't over, not by a long shot. There was an image in the wardrobe mirror: me. I was standing hand in hand with someone. A boy? It looked like it.

And we were laughing.

Chapter Twenty-Four

OF course I wanted to go downstairs straightway and tell Mum what I'd seen and I proposed to do just that. Despite my aching head, I got myself up, ran out of Ethan's room, turned left on the landing and at the top of the stairs I skidded to a halt. What would the repercussions be if I told Mum? How badly would Ethan get into trouble? What if it was really badly and she sent him to live with Dad whilst we waited to leave? There'd be just the two of us left then. Another thought: what if she told the police? Young as I was, I thought that was possible. He'd get taken away, put in prison. For how long? It could be months, years even. I couldn't tell her. Besides, it would feel like snitching. *Tell-tale! Tell-tale!* I could imagine Ethan yelling it at me. I had one option and that was to encourage Mum to leave – she was our only hope, our means of escape. All she had to do was get in touch with Carol first.

The weeks passed, I kept away from Ethan, certainly away from his room. I still found it so hard to believe that he was capable of what I'd seen. I considered talking to him about it, but quickly thought again. He wouldn't talk to me. As for Carol, why wasn't she replying to Mum's emails? Was it really so vital that she did? Couldn't we just leave anyway? Mum was adamant we couldn't. "It's not fair to do that, besides I haven't found the ideal place for us yet."

As far as I was concerned the gutter was preferable to Blakemort. I tried to talk to Dad too, but he just told me not to worry, that Mum was sorting it. "It can be hard to keep up with affairs back home when you're travelling, but I'm sure Carol will be in touch soon. Perhaps it's best to wait until after Christmas to contact her."

He said what I dreaded hearing: that we had to spend another Christmas here.

Mum was looking forward to seeing Aunt Julia again. Apparently she'd split up with her boyfriend and was a bit down about it. "She really thought he was the one," Mum told me. "It's funny how we can be so wrong about people." It was; about people, houses, and those closest to us. I was still so worried about Ethan.

"Mum, Ethan's room…" I began.

We were sitting on the sofa, trying to watch TV but the signal kept dipping in and out, making it close to impossible.

"What about it?" she asked.

"Have you been in there lately?"

She laughed. Well, it was more of a snort really. "I daren't. Teenage boys rooms are something to be feared, darling." If only she knew how much. "No," she continued, "Ethan's a big boy now, he can clean his own room. I don't see why I should do it. I do enough around here. If he wants to live in a pig sty, let him."

Christmas was drawing closer and there was still no word from Carol. Mum wanted to put the decorations up and so we went to nearby Wilderness Woods to buy our tree, hoping for one that wasn't quite as forlorn as last year. It certainly looked abundant as we dragged it through the hallway, pine needles littering the floor although their clean almost antiseptic smell failed to penetrate. Once positioned upright, the tree's glamour decreased dramatically. Nonetheless, Mum retrieved the box of Christmas decorations that she kept in one of the spare rooms and we began to hang ornaments from its branches, Ethan dropping one of her prized baubles, made of Murano glass, one that Dad had bought her whilst they were on honeymoon in Venice. There were tears in her eyes as she picked up the jagged pieces.

Again we adorned picture frames with tinsel but, as soon as our backs were turned, they slid off. Mum bent to retrieve one of the garlands and then frowned.

"What's the matter?" I asked.

"It's nothing, it's just… how strange. Look at this picture here, it appears as if the canvas is cracking, distorting the entire thing, making it look wavy instead." She lifted a finger and scraped at the surface with her nail. "How odd, the paint is flaking too." Examining other pictures, she found the same thing. "It must be something to do with the heating," she surmised, looking for excuses again. "That bloody heating!"

"Perhaps we shouldn't bother with the tinsel," I suggested.

She nodded. "I think you're right, we shouldn't bother anymore."

Mum went into the kitchen to do some baking instead, humming that tune of hers. Later, when I went in to find her, she'd done no baking at all. Instead she was sitting, smoking a cigarette, shards of Murano glass lying on the table in front of her.

* * *

Aunt Julia was due down on Christmas Eve Eve (as we called it). Christmas Eve we were spending with Dad and Carrie, to be dropped home that same evening. I was dreading the big day, absolutely dreading it, hating the Christmas tree in the drawing room that looked so out of place, a season that should be happy but which, at Blakemort, never was. And none of it was helped by Dad's news – Carrie was pregnant, by over three months. We had a half-brother or sister on the way. Ethan was pleased, even I was secretly pleased, but Mum was shocked, truly shocked. As she broke the news to us she was trembling. When Aunt Julia arrived a few hours later she must have been informed too because she bypassed us and went straight to Mum, the two of them disappearing to talk. Whilst they did I went into Mum's office, sat at the computer and opened up her email account, I wanted to see if it was true, if she'd really been emailing Carol. I'm sorry to admit it but I thought she could be lying, actually lying, that she'd been as seduced by this house as Ethan was. It took me a fair bit of scrolling but sure enough she'd sent various emails, latterly typing, *'What's wrong, Carol? Is something wrong? I really need to hear from you. I hope you're having the time of your life and I understand you're busy, but it's been so long. Please, just let me know that you're okay.'*

For some reason, those words caused alarm. *'What's wrong, Carol?'* I hadn't thought anything to be wrong before. As Dad had said, she was simply preoccupied with her travels, but what if she wasn't? What if something *had* happened to her? Would that mean we'd be stuck here, that we'd never escape?

My hand started typing a fresh email – I couldn't stop myself. *'What's wrong, Carol? What's wrong, Carol?'* I typed it over and over again. It seemed whoever controlled my hand previously was back; at least I presumed it was them. I then hit 'send' or rather I was made to hit 'send'. I thought that would be the end of it but it wasn't. I was directed to the Internet search bar and my hand typed in *Occult Symbols*. I tensed. Wasn't Occult a bad word, something to do with the devil?

Various pages came up and my hand clicked on the first one – a Symbol Dictionary – there were so many symbols, including a reverse cross, like the ones in the graveyard, its long stem pointing upwards. A symbol for Baphomet, I read, although who or what he was, I had no idea. The star I'd seen too, it was known as a pentagram. There was one on its own and one in a circle. I clicked on the pentagram in the circle and read the following description:

The pentagram is a five pointed star commonly associated with Wicca, Ritual magick, Masonry and Satanism.

Satanism – Satan – that was definitely another name for the devil! And the word 'magick' spelt the wrong way but for a reason perhaps, because it was exactly that – the wrong type of magic? But the pentagram I was looking at wasn't quite right; the one I'd seen was the other way round – reversed. My hand travelled upwards again and typed in *reversed pentagram*. I clicked on another page to read:

… it represents Satan or the world of matter ruling over the Divine, or Darkness over Light.

That was the sentence that jumped out at me, that I was

meant to see, that I remember so clearly. The reversed pentagram was a symbol used to encourage evil and it was carved into the very fabric of Blakemort, the grounds too – the house itself encircled, nature in league with whatever forces presided, encouraging the weeds and bushes to grow that way, to enclose us. Beads of moisture raced down my forehead. I had to go and tell Mum. Show her what I'd found – the *evidence*.

Snatching my hand back, I stood up, determined to do just that, and then heard a ping as an email landed in the reply box. After a brief pause, I sat down again. Was it? Could it be? Carol was answering at last? I swallowed hard, began to read.

'*Who is this? Why do you keep typing the same thing over and over again? Surely you must realise, Carol passed away years ago.*'

Chapter Twenty-Five

"MUM! Mum! Come and see, you have to come and see!"

I was yelling for all I was worth, tripping over my shoelaces, as I ran across the hallway. From the kitchen Mum emerged with Aunt Julia, her eyes were red, she'd been crying – again. Why couldn't she just be happy for Dad and Carrie? Why did everything have to be about her? I shook my head, surprised that I'd become so easily distracted. I had to focus – there was something to tell, something important.

"Carol's dead!"

Mum stared at me. "What?"

"Carol's dead. I was sitting at your desk and I thought I'd send her an email. I asked if she was okay and I had a reply, Mum, a reply! She's not okay, she's dead."

Why I was so euphoric I don't know – it was bad news, the worst.

Mum glanced at Aunt Julia and then looked at me. "Let's go and see what you're talking about."

Oh, the ghosts, the clever ghosts! They'd erased the email! Why hadn't I printed it off? I knew how to do that.

I'd seen Mum do it a thousand times.

"Is this your idea of a joke?" Mum said, caught between confusion and anger too.

"No, it's true! I had an email. Honestly. It said she's been dead for years."

Aunt Julia endeavoured to come to my rescue. "Perhaps she erased the email, Hel, by accident, I mean."

Mum ignored her. "I don't know what you're talking about, she can't be dead. She can't. If she is who the heck am I paying rent to?"

Aunt Julia had been inspecting the computer too. She'd gone onto the Internet page I'd been reading. "What's this?" she asked, baffled. "Why are you looking at stuff like this, Hel?"

Mum looked to what she was pointing at. "Me? I wasn't…" Her face clouded. "Is this you, Corinna?"

"I… Yes. I've seen that symbol before, I wanted to know what it meant."

"I don't think you have, why would you have done? It's nasty, plain nasty. There's no way you've seen it before."

She was getting angrier, her cheeks flushing.

"You need to find out what happened to Carol," I said, standing my ground.

"Carol's fine, she's busy that's all. She's certainly not dead. What a thing to even suggest. I'm disappointed in you, Corinna, very disappointed."

Aunt Julia interrupted. "I've seen that sign too… I was going to tell you."

Mum's confusion increased. "What are you talking about?"

"That sign, the pentagram with the circle around it, I've seen it here, in the graveyard."

"Graveyard? What graveyard?"

"It's also in the attic," I blurted out. "Carved into the window frames."

Mum threw her hands in the air. "What's wrong with you both? You're both spouting such nonsense."

"I don't know about the attic, Hel," Aunt Julia's voice was only slightly hesitant, "but there's a graveyard in the grounds, closer to the woods than the house but… even so. There are crosses in there, strange crosses."

"They're inverted," I said. They both looked astonished I'd come out with such a word but then Aunt Julia nodded.

"Yes, Corinna's right, they're inverted, and there are names carved onto them, unusual names, as well as those symbols."

"You knew about this?" There was shock on Mum's face.

"As I said, not about the attic, I had no idea."

"I can show you where in the attic," I piped up, but Mum was still looking at Aunt Julia.

"You knew about the graveyard, about the fact that there's a bloody graveyard on our grounds?"

Aunt Julia's face was as red as the top she was wearing. "Yes."

"When did you find out?"

"Erm… quite a while ago."

"When?"

"A couple of years."

"You've known for a couple of years and yet you've said nothing?"

"No."

"Why not?"

Another look passed between Aunt Julia and me – my co-conspirator. "I had my reasons, but I think it's time to tell you now."

It was, and time for me to tell what I knew too.

* * *

Mum and Aunt Julia went into the attic. Half of me wanted them to, the other half was scared they'd never emerge, but they did, with Mum looking completely shell-shocked, what she'd discovered eclipsing for the moment what she'd found out about Dad and Carrie. I hadn't told her everything I'd experienced here, I stuck to cold, hard facts. One of them being what was in Ethan's wardrobe. That was their next port of call. Ethan was stunned when they burst in, as he'd been playing one of his games, totally immersed, and it took him a few seconds to register what was happening.

Mum went straight to his wardrobe, opened it, and gasped in horror.

"What the fuck…?"

"Oh, God!" Aunt Julia couldn't believe it either.

Mum might have been cross with Aunt Julia for hitting Ethan that day in the graveyard but she looked as if she was the one who could slaughter him now.

"What's wrong with you, Ethan?" she screamed. "What the hell is wrong with you?"

To be fair, Ethan didn't look as if he knew what was wrong with him either – he stared at the contents of his wardrobe, just as stunned.

"Get out," Mum said. "Get downstairs, out of this

room. I'm calling your father."

She followed him, practically on his heels. Phoning Dad, he didn't answer the phone. "Typical!" she said. "He's probably too busy with that tart of his."

"Mum," I reminded. "She's his wife."

"Who cares? Who the bloody hell cares?"

We were all in the drawing room, Mum and Aunt Julia on one faded sofa, Ethan and me occupying the other. The Christmas tree purchased only a week before and fed plenty of water, looked as if it wouldn't last another day. As for the mould, in some places the walls appeared to be an inch thick with it.

"We have to get out," Aunt Julia was muttering, wringing her hands together. I'd focused mainly on Mum up until then but I realised she was just as agitated.

"We have to find out what happened to Carol first," Mum countered. "That's imperative."

"Is there anyone else who knew her – that you know too, I mean? Maybe you can get in touch with them."

Mum shook her head. "She's an old friend from college. I've lost touch with a lot of people from those days."

"Does she have a sister or a brother?"

"A sister yes, Rose, Rose Mathieson. That was her married name if I remember correctly. She's a few years older than Carol. I could try and contact her, look her up in the phone directory, try all the bloody Rose Mathieson's until I get the right one."

"Or we could email again," I suggested, fearing her plan may take a lifetime. "I'm telling you I got a reply."

"But who was it that replied if not Carol?"

Aunt Julia looked at Mum. "I suppose there's only one way to find out."

Mum considered her words. "Okay. Let's do it."

We all trooped through to the morning room, ill-named because night had fallen, had really taken hold. En route, I thought I heard a tinkling of piano music. It was such a solemn tune, familiar too, the hymn Mum tended to favour: *Silent night, Holy night, All is calm, All is bright.* They knew how to mock, those spirits.

Mum sat at her computer and emailed the same address as before, I read as her fingers flew over the keyboard.

I am truly sorry to hear Carol has passed. Could you tell me the circumstances surrounding her death please and when it happened? I'm an old friend of hers and I rent the house she owns – Blakemort. I've been renting it since December 1999 and if she's dead, I'd like to know who I'm paying rent to. I'm very confused. I've emailed this address several times but never received a reply until this evening.

Regards,

Helena Greer

Mum sent the email and we waited with baited breath, even Ethan, who was clearly as bewildered as the rest of us.

"She won't reply," Mum said, chewing at her nails. Anger flashed through me. Why'd she have to be so defeatist?

We waited and we waited, I was beginning to give up hope too and then a reply pinged back.

Dear Helena,

My name is Dianne and I was Carol's former partner. She died shortly after leaving the house. It was suicide. She committed suicide. As for owning Blakemort, she didn't. I don't know where you got that idea. She rented it as you apparently do. You say you've emailed this address several times before but I've never received any correspondence from you until this evening. Perhaps they went straight into the spam folder, I'll have to run a check on that. If you'd like to discuss this matter further, I've included my telephone number in the subject line of this email.

Thank you for getting in touch,
Dianne Parker

Reading the email a second time, Mum grabbed the phone and started dialling.

* * *

Back in the drawing room, Mum was pacing up and down.

"Dianne doesn't know who we're paying rent to, she's got no idea at all."

"How'd you pay it?" Aunt Julia asked, biting at her nails too.

"Just before she left we arranged that I'd send a cheque every couple of months to a PO Box address Carol supplied me with. And yes, before you ask, the cheques have been cashed, every single one of them. It's quite a relaxed arrangement, I suppose. But that's Carol all over. She's very relaxed."

"Doesn't sound it to me, not if she took her own life."

"No, there is that."

"Do you know why she did it, did Dianne say?"

Mum shook her head. "She was stunned when the news came through. They'd split up by that time you see, run into problems. Theirs was a bit of a rocky relationship apparently. Poor Dianne, I think she feels guilty about what happened, responsible in a way."

Aunt Julia murmured as if in agreement. "How long did Carol live here?"

"Not even a year, although she gave me the distinct impression she'd been here a lot longer than that." She shook her head. "But then, as you know, she also gave me the impression she owned it. I didn't think to delve deeper, to ask too many questions, why would I? She was my friend, I trusted her." Sighing deeply, as though exasperated, it was a moment before she continued. "As I now know, before she moved in she was living with Dianne. When things started to go wrong, Carol wanted her own space. This place came up, it belonged to a friend of a friend, and the rent was low, *irresistibly* low." Mum paled further when she said that, at the parallel of it. "Carol thought it was ideal. With plenty of room to stack her canvasses, she could really spread herself out." Again she was quiet. "I can't believe she's dead, Ju. We used to have such a laugh, Carol and me, in our art school days. She was so talented, she specialised in fine art, you know. Portraits mainly. Dianne hardly ever visited Carol at Blakemort. She didn't like it. She found it… *oppressive*. But Carol seemed settled, until she decided completely out of the blue to up sticks and leave, that is."

"How did she…?" Aunt Julia's voice trailed off.

"It wasn't here," Mum rushed the words out, keen to dispel that notion. "She didn't kill herself here. She told Dianne she was going to live and work abroad, just like she told me, that she wanted to do a fair bit of travelling in-between, see and paint the world, get her head straight, her priorities right, that kind of thing, perhaps even settle permanently overseas. But she never left the country. She caught a train to London, checked into a hotel, one of those big, anonymous ones, stayed there for quite a while actually, a few weeks, and then…" Mum closed her eyes briefly, "hung herself."

Aunt Julia's expression was as pained as Mum's. "Did you say she specialised in portraits?"

"Yes, why?"

"When we went into the attic, I noticed some canvasses stacked up against the wall. An old sheet was thrown over them but it had slipped off, they were easy enough to spot. Whilst you were looking out of the window at the graveyard I went over to look at them, they were portraits too. I didn't like them."

"Why not?" Mum asked.

"Because the subjects all had their eyes closed as if… as if they were dead."

Like the photos then – the ones I'd seen in the attic and those they'd subsequently seen in Ethan's wardrobe.

"What… who are these people?" Mum's voice was a whisper.

"God alone knows," Aunt Julia answered.

I pressed my lips together. It was either God or the antithesis of God.

"There were quite a few paintings," Aunt Julia elaborated. "Old people, children as well, some of them were modern, others historical, dressed in… you know, strange clothes, Victorian, Edwardian. I'm no expert, but I think some clothing dated back even further than that. And all of them had that one thing in common."

Mum stared at Aunt Julia for a few seconds and then repeated her sister's words of earlier. "We have to get out."

Although despair was apparent in her voice, her words were like music to my ears. She tried calling Dad again but got no reply.

"Let's just take the car and go," Aunt Julia suggested

when Mum replaced the receiver.

"But what about all our stuff?"

"Your stuff?"

"All our belongings, I can't just leave everything."

Aunt Julia seemed as small as Mum suddenly, no longer statuesque. "I… I don't know, Hel."

Mum shook her head, came to a decision. "I think we're panicking. We do need to leave but perhaps not tonight. Let's… let's just hang on 'til tomorrow. It's really icy and… well, country roads can be dangerous when they're icy. Paul's intending to take the kids out in the morning, so let him do that whilst we pack the essentials. It's much more sensible to leave in daylight. We'll be calmer too, able to think more clearly. It's important to stay rational." Focusing on Aunt Julia, she asked, "I know your place is small, but can we go to yours? It'll just be for a few nights, until we find out what's going on here." Aunt Julia said, "Of course." and Mum sighed in relief.

"We can all go to my room tonight, bunk down tog—"

"Not your room, Mum," I interrupted. "Can't we light the fire and stay here?"

Mum glanced at the ceiling, no doubt thinking about the symbols engraved in the window frames directly above her bedroom and didn't insist otherwise.

Chapter Twenty-Six

ON Christmas Eve there was more terrible news. We learnt that Dad and Carrie had been in a car crash. He wasn't badly hurt, thank God, but she'd received quite a jolt, and there were fears for the baby. We wouldn't be seeing him as planned because he was remaining in hospital by her side. Carrie was distraught, Mum told us, and understandably so, as was Dad.

"I couldn't tell him about Carol," she continued to explain, the rest of us huddled on sofas, shell-shocked too, "or about the house. How could I? He's got enough to deal with. We have to take care of ourselves."

We started packing, just a small suitcase each, Mum helping Ethan or rather just grabbing clothes from his floor and stuffing them in. What presents we had were put into one of those big blue laundry bags. Mum said we could take them too. As for me, I was quite capable of packing my own suitcase and Aunt Julia had barely unpacked. Alone in my room, the whispering started.

You can't leave. You can't.

"Yes I can, I bloody can!"

I'd never sworn before, not really, but I thought I'd give

it a go.

There was laughter, the kind I never wanted to hear again. My resolve hardened. Once I'd left and got out of there, I wouldn't go back, I'd refuse. Mum could send in the removal men to get the rest of our stuff surely? We didn't *have* to go back.

I turned to get more clothes and tripped over a pile of books on the floor, books that hadn't been there before. I fell to my knees, landing heavily. Raising my head, I looked around me. Who'd done that?

"You can't stop me," I repeated. And that's when I saw it, even though to this day I try and tell myself otherwise, that it's just not possible – that my eyes were playing tricks on me, fear causing my imagination to go into overdrive. The walls surrounding me were breathing – that's right, *breathing* – in and out, slowly so slowly as if all four had a heartbeat. I gasped and staggered to my feet, continued to pack, but not so carefully this time. Like Mum I just threw things in.

We met on the landing, all four of us, and eyed each other.

"Ready?" Mum asked.

We nodded.

She took the lead. "Be careful coming down the stairs, hold on tight to the bannister."

None of us needed telling.

Walking across the hallway, I could sense so many pairs of eyes on me. *We're leaving.* I fired the thought like an arrow. *And there's nothing you can do about it!*

Fear gave way to elation; Mum and Aunt Julia were on my side at last and Ethan too, in his own way. He was scurrying just as fast as the rest of us.

I half expected the front door to resist, but it didn't, it yielded easily enough – something else that ignited hope.

The car! There it was, our means of escape. We chucked our bags into the boot and bundled into its worn interior. Mum inserted the key and turned the ignition. It started first time and I exhaled in relief, not aware until then how hard I'd been holding my breath.

We're on our way! We're finally on our way.

And I wasn't going to look back, not even a glance.

Moving forwards it became obvious that something was wrong. The car was dragging, making a strange noise. Mum stopped the car and I tensed. We all did.

She got out and went to inspect.

"What is it?" called Aunt Julia.

Mum had bent down but then she straightened up, fury and confusion on her face.

"It's the tyres," she replied, "there's no air in them, they're flat, every single one!"

* * *

I was glad to see Mum still determined. She stomped back into the house, muttering something about a taxi, Aunt Julia following her, Ethan and me following them.

"I've got a card for a local taxi firm somewhere, I'll try and find it," Mum said when we were in her office.

"And I'll phone the train station," Aunt Julia offered. "As it's Christmas Eve, trains will be a bit on the sparse side."

We stood by as they carried out their respective tasks, both of us nearly jumping a foot in the air at the sound of a loud bang – the front door slamming.

Mum was shaken too. "Did you leave the door open?" she asked us.

Ethan held his hand up. "Yeah, I… I think so."

"So why's it banged shut? There's no wind."

Aunt Julia gasped. "Has someone come in, do you think? The same person who sabotaged the tyres!"

Mum glanced at us; clearly worried we'd be frightened by her words. "We don't know the tyres were sabotaged. It could just be… coincidence."

It was obvious Aunt Julia didn't believe that for a minute.

"I'll go and check," Mum appeased, leaving the morning room and walking into the hallway shouting 'Hello'. There was no reply. Not one that she could hear anyway.

I've told you, you can never leave.

"Mum," I called, galvanized into action by the whisper in my ear, "we need to phone the taxi! Right now." We couldn't delay. We *shouldn't*.

Mum returned. "Yes, yes, I know that." She started searching her desk. "Where's that card, where is it?"

"Was there anyone there?" Aunt Julia asked, still fretting about an assailant.

"Of course not," was Mum's terse reply.

Aunt Julia started ringing the station to check the train times, looked at the phone in confusion, and dialled again. "I think your phone's up the creek, Hel. I guess we'll just have to take pot luck."

Mum only briefly looked up from the drawers she was rifling through.

"I'll check the Internet for train times instead," Aunt Julia decided.

"Yeah, we can look up a taxi firm online too, order one

that way."

Aunt Julia started frowning again.

"What's wrong?" Mum asked her.

"The page won't load."

Straightening up, I think Mum wanted to scream. "What the bloody hell is wrong with everything today? Nothing's working!"

The phone started ringing.

"I thought you said—"

Aunt Julia shrugged. "I don't know, Hel… it was making a strange crackling sound when I tried it."

Mum answered it and immediately her face was one of concern. "Oh, no," she was saying. "I'm sorry, so sorry. Truly, I… I can't believe it."

A few minutes passed whilst Mum continued talking, she'd turned her back on us, her voice so low it was barely audible. Putting the phone down, she looked at each one of us. "That was Dad. Carrie lost the baby."

Her announcement was as stark as the news.

"Oh, no," Aunt Julia responded. I was too shocked to say anything, so was Ethan.

After a few moments of silence, Aunt Julia took the phone from Mum. "I'll call the station again, check those train times."

Once more the phone was dead.

"Damn it! I don't understand." Her nostrils flaring in anger, Aunt Julia looked at Mum. "You know what, let's just bloody walk shall we? I don't care how far it is!"

Still reeling from Dad's news, Mum sank into her office chair. "Poor Paul, poor Carrie, I feel so bad."

"Well, it is sad, but—"

"No, Ju, I mean it, I feel awful."

Aunt Julia didn't ask it, I did. "Why, Mum?"

I don't know if Mum even realised it was me who'd spoken; she was staring into the distance, a tear trailing down her cheek. "Because I wished for it to happen. I sat in that kitchen, distraught, and I wanted them to be as distraught as me. I *hated* the fact that they were happy." She burst into heart-rending sobs. "What a terrible person I am, what a terrible, terrible person! It's my fault. Everything's my fault."

Aunt Julia rushed to console her. "It wasn't your fault, how could it be?"

Mum continued crying and I felt like joining in – somehow I knew all hope of leaving Blakemort that day was lost. Mum had retreated into herself; so far even her sister couldn't reach her. She pushed Aunt Julia away slightly and stood up.

"I… I just need to lie down. You don't mind do you? I'm sorry…" Her voice trailed away as she left the room.

Aunt Julia turned to me, defeated. "We'd better get the bags in from the car."

* * *

I forced myself to go and see Mum later that day. Standing in the doorway, I looked at her, my shrunken mum, lying in that bed, her eyes fixated on the ceiling, she was humming, incessantly humming.

"Mum," I called but she didn't respond. "Mum," I said again, much louder.

Finally she noticed me. "Go downstairs, sweetie. Go and see Aunt Julia. We'll leave soon, I promise. But not yet, I can't go anywhere just yet. Run along."

I wanted to hug her, to tell her not to worry about anything, that we'd look after her, Ethan, me and Aunt Julia too, help her to move on like Dad had moved on. But I wasn't brave enough to go further into the room. I wish I had been. I wonder sometimes if a hug there and then might have changed everything.

I went downstairs. Aunt Julia and Ethan were sitting in front of the fire playing a card game. Despite his teenage years, Ethan looked like a little boy again, lost. We all were, perfect fodder for that house in so many ways.

All too soon, afternoon gave way to evening. It was getting later and later, and, despite ourselves, we were growing heavy-lidded. The house around us was quiet. Everything was quiet. *Silent night.* I started biting my nails, something I never did. It felt like we were in the eye of the storm, waiting for something to happen.

Which of course we were.

Aunt Julia yawned widely and then suggested we go upstairs too, that if Mum still wanted to be alone, the rest of us could bed down in my room together.

"We'll be just across the landing from your Mum, close enough, you know… if we're needed."

I nodded and Ethan shrugged. Seeing that she forced a smile, rose and stretched again – making a bit of a show of it. Just as quickly she seemed to double over.

"Ow!" she yelled, her hand reaching behind her. "My leg!"

"Your leg?" I jumped up too.

"The fire! My leg is on fire!"

How? She was close to the fire, but not that close. Had it sparked and we'd not seen it?

Without questioning further, I rushed over, Ethan did too, me at least expecting to see all sorts of horrors, but there was no evidence whatsoever of scorch marks on the trousers she wore, despite her insisting otherwise, her face a mask of bewildered pain. Helping her to the sofa, she continued to complain of burning, tears in her eyes as gingerly she rolled up her trouser leg. Again there was nothing, although an acrid smell filled the air, reminding me of meat left too long on the barbeque.

I looked around, at the four walls that enclosed us, desperation rising, but who was there to help? No one living, no one dead either. The house had seen to that.

"Aunt Julia, did you ever see Carol? Do you know what she looked liked?"

"Carol? Why are asking me now?" Her breath was coming in short, sharp pants.

"I just… want to know."

"I saw a picture of them together once. She's got short hair, shaggy, pale skin, freckles, pretty in a plain sort of way." Again she gasped, "My leg bloody hurts!"

Short hair, shaggy – the woman standing behind Mum at the window, screaming. Was that Carol? The woman we thought we were renting off, the dead lady, the one who'd committed suicide. I gulped.

"We need to get out." How many times did it have to be said?

I looked at Ethan and he looked at me. He knew it was crucial too. But what could we do? Children are so helpless – at least we were. There was a single scream.

Forgetting her own pain, Aunt Julia sat bolt upright. "Helena," she whispered, and then to me, "Help me up, for God's sake, help me up!"

Quickly I obeyed, so did Ethan.

"We've got to go upstairs," she continued.

Standing at the bottom of the stairwell, we looked upwards. It was dark. Why had Mum turned off the lights? I went to the light switch, flicked it, but nothing happened.

"I think the lights have blown again," I said. "We've got a torch."

"Where is it?" Aunt Julia asked.

It was Ethan who answered. "It's in the kitchen."

"Run and fetch it," she instructed but he didn't move an inch.

I volunteered instead.

As I ran, I refused to look towards the music room, which was also in darkness. Again, there was the sound of a piano playing, mixed in with laughter, not just from the spiteful boy, but so many spiteful others. *Fuck you,* I thought. Like 'bloody', the word sat well with me.

The torch was kept in the utility cupboard. I went straight to it, pulled it open, and searched around. The light was on in the kitchen but it had sunk very low. I needed that torch! Where was it? Behind the bottles of bleach, perhaps? There were so many of them, as if Mum had been stockpiling. Using them to clean the mould, the yellowed kitchen surfaces, and the general layer of grime, invisible to the eye mostly, but there, always there and easily sensed, even by the non-psychic. I knocked several bottles over, they made a loud thud as they fell to the floor but finally my hand closed around the cold metal of the torch. In my hands now, I switched it on, turned and the light bounced off the window, but more than that, a shape at the window – that of a man, peering in and glaring at me, blaming me, as he'd blamed Ethan – but what for?

How were we to blame for any of this?

A scream lodged in my throat as I continued to stare, as others joined him, so many others.

You're bastards, all of you!

And you! The words flew back at me. *You're Corinna Bastard.*

I shook my head, blinked my eyes. Argued no more. Instead I got out of there, fled to the hallway, to the foot of the staircase.

"Oh, there you are!" There was so much relief in Aunt Julia's voice when I returned, as if she couldn't believe I *had* returned. "Come on, help me upstairs."

She was limping, heavily. She placed one arm around me, and the other around Ethan, the light bouncing erratically off the walls.

"We're coming," she called ahead. "Helena, don't worry, we're coming."

Upstairs, the torch was barely sufficient, and the smell that hit us was the same as that which had been in Ethan's room, only intensified.

The smell of death.

Yes, I'd grasped that; I didn't need one of the unseen to tell me. And then the words hit home. Whose death were they talking about?

From downstairs something burst into life – a chorus of voices singing.

"What the hell is that?" Aunt Julia screeched.

"It's the TV," I quickly replied.

She turned towards me. "Did you leave it on?"

"No."

"Ethan?"

"I never touched it!"

It was a Christmas song, not a hymn, a pop song, Live Aid: *Do they know it's Christmas?* Just as quickly it died down, the TV switching itself off.

Aunt Julia was shaking. I could feel how violently her body trembled. "Let's focus on your mum," she said. "Helena, Helena, we're here."

We approached the bedroom and the door was shut. Earlier it had been open.

Aunt Julia released us and fell against it, resting her head briefly. She seemed exhausted, no life in her at all. "Darling, are you asleep?" she called. "Helena?" There was no reply. She turned to us. "We have to go in."

I took a step back not forwards. "I can't," I breathed. "I just can't."

"Don't be stupid," she said and I bristled. She'd never called me that before. "Give me the torch."

"Yeah, go on, stop mucking about." There was spite in Ethan's voice too.

I handed over the torch but reluctantly. *Let them go in*, I thought. *Let whatever's in there consume them.* That will show which one of us is stupid.

Don't.

The word flew at me.

Stay calm.

My hands either side of my head, I wanted to scream. What were these voices in my head? Who did they belong to?

Carol?

My own thought was met with no reply. Instead there was silence again as Aunt Julia and Ethan moved into the dark chasm of the room.

"Helena," Aunt Julia called.

"Mum," said Ethan.

The two of them lowered their voices to whispers.

"Where is she?"

"I don't know."

"She can't have gone far."

As Aunt Julia had said, she couldn't have gone far, she was in no fit state. I turned to the left, walked towards the staircase that hid itself away, stood at the bottom of it, and stared upwards again. I could hear something – a faint humming, drifting towards me, echoing in my ears. How I wish she'd stop humming that damned hymn! That hateful hymn! I didn't want to hear it. As much as I used to love Christmas, I hated it now and everything to do with it – people pretending to be happy when they weren't. Mum pretending to laugh and smile when she'd split with Dad, telling us we'd be okay, that we were still a family, a happy family.

She's a liar!

It wasn't my thought but I couldn't disagree. That's exactly what she was. I started climbing, my tread sure, my eyesight adjusting. Whereas before I'd needed the light, now I knew every tread, every square inch; I could have navigated them blindfolded.

The attic door was ajar, always ajar – that strange mix of 'come in' and 'go away' – and I pushed it further open. The light was working; it was on, but more sickly than ever, as diseased as the house, as the ground it stood on. *Death. Always death.* We'd been surrounded by so much of it for so long.

I could hear Mum but not see her, not yet. What I could see were shadows, more than ever before, gathering again for another performance, eager to enjoy the show.

There were flies too, hordes of them, not in the air, but crawling over surfaces, their movements not fluid but strangely jagged as though they were part of an old black and white film, the kind that flickers constantly. In the rafters, something fluttered, not a fly, much bigger than that. I steeled myself, inhaled. Let it swoop at me. Let it dare!

"Stop that noise, Mum," I said, my voice impressive, bold.

The humming continued.

"Stop it," I repeated.

When still she refused, I crossed to the box that Ethan had previously opened and reached into it. Immediately my hand closed around the smooth glass of a paperweight, one that Ethan hadn't stolen for his morbid collection.

Accompanying the humming was whispering, soft at first but becoming frenzied.

Do it, do it, do it! Kill her, kill her, kill her! Do it, or we'll kill you!

And then another whisper, more timid: *Don't give in.*

Yet more: *You can't leave. You can never leave.*

The soft voice again: *Try. You have to try.*

I closed my eyes, becoming even more confused. *Try what?*

To kill her.

It was those words that were the clearest.

There she was! I could see her at last. Sitting in the middle of the room, dead centre, with all those strange, spider-infested clothes scattered around her and swaying back and forth, her eyes closed and humming – my mother, my beautiful but weak and lying mother.

It's my fault, she'd said. She'd actually admitted it.

Everything's my fault.

Something fluttered above her head now but just as quickly it disappeared. On her hair a fly landed, seemed to settle.

I clutched the glass weight tighter and continued forwards, started to hum too. *Silent Night, Holy Night.* No, Mum, no. There was nothing holy about this night.

There was a tugging at my hand but easily I shrugged it off.

Don't, don't, don't.

Ignored too the accompanying pleading.

Even when I stood before her, Mum didn't open her eyes, didn't bother to acknowledge me. Typical of her, she never acknowledged anything.

It's your fault, all this torment. You're to blame.

I lifted my hand, higher, higher still and then, as the whispering turned to laughter, to cheers, to a resounding applause, I brought it crashing down.

Chapter Twenty-Seven

ALL hell broke loose. There were footsteps behind me, screams from both Aunt Julia and Ethan, wild fluttering above, then more screams, but not from the living. Some frantic, others whooping with joy. Amidst all this, Mum never stirred. As for me, I was screaming too; such a strange sound, distant, disconnected, but me nonetheless, my mouth wide open. The object was still in my hands and there was red, so much of it – blood on the floor and blood soaking my mother's hair as her body crumpled, not matching the shade, but turning it darker, so much darker, blacker than black. This was no vision, not like the one I'd had in the drawing room. This was real.

Desperate to regain some kind of control, I threw the glass weight as far from me as possible; heard the thud as it landed in some far corner. I threw myself too, across Mum's body, yelling out for her, praying fervently that she'd be all right.

"What have you done? What the hell have you done?" As much as she was able to, given her perceived injury and all the junk that was in the way, Aunt Julia rushed towards us.

Ethan stood perfectly still. "It's the house," he kept repeating. "It's the house."

Mum stirred. One hand reached upwards and came away smeared. She looked into Aunt Julia's eyes not mine. "Get me out," she managed. "Get us all out."

Thank God Mum wasn't like Aunt Julia, that she was slighter. Between us we managed to hoist her up, Aunt Julia still wincing with every step she took, crying out on occasion. She turned her head to look at me… no, not look… she glared.

"Lead the way," she instructed.

Don't hate her back, don't hate her back, don't hate her back. The words were spinning in my head. *Don't give it anymore to feed on.* And I had, I'd given it plenty. Mum and Ethan too, they'd given it apathy – just as nourishing. But here's the thing – the thing that only now I'm starting to admit. That moment when I held the paperweight up high, my mind had been clear, not encroached on at all. When I brought it down with all my might, not once, not twice, but several times, I'd been elated, the happiest I'd ever felt – powerful, in control for once, and hungry for more. I'd been evil, I'd tasted it, and it was delicious, like the best treat in the world, better than chocolate ice cream, than birthday cake, so much more satisfying. Even the coldness within me had warmed; I was on fire, *glowing*. The boy, that spiteful boy, and me, we were the best of friends after all. And *that* was the worst thing that happened that Christmas. I'd succumbed, become a part of the house – *Corinna Bastard*. There was no one to blame, no unseen entity, no assailant, no possession of any sorts, not this time. It was me, all me. When was I lost? The minute I'd run through the music room door with its blackened surround? I don't think so. But something had set me on my way. And in that room with the eaves windows, I'd almost reached the point of no return.

Ethan broke my reverie, he pushed past me and took the lead, but surprisingly he reached backwards to grab my bloodied hand, to pull me forwards. I think it's the first proper contact we'd had in years, besides a push and a shove, that is. Perhaps he was worried I'd change my mind, run further back into the attic to hide alongside the others. Afraid of the repercussions I would face from the living. I was tempted; believe me, so very tempted.

Again, somewhere in the house a door banged. I was terrified the attic door would shut too and close us in. Those within would fall upon us like ravenous beasts, desperate to gorge themselves on our flesh, to drink from our veins, but that didn't happen. We shambled through it, all four of us, the walking wounded, Ethan flicking on the torch again to light the way. Having been such a commotion, there was again no sound at all; everything was still, so still. I couldn't decide which was worse. We had to go single file down the stairs. Mum only just managing to stay on her feet, colliding with the wall every so often, Aunt Julia ever vigilant, turning round to steady her. On the landing we bunched together again. There'd be plenty of questions fired my way soon but now was not the time.

"Come on," Aunt Julia instructed. "We have to keep moving."

There was another bang and then another.

"Who's here?" Mum's voice was still slurred, as if she was drunk. "Who could it be?"

"No one, Mum," I said, trying to offer what comfort I

could. She ignored me. "Mum," I said again, more piteously this time. I had to have one word from her, just one, to tell me it was all right; that she didn't hate me, that she loved me still.

How can she love you now!

"Stop it!" I yelled. "Stop it!"

Before anyone could react to my outburst, light flooded the landing, the bedrooms too, the radio in Mum's bedroom and the TV from the drawing room both started blaring. There was silence no more. The sound was deafening.

"The electrics," Aunt Julia had to shout to be heard. "It's just the electrics, they're as dodgy as the heating. Follow me."

Again we hurried forwards, as much as we could, taking into account the state Mum was in, but then, halfway down the stairs, she stopped.

"Who's that?" she said, her eyes narrowed as though she was trying to focus. "Carol, is that you?"

I could see nothing. "Mum," I urged.

"Carol, it is you! We heard you were dead, that you'd committed suicide. What nonsense! You're here, you're alive!"

"Hel, there's no one there." Aunt Julia tried to reason with her too.

Mum held her hands out. "There is, Ju, can't you see her?"

"Hel—"

"Wait! She's speaking, she's saying something."

I strained to listen too.

I am dead… I'm here. I tried to warn…

Warn? That word struck me.

"It was you, wasn't it?" I shouted. "That wrote those words, that guided my hand?"

Aunt Julia looked at me as if I was mad.

"There's no-one there," reiterated Aunt Julia, her voice a hiss.

"Hang on," Mum said, "just hang on."

"It's that blow to the head, that's what this is." Aunt Julia was still searching for logic, but I noticed Ethan was listening, intrigued too.

"She's telling me she's sorry," Mum continued. I was amazed she could hear so much better than me. "She wanted to get away, escape, she was desperate. She sacrificed us, offered us up as a replacement, but the guilt was too much. What she'd done, the selfishness of her actions, it overwhelmed her. She's sorry. Over and over again she's saying she's sorry, that she's here, she's still here. That it's hell."

I tugged at Mum's sleeve. "Ask her who the house belongs to?" Maybe that was the key I was looking for, the knowledge that would release us; the mystery owner.

Mum faltered and silently I urged her to hurry. After a moment she spoke again.

"It doesn't belong to the living, that's all she'll say. It's nobody living."

Aunt Julia had had enough. "We're getting away from here. The next house isn't far. What do you think, a mile or two? We have to reach it. Come on."

Mum turned to her, her eyes wide, and full of terror. "Ju, she said the house won't let us go, it'll trap us."

"Rubbish! A house can't trap you."

But it could, in many ways.

Starting to move again, my foot slipped and Ethan

reached out to grab me.

"Careful," his voice a loud whisper. "You know you have to be careful."

Downstairs, other noises filled the air, ones that only I could hear. Party noises, people talking, laughing and clinking glasses. Piano music too, definitely piano music, the keys being pounded, not a hymn this time, instead it was an erratic, savage cacophony. We were hurrying towards the door but I couldn't ignore what was happening in the music room. There was definitely a party going on, but not one you'd ever want an invite to. So many filled the room, figures that were becoming clearer, more defined. All wore gowns, like the ones in the attic, some with their hoods up, others wearing masks instead, hideous masks, a few with long beaks, made of something white, could it be bone? It reminded me of bone.

The sight stopped me in my tracks.

"Come on, for God's sake come on," Aunt Julia instructed, but I couldn't move. The shadows, the shapes multiplied, filling the kitchen too no doubt, as well as the other rooms, and in-between them were more shapes – people without cloaks and masks. Naked, the only thing that covered their bodies were sores – black and foul looking, beginning to burst, oozing long thin strands of white. Could it be maggots? Bile rushed upwards but I gulped it back. Such wretched beings, their hands were either side of their faces, as Carol's had been, and they were screaming.

One broke away from the rest – the spiteful boy – no longer a shadow, an outline, or a mere sensation; he was as solid as you or I – as vital. I was surprised at how sweet his face was – his dark eyes framed by long lashes, dimples in both cheeks and creamy white skin without so much as a blemish. I'd never imagined him that way. Never. His smile too… it was beguiling.

It's Christmas Eve; do you want to join the party?

I refused to be taken in by him.

Go away.

Come on, it's fun. We're friends, the best of friends.

I'll never be your friend.

Why's that? Because you hate me?

I hesitated.

Go on. Say it. Say that you hate me.

Again I refused.

Hate is welcome here, as welcome as you are.

I'm leaving. I'm going.

The boy simply shrugged.

Go on then. But you'll return. Making a wide arc with his hand, he grandly gestured to those behind him. *You have to. You're one of us.*

I stepped back, took another and another, crashing into Ethan again.

"Careful!"

I turned and looked at him with tears in my eyes. Incredibly, he softened.

"It's all right, we're going. You'll be all right." At last he was acting the part of the protective big brother. He wasn't calling me stupid. None of this was stupid. It wasn't imagination either. I'd seen. I'd actually seen. And I didn't want to see anymore.

Aunt Julia opened the front door as figures spilled into the hall – the house was bulging with them – and their laughter… oh, their laughter. It would sound forever in my head.

They were at our backs, driving us forward, not concerned at all by our departure. And that was what was so frightening, much more than if they'd blocked our path. Their confidence echoed that of the boy's: *you'll return, you have to.*

Outside the cold air hit us. The trees that surrounded us, the bushes – *in a circle, you're in our circle* – swaying, despite the stillness of the night. And in amongst the trees were more hooded figures, swaying too, and chanting, endlessly chanting.

Legion. Legion. Legion.

"I feel sick." It was Mum. She came to a sudden standstill and heaved violently, the contents of her stomach spilling everywhere. At the same time her legs buckled.

"We have to get you to hospital," Aunt Julia was muttering, her voice shaking as much as she was, her eyes wild. "The car, if only we could use the car."

"Walk," Mum croaked. "Just help me to walk."

Behind us the door shut, groaning as it always did. Unlike last time, I looked back, my gaze irresistibly drawn. The dead filled each and every window, the lights a dull flicker in some rooms but fully ablaze in others, as if flames were devouring them. And Carol, poor apologetic Carol, who'd sacrificed us to save herself, she was no longer screaming but dangling from the ceiling of the upstairs spare room, her legs jerking violently and those around her ecstatic to see it. I didn't need to be in the room to hear the snap as her neck broke, to see the terror, the despair on her face, the sheer hopelessness, or hear the words that were meant solely for me.

This could be you.
This could be you.

This will be you.
It will be.

Unable to look anymore, I followed the others, onto the road that led into Whitesmith, the village proper. The time was one minute past midnight on Christmas Day and white flakes began swirling in the air before us. It was snowing at last, that yearned-for snow, but there was no joy in it. It was just another mockery.

Epilogue

MUM was okay – there was no lasting damage. Knocking on the door of the first house we came to in Whitesmith, the resident was shocked but kind, quickly dressing and taking us via her car into Eastbourne, to the accident and emergency department, her windscreen wipers frantic as the snow became heavier. At the hospital, the usual questions were asked and Mum said it had been an intruder who'd attacked her, who, when rumbled by us, had escaped. So fluently she lied and I was grateful for it, for her protection. Aunt Julia wanted to interrogate me later, in a bid to understand why I'd done what I did, but Mum was stern with her and told her to leave it, just like she'd done once before. She said that she'd deal with me. But she never did. Deal with me, I mean. She never even told Dad.

The story about the intruder served us well, Mum saying that was the reason she couldn't bear to set foot in the house again, and nobody sought to question it. The removal men were sent in to retrieve our items and they were put in storage, whilst we spent the remainder of the festive holidays between Dad's house and Aunt Julia's. During that time I kept catching my aunt eyeing me suspiciously, fearful I was going to attack her next. The bond between us broken, we were yet another casualty of Blakemort, our relationship strained to this day. That stuff we had in storage? Most of it was sent to the tip. We moved into our new house in Lewes in mid-January, a humble two up, two down, but none of us minded. How can you mind normality?

We got on with our lives and Mum's work gradually began to pick up. She even started dating again, but so far she hasn't settled with anyone permanently. 'I like my freedom,' she once told me. I liked mine too, what I have of it.

When enough time had passed, two years, maybe three, I summoned up the courage to ask her. "Mum, what are we going to do about… you know… everything that happened?"

"We bury it, that's what we do, sweetie, and we carry on, we smile, we laugh, and we counteract it. One day it will go away. If we don't talk about it, it will just go away."

We counteract it. It was sensible advice. But at night, when I lie awake, listening to the sound of traffic in the distance, questions go round and round in my head; primarily to whom did the house belong? Not Carol, but someone else – someone not living – Legion perhaps, a collective. But what kind of collective, a satanic coven or a cult? As an adult I know that Legion has connotations with the demonic. When a person suffers possession it is often Legion who speaks through them, a multitude, a mass, demon upon demon – could it be that the same applies to Blakemort? That it was built to house Legion? Blood the cement holding it together. And the spiteful boy, who was he? A leader? How could such evil be wrapped in such beauty?

Ethan never mentioned the house again either, nor his macabre collection. He developed a healthy interest in girls instead. Between them and exams his attention was focused.

I studied hard at school but I also read about my psychic ability – it wasn't diminishing but it certainly wasn't developing either. It seemed to be stuck at some sort of stalemate. After our time at Blakemort, I still sensed things but nothing as malevolent, nowhere near. Thank God. And then I left school, started working, and met a new set of friends – one in particular, with a more defined ability than mine. A friend who 'saw' as a matter of routine, who insisted I had nothing to be embarrassed about; someone who heard every word the spirits uttered, who offered me an opportunity to use my gift for the greater good. The thought really appealed to me – helping those that are grounded. There are just so many in need…

I started working for Ruby, met Theo and Ness too, and became part of the Psychic Surveys team. I even met my boyfriend, Presley, through Ruby's boyfriend, Cash; they're brothers you see, ordinary people, not psychic at all. Or at least I don't think they are. There's a school of thought that says everybody has a psychic ability – Theo's school of thought to be precise. She says it's in each and every one of us but most shut it down, are taught to do so as children. Any lingering insights they have earning them the title of 'stupid', or 'weird', just plain weird. How many times was I called stupid as a kid? As you know, plenty. You shut down or you shut up. It seems most people cannot contemplate a spiritual world existing alongside the material one, not unless it's within the restraints of religion. But it's there all right and at times the veil is perilously thin. I suppose that explains why Mum saw Carol, and why she tolerates what I do now, although if I start to tell her about a case she'll often change the subject. Thinking about it, she changes the subject every time. She just smiles at me. Always she smiles. As I do. Like mother, like daughter.

I've mentioned before that Ruby, Ness, and Theo don't know about Blakemort, or that I've seen and heard too in the past. I haven't been brave enough to explain. Is it still standing? That house marked by death. None of my family have been back; haven't been anywhere near it. When we go out, we head the other way. And only briefly have I searched for it on the Internet – there was nothing of course, no mention at all, not then and not now, as if the house doesn't exist. But it does exist, and I live in fear of Ruby saying, "Hey, Corinna, I've had a call, there's a couple renting a house nearby. They're complaining of the usual, you know, cranky heating, whispering, and footsteps. Do you fancy coming along with me to investigate? It's close by, in the village of Whitesmith. It's got a strange name, it's called Blakemort."

What will I reply? "It's not in Whitesmith, Ruby. It's a lost house in a lost village, and home to the lost. I know because I used to live there, it was once my home too."

That phone call's coming.

I know it is.

The End...

Psychic Surveys Companion Novel
Book Two

THIRTEEN

Prologue

1972

"GO away, let me sleep."

The hand tugged at my bed sheets.

"I told you to stop it! Leave me alone."

But, Ness, it's snowing. Come over to the window and see.

"You said it was snowing an hour ago and it wasn't."

I said I thought it was going to snow, but now it is, it really is.

"So what," I responded, unable to help the petulance in my voice.

Don't you like snow?

Of course I liked snow, what child didn't? What I didn't like was being teased, and she was teasing me, she definitely was. She *always* teased me.

You're no fun, do you know that, Vanessa Patterson?

"And you're annoying, do *you* know that?"

You're lucky to have snow in your world, to be able to go out and play in it.

"Play in it? It's nearly midnight!" As if Mum would let me go and play at this time.

I can go though. She's got no control over me.

"No one's got any control over you."

She laughed, a tinkling sound, mischievous.

You're jealous really, aren't you?

"Of you? No."

You are, because Mum can't touch me, she can't hurt me.

"I said I want you to go away!"

You should stand up to her, be a little braver.

"Don't tell me what to do."

You should tell her about me.

Incensed by her words, I sat up, any attempt to sleep shoved to one side. "How can I tell her about you?" I hissed. "You know what she's like."

Again she laughed. *I know exactly what she's like.*

"Then don't be so daft."

The shape, the figure, my twin – my *dead* twin – left me and drifted over to the window, where she tugged the curtain aside. It amazed me she could do that, that she could actually touch things, interact – someone, *something* like her. She had no substance, was barely an outline at times, part of the spiritual world, not material, so how was it possible?

I told you it was snowing.

Unable to resist, I peered beyond her and into the night. She was right. It was! It really was. She hadn't been teasing after all. Big fat glorious snowflakes were pirouetting past my window, offering such a contrast to the darkness of the sky.

I leapt from bed and ran over to the window too – thick snow was covering the ground, the shed, the hedges and the tops of the garden walls.

You want to go outside, don't you?

I did. I longed to.

Even at this hour?
"Even at this hour."
Mum will be asleep.
"What about Dad?"
Him too.

And my brothers and sisters, would they be asleep too? I had five siblings – five that were living that is – the two older girls shared a room, so did the three boys. It was just me in a room on my own, and I say alone, but more often than not I wasn't.

Come on, get your shoes on and come with me.

I'd need my shoes, my coat, my hat, my gloves and scarf, and then I'd need to tiptoe down the stairs as silently as my twin; I'd need to *glide*.

She was right about me. I *was* jealous sometimes. I wanted to move around like she did; I wanted to hide, to disappear at times, to boldly face the disapproving glare of my mother, to shrug off the stifled laughter and nudges of my siblings. I was the youngest of the six children; that is, *we* were – my twin and I. I was also different from them, although I was learning to keep those differences to myself. I had to for survival's sake. My twin had asked me to tell Mum about her, but I'd tried once, she knows that full well. I'd said to Mum that my sister was still with us and that I saw and spoke to her often. I don't want to think about what happened next; how hard I was beaten, whilst my twin looked dolefully on. She was denied, just as I was – both of us feeling like outcasts.

Ness, don't think about that. Think about having fun instead!

She was right. I had a tendency towards the maudlin. 'A sour child,' was how I'd heard my mother describe me once, the intimation clear: I was a curse rather than a blessing.

Glancing again out of the window, at the world in white, I had to say the idea of having fun did appeal. I didn't mean to be sour, I honestly didn't.

"Come on, then," I said, crossing over to my chest of drawers and pulling out some warm clothing. "But we have to be quiet, promise me you'll be quiet."

I'm always quiet!

That was a lie. As I've said before she could interact with the material world on occasion, although I know it took it out of her. When she did I wouldn't see her for ages, sometimes up to a week – she had to rest, that's what she'd tell me when she eventually resurfaced. But on that occasion when Mum was hitting me, she'd interacted then; she threw Mum's favourite vase against the far wall, smashing it to pieces. That had stopped Mum in her tracks. More than that, it had caused her to flee from the room. Ultimately, it also caused her to hate me more.

She doesn't hate you.

"She does," I murmured back. But in that moment I didn't care, not when there was fun to be had.

Together we left my room. The landing was in darkness, no sound at all in the house except the low hum of snoring from my parents' room. Everyone was fast asleep.

God, I was excited. Such a rare but welcome feeling and all because of the snow. It has such magic to it, being both soft and pretty. I dream of it snowing in wintertime, of the outside looking just like a Christmas card. Living in the south it's rare, but tonight it was here and I didn't want to wait until morning to go out in it. In the morning, it might be gone.

I giggled. My twin swung around, almost as startled by the sound as I was.

Shush.

"Sorry," I whispered, but in truth I wasn't sorry at all. I *wanted* to giggle.

There's a creak at the top of everyone's staircase, isn't there? Certainly there was at the top of mine, but I knew where it was and how to avoid it. On the first tread, I clamped my hand around the bannister and used it to guide me, although my eyes had adjusted quickly enough to the darkness – they always did.

At the bottom we stopped and looked around us. There was still silence.

Go on then.

I crossed over to the door, placed my hand on the latch and pulled. As soon as the door opened a blast of icy air enveloped me, sharp and invigorating. As for the snow, it was falling in earnest, transforming what was once an ordinary street on the outskirts of town into a winter wonderland. With no one to disturb it, the snow was immaculate, sparkling – not just on the ground, but the air glittered too. I wanted to fall to my knees and breathe it in; taste how pure it was. But my legs moved backwards instead of forwards.

My twin was horrified.

What are you doing?

"I can't."

Why?

"Mum."

She's asleep!

She was, but she was a restless sleeper. So was I, and because of that I'd catch her coming into my room at night to stare down at me, my eyes screwed shut in pretence of sleep, but knowing the disgust and disappointment that would be on her face.

"I have to go back."

Straightaway, my twin started to plead.

She won't know. I promise. Come out, just for a few minutes.

"She *always* knows."

In some ways Mum was as intuitive as me.

Ness, come on.

Ignoring her, I closed the door on such an incredible sight, and with my heart breaking just a little bit I turned around and retraced my footsteps.

Ness!

Go away.

Often I spoke out loud to her, but not on this occasion, not here on the stairs.

If you don't stop, I'll… I'll throw something, and cause a commotion.

I stopped and glared at her. *Don't you dare! Don't you bloody dare!*

I hate swearing, even now as an adult I abhor it, but I swore then. My twin recoiled. She knew I meant it, knew I'd freeze her out if she continued to threaten me. I'd ignore her and could keep it up for days, weeks even. She hated that, more than anything.

Sulkily, she followed me to my bedroom, where I closed the curtains, tore off my clothes and returned to bed, any thought of midnight capers – of fun – banished.

You're a spoilsport.

"Shut up."

Just five minutes, that's all I was asking.

"I have to sleep."

But the snow…

"So what about the snow! Why should it even matter to you? You can't feel it on your skin; you can't taste it on your tongue or build anything with your hands. You're dead!"

There was a pause, and then a heavy sigh as I pulled the sheets over my head.

Do you know something, Ness?

"What?" I mumbled from beneath the covers, just as sulky as her.

Sometimes I think I'm more alive than you are.

Chapter One

1987

MINCH Point Lighthouse on Skye's most westerly tip – what a place to find yourself during a month as fierce as November. It's such a beautiful island, so dramatic, with the scenery far exceeding my expectations. When it can be seen, that is.

Right now, the rapidly fading light as well as the lowering clouds have conspired to obscure the mountains to one side and the sea that rages in front. Even the sky looks as if it's been swallowed up. All I can hear is the slashing rain and the birds that live at the cliff's edge shrieking in protest – thousands of them, getting as battered as I was.

"We'd better hurry," my companion shouted, a man a couple of years younger than me, twenty-three to my twenty-five, and a typical rugged Scot: tall – well over six foot, with wild hair that he constantly pushed out of his eyes.

Rather than answer him, I lowered my head and pushed forwards, having to battle with the elements every step of the way. Who knew that rain could be such a harsh foe? In the south it's never as bad. This is *hard* rain, merciless.

How do the natives stand it?

The first structure – some kind of cabin – stood apart from the main building, Angus having parked his car as close to it as he could. It might have only been a few yards, but I doubted whether I could actually reach it. This rain was going to drive me to my knees.

"Ouch! Shit!"

I tripped over a boulder – the ground being littered with them. I wore boots, jeans, and a black quilted coat, all of which got soaked. As for my jeans, one knee ripped.

Immediately Angus offered his hand. "Here, Ness. I'll pull you up."

Within seconds I was on my feet again and I glanced down at my injured knee, noticed a red smear – blood. But I had no time to deal with it; we needed to get this over with.

The cabin walls looked solid enough but the windows were smashed and the door had long since blown away, smashed to pieces perhaps on the rocks below. Even so, it offered a semblance of respite, one that I was grateful for.

"Away in with you, Ness, we can wait here for a while, catch our breath."

"A while?" I'd wait here all night if needs be. This wasn't just 'fine Scottish weather' as Angus's mother had insisted when we left her house nearly an hour ago to come here, 'a wee bit of a drizzle' – this was a full-on storm!

Standing just inside the cabin, shaking the water from my hair and clapping my hands frantically together in a bid to warm up, I tried but failed to stop myself from snapping at him. "Why couldn't this have waited 'til morning?"

His reddish hair plastered to his face, as my dark hair

was plastered to mine, he looked part sheepish, part determined. "It's not the same in daylight, it's at night this place comes alive." Sheepish started to dominate. "Sorry, that's a bit of a conundrum, isn't it?"

Not sure how to answer that, I dug my torch out of my coat pocket instead and shone it along a short corridor that ran to the right of me.

"Oh Christ, look! There's still furniture in here. A fridge it looks like, with some sort of mould all over it, a table and chairs too." Changing direction, I shone the light directly in front of me. It was another room, smaller, with a toilet and sink in it, a *filthy* toilet and sink. Sludge or slurry covered the floor. I wrinkled my nose and had to look away. "Charming."

"Aye, that it's not," Angus agreed, or at least I think he was agreeing.

Curiosity got the better of me and I made my way down the corridor. A few steps later, I was standing in the main room. It was compact in size, the fridge not covered in mould as I first thought, but rust. A microwave, perched on top of it, had suffered a similar fate and in one corner there were bunk beds, duvets and pillows still present, although forming a crumpled, festering heap. The floor was littered with rubbish, which included old carrier bags, blankets that were in as bad a state as the duvet and pillows; bottles that had once contained alcohol or water; food wrappers and cigarette butts. On a round table lay a single plastic spatula, and facing the bunk bed were three cheap Formica units, with a sink and a hob set in. I wondered if water still flowed from the taps and crossed over to see. The cold was difficult to turn. Angus saw what I was doing and decided to help.

"Here you go," he said, "it still works."

There was a bang in the pipes somewhere, after which a sludgy mixture poured forth. I eyed it in the beam of my torch. "After a fashion," I replied. When he'd turned the tap off, I shone my torch at him, aiming low so as not to blind him. "What is this building?"

There was both excitement and fear in his eyes; a look I've seen often enough, especially when people first find out about me, when they realise what I am: a psychic, someone who can sense – who can see – the dead. Such a discovery tends to ignite both emotions, *twin* emotions.

"This is the cabin, or the bunkhouse if you like. It's where a young lad, or a couple of lads, assisting the lighthouse keeper would live. It's that bit removed from the main structure."

"It's more private?"

"Aye, for all parties concerned."

Inadvertently, I kicked a bottle lying in front of me. "But that was a long time ago, wasn't it? Since then I gather it's just been used for parties."

Angus shrugged. In the half-light he looked so much younger than his twenty-three years, a stark contrast to me who always feels double my age, weighed down by this supposed 'gift' that most of the time hangs like a weight around my neck. "There's not many come to party here, to be honest." He paused. "Not after what happened."

A ghost – that's what happened – or rather something supernatural. The very thing that lured bored teenagers to the lighthouse in the first place: the rumour that it was haunted. A building abandoned in the seventies – *suddenly* abandoned – by all those who lived on site: the lighthouse keeper, his family and whoever worked for him at the time

– a lad or lads, as Angus had inferred. And it was never lived in again. It was just… abandoned. All tools downed and belongings left behind, with no reason for the sudden flight ever found.

I was here because the property was for sale and a hotelier was interested in buying it, but not until it had been 'cleansed' – especially of its recent reputation. As well as being a native of Skye, Angus was the nephew of this London-based hotelier, who'd got in touch with me because of a case I'd been working on in my hometown of Sussex, assisting the police who were investigating the murder of two children. The information I'd provided, after contacting one of the victims psychically, led to the unearthing of their bodies in a lonely woodland spot. A grisly case, it continued to haunt me – the sound of the child crying, her loneliness, her sheer terror and bewilderment, how pitiful she'd been – but then so much haunted me, the child's cry was just one of many. Because of my success with that case my name had been leaked to the local press; something the constable in charge promised wouldn't happen. I worked so hard to play my involvement down, to *deny* the extent of it, to try and prevent it from ever reaching the attention of my remaining family. It had, however, reached the attention of some people, the hotelier for one – who'd finally persuaded me, via Angus, to investigate. Vast sums of money had been offered, but I'd only accepted enough to cover travel expenses, with lodging expenses being non-existent as Angus's mother was hosting me. The case of Minch Point Lighthouse, and what had happened here, as well as the Isle of Skye itself – more remote than anywhere I'd ever been – intrigued me. And if I could help the living as well as the dead… well, it made my 'gift' easier to bear.

A crash from outside made me jump.

"Is that thunder?" I asked.

"Probably."

I was incredulous. "So now there's going to be thunder and lightning?"

"You're not frightened of a bit of lightning are you?"

"Well, no… not unless I get struck by it."

"Does that tend to happen often with witches?"

At once my hackles rose. "What did you say?"

He coloured. Even in the dim light I could see that – his cheeks flaming as red as his hair. "I'm sorry, I didn't mean to—"

"I'm not a witch and neither am I a performing monkey. If you ever refer to me as such again, I'm leaving. You can solve the mystery of this lighthouse yourself."

"But my uncle—"

"And you can explain to him why too."

"I'm sorry, I really am."

I wasn't about to backtrack just because he'd issued an apology. "You should be."

"About what happened here—"

"Tell me."

"It didn't actually happen here, in this cabin I mean, it happened in the main building."

"We'll explore the main building soon enough."

"You're a tough wee thing, aren't you?" he said.

"And that worries you, does it?"

He looked amused, or it could have been bemused. "Actually, I'm impressed."

"And don't get any romantic notions either of wooing this 'tough wee thing'. I'm here on a job, that's all."

THIRTEEN

He almost spluttered when I said that. "Perish the thought," was his eventual response as he turned from me and walked over to the window to stare outwards at the sea.

"I'll make no secret of it," he started to say, just as a bolt of lightning lit up the sky. "I used to come here plenty as a youngster too. Ach, can you blame me? Can you blame any of us? You're short on entertainment when you live in a place like this, believe me. And the lighthouse, well, it's remote; it's got shelter, plenty of dark corners if you fancy a smooch with one of the lasses. You can get up to what you like because the adults tend to stay away." Facing me again, he carried on. "Obviously there's drink involved, beer, cider, whatever the kids can get hold of. In my day it was cider, but the hard stuff creeps in now, as you can see by the bottles at your feet: gin, vodka, whisky, and occasionally drugs."

I raised an eyebrow at this but let him carry on.

"For years there's a game we've played at the lighthouse called Thirteen Ghost Stories. Have you heard of it?"

I shook my head, whilst he glanced fretfully over in the direction of the main complex. Another roll of thunder made him flinch this time, not me.

"It's a sort of ritual, I suppose. A bunch of us gather together and light thirteen candles – you know, those wee tea light things."

"Yes, I know," I responded.

"You sit in a circle, and each of you takes turns in telling a story."

"A short story I presume, as there's thirteen to get through?"

"Aye, mostly it's just a few paragraphs, although Maire

MacTavish used to go on a bit. She's an author now by the way, written a romance book. Have you heard of her?"

"I don't tend to read romance." At least not anymore.

"You don't? Now there's a surprise. Anyway, as each ghost story is told, you blow out a candle, counting all the way to thirteen. You can imagine it, can't you, the room getting darker and darker, the shadows around you becoming more menacing."

I could, the stories getting wilder too, macabre even.

"The best story is always saved 'til last. In my time it was Gordy Ballantyne who usually bagged that honour, he had a brutal mind, so he did. The stuff he'd make up, whoa, even now I try not to think of it. He was into blood and guts, was Gordy. Once he'd terrified the shit out of us – oops, sorry, excuse my language: the living bejezus; he'd blow the last candle out. By this stage, the darkness," Angus paused, took a breath, "…was intense."

"What would happen then?" I realised I was holding my breath too; there was even a break in the weather – a lull – as if the rain, the wind, and the sea itself was curious.

"Angus?"

"Nothing!" he declared. "Absolutely bloody nothing. We'd all fall about laughing, some would start chasing each other around the room, shouting 'woo woo' at the tops of our voices, tickling each other, laughing, joking, and a fair bit of flirting too. And that was it, honestly – there was no drama, not really. For years that game's been played here. And it was fun, just a wee bit of fun." He lowered his head, solemn all of a sudden. "Until now that is. This new generation, they might be wilder in some ways, but basically they're good kids. And Ally Dunn, she's not a liar or a drama queen. I've known her all her life. She's changed, all those involved that night have changed." Once more he stared out of the cracked window. "I'm wondering if they'll ever be the same again."

Chapter Two

1972

COME on, play the game; I want to play it.
"Mum's only in the kitchen."
So, switch to thought instead.
I did as she asked. *What's the point though?*
The point is that we all need a name.
I don't know your name.
Ask her.
Ask Mum? I don't think so!
Make one up.
I've made up hundreds for you in the past; you don't like any of them.
That's because… because…
None of them are your real name.
I'd hit the nail on the head.
It's not fair! It's so not fair!
Oh, please don't start.
It's not though, is it? I didn't ask to be born dead.
I winced; it always came back to this. *I'm sorry I lived.*
And I meant it, I honestly did. Perhaps I would have felt differently if I were 'normal', like my brothers and my sisters who all got on well enough with my mother. But I

wasn't. And yes, that made me sorry at times that I continued to breathe.

It's all right, Ness, don't get sad.

As guilty as she made me feel, as frustrated, even as scared at times, she cared this twin of mine and she wanted me to care for her too. I was born ten years ago and I was supposed to have a sister – an *identical* sister. When my mother realised what had happened to one of us, she'd screamed apparently, wouldn't stop screaming. It had been a difficult pregnancy – I remember Mum referring several times to how ill she'd been whilst carrying us. It'd been a difficult birth too. Not to have a full return on it must have been a harsh blow. One of my brothers, Ollie, had once elaborated further on this tale of misery, had seemed to take great delight in telling me. It wasn't just grief that did for her apparently, she'd haemorrhaged too, losing blood and becoming weaker. The doctors whisked both babies away, but what they did with the deceased I don't know. Afterwards, Mum was ill for days, weeks even. The whole experience had changed her entirely.

Very early on I realised she could hardly stand to look at me; certainly I can't remember ever being hugged or kissed by her. I have a theory about this: instead of appreciating what she'd got, Mum dwelt only on what she'd lost. I was always such a painful reminder. Then, as time wore on, it became clearer what else I was. A young child doesn't know how to lie, to pretend that what's happening isn't – and the gulf between us widened.

My twin was talking again.

I like the name Mary.
Mary?
Does it suit me?

No, you're not angelic enough.
She laughed at that.
Lorraine?
I screwed up my nose. *I don't like Lorraine.*
So what? It's my name, not yours.
You haven't got a name.
Yet, she reminded me. *Okay, okay, Sandra.*
Maybe.
No, I've gone off that already. Carrie?
Carrie's good.
Shall I be Carrie?
If you want to, it's up to you.
Ness, you need to take this seriously.
Carrie's fine.
You're not taking it seriously!
I am. I like Carrie. We haven't had that one before.
But would Mum have chosen it?
Mum? I've told you, I don't know.
What name would Mum have chosen, do you think?
She can be relentless at times.

Getting up to turn the volume on the TV louder, she knew what I was doing: trying to drown her out. From being a vague outline, she materialised more fully to stand in front of me. Like looking in a mirror; she had the same straight black hair, a heart-shaped face, pale skin, and dark eyes. Only one thing was different – her stormy expression.

Ask Mum!
I can't.
I want you to ask her.
It'll only upset her. Or make her angry, one of the two.
Ask her or I'll scratch you!
You can't hurt me and you know it.

I can! I will!

She never used to get so angry, upset yes, but not angry, not whilst we were growing up. It sounds odd saying that my twin was growing up too, but she was, in the spirit world at least. It wasn't that I didn't care about how frustrated she felt at times; I did, especially with regards to my mother. She seemed to *crave* her attention. My father, brothers and sisters, she didn't seem so bothered about, but then neither was I to an extent.

Ask her, Ness.
Or what?
Or… or… I'll make the TV go blurry.
Big deal.

I didn't like giving in to her too often, if I did, it encouraged her and she'd be worse the next time. I turned from her, from the TV, and settled back into the sofa, carrying on with the book I was reading as part of my homework – a somewhat dull book, written for kids, but not able to capture a kid's imagination; a shame because I loved reading usually.

Hanging around for a few minutes, huffing and puffing, she then disappeared. *Good*, I thought, *she's left me in peace* – for a short while at least.

I should have known better.

She appeared again, dashing the book from my hands. That's what she'd been doing during her brief absence, gathering enough energy to do that.

I jumped up; glad that I was alone in the room, that no one else had seen it.

Why'd you do that?
You're mean.
I'm not.

You are.

Because I won't ask Mum? Of course I won't. You know what she'll do.

But I need to know.

No!

Ask her or I'll hurt you, I will. I can do it. I'm strong enough.

Her insistence – her *threats* – incensed me further. I wouldn't do what she asked, never! Besides which, who could hurt me more, her or Mum? Mum wasn't averse to beating me, and sometimes those beatings were severe – as if she was trying to beat my 'ability' right out of me, perhaps in her own way, trying to save me. That's how she always justified it. Not that she ever said as much out loud. But sometimes I could catch what she was thinking – *I'm doing this for her own good, something's not right with her, something's very wrong, I have to do this, it's for her own benefit* – and all the while Dad would stand by, not joining in, but not stopping her either. Only once did he do that, after my Aunt Jean's funeral when I'd seen her spirit at the wake, when I'd said I'd seen her, when I'd made that mistake. Dad had to pull Mum off me then, fearing that she'd go too far, that she'd send me to join my twin. Every other time he endured, as I endured.

I stormed past my twin, warning her not to follow.

I WANT TO KNOW MY NAME!

When I didn't reply, she screamed again.

FIND OUT MY NAME!

I swung round, as enraged as her.

"You haven't got a name! I expect Mum didn't bother to give you one and if she did, she never told me, no one has. I don't even know where you're buried, *if* you're buried that is. You might not be. You're just... nothing. Do you hear me? You *should* be nothing!"

I realised my mistake too late.

"Not this again."

Drawn by my shouting, my mother had entered the living room. As I swung round, she was there in front of me, her face a mask of barely controlled fury, and I cowered in her shadow. Why had I done it? Why had I started screaming? What had possessed me?

You, you possessed me!

I glowered at my twin; she'd hurt me after all, by proxy.

Mum's hand came out to grab me by the scruff of my neck, I knew that any moment that same hand would hurl me across the room and I'd go smashing into the wall. And then she'd grab me again, by my hair or the collar of my blouse and she'd stand me up in front of her, freeing one hand so that she could slap my face, not once but several times.

I started whimpering. "It's because she wants to know her name, she *needs* to know."

No matter what Mum did to me, nothing could hurt as much as her words.

"A mistake, that's what she was, as were you. You should have both died that day."

Chapter Three

THERE are some games that shouldn't be played, the most obvious perhaps being the Ouija. The reason for that is because there's a belief system involved – and belief has a habit of opening doorways, ones that should remain firmly shut. This game that Angus was telling me about – Thirteen Ghost Stories – sounded more like a ritual. He'd even called it that himself, carried out in this same place, in the same manner, time after time, year after year, mostly by kids, the young, the innocent, the *enthusiastic*, their hearts and minds willing something to happen, throwing caution aside for the sake of a thrill, praying even. *Come on, come on, whatever's out there, break through the veil that separates us, we're desperate to see you.* The energy, the thoughts, the hopes, and the dreams build up, until finally something in the darkness *does* takes notice. They stop, they listen to your pleas, and they step forward, eager to see you too. Not always for the best of reasons.

The man who stood in front of me mentioned that all those involved that night had changed, but he'd changed too. Just minutes beforehand, he'd been gung-ho about bringing me here and showing me around, intrigued to see what I could sense. But now, with his eyes on the main

THIRTEEN

building, reticence had set in.

"How long is it since you've been to the lighthouse, Angus?"

He rubbed at his chin. "It's the kids that come," he repeated. "Not the adults."

"So a few years then?"

He nodded.

"And what happened to Ally Dunn, it was two months ago?"

"Aye."

"Any chance of seeing her at some point?"

"We can ask her mother."

There was something else I needed to know, something that risked unsettling him further. "Angus, has there been a known death at the lighthouse?" According to the research I'd been able to do prior to my visit, there hadn't been, the hotelier and Angus's mother confirming that, but I hadn't asked Angus outright yet, and I'd deliberately used the word 'known'. Not everything catches the eye of the media, especially on an island like this: remote and with a strong sense of community. Some things get hushed up.

He didn't answer straight away, in fact, he didn't answer at all. Another almighty roar captured our attention, the wind so loud it hurt your ears.

"We should get going," Angus yelled.

"To the main building?"

"Aye."

The lighthouse complex proper, not this single cabin that, although abandoned too, seemed benign enough. Perhaps 'benign' wasn't quite the right word, for, while I could feel nothing of a tangible nature, it certainly had a simmering quality – a precursor perhaps to what lay ahead.

As we left the building my eyes were drawn back to the fridge, the microwave, which were covered in rust. I shone my torch at them again. *Diseased*, that's what they looked like, as did this building, and the buildings that surrounded it.

That thought having formed in my head I couldn't wait to leave, to take my chances with the great outdoors again, with what was natural rather than otherwise. That's the thing, you see, there are those that think because I'm psychic I welcome what I see, that I take it in my stride, and it's simply part of who I am. That's not the case though. To date, I've not met a single person with abilities similar to mine who actively welcomes it. If anything, I've seen madness in their eyes, and desperation. I've recognised that in myself too.

The cold rain was at once enlivening and repellent, and we'd get soaked again dashing from here to there, but what did it matter? I only hoped that when we got back Angus's mother had plenty of hot water, so I could take a shower and warm my bones. There'd been grass beneath my feet en route to the cabin but now there was gravel, no crunch could be heard as such. It was the change in texture that was obvious. I tried to look up, to get an impression of the building before me, licking my lips as I did and noticing the salt on them. It seemed sizeable enough, laid out over two floors rather than one. The door was intact and Angus shoved against it with his shoulder three or four times. When it opened – quite suddenly – he stumbled, falling across the threshold. On his feet again, he shut the door behind me, having to fight to do that too as I shone the torch around. A smell was the first thing to assail me, one that made my eyes water. It was a mixture of things, damp, rot and mould, but there was an underlying sweetness to it, one that was sickly rather than pleasant. Swallowing hard, I continued to peer into the gloom.

What a mess – an *unholy* mess you could say. There was a sofa and two armchairs, both of them vomiting stuffing. A low coffee table had been turned over and rag-like curtains hung at the windows. On the floor, torn pages were scattered everywhere.

"They're from school exercise books," Angus informed me when I remarked upon them. "I suppose you could call it another ritual. Students come here at the end of their school year and they tear their books to pieces. It's a sort of celebration if you like, a release."

I supposed it was.

As in the cabin, there were empty bottles too, scores of them, and the wallpaper looked as if giant fingernails had travelled up and down it, scoring it again and again. Directing my torch upwards, I noticed that the ceiling had cracks in it, reminding me of a spider's web.

As I'd had to do in the cabin, I kicked a path clear in front of me. "How many rooms are there in this building altogether?"

"There's this room, which is the living room."

"Obviously."

"A kitchen of course, a utility room, three bedrooms and a bathroom."

"How many children did the keeper have?"

"Two. A boy and a girl."

"Is this where you played the game, in the living room?"

He shook his head. "No, we used to play it upstairs in the bedroom."

"Whose bedroom?"

"Not the main bedroom, it was one of the kids'."

"Any reason why?"

He shrugged. "The main bedroom belonged to the mum and dad, it seemed a bit… pervy, to go in there, where they, erm…" A burst of laughter escaped him. "Teens, eh? It's funny the way we used to think."

I couldn't help but smile too. "Tell me about the family."

"I never knew them, but according to everyone round here they were a strange lot, insular, you know? Och, don't get me wrong, island folk can be like that, non-island folk too. There's plenty who away up to Skye to escape, those who want to keep themselves to themselves, but as keepers of the lighthouse, you'd think they'd mingle. They're a vital part of the community with an important role to play. Caitir and Niall were the kids' names, the girl was the elder of the two, but they never went to school, they were taught at home. The family lived here for around five years, until 1977. They'd come from Barra—"

"Barra?" I interrupted. "Where's that?"

"It's a Hebridean island, a real outpost, but where they went to, no one knows. It was a cold day in winter when they ceased whatever they were doing and left, they didn't even bother to turn the TV off. It was still on full blast when it was discovered what had happened." Clearly he disapproved. "It's against the rules you know, to do that, for a light keeper to just leave. Someone needs to remain on site at all times to ensure the light comes on when it's supposed to. Later, one of my dad's friends checked with The Northern Lighthouse Board whether the Camerons had been reassigned elsewhere."

"And?"

THIRTEEN

"They hadn't."

"Little wonder. What about the boys that helped Mr Cameron? Did they leave too?"

"It was just the one boy by that time, a young lad called Liam, and he'd been dismissed a few months earlier. Mr Cameron said he had no need of him, that it was a waste of money employing him, that he and his wife could manage well enough."

"Is Liam still on the island?"

"No, he left at the first opportunity, a lot of the youngsters do, to be fair. They go to Glasgow or Edinburgh. Unless you're into farming, there's not much to stick around for."

"Has Liam still got family on Skye?"

"Aye, his dad's here, Ron McCarron."

"Perhaps I can talk to him."

Angus snorted. "Good luck in finding him sober enough to make sense."

"Oh," I responded.

"Oh indeed."

"When was the lighthouse put on the market?"

"Only recently, a whole ten years later. In this part of the world, things have a tendency to move slowly, business included. As you know, my uncle really wants to invest in it. He said it'd make a mint as a bespoke guesthouse, that the punters would love its quirkiness. There are those on Skye that doubt that, who think it's in too remote a location to stay busy all year-round, but Uncle Glenn insists that's not a problem, that people will flock here, come rain, shine, hail or snow. And they may do if what happened to Ally gets fixed."

I nodded, mulling over in my mind what he'd said and

what I knew already. Ally Dunn had barely spoken a word in the two months since she'd been here. She and a group of her friends had sat upstairs, as so many had done on so many occasions before, and played Thirteen Ghost Stories. There'd actually been thirteen of them that night according to Angus, usually there were a lot fewer, each of them telling a story, and, as they'd counted upwards, got closer to thirteen, things started to happen. Several of the teenagers experienced blinding headaches, another two felt sick, one to the point of retching. One girl swore blind that the teenager next to her had pinched her, whilst a boy felt someone blowing into his face, a short sharp puff that caused his eyes to water profusely. But, of course, it was Ally who'd suffered the most.

"Poor Ally," Angus was saying, looking around him, at the shadows that seemed to be on the increase. His hands were in front of him, the fingernails of one hand scratching the palm of the other – a nervous habit perhaps? If so, I didn't blame him. Just as he was nervous, I was too. I wasn't sure what was here, yet – but there *was* something. And its energy… was it dark or was it troubled? There's a difference as far as I'm concerned. Troubled I could identify with more, whereas the dark verges on something I don't want to believe exists – worse than any human savagery, it's something inhuman.

I took a breath, reminding myself what I was here to do: to discover if this place was haunted or if what happened to Ally Dunn was the result of teenage imagination, which is fertile enough at the best of times, never mind the worst. "I need to know everything you know."

"Well, it was… erm… Christ, it's hard to get the words out, you know, standing here…"

THIRTEEN

"But here is where it happened?"

"Like I said, it was upstairs, in the one of the kid's rooms."

"Which kid?"

"The girl's."

He meant Caitir's room – a private room, a sanctuary, or at least it should have been.

I glanced upwards at the ceiling, at the cracks similar to a spider's web and made a decision. "Then we'll do the same, Angus, we'll go upstairs. You can tell me there."

Chapter Four

1973

NESS, Ness, don't cry. Mum really doesn't hate you.
 She does!
 She doesn't, she just gets… angry sometimes. So do you.
 Me?

I was upstairs again, in my room, the only place I could find respite from the rest of my family, where they didn't usually bother me. Only my twin *bothered* me. There'd been yet another argument between Mum and me, or rather Mum had laid into me for yet another perceived slight. I'd been lying on my bed sobbing, but at my twin's words I sat bolt upright. "This has got nothing to do with me. This is her fault, hers and… and yours."

Her pale eyes clouded, as her shoulders wilted. *Feeble*, I thought, *that's what she looks like*, and then immediately felt guilty. Another thing that had been pointed out to me several times by my mother was that I'd been the twin who took all the nutrients from the other one. 'Greedy,' she'd called me once. I'd had to bite down hard on my tongue so I wouldn't retaliate. How the hell could anyone blame a foetus! But I had been greedy, even if unwittingly, stealing my sister's life force to bolster my own. Staring at her, I started to reach out, to touch her arm, an apology forming on my lips, but I stopped, and couldn't go through with it. Instead, I snatched my arm back and threw more words at her.

"I wish you'd all leave me alone."

Ness—

"Mum, Dad, my dumb brothers and sisters, but most of all I mean you. How can I ever hope to be normal when you're always hanging around?"

The way she sat there, huddled on the edge of my bed, only served to infuriate me more. She was doing it deliberately, I was sure of it, acting all pathetic in order to try and make me sorry for her, to admit how horrid I was being. It wasn't going to work, not this time. I shoved my face into hers, expecting her to recoil, and was surprised when she didn't.

"I hate you, do you know that?"

Ness, don't.

"I don't want to live with ghosts."

But it's your gift.

I laughed, such a bitter sound. "Being able to see you, to see others, is *not* a gift!"

It is, Ness.

She always said this, always!

"If I could unsee you, I would."

You can't unsee things. That isn't even a proper word.

"How do you know? How the heck do you know? You don't go to school."

I'm not stupid; I know a lot of things, as much as you do, if not more.

"Then keep it to yourself and don't bother me with it."

She was the one who tried to reach out, but I reared back.

"Don't touch me," I spat.

In truth, what always surprised me whenever she did touch me was the warmth of her. She wasn't cold at all, not like I expected her to be, she was as warm as anything living.

You don't always hate seeing me.

"I do," I replied, wiping at the tears that threatened to spill.

Sometimes we have fun.

"No we don't!"

But that wasn't strictly true. We *could* have had fun together, plenty of it – like that time last year when the snow came, we could have gone out together, played and laughed. God knows I had very few friends as well as a family who either treated me as an outcast or a joke. Yes, there had been some who'd tried to befriend such a solemn child, but when you think your own family doesn't like you, you simply can't believe that strangers will either. And so it's easier to shun people before they shun you, it's easier to be alone. Especially when you *weren't* alone. When you could see others hovering around the little girl that's smiling at you or the boy who's asked you to join in a game of tag – attachments, spirits, some inviting you, or rather pleading with you to help them, to acknowledge them, to admit you can see them. The despair on their faces as you shake your head, as you walk away, their terror that someone might never see them again, that wasn't fun, none of it. It was too much for someone who was just a little girl as well.

Ness.

She was tugging at me now.

Ness, everything will be all right, if you'd just accept me.

THIRTEEN

Anger caused my chest to heave.

I'm the only family you really need.

My breath was coming in short, sharp pants.

The only friend.

Was she being serious?

We're a part of each other, Ness.

Still she was tugging at my sleeve, desperate for me to answer.

Finally, I raised my head and looked her straight in the eyes again.

"I hate you."

She was even more pitiful than before.

Don't keep saying that.

"Why not? Tell me a good reason why I shouldn't?"

Why? Because you're beginning to sound just like Mum, that's why.

Chapter Five

THE hallway was also littered, ankle-deep in places, and that terrible smell… it really was sickening, a real stench. We needed more light, the torch was useless against such inky blackness, but it was also the only thing we had. Ironic really, that more light was needed at the lighthouse. It defied its existence alone on the cliff top and it defied its name too.

"Why was this lighthouse decommissioned?" I asked, as we found the stairwell and began to climb, Angus insisting on going ahead of me. "Was another one built?"

"Aye," he couldn't keep the shiver out of his voice, "there's one further up the coast, just a tower, no big house or cabins attached to it and therefore much more cost effective. After the Camerons left, this lighthouse was converted to automatic operation for a while, but the light kept failing, and for no reason that they could fathom, so it was decided to build another. That one works well enough. Mind you, with satellite marine navigation coming on in leaps and bounds, by my reckoning, in ten to twenty years, there'll be no need for lighthouses at all. There'll be loads of them up and down the country, left like this, abandoned, the new tower a few miles away included, the lights turned off forevermore."

It was a sobering thought.

At the top of the stairs, on the landing, we stood side by side. More darkness stretched before us, and in that darkness were deeper patches – doorways to bedrooms, which at this moment felt like they harboured other dimensions, ones we weren't equipped for.

Striving to keep my breathing calm, to keep it even, I nonetheless had to reach into the pocket of the coat I was wearing. In it I'd placed a great big chuck of obsidian, my hand closing around it and feeling how solid it was, how cool, its black shiny surface as smooth as glass. A lucky charm, a talisman, call it what you will, it gave me comfort. Renowned for its ability to repel negativity, to protect a person from psychic attack, it was also supposed to have healing qualities, helping to release lower or negative emotions – I hadn't found it much good for that, but it was certainly a stone I was drawn to at the moment, more than tourmaline, which was widely considered the queen of the protection stones. It was *my* stone and without it I felt exposed. Having drawn strength from the crystal, I inhaled again and composed myself as much as possible, given the circumstances. That feeling that there was something here – besides Angus and myself – was becoming more apparent. There *was* something and it was watching – hiding in shadows that were darker still.

"Come on," Angus said, either getting braver or wanting to get this whole shebang over and done with as quickly as possible. "The girl's room is this way."

My conflict continued. Should we be doing this – going into what might be the epicentre? Maybe it was best if I went alone, I didn't want anything to happen to Angus.

Another option: we could call the whole thing off and seek more advice. It's not as if I fancied putting myself in danger either. But here we were – just feet from Caitir's room. It might be possible to make contact, and if we did, we could wrap this whole matter up tonight and what few days I'd booked here I could enjoy instead, taking long solitary walks beside lochs and along cliff tops, immersing myself in the beauty of Skye, which might prove healing too. Hope – how it spurs a person on. And despite my fear I *was* hopeful. I also reminded myself of other encounters I'd had previously; spirits that seemed as dark as this one, as spiteful, and as mischievous. They'd all been human once, humans who had suffered, and in the spirit realm were suffering still. That was what kept them grounded. So often – as with the girls in the woods, certainly the one I'd managed to contact anyway – it was shock, hurt, despair and disbelief at what had happened to them, that people, living and breathing, could inflict such cruelty, could be so merciless. What if, like her, something terrible had happened to whoever was grounded here: what if it was experiencing a similar range of emotions and having lost faith in this world, had lost faith in the next too? If so, that might be why it had hit out – at Ally Dunn, at the other teenagers. It had simply had enough of being teased, even if that teasing was more attributable to youthful ignorance than malice. If I could release its spirit, not leave it lingering in such a lonely, desolate spot, anger and fear growing ever more potent, then I had to try.

That little girl in the woods – she was never far from my mind, or her expression as her body was eventually found, as she'd hovered above it, staring down into milky eyes that had once shone with vitality, at a perfect complexion now mottled and dirt-encrusted. The girl was sad, of course she was, but she'd been relieved too. Finally there was resolve and because of it she could let go, her sadness fading entirely as the light wrapped itself around her. The second girl in the woods, her friend, I'd tried so hard with her too – but you have to be ready for release, you can't force it. As free-will exists in life, it seems to exist in death too. We may have found her body, lying right beside the first, but her spirit continued to elude me – she was there all right, she was grounded, but she refused to come forward. But I've made a promise: one day I'll go back to those woods, as lonely a place as this, and I'll go alone, with no police officers in tow, and try again to coax her.

Having bypassed the two other bedrooms, the bathroom as well, Angus pushed the door to the third bedroom open. I don't know what I expected; perhaps a rush of energy as whatever was grounded hurled itself at me, a mad keening perhaps from something barely visible, a burst of emotion that would force its way down my throat to broil in the pit of my stomach. My imagination runs riot as much as the next person. But there were no spectral hands to tear at my hair, no hollow eyes that bored into mine, there was nothing – absolutely nothing. It was just a dark space, into which we stared blindly – Caitir's room, only a very little of her energy lingering: the innocence, the sweetness, and the fear.

Who'd she been afraid of?

Who or what?

Outside the wind had picked up. I pictured it curling itself around the building, tendrils desperately seeking portals they could rush into, entering at last, in belligerent triumph. I envisioned the mist too as it crept stealthily inland, intent on suffocating us.

I gulped. "Angus, I think we should come back in day—"

It wasn't him who interrupted me; it was a high-pitched cry that rang on and on.

"It's just the weather," he said.

"I know that."

"It can sound pretty eerie at times."

That was the understatement of the year. But he was right, it *was* just the weather and I needed to keep calm. This was my profession. I couldn't run at the slightest hint of unease. I discarded entirely what I was going to say earlier. "Let's go further in."

We did, Angus at my heel.

"Shall we close the door?" he asked.

"Leave it open."

"The wind might catch it, that's all."

It might. We'd see.

"So now, tell me everything that happened," I said, steeling myself, imagining not what was lurking, or the elements as a living beast, but a swathe of pure white light, drawn straight from the beating heart of the universe, bold and brilliant. A shield, that's what the light was, one that no dark force had the power to penetrate. Immediately, I could feel my shoulders relax and my jaw unclench. I could do this. We were safe… or safe enough.

"It was a wild and stormy night," he began, "similar to this one…"

Immediately I reprimanded him. "Angus! Come on, kill the jokes."

"Sorry," he replied, laughing and then he paused again. "Actually it's not a joke. It *was* a wild and stormy night, as many of them are on Skye. The kids had gathered here again, probably a couple of the older ones had borrowed their parents' cars or something and were looking forward to another night of partying. But I think they looked forward to the game the most – I know we used to, when we were young. It added that extra bit of spice. They'd drank, mucked around a bit, the usual, and then they'd settled down – this is along the lines of what I've been told, by the way, by one of the lads who was here. I can't give you a blow by blow account, it was hard enough getting this much out of him."

"Okay," I conceded, shivering a little. "It'll do for now."

"The candles were lit, thirteen of them, and then everyone took their place, sitting in a circle. The first person told their story, blew out the candle, the next, and the next, and so on. There'd be giggles, a bit of elbowing to hush the gigglers up, one teen clutching onto another, any excuse, eh? But as the stories continued, the atmosphere must have changed, that clutching became pinching, people no longer laughing. They'd started to accuse each other of stuff, getting tetchy. During all of this, Ally had grown quieter, those either side of her, Isabel and Craig, had noticed but not said a word, to her or each other. It was as if she'd gone into a trance, Craig said. She was just… staring."

Coming to a halt, it took a few seconds for him to continue.

"Finally they got to the last story, which is always a tense time. Soon the room would be in complete darkness. It was Isabel's turn to tell it, but she didn't want to, she'd got scared, the way that everyone was behaving, not sitting as quiet as they usually do, as rapt, but getting aggressive with each other. Most of all, Ally was unnerving her, her being as still as a statue. I think Isabel made some joke about not bothering with the last story, leaving the candle to burn, but the response to that was aggressive too. She was told to 'bloody get on with it.' So she did, trying to string it out a bit, to make sense of what was happening around her, but just as there's a beginning and a middle, there's an end, and so she leant forward to blow the candle out. And that's when it happened."

"What?" I asked.

"In the darkness Ally started screaming, started to tear at herself, her clothes, and her hair. She jumped up, pushing off Isabel who was trying desperately to calm her, Craig too, and almost hurling them across the room. Her strength was superhuman, Craig said, but then he had been drinking. She continued to scratch at herself, to spit and snarl, and then she stopped. Started howling instead, falling to her knees, her hands covering her face, as if trying to protect herself, all the while screaming *No! No! No!*"

My teeth began to chatter. The room was like an icebox.

"It took almost all of them to drag Ally out of this room, every single one shitting themselves by now, unsure of what she'd seen but knowing she wasn't playacting, that whatever was going on was genuine. They'd also had their own terrifying experiences to go by. As another boy said, Murdo, the air was like a firecracker, he could almost see it sizzling in front of him. They got Ally into one of the cars, three of them in the rear seats pinning her down and drove her back to her house. They were scared of what her mum and dad's reaction would be, but they'd rather take a chance with that than stay at the lighthouse. By the time they got her home she'd calmed down… and I mean seriously calmed. She was virtually catatonic. Gradually the kids dispersed, some made their own way home, others wanted their parents to come and fetch them, and Ally's mother obliged by calling them. They were shaken. They still are shaken. No one knows what happened here really, especially to Ally, and she's not saying. Ness, tell me, what can you feel?"

"Something."

"What kind of something?"

I looked around yet again; the darkness as thick as ever, the wind still moaning.

"Something that's gone back into hiding, but not for long."

Things like that never hide for long.

Chapter Six

AFTER several more minutes spent acclimatising, I reached a decision. If this thing was proving elusive, then perhaps there really was little point in hanging around further, especially as doubts had been planted in my mind as to the nature of what it actually was. I needed to find out more about the history of Minch Point – knowledge was armour too – and it'd be handy to have more light, daylight that is, to get a proper grip on where I was.

"Come on," I said. "Tomorrow I'll—"

The door that I'd asked Angus to leave open, slammed shut.

We both swung round to stare at it.

"It's the wind," Angus said finally.

"Not this time."

"How do you know?"

"I'm a psychic, remember?"

Right then the tension in that room was mounting, like a rubber band being pulled tight at both ends, and bound to snap.

"First things first," I decided. "Try the door."

It must just yield, and if it did, we'd scarper.

No such luck.

"It's stuck fast," Angus said. "I don't understand it. There's no lock on it or anything."

"Damn," I muttered under my breath. There was nothing for it but to turn and face the darkness again. *Bright light, Ness, visualise bright light.* I had to surround both Angus and myself in it, head to toe. And stop being afraid. That was imperative. I *mustn't* show fear. "Whoever you are, whatever you're doing here, we mean no harm. We've come to help."

"We?"

I shot Angus a glance, one meant to silence him.

"My name is Ness Patterson, I'm what's called a psychic. I can see those that reside in the spirit world. If you're trapped here, if you're bewildered or you're in pain, I'll do my best to help. Communicate with me, tell me why you haven't passed, why it is that you remain."

Here's the thing: it's hard to know what to say to a grounded spirit – so often they're wary, they're terrified, they're the ones that are afraid of us. I've witnessed other supposed psychics go steamrolling in, baiting them, blaming them almost for having the temerity to remain. They make no effort whatsoever to understand the reasons why. I've seen too how the spirit reacts, how it strikes out, plays to the gallery, no matter how unwittingly. I've seen it and I don't like it. It doesn't solve a thing. And so I've developed a different technique: to go in with light, love and understanding, to realise that fear is often at the bottom of the problem – no not often – it *always* is. Fear is key.

Whatever I was addressing showed no sign of responding.

"Please talk to me. Not out loud, I don't mean that, I

can hear thoughts well enough. Aren't you lonely here? There's no need to be. You're spirit now, and that's where you belong, in the spiritual world. Tell me, in the darkness, can you see a light? A bright light that is, like no light you've ever seen before, can you see it shining?"

No response, the tension still at breaking point, the wind around us as agitated as ever.

Perhaps what the entity needed was time to consider my words? That was okay, that was understandable. A two-way communication could take time.

With Angus still standing obediently beside me, I reiterated what I'd said previously.

"I really do want to help. I'm here for no other reason than that. I certainly don't want to upset you. If you let us go, I'll return – that's a promise. I won't abandon you."

Exhaling, I turned to Angus. "Perhaps the door will open now."

"I bloody hope so."

He gave it a yank, but it refused to budge. He tried several more times. "It's not moving," he complained, just as it flew open. "Oh," he exclaimed. "It's not stuck anymore."

Stuck? Surely he must have realised... Instead of contradicting him, I muttered "Good", sighing in relief that my words had had an impact. I started to make my way over to the door. We'd be out of here soon enough and I could breathe again.

Breathe?

It was only when I realised my breath was caught in my throat that the visions started – so many of them; an assault, filling my mind, one after the other. *Horrific* visions. Images I couldn't bear to see, but couldn't escape either. It's easy to shut your eyes, but your mind's eye? I hadn't learnt that trick yet. I was an easy target – a sitting duck. Whatever was in the room with us was having such fun. God, those visions, they made me quake in my boots. Torture, people, animals – *children* – being torn apart, mutilated – innocent things, vulnerable, their eyes wide open in terror, mouths screaming.

"Stop. Stop. STOP!"

I didn't know what Angus was doing while this was happening, probably looking at me with that bemused expression of his. He couldn't see what I could see. At least I didn't think so.

"Angus," I croaked, my voice sticking in my throat, "get out. We have to get out."

"What is it, Ness? What's happened?"

So he *was* oblivious. Thank goodness.

"Have to get out," I croaked again.

"Aye, of course, the door's open now."

"Please, help."

What I want is for him to *drag* me out. I can't seem to move of my own accord.

"Angus!"

"Aye, lass, I've got you. It's okay, I'm here."

With his hand on my arm, he forced me forwards. These visions – when would they end?

Stop it! Please! Why are you doing this?

Mentally I implored, but whoever was responsible, wasn't listening. On the contrary, it was as though they *thrived* on this sort of thing – the sick and the twisted. How could they? I don't understand and I'm *glad* that I don't. But seeing is torture too.

The threshold of the doorway is too far away, every step

it takes to get there nothing less than agony. *Come on, Angus! Come on.* These visions are going to kill me. Why is it always the children that suffer the most? I'm sure my airways are on the verge of closing completely, that my heart will beat too fast, will buck like a wild horse. *Angus!*

I lashed out. Doesn't he know the pain I'm in? The fool!

"Hurry! I've told you to hurry!"

I want to hit him, hurt him, claw at him, and draw blood. Stupid man! Stupid, stupid, man!

"Ness, for God's sake, calm down will you." As my fist connected with his jaw he yelled out. "For Christ's sake, what's wrong with you?"

"I… I… GET ME OUT!"

His grasp on me tightening, he hurled us over the threshold, one hand releasing me temporarily so that he could close the door behind us.

"Come on." His voice is a mixture of so many things, shock, fear and anger. "You can explain what's just happened, why you attacked me, later."

Looking into his eyes, I can't see the colour of them in the darkness, but I can see how wide they are – probably as wide as my own.

Explain?

How do you explain hell?

* * *

"There now, there now, get this down you."

Angus's mother, Eilidh – pronounced *Ay-lee* I'd gathered listening to Angus referring to her previously – had tried to get me to drink a cup of tea, but I could barely hold the cup I was shaking so much. Having eyed me for a few seconds, she clearly thought something stronger was needed and handed me a tumbler of whisky instead.

"It's Talisker of course, Skye's own. My advice? Knock it back."

I did as she suggested, the fiery liquid initially burning my throat and making my eyes water, but gradually giving way to a more pleasant smoky warmth, one I was grateful for – in the confines of Caitir's room I thought I'd never be warm again.

I could feel Angus staring. He was sitting across the table from me, in a room full of chintz: his mother's dining room. I could barely lift my eyes to meet his, but I had to.

"Angus," I began, but then stopped. His jaw looked pretty bruised and there was a scratch under his left eye. "Oh God, I'm sorry, I'm so, so sorry."

"What happened? Why'd you do it?"

His bewildered look made me feel even worse. Eilidh, I noticed, turned her gaze away, leaving it to us to sort out. I was grateful for that at least.

"Just before we left the bedroom I started to see things, terrible things."

"Like what?"

I was curious. "Did you not see anything at all?"

"Just you, going ape."

"I… well… yeah… They were visions…" I couldn't bear to recall them, but somehow I had to try. "Terrible scenes of torture and degradation. Things I could never imagine, not in a million years. They just… flooded into my mind, one after the other."

Eilidh was looking at me again. "Why?" she asked, as bewildered as any of us.

"I don't know why," I answered and it was true, I

didn't. I'd never dealt with anything like this before. "I think whatever's there, it's bad. It's…" How could I say this? "It's pure evil."

"Pure evil?" Angus repeated. "Isn't that something of a conundrum?"

A wry laugh escaped me. Yes, I supposed it was. "What I'm trying to say is, I think it's some sort of—"

"Demon," Eilidh finished. Her voice, the kind of voice you hoped belonged to a woman such as her, petite, in her early to mid-sixties, and so very homely, no longer sounded soft and sweet. The solemnness in it echoed my own.

Even so, hearing her actually say the word, I backtracked. "I don't know whether it's a demon or a spirit. If it is a spirit, it's a very disturbed one. Eilidh, Angus, the history of that place, the 'real' history I mean, that only the islanders know, I have to find it out."

"Aye, lass, you will, you will," responded Eilidh, back to being homely again, "but not tonight. It's rest you need. Now come on, away to bed with you. I'll show you the way."

Rising from my chair, I started to follow her, but not before offering a still perplexed Angus another apologetic smile. Thankfully he smiled as well.

"Sleep well," he said.

"You too."

Upstairs, on the narrow landing, one that was bathed in the warm glow of a sixty-watt bulb, Eilidh stood in front of my room, smiling too. "I've put a glass of water by your bedside. If you'd like me to leave the landing light on tonight, that's fine, I can do that."

I shook my head. "It's okay; I don't mind the dark normally."

"Not you, no, but…" She stopped what she was saying and gave a little cough. "Well, you've a lamp in your room anyway, you can leave that on if you've a mind to."

"Thanks," I whispered, still staring at her as she turned and made her way back down the stairs.

I was curious. If it wasn't me that's afraid of the dark, who did she think might be?

Chapter Seven

STILL the images come. Even in sleep there's no escape. They're not as bad as when I was in Caitir's room, they're more diluted somehow and a part of me realises that I'm asleep – that this time it's a dream, not real at all, and that at some point I'll wake up. I'm trying so hard to wake up, to walk through the door that separates the world of dreams and reality, but every time I approach it, every time I get close, the door slams shut, traps me again.

I'm not going to be at the mercy of whatever's causing this. I refuse to be.

I remind myself what I have to do: imagine white light, pure and impenetrable.

Pure?

Hadn't I mentioned the word 'pure' earlier?

Pure evil.

Oh, the things I'd seen. Had Ally seen them too?

The things I was seeing…

Instruments of torture, ancient and rusted, forged in fire with the sole intention of causing pain. Agony, the screams and cries of all those that had ever been subjected to such instruments combining to form one single terrible sound that never faltered, that rang on and on and on. In the dream I hold my hands to my ears, attempting to drown that sound out, all the while knowing it's in vain. I fear for my sanity – such images have the power to destroy you, they can leave you a gibbering wreck confined to a white-padded cell for the rest of your life, they'd torment you, ceaselessly, in the lonely reaches of the night, and during daylight hours too. Was the light strong enough to combat this?

Of course it is! The light is all-powerful.

But do I believe that, do I really?

If only I didn't feel so alone.

You chose to be alone.

No, I didn't, not like this.

I've got to wake up. I have to. This dream is dangerous. This dream will… change me. I'm vulnerable whilst asleep. I'm a victim, waiting to be devoured, to be swallowed whole.

I have to reach the door, just as I did before, although there's no Angus to help me.

You attacked him!

Yes, I did, but I didn't mean to. I didn't even wholly realise… My hands just… struck out.

You lost control.

I shake my head. Control was taken from me – there's a difference.

The door, Ness, focus on the door. I'm trying to, but what waits on the other side? More darkness?

It's okay; I don't mind the dark normally.

I'd also said that earlier. Who to? A mother. Not my mother. My mother's dead.

Angus's mother!

Of course, I'm getting so confused. It's hard to think

straight, to think at all.

I'm not afraid of the dark, but someone doesn't like it; Eilidh was right about that.

No, no, no, I can't think of her now. I mustn't.

But her voice is suddenly all I can hear.

Ness, Ness, is that you?

I must wake up.

Ness, I don't like the dark.

Pinching is supposed to wake a person up; I'll try pinching my hand.

You know how I hate it.

Pinching harder, I'm clawing at my skin.

My dark isn't like your dark. There are things in it.

My hand feels sticky. Why is that? Is it because I'm bleeding?

I can't see them, Ness, but I know they're there. Just because you can't see something, doesn't mean it doesn't exist. These things, they wander round, looking for someone to latch onto. They're relentless. They need constant feeding; they need nourishment.

There *is* blood; I'm covered in it. It's dripping onto the floor, surrounding me, so much of it. Not dripping, it's pouring.

If they see me, Ness, if they see you... Ness, please, don't leave me alone in the dark.

I have to wake up! I have to!

I'm going mad trying to hide from them. If I had a name, an identity, it might be different, but I've neither. So I'm lost too, as lost as they are. Ness, what's my name?

NESS!

Chapter Eight

SITTING at the dining table with the morning's post-storm light doing its utmost to brighten the room, my body is shaking as much as it ever did last night. Clearly this wasn't lost on Eilidh, who was busy setting three places for breakfast.

"There's no law against having a wee dram in the morning too, not in Scotland."

"What? Oh, Eilidh, I'm sorry… no thanks."

She waved her hand in the air. "Och, take no notice of me, I wasn't being serious. Now, what would you like for breakfast? I've sausage, a lovely bit of bacon, black pudding—"

"Oh God, no." I couldn't help but grimace – after the visions, and the dream too, with helpless people treated as nothing but meat, the blood there'd been, there's no way I'll be able to eat what she's offering. "I don't mean to be rude. It's not that I'm a vegetarian…"

Continuing to stare at me for a few moments, those grey-green eyes of hers so penetrating, her smile returned. "Scrambled eggs it is."

"Thank you," I muttered, intrigued again. It's as if she *knows* the details behind my refusal. She doesn't. She knows the bare minimum. If anything, she's *resisted* being told.

On her way into the kitchen, she bypassed Angus – his red hair as awry as ever, and matching the stubble on his jaw, which masked the bruise I inflicted at least.

"Morning," he sounded cheery enough. "Did you sleep well?"

I couldn't see the point in lying. "Not particularly."

"I thought not."

"Oh, how come?"

"I went to the bathroom in the night, to get some water. When I passed your room, you were… I'm not sure how to put it really… yelping."

"Yelping?"

"Aye," he continued, unabashed. "I did the decent thing and knocked on your door, obviously you didn't answer it, but it stopped the yelping anyway. Nightmare?"

"A nightmare? No, of course not, I yelp in my dreams for fun."

My sarcasm caused a burst of laughter. "That's all too easy to believe, I'm afraid."

I smiled also before lowering my eye. "That bruise on your chin—"

"Aye, aye, you can pack a punch for a wee 'un. Seriously though, it doesn't matter; I don't want you to fret about it anymore. Bruises fade."

Once again I tried to explain. "The visions were relentless. What was happening in them, I… it made me angry, really angry, I mean, which could be why I hit out."

He frowned. "You don't actually know?"

"Why I hit out? No, I don't, not for sure."

"A spirit can make you do that? It can possess you?"

"*If* it was a spirit."

"Oh aye, that's right, and not the devil himself."

"I wouldn't go that far," I said, struggling to smile this time.

His expression softened. "It's tough, what you do, isn't it?"

"Not always." And that was the truth; sometimes it was actually very straightforward.

He seemed to mull over my reply before answering. "I know I can't see what you can, but you're not alone. Not here anyway. Have you heard that the Scots are a fey race?"

My smile was a little wider this time. "I have, yes."

"Aye, well, it's true, some of us are. And those of us that aren't, well, we don't doubt our own people."

"But I'm not one of you," I pointed out.

"Aye, you're a Sassenach."

"A what?"

"A Lowlander, an English person."

I screwed up my nose. "Ah, I see, sorry about that."

"S'okay, not all the English are bad. We're quite fond of some of them." More seriously, he added, "What I'm trying to say is we won't doubt you either."

"Why?" I asked. In his own way, Angus was as intriguing as his mother.

He sat back in his chair and shrugged. "Because when you live here, in God's own country, it's hard to deny that there's something else out there." Slowly, he shook his head. "Up here, it's as if you're closer to something bigger, something good, sacred even."

"We're not talking about something sacred though."

"Aye, but good and bad go hand in hand sometimes, don't they?"

Before I could reply, Eilidh returned, two plates containing eggs and toast in her hands.

"What's this?" Angus looked puzzled. "Is there none of that bacon left?"

"There's plenty."

"But—"

"Stop you're mithering, son, and eat whilst it's warm. You've a busy day ahead."

* * *

The weather may have cleared somewhat, but it was still a drizzly day, grey cloud concealing so much. Standing on Eilidh's doorstep with nothing but hills and sheep surrounding me, it was at once beautiful and oppressive.

"Cloud Island," muttered Angus, coming to stand beside me.

"Sorry?"

"The word Skye is Norse, it means Cloud Island, named for the whirling mists that you're admiring right now." He sighed. "It's as if this island wants to hide sometimes, to keep itself separate from the rest of the world, and, as I may have mentioned before, the people that live here are the same. Ness," he continued, an earnest look in his eyes, "whatever happens on Skye—"

"Stays on Skye. I know the saying."

"We're a private people. If there is something… *unnatural* happening, we'll be the ones to deal with it."

"Naturally," I said, smiling.

He smiled too. "With your help of course."

"A Sassenach?" I teased and then thought about it. "You know for a fey race, I'm surprised there's not a psychic

THIRTEEN

amongst you."

"Maybe there is, but people only like to admit so much."

His words dismayed me. Even here, in God's own country, you couldn't be true to yourself – different *meant* different, whatever the location.

"So, what's on the agenda for today?" Angus asked. "Another trip to the lighthouse?"

"Not yet," I started walking towards his car, waiting patiently at the passenger door. "I'd really like to speak to Ally Dunn first, or at least her parents."

Angus didn't look too hopeful. "It might be best to build up to Ally Dunn. What about some of the other teenagers?"

"Let's try Ally," I persisted. "At least give it a go."

Having joined me at his car, Angus climbed into the driver's seat. "Aye, I suppose we could. I know Ally's parents well, I could pave the way."

"Do they know about me, why I'm here?"

"I haven't told them yet. A few of the other parents of the teenagers know though and they seem willing enough to have a word. Are you sure you don't want to try them first?"

In the seat beside him, I remained resolute. "I'd like to cut to the chase. There's only so long I can stay on Skye."

Smiling, he started the engine, which clunked loudly before springing into life. "You know there's those that come to Skye and never leave. They find it suits them here."

"And there are those that flee at the drop of a hat, remember?"

Again he burst out laughing. "Okay, Ally Dunn's it is.

They live over near Dunvegan, just a few miles away."

It may have been just a few miles, but on Skye's winding roads – that ribbon through the rise and fall of craggy rock, heather and sheep – the journey seemed to take forever, leaving me a little nauseous into the bargain. Similar had happened yesterday when Angus had picked me up from Inverness Airport. We'd then driven seventy miles across some of the most amazing terrain I'd ever seen before taking the car ferry over Loch Alsh to reach the island. Our journey far from over, it was another fifty-something miles to the township of Glendale, where he and his mother lived, more magnificent views at my disposal, particularly the brooding Cuillin Mountains capped in tumbling cloud, which held me spellbound. But those twisting, turning lanes, they were something to be endured. By the time we'd reached Eilidh's, I was feeling a little worse for wear as well as extremely tired – not the best state in which to kick-start a psychic investigation in hindsight.

During that same drive, the conversation between us had been slightly stilted; as well it might be considering we were two strangers meeting for the first time. I'd also deliberately refrained from asking too much about Minch Point Lighthouse, at least until I'd actually set foot in the place, not wanting to encourage preconceptions, but now it was different, I *had* to know more and this journey was as good a time as any to pump Angus for information.

He replied knowledgeably enough, but it was the more technical details he was familiar with: that it was first lit in July 1909, that the tower itself is 43 metres tall, and the light – when it had been working – could be seen from twenty-four miles distance. There was also a foghorn, but that was disabled now too. It was just an empty building,

THIRTEEN

falling into disrepair.

"And through the years, as far as you know, Angus, various keepers have lived there without incident?"

He glanced briefly at me. "Aye, right up until the Camerons."

"Are any of those that lived there still on the island?"

He shook his head. "The lighthouse keeper before Cameron was Donder McKendrick. He retired to the mainland, near Inverness I think, a good while ago. Went to be closer to his daughter. My mother knew him and his wife, nice enough people apparently."

"It might be necessary to pay him a visit."

"If he's still alive," Angus began and then paused, trying hard to suppress a smirk. "Not that that's strictly necessary for you, is it?"

His teasing was good-natured enough. "Believe me, if they're alive, it's easier."

His voice grew more serious. "You know, Mum and me, we're happy for you to stay as long as you like. I know it's not a big house, but hopefully you're finding it comfortable."

"It's very comfortable, thanks." And it was – a traditional white house, as so many of them were on Skye, with a slate roof. It was warm and cosy, and in it I was made to feel at home rather than a jobbing visitor. Only Angus and his mother lived there, his father having died a couple of years before, his spirit not lingering I was glad to note, only a sense of his beloved presence. "But I do have other work to get back to."

"With the police you mean?"

I nodded. "I also work for Brighton Council on an *ad hoc* basis."

"They need a psychic too?"

"Not every tenant pays rent."

He bellowed with laughter. "I think I've heard it all now, the local council involved in spirit eviction! Your work with the police though, that must be interesting at times."

"At times."

He must have caught the more sombre note in my voice as he turned to look at me more fully. "Do you get results?" he asked.

"Mostly… Angus, watch the road will you, there's a car coming."

The car was actually a fair distance away, nonetheless I was glad of the excuse it gave me to cut Angus off.

We passed the road sign for Dunvegan. "Does Ally live in the village?"

"A wee bit on the outskirts. We're not far now, another mile or two."

The drizzle had become rain, the clouds even lower than before, and the sheep at the side of the road looking sodden and forlorn. Desolate was the word that sprang to mind as I peered outwards at the grey, barren scree slopes. If it was beautiful, it was a melancholy beauty. This was a land that was hard to live in; I'm not sure I'd be able to. A land in lockdown for many months, enslaved by the elements. In it, some things would never be able to prosper. Other things, however, would prosper well enough.

"That's the Dunns' house," announced Angus, "right up ahead."

It was another white house, but one that wasn't as pristine as Eilidh's, the patch of garden that surrounded it once neat perhaps, but which had clearly been left to its own devices recently with grass left wild and the weeds running riot. There were five windows at the front, two downstairs and three above in the eaves. At every one of the windows the curtains were closed, despite it being close to eleven on a weekday morning. As Angus stopped the car and we approached the front door on foot, I could feel the unease in the air. I should think anyone could.

I turned to Angus. "Are you okay?"

"Aye, I'm fine," he replied, but I could tell from his slightly worried expression that I was right, he could feel it too – a cloud of another kind that hung over the house.

While Angus rang the doorbell, I hugged the obsidian in my pocket.

Chapter Nine

"ANGUS Macbrae, what can I do for you?"

"Molly, hello, I've…erm… That is *we've* come to see you and John, to talk about Ally."

Molly Dunn raised an eyebrow as she shifted her gaze from Angus to me, clearly unimpressed with this intrusion. "Exactly who does 'we' consist of?"

"I'm Vanessa Patterson," I said, smiling as I held my hand out. "If we could come inside, I can explain who I am and what I'm doing here."

She seemed appalled at the idea. "You can't come in. It's… it's… not a good time."

"Molly," I persevered, "I don't think it's been a good time for the last two months, has it?"

"What? I…" At once her resolve broke and her face, far too haggard for someone of around forty, fell into an expression of despair. "How do you know that?" she whispered. "What's Angus been saying?"

"Only the truth," I assured her.

"She works with the police," Angus blurted out.

Molly's pale eyes widened, "You're a detective?"

I bit down on any retort I might have had for Angus and admitted what I was, there and then, on the doorstep. "I'm a psychic. That's the capacity in which I work for the police."

"This is *not* a police matter," she growled, her nostrils flaring slightly.

"I know, I know… Look, if I could come in, I can explain."

"John isn't at home."

"Then perhaps we can talk to you first, Molly? Please."

I'm not sure I would have pushed so hard if I hadn't sensed quite how desperate she was, that this entire matter was. Something was building, but what climax it was rushing towards I still had no idea. Nor how much time was left before it peaked.

"Molly," I continued. "We just need to talk."

Perhaps she sensed how desperate I was too, as she stared at me for only a few more seconds before dropping her gaze and standing aside. Glancing briefly at Angus, who nodded, I sidled past her and down a narrow hallway.

"Turn right," she instructed, "into the living room."

A pleasant enough room, despite the darkness, there was no sign of Ally; maybe she was upstairs in her bedroom. Tilting my head, I noticed a spider web crack in the ceiling, just as there'd been in the living room ceiling at the lighthouse.

Molly and Angus followed me into the room, Molly indicating for us to take a seat. Her eyes kept flickering upwards, as her teeth agitated at an already sore lip.

"The curtains," I said, feeling the need for some light, however pitiful.

"She doesn't like me to open them."

"Ally?"

A sharp nod was her only reply.

"Angus has briefed me on what happened that night at the lighthouse—"

"Briefed you? You said you weren't a detective."

"I'm not, I'm sorry, he's *told* me what happened."

"What he knows of it," she corrected.

"That's right. Perhaps you can tell me what's been happening since."

I could feel how tense Angus was beside me and wished I'd come alone so I wouldn't have to worry about him. But then it was only because of him that I'd managed to gain entry into the Dunn household at all, and so decided to be grateful, although the police angle he was promoting, I'd have to have a word with him about that. Police, psychics; neither were popular. The last thing I needed was a double whammy of distrust.

"Molly?" I prompted when she fell silent.

"It's difficult," she whispered, her eyes again flickering upwards.

"If it's possible I'd like to talk to Ally too at some point."

"Ha! Good luck with that! She hardly talks to anyone anymore, not even me."

I seized the moment. "What does she do?"

"She sits, that's all, and stares at the wall. She hardly eats, hardly drinks, and there's no hope of getting her to school. The teachers are being very good, they provide me with material to home school her, and I do, I sit and I read through everything with her, but she barely acknowledges me. Their patience is going to run out soon."

"And your patience?" I ask.

"Mine? I'm her mother!"

She'd taken offence, but I ignored that. "Molly, as her

THIRTEEN

mother, this is the hardest of all for you. Has she said anything at all about what happened at the lighthouse?"

"Nothing. But when she sleeps, she dreams, and when she dreams, she mutters. She sounds frightened, as if she's trying to escape something. Sometimes she lifts her hands and bats at something above her, turning her head from side to side and yelping."

At the use of that word, I sensed Angus looking at me – he'd said I'd been yelping too last night. I ignored him, my entire attention on Molly. "Go on," I said.

"I woke her once, during one of these dreams, and she lashed out at me." Her voice was trembling as much as her body. "John heard the commotion and came running. He had to pull her off me. Oh my girl, my poor wee pet, it's awful, just awful."

Her words ended on a sob, one that galvanised Angus into action. He jumped up to stand awkwardly by her side. "Will I get you a cup of tea, Molly?"

"No, no." She waved her hand at him. "Tea won't help. *Nothing* helps." Wiping at her eyes, she lifted her head to stare at me again. "Whatever happened at the lighthouse, it was bad, very bad. I keep thinking she might be… that's she's…"

She didn't have to say it, I knew what she meant – possessed. I hoped not, but I couldn't deny it either, not until I'd talked to Ally. If she was possessed, what by? It could still be a spirit. I'd heard of such things happening before, but not encountered it personally. If it was something non-spirit… I swallowed. Was I out of my depth here?

A loud thud from upstairs captured our attention.

"Is that Ally?" I asked.

Molly nodded. "Her bedroom's just above."

"The cracks in the ceiling…?"

"They weren't there before," she admitted. "As much as John and I are frustrated, Ally is too, I think. There are times when she barricades herself in, and when she does, it's as if she's hurling herself from wall to wall in some mad frenzy. I've shouted through the door, I've pleaded with her to stop, but she won't. And she can keep it going for ages. The screams and the yells, it's heart-breaking to hear, truly heart-breaking. Before this, she was so lovely; she was bright, funny, and sociable. She was our angel."

Molly was crying again, sobbing, Angus still hovering uncertainly by, feeling just as bad as I did. More than ever I had to get to the bottom of what was happening. My gift could go some way towards enabling me, and so I had to use it accordingly.

There was one more thing I needed to know before I headed upstairs.

"Have the church been involved in what's happening here?"

"We're not church-goers," she replied. "It's not that we don't believe, but we've never been regulars. The Reverend Drummond is the minister at our local church and he's itching to get involved. I know it. He's heard rumours, you see, people love to gossip around here, you can't escape it. But I don't want the church involved, the police, or any of the authorities, I don't want them thinking that we've done something wrong, that all of this is our fault. It isn't. We're good parents. We've done our best by her. We love her, so much. I can't fob the school off for much longer though. They'll be the ones to involve others, I know it. And if that happens, if she's taken away from us…"

THIRTEEN

"Molly, I'm not the authorities, I'm just a person who thinks I can help."

"Because you're psychic?"

"Because I have a connection with the other side, because I can see."

She sniffed and blew her nose on a tissue that Angus had handed her. "And you won't breathe a word of this to the police, to Reverend Drummond either? You won't take this off-island? You have to promise me, mind. You have to say it."

"I promise."

She settled back in the armchair, confusion, wariness and hope battling inside her – hope eventually winning out.

"Then go upstairs," she said, her voice a mere whisper. "See what you can do."

* * *

Angus wanted to come with me, but I insisted he stayed with Molly, get her that cup of tea after all, and to make sure there was sugar in it. He was reluctant but he agreed.

"I'm here if you need me, just… shout or something, and I'll come running."

"Thanks," I said, appreciating his concern.

Leaving them, I stood at the bottom of the stairs staring upwards. It was dark up there, with no light allowed to infiltrate. I had such an urge to rush around and start drawing the curtains back, but if I wasn't given permission to do that, it was an urge I had to dampen.

I climbed one step at a time. It was like wading through treacle. How could the Dunns stand it? The atmosphere, charged as it was with fear and bewilderment, was utterly depressing. No wonder Molly — let alone Ally — was in such a state. At least the husband could escape during the day, thanks to his work, but the prospect of returning here, night after night… I'm not sure I could do it.

Either side of me, on the walls, were framed pictures, a huge variety of them, all of them validating what Molly had said, that they were a happy family, or had once been. Staring at them gave me a chance to get to know what Ally looked like, although it was Ally through the ages that they depicted, as a sweet baby, a cute toddler, Ally at a slightly awkward pre-teen age and as a full-blown teenager, but still smiling, still laughing alongside her parents. She was sixteen now — an only child — a *treasured* only child. How wonderful that must have felt. How terrible for it to have gone awry.

Leaving her bright youthful face behind, I reached the landing, turning in the direction of her bedroom. God, I wished they'd let the light in — it really would help. I'm not afraid to admit, I felt scared. I felt vulnerable and alone too. What was it that I was going to encounter in that lair of hers? Not the smiling Ally that filled my mind, that was for certain.

Refusing to think, determined to act, I forced one foot in front of the other. The closer I got, the denser the atmosphere became. Once again my breathing became erratic and I had to stop several times to force myself to inhale to a count of four and exhale for the same amount. My heartbeat steadier, I positioned myself in front of her door and knocked.

As I expected there was no reply.

"Ally, my name's Vanessa Patterson, I've come to talk to

you about what's been happening lately, about how you've been feeling. I'm not here in any official capacity, please don't worry about that, I'm here as someone who wants to help. You've nothing to fear from me, nothing at all." As with the dead, initially my job was all about cajoling.

Once more I was ignored, so I decided to force the issue and twisted the handle. Molly said that Ally barricaded herself in during more troubled times, I was glad to note that this wasn't one of them as the door yielded easily enough. I entered, my eyes searching for her in the darkness. There she was, sitting on a chair by the window, not staring out of it, but staring at the closed curtains, so still that for a moment I gave in to panic. "Ally, are you okay?"

The slightest of movements reassured me she was still alive, and that she could hear me well enough. Although instinct screamed at me to leave the door open, and therefore the path to escape clear, I closed it, thinking that in her current state she might prefer it.

"Ally," I said again, edging my way over to the bed and sitting close to where she was. "I should come clean about who I really am. I'm a psychic. Do you know what that means? Shall I explain?" When there was no answer, I did just that, wondering if that at least might provoke a reaction. It didn't. She was statue-like.

I looked around her room, took it all in. Only the bed was unmade, otherwise it was fairly neat and tidy, Molly steadfastly refusing to let her daughter reside in squalor – picking clothes up if they were left on the floor, changing sheets, polishing surfaces, vacuuming. I could see her now, in my mind's eye, carrying out such mundane tasks, and all in the darkness. The walls, which Ally would hurl herself against on occasion, may well be scuffed, but it was impossible to tell without the light on. I inhaled. There was no stale sweat, no smell of grime. What there was, was an underlying sweetness – the same unpleasantness to it as the smell at the lighthouse – a *connection*.

"Ally, what happened? Tell me. Whatever you say, I'll believe you, no matter how outlandish you might think it is, how crazy or weird. I'm on your side."

I have a good amount of patience, you need it in my job, but there were also times when you have to make a judgement call. It was time to explain further.

"Ally, I've been to the lighthouse too, last night. I went up to Caitir's room, where you and your friends played Thirteen Ghost Stories. I sensed there was something there."

At last a response – a mumble that I couldn't quite hear.

"Sorry, Ally, could you repeat that?"

"Did you play the game?"

Her voice was croaky, as if her throat had become as rusty with disuse as the pipes at Minch Point. "No, I didn't play the game, but I tuned in, and I had an experience too."

No verbal reply this time, but she did turn her head further towards me. I was able to study her profile a little better, a pretty girl, or she would be if she didn't look so strained – even in the darkness I could tell that. She was as worn as her mother. What should I do? Describe what I'd seen? I'd have to, but a significantly watered-down version. The last thing I wanted was to remind her of how vicious the visions had been.

"Ally, as I was leaving Caitir's room, images started to fill my mind, they came in rapid succession, one after the other, like a movie reel. These visions…" I paused. It's not as if I wanted reminding either. "They were… nasty. Very. Did you see something too?"

She issued another mumble, forcing me to lean closer to hear what she was saying.

"Animals, cats, my favourite, dogs too, blood, hurt, all of them. So much blood."

I shuddered at her words. "I know."

"Kids, younger than me. Kids my age too. Friends. Screaming. Crying."

And not just that, there was also the pleading, the begging, and the sheer lack of any mercy shown. It seems we *had* seen similar visions, and once seen, how could we forget? I wanted to bleach my mind, to scrub away the scars they'd left, but it was impossible. Such sights destroyed innocence. They left you feeling corrupted. No wonder Ally was suffering. But there had to be a way back – for both of us.

"Ally, whatever you saw, it's important to remember that it's over now. The images, the horror will fade with time. Here's what I do: whenever I remember, I replace it with another image, with something positive, something I love. You could try and do that too. Keep pushing the negative away, until eventually it recedes, and loses its power. Right now, what we've seen is holding us in its thrall, it's making us afraid and we can't afford to be. Fear is what keeps negativity thriving." When she failed to answer me, I dared to do something: I reached out and touched her shoulder. Inwardly I gasped. She was so cold, despite it being warm enough in the room, like a carving made from ice. "Ally, listen to me, please, you're not alone with this, I'm here now. Together we'll beat it."

"What do you love?"

I retracted my hand. "I'm sorry?"

She turned more fully, dark hollows for eyes giving her a ghoulish look. "What do you love?"

"I… erm… love lots of things. I love…" Damn it, but I had to struggle to answer this surprising question. "Chocolate." A small laugh escaped me, one with a nervous edge to it. "Doesn't everyone? A cup of tea with milk and one sugar; I love films; I love reading. One of my favourite books used to be *Jane Eyre* by Charlotte Brontë. Have you read it? I love animals, all animals really, no favourites there. I used to knit. Not so much anymore, but when I was younger. It helped me to focus somehow and having something nice to wear as a result of it was an added bonus. I—"

Those hollow eyes met mine. "*Who* do you love?"

Her voice sounded croakier than ever, scratchy almost

"W…who?" I repeated, stumbling slightly over the word.

"Who do you love?" She was glaring at me now.

"I… I love…"

"Who?"

"I…"

"WHO?"

"Stop yelling, Ally, stop demanding. That will get us nowhere."

She thrust her face forward, such a sudden action that I couldn't help but be alarmed by it. "Who do you love?"

Quickly I gathered myself. "Ally, this isn't you speaking. I think what's happening—"

"Your brothers?"

Again I was taken aback. "My brothers? Yes, yes of course."

"Liar!"

"Ally, whatever's in you is trying to take control."

"Your sisters?"

"Yes, Ally, I love my sisters. I do."

"Liar!"

I started to rise, but my legs felt like lead. *Get a grip, Ness, get a grip.*

"Your father?"

My breathing, I couldn't keep it steady anymore. "Ally, I'm warning you, I won't listen to any more—"

"Your mother?" At that a sly smile spread across her face. "Do you love your mother?"

I was able to stand at last. Ally knew nothing about my family, and nor did whatever it was that had hold of her. Towering over her as she sat in her chair, seemingly relaxed, casual even, I did my utmost to rein in the feelings – the memories – that were trying to overwhelm me, as horrific, *personally* horrific, as any of the visions I'd had at the lighthouse. "Ally, I know you're in there. Fight this thing. Don't be afraid."

She laughed – a cackle that didn't belong to her, but to something far more ancient. "I'm not afraid, you are. You're terrified. And your weak spot, I've found it."

"Leave my family out of this."

Ally refused to obey. "Your poor mother, what a torment you were to her."

"I've told you, I won't listen."

"This thing she'd spawned, as terrible as I am, an abomination. How it hurt her."

As I'd forced my legs towards Ally's room, I now had to force them to move away, from her and from the darkness that clung to her. But shock had rendered me slow.

"You drove her to an early grave."

How far the door was – an ocean of carpet separating us.

"You hurt your twin too, so bad."

Thrusting my hands out, I imagined a rope in front of me, and someone at the end of it; a friend, not a foe, hauling me towards the door. I had to go and come back stronger.

Stronger? What a joke! I'd never felt so weak.

"Remember, Ness, how you hated them."

Reaching my goal, I could barely see for the tears in my eyes. If I expected the door to be stuck again, it wasn't. It opened and I fled, but not before Ally issued her last words.

"And remember this: they hated you too."

Chapter Ten

1974

WHAT'S wrong with Mum?

I shrugged. "Don't know. Don't care."

She's being sick all the time.

"I told you, I don't know. How would I? She barely speaks to me."

Well, something's wrong.

I ignored my twin and her concerns, and continued to read my book – I got through so many, confined as I was to my bedroom, by choice as much as anything. Today, I was alone in the house with Mum. My father was at work, and my brothers and sisters were either at work too or school. I wasn't at school because I had a stuffed-up nose, a headache, a sore throat and blocked ears. Normally I never missed a day even when I wasn't feeling well. Mum always insisted I went. But, when I'd gone into her room to complain how I felt this morning, she'd just waved her hand at me, and said it was fine, that I could go back to bed. I couldn't believe my luck. I hadn't questioned it, hadn't hung around for a minute longer than necessary in case she had a change of heart, I'd simply raced out of her room and back into mine, closing the door behind me.

I had a whole day to myself – no teachers, and no one to ignore me in the playground. Bliss! I could read to my heart's content, do some colouring in, sleep even. I really did feel ill. What would have made it perfect was if my twin had kept away too. Some days she did, but today was unfortunately not one of them. She was worried about Mum and to be honest, I was a little bit too. I could hear her in the bathroom retching; it was a horrible, gurgling sound. As much as I tried to focus on my book, I couldn't. She'd shown some mercy towards me earlier, perhaps I should go and show some sympathy towards her.

I looked at the shadow of my twin, thought I saw her nod in approval.

"Okay, okay, I'm going," I said, shutting my book perhaps a little too hard. It was *Jane Eyre* – the story of another lonely girl – and I was really enjoying it, although the last chapter I'd read, where poor Jane had been locked in the Red Room by the terrible Mrs Reed had left me somewhat reeling. Leaving my room, I tentatively made my way to the bathroom and knocked on the door. Rather than vomiting, Mum seemed to be groaning, as if she were in considerable pain.

"Mum, it's me. Are you okay?" Stupid question really, but still I asked it. "Mum, do you want me to get you a glass of water?" Another stupid question, she was in a bathroom for goodness' sake, there was water enough in there! "Mum, say something. Please."

My twin was by my side. *Try the handle; see if the door will open.*

It did, something that caused both fear and more trepidation.

Taking a deep breath, I entered the bathroom. The first

thing I saw was blood – *the red room* – the tiles, normally a pale grey, were covered in it.

My hand flew to my mouth. "Oh God, Mum! Are you dying?"

Despite everything, that realisation was shocking. I was a child – I couldn't lose my mother! Terror drove me forward. "Mum, it's okay, I'm here. Tell me what to do."

She was slumped on the floor, her head resting against the side of the bath. Doll-like, her face was pale and waxy and her arms hung limp by her side. Not caring about the blood, I knelt beside her and reached out.

"Don't touch me!"

Her words stopped me in mid-action. "Mum!" I implored.

"Call your father."

Lowering my hands, I nodded. "What shall I tell him?"

"The baby…" her voice was low, guttural even, "…the baby's dead."

"Another one?" I gasped. I couldn't help myself.

"Yes!" she spat. "Another one."

I swallowed. "Ambulance," I muttered. "I'll call an ambulance."

"CALL YOUR FATHER!"

I pushed myself away from her, stood up and ran from the room, slipping on the bloodied floor as I went, crashing onto the landing, leaving footprints behind me on the oatmeal coloured carpet. Once downstairs, I dialled my father's office number with trembling fingers – it took three attempts before I made a connection. When he answered, I told him as best I could what was happening. He kept telling me to slow down, but I couldn't. Finally, he told me to go back upstairs, to stay with mum, that he was on his way, and would be there as soon as possible. I think I heard him swear as he replaced the receiver.

At the bottom of the stairwell, I stopped. I didn't want to go back up there. What was the point? She didn't want my help. I had to though; Dad had said so.

Once more in the bathroom, I saw that Mum had tried to straighten herself up, saw too how wet her cheeks were, and the tears that glistened there. She was sobbing, snot running from her nose, which she wiped at with the back of her hand.

"I'm sorry, Mum." I didn't know what else to say.

"Probably just as well," she managed.

I frowned. What did she mean?

"Like you. If it was like you."

"Like me?"

"Wrong! All wrong."

I took a step back, not sure if I could bear to hear what she was going to say. Not again.

She continued to mutter. "No more of this, I want no more. My luck ran out with you."

Tears blinded me too. "Mum, don't. Please don't."

But she was in her stride.

"I believe in Jesus, Mary and Joseph. I believe in God. It's what normal people believe in, self-respecting people. I *don't* believe this world is full of ghosts, of people long gone, that they walk alongside us, that they try and communicate, that they're lost somehow, that they need our help. It's not true, none of it. You're a liar, and you always have been. You just make it all up. I don't believe I'm capable of producing something like you."

She'd said *something* this time, not even *someone*. Anger overtook despair. "But you did though," I replied, shaking with the injustice of it all. "You produced two of us."

"DON'T YOU DARE TALK ABOUT WHAT HAPPENED!"

I could see my twin. She was standing beside my mother, staring down at her, with such sadness in her expression. "Look," I said, lifting my hand to point. "She's there right now, my twin sister, she's standing beside you and your words, they're hurting her too."

"The filth that comes out of your mouth."

"It's true! Look up. Can't you see her? Can't you sense her? Look at where I'm pointing!"

I don't know if it was something in my voice, a thread of steel perhaps, but she obeyed and for a moment, a brief moment, I thought I saw her eyes widen.

"You *can* see her, can't you? What's her name, Mum? What did you call her? She wants to know so badly."

Slowly, very slowly, my Mum turned back. Her voice when she spoke was loaded.

"I will continue to clothe you, I will continue to feed you. I will do my duty, as the state requires. But the minute you're old enough, you leave. Do you hear? I want you gone."

All anger, all defiance spent, despair engulfed me yet again.

I took another step back and then fled from the room, leaving my mother, my twin, and another sibling who'd never live in this world, but who hadn't lingered at least; who'd had the good sense to fly back to where he or she had come from: a better place than this.

Because this – my home – was nothing less than perdition.

Chapter Eleven

"ANOTHER cup of tea, Ness?"

"No thanks, Angus. I'm done now, I'm okay."

"You sure? You still look really pale."

"I *am* pale," I replied, smiling a little. "My skin never seems to tan, not even in the height of summer. Seriously, I'm fine. It's just… I've things on my mind lately."

"The mystery of the lighthouse?"

"That's certainly one of them."

Having escaped Ally, I'd managed to pull myself together, heading downstairs, past all those smiling photographs of the perfect family, ignoring every one of them, using the time I had to compose myself instead. The last thing I wanted was to burst into the living room looking as shaky as I felt. Ally wasn't to be blamed for what had happened, she was an innocent being used as a pawn. Molly was, of course, curious as to how I'd got on.

"I need to find out more about the lighthouse," I'd said to her, "speak to other parents of the teenagers involved, get a more rounded picture of what happened." I hadn't looked at Angus when I said that, I was too embarrassed. That had been his suggestion after all.

"And then what?" she'd asked.

"Then I perform a cleansing."

"An exorcism?"

That wasn't a word I tended to use. "A cleansing is more of an holistic approach," I explained. "I'll use light and love to combat whatever it is that hides at the lighthouse."

She'd frowned at that, not as impressed, I suspected, than she would have been if I'd admitted to an exorcism. I explained further than it was the Catholic Church that tended to carry out exorcisms and if she didn't want the church involved, the authorities…

"Okay, okay," she said. "I understand what you're trying to say. But this cleansing, is it as effective?"

"It has been in the past." And it was true, but no two cases were ever the same. People were unique, so were spirits.

Having said goodbye to her and climbed back into Angus's car, my façade crumbled, tears stung my eyes as I screwed them shut. As he'd been when Molly had got upset, Angus was all concern. "What's wrong? Come on. Come here. You need a hug."

How much I needed it he'd never know.

Once he released me, I dried my eyes and he'd driven us to this café, a short way from Ally Dunn's house, and plied me with tea, brushing aside any apologies I might have.

"Right," he said, watching me as I pushed my cup away. "Is it the lighthouse you want to go to next or to see a few more parents?"

"Not the lighthouse, not today." I needed to be more stable than this before I returned there. "Let's piece together what we know already, and try and make some sense of it."

"Sounds like a plan," Angus agreed.

"Angus," I said, worried suddenly. "Are you okay to help me? I don't mean to sound rude or anything, I'm grateful for your help, but don't you have a job to go to?"

His face fell slightly. "Actually no, not right now. You could say I'm in between jobs."

"What did you do?" I asked. "And what are you going to be doing?"

"I was working in an architect's office, in Edinburgh actually, as an architectural technician. But it's not my true calling. Uncle Glenn said I could manage Minch Point when it's a guesthouse. I like meeting people, I like being on Skye. I thought I'd give it a whirl. To be honest, I couldn't wait to ditch my job. "

"So you've a vested interest in this case too?"

"Aye, well, yes, I do now. I'm counting on it. I'd like there to be a steady stream of guests, but also, I don't want the lighthouse to suffer from an ill reputation any more than my uncle does. We'd be finished before we even got started. For my uncle it's an investment opportunity, but for me it's much more than that."

"I wish you all the luck."

He smiled. "I wish us *both* luck."

My smile was a little more strained. "Okay, back to basics. We know that the Camerons lived at the lighthouse, that they abandoned it a decade ago, that it's been used as a playground for kids ever since, and that those kids, including you at one point, played a game there: Thirteen Ghost Stories. It's become something of a ritual."

"All correct," Angus replied.

"Around two months ago whilst playing the game, Ally Dunn, and even a few of the others, experienced something. They've been different ever since."

"Aye, the others are more subdued, but they still manage to get up, go to school and socialise to an extent. It's Ally that's been affected the most."

"I wonder why that is?"

"I don't know."

"And none of them have been back since?"

"Not that I know of." He paused. "Ness, what happened when you went to see Ally? You haven't really said."

"It's not easy seeing a kid so distressed, you know," I replied, palming him off a little.

"I understand that. But did she say anything… you know… to upset you?"

This man, was he as fey as his mother?

"No, it's fine. It's just… A lot of negative energy clings to Ally, it can have an effect."

"Oh aye, I'm sure," he conceded, nodding gravely.

"We also know that whilst the cabin boy, Liam, moved away soon after his dismissal, his father, Ron McCarron, lives here still and, despite what you said about finding him sober, I'm going to need to speak to him, see if there's any way I can contact Liam."

Angus didn't look too sure. "It's a long time ago that Liam worked for the Camerons."

"That's as maybe, but he lived there, alongside them, at the lighthouse, he'll have more of an insight than anyone."

"Aye, I suppose. It's worth a shot."

Anything was at this particular point in time, because whatever was happening in this corner of Skye, it wasn't getting any better.

* * *

The afternoon was spent visiting the parents of Isabel Croft, Craig Ludmore, and Grant MacIver. Considering prior arrangements to do so were hastily made by Angus via a phone call, we were greeted amicably enough, even keenly I'd say, certainly by Isabel's mother and Grant's father. When we were ushered into various living rooms, the story was the same – their children, all of whom were still at school during our visit – were much quieter than usual, they'd lost their spark, their zest, they were more nervy instead, jumping at anything and everything. Isabel's mother, Beth, had also found sheets of A4 paper in her daughter's room, reams of them, the number thirteen inscribed on every inch of space, the paper jagged in places where she'd gripped the pen so hard.

"She'd hidden these sheets of paper," Beth explained as Angus and I sat on her sofa, "on top of her wardrobe, in her wardrobe, under her bed. Why would she do that?"

"Did you ask her why?" Angus enquired.

She shook her head as if the thought had never occurred to her. "No, no, I didn't. I suppose I felt… it would upset her somehow. I put them back where I found them. She's added to the pile since, there'll be no room for anything else in her room at this rate."

Grant's father told us how, when his son came home from school, he shut himself away in his room, only emerging to grab dinner and use the bathroom.

"At least he goes to school," Angus tried to soothe.

"Aye, that he does. But he used to be a sociable lad, sitting with his family in the evening, telling us all about his day, and what he's been up to. I miss him you know. We used to go fishing together at the weekend. Suddenly he doesn't want to do that either."

"It could be just a teenage thing," I venture.

"He's been a teenager for a while now," was Mr MacIver's reply. "As I said, this is a sudden change, ever since that business at the lighthouse."

"It's an odd place," Craig's father told us when we visited his house. "You know about the shipwreck, don't you, which happened soon after the lighthouse was built?"

Angus nodded. "You think it's relevant?"

"I never used to, but I'm beginning to wonder."

"Mr Ludmore," I asked. "What happened exactly? Did many people die?"

"Oh aye," he said, "all those on board. Thirty-six to be precise, the bodies that were recovered either sent home or buried here on the island. I think the youngest deckhand was recorded as being no more than thirteen. A tragedy it was, and no matter that it was so long ago, the weight of that tragedy remains. The lens, a Fresnel lens too, supposedly one of the best – it either failed that night or the clouds were just too thick for the beam to penetrate, no one knows for sure. It's not a great beginning for a new lighthouse, is it?"

It wasn't – it was dreadful. "Any other shipwrecks of note?"

Mr Ludmore shook his head. "A few incidents, but no more deaths."

Mrs Ludmore, who'd been in the kitchen, came in to join us, a laden tray in her hands. "You talking about the shipwreck, Alan?" She exhaled heavily as she put the tray on the table in front of us and began to pour into china cups. "The blue men at work again."

I was lost. "The blue men?"

"Aye," she said, handing me a cup, "the blue men. Storm kelpies, in other words. It's said they inhabit the waters around here, playing havoc with sailors, and causing boats to overturn. There've been several people who've sworn blind that they've seen them in the past, when the weather's fine, just floating on the surface, sleeping. But they can conjure storms too, whenever the mood takes them, when they want fresh bodies to feast on."

"Och, Meg, away with you!" chided Mr Ludmore. Looking at me, he shrugged as if in apology for his wife's flight of fancy. "It's a myth that's all, but aye, there's many around here that believe in the blue men well enough."

"Belief is a powerful thing," I said. And perhaps not to be dismissed, nor all this talk of conjuring. Certainly something had been conjured at the lighthouse, perhaps feeding off any negative energy that remained from so many deaths – thirty-six of them and the youngest victim only thirteen. That number, how it kept recurring.

"Is the boy buried locally, the lad who died because of the shipwreck, do you know?"

"Aye," Mr Ludmore answered, "he's got a headstone at Kilchoan Cemetery, in Glendale. Angus, you must know it? It's in your neck of the woods."

"Aye, I know it."

"Perhaps we can stop off there on our way home?" I asked Angus.

"Of course, if you want to."

I did, I planned to touch his gravestone and see what I could glean from it.

Still on such a delicate subject, I remembered something I'd asked Angus the previous day, to which I hadn't yet got an answer. "Aside from the shipwreck, have there been any more known deaths at the lighthouse? In more modern times perhaps?"

Mr and Mrs Ludmore looked at each other and then at me. "Are we talking murder here?" Mr Ludmore said.

I inclined my head a little. "Not necessarily."

"There's been no more deaths that I know of," he replied.

"Not at the lighthouse anyway," Mrs Ludmore added. "But there was another death. What was it, three or four years after the Camerons left. Not murder but not natural either."

My ears pricked up. "Oh?"

"A few miles from the lighthouse, following the coastline to the north, it was to do with a young girl. She threw herself from the cliffs, committed suicide in other words."

"How old was she?"

"Young, not even twenty."

"Do you know why she did it?"

"Not even her parents knew that. They were devastated, moved away soon after, wanting a fresh start, I should imagine. The one thing they did say was that she'd changed, and that that change had been quite sudden. She'd become moody and withdrawn, had stopped communicating with them. The lighthouse was empty by then, as you know, I'm wondering if she went there with her friends too, if something happened to her like it did to Ally, and to our kids. Oh God," her eyes widened, as her hand flew to her chest. "I've only really just put two and two together. What if, what if—"

Mr Ludmore immediately tried to soothe his wife. "No child of ours is going down the same route, don't worry yourself, lass. Don't even *think* it. And that girl, Moira her name was, she was a wild one. Och, I know her parents thought she was meek and mild, but come on, love, you know as well as I did that she had a reputation. She'd been giving them cause for concern for a long time, it didn't happen as suddenly as they claimed."

Angus broke into the conversation. "We shouldn't speak ill of the dead. Moira, she was… She was all right."

I turned to look at him. "You knew her?"

"Aye, I was a kid, barely sixteen when she died. Hung about with her sometimes in a big group, not that she ever noticed me." He paused and gave a wry laugh. "You couldn't help but notice her though. She was beautiful with long blonde hair, a tinkling laugh, and eyes that would sparkle." He fell into a silence, and not just any silence, it was mournful.

Gently I probed further. "Angus, did you hang about with her at the lighthouse?"

"On one or two occasions. Moira wasn't long into drugs before she died. They weren't easy to get hold of back then, not here, not on Skye, but there were rumours that she was dabbling, that somehow she'd found a supplier."

"Do you know what kind of drugs?"

"Again it was rumour, but I did hear mention of LSD."

I was surprised. "Wasn't LSD out of fashion by then? Heroin's more popular now."

"Scotland isn't like the rest of the UK," was his answer. "I heard it was LSD."

"Okay," I conceded. "When you were with her, did you ever suspect she was high?"

He shook his head. "No. Whatever she did, she didn't do it around me."

I sighed. All drugs were dangerous, but LSD was one to

be particularly wary of. It could cause nonstop hallucinations, and depending on the dosage, they could be either subtle or severe. If she was hanging about at the lighthouse, if she was ever high whilst she was there, she could have seen what I'd seen, what Ally had seen, she could have opened the door in her mind so wide it had been impossible to shut again.

"The house where Moira lived, is it still there?"

"Aye," Mrs Ludmore said, "it's still there."

"Who lives in it now?"

"No one."

"It's abandoned too?"

"It is. There's no shortage of houses on Skye, or land to build them on. Why live where there's been trouble?"

The people on Skye clearly believed in karma as much as they believed in the blue men. Superstitions and fears ran deep. But it wasn't just here. It was everywhere I'd ever been.

Having finished my tea, I checked my watch. It was nearly three o' clock – the day was already on the wane. We left the Ludmores' shortly afterwards, and they, as Mrs Grant and Mr MacIver had done, agreed that we could come back and talk to their children if it proved necessary, although Mrs Ludmore showed more reticence than the others.

"I wish you the best," she'd said, "in tackling what's out there. I don't doubt for one minute that you're as gifted as you say, I've known one or two similar to you in my time, but…" and here she'd paused. "All that talk of Moira, I'm more worried now than ever. I want to protect Craig, not involve him any more in what's happening."

Mr Ludmore had spoken next, his blue eyes beseeching.

"What exactly is happening, do you actually have any idea? Because I'll tell you something, I'm flummoxed. Is it a ghost? One of those who was shipwrecked, or all of them perhaps?"

"I don't know what it is," I answered, standing on their doorstep, shivering with the cold. "But one thing I want you to know is I'm doing my best to find out."

Mrs Ludmore shuffled slightly. "It must be hard, having the sight. I wouldn't want it."

"I don't have any choice," was my reply.

"Aye, I don't suppose you do."

Finally on our way again, I checked my watch a second time.

"What's worrying you?" Angus said, as we sat in the car, the heater turned up high.

"The light and how it's fading."

"It is. It'll be full dark soon."

"I'm wondering what to do next, find McCarron, go to the graveyard, or visit Moira's house."

"Moira's house?" he visibly jolted at that. "Why?"

"Because the Camerons disappearance and her suicide might be linked."

"I don't see how."

"Nor do I, but there's only one way to find out."

"Moira's dead," he muttered.

"And guess who can speak with the dead? Come on, then. Moira's house it is."

Chapter Twelve

THE further we drove, the harder it rained – battering the windscreen and the side windows, as if livid at what we were doing: stirring things up further.

"So come on," Angus said, squinting as he drove. "What's your theory regarding Moira?"

I angled my head to look at him. "Angus, you seem slightly het up about my decision to go to Moira's house. Were you fond of her by any chance?"

"I told you, she was bonny."

"You fancied her, you mean."

Briefly he looked at me, his cheeks matching his hair. "You're incredibly blunt, do you know that?"

"And you're transparent."

"That's as maybe."

I tried unsuccessfully to suppress a smile. "So it's true, you did?"

He snorted. "I don't know what red-blooded Scotsman wouldn't."

"Redheaded *and* red-blooded? An explosive combination," I remarked.

He smiled too this time. "Aye, well, maybe you'll find out one day."

"Let's focus on Moira, shall we? Do you have a picture of her?"

He shook his head. "No, more's the pity. I'd have liked a picture, but it doesn't matter, not really, I remember her as though I can see her still." Once again he described her hair, her eyes, the angel that she was, in his eyes as well as in her parents'.

"But she had a wild streak?"

"She was fun," he insisted. "Old people often confuse the two."

"Drugs aren't necessarily fun." I might sound like a maiden aunt rather than a young woman, but drugs were taking it one step too far, especially in the circumstances.

"The drugs may have had nothing to do with her suicide," he replied, just as insistent. "If that's what it was."

"What do you mean?"

"It could have been an accident. She could have gone walking too close to the edge, the cliffs round here give way sometimes, and crumble. It's so hard to believe she'd kill herself; she was always so full of life. It wasn't just me who adored her, everyone did."

"Did you see her towards the end, when she'd supposedly changed?"

"No." With that he emitted a heavy sigh. "Tell me, how does anyone get that low?"

"They just do," I replied, as he brought the car to a stop. Switching off the engine, he sat where he was, staring blindly ahead. "Are you okay?" I asked.

"I'm fine. We're here. This is it."

"Really?" I said, squinting as he'd done earlier.

"You can barely see her house in this weather, but it's there, a few yards away."

THIRTEEN

Back on the coast, the weather was as wild as it had been the previous night – another storm riding in angrily on the shoulders of the last one. The thought of getting out of the car and exploring didn't exactly appeal, but if I waited for the weather to clear, I might be waiting until springtime. He seemed to read my mind.

"It's now or never," he said. "This is settling in for the night."

"I don't know how you stand it really, such awful weather, such a lot of the time."

A smile dissolved all worry from his face. "You stand it because when the sun does shine, there's no better place on earth to be. The big sky, the mountains that surround you, the sheer space that's here, and even weather like this. It's an extension of the landscape. It's magical and alive. Aye, that's what draws you back, what keeps you here – some of us anyway – the magic of it all."

"The magic?" I repeated, feeling even colder than I had before.

"That's right," he continued, oblivious to my sudden change of tone, "it gets in your blood. You become a part of it; it becomes a part of you. Man and his surrounds meld."

"I need to get out. I need to breathe."

"Ness?"

I was being serious – I did need to breathe. Fresh air, cold air, I wanted to stand in the rain, and get soaked to the skin. Outside, where just a minute or two ago I'd baulked at being, suddenly felt wonderful. Breathing deeply, I tilted my head and let the rain plaster my hair to my face, let it wash over me. I understood what he was saying about magic, but there was good magic and there was bad magic, white and black. In such a beautiful place, something ugly had reared its head. And it wasn't to do with the spirit world. Suddenly I understood that. There was no point in going to Kilchoan Cemetery to stand over a slab of stone. The ghosts of those who'd been shipwrecked weren't responsible for this, perhaps not even forlorn Moira. What was responsible was something infinitely darker. Despite that, our trip to the deceased girl's house hadn't been in vain. Even if Moira's spirit had flown – and I sincerely hoped it had – the emotions she'd experienced just before she'd fallen to her death, *whilst* she'd fallen, were certain to have left behind a residue – and that might give me an insight into whether her death had been accidental or intentional. If the latter, she'd have been in agony. *No one* contemplates his or her own demise without being in agony. So what had been the cause of it?

Angus had joined me. "Ness, did I say something—"

"Let's go."

"Where?"

"To the house and then the cliff tops."

"The cliff tops, in this weather? Are you mad?"

I ignored his warning and started to walk, having to fight the wind that wanted so desperately to spin me round and send me the other way. There were no other houses nearby; Moira's stood quite alone. Once again, it was the perfect breeding ground. At the house I peered through the broken window into a dark and abandoned interior. A haven for spiders and other wildlife perhaps, but all furniture, all personal belongings, gone.

"Can you get the door open?" Like last night I had to shout to be heard.

"That'll be breaking and entering!" Angus declared.

"I need to get in there."

"Shit. Well… okay."

Although reluctant he obliged, heaving his shoulder against it. *Come on, come on,* I silently urged. Thankfully, it didn't take long to give way. Standing aside, he let me enter first and then followed, shaking the rain from him as a dog might, sending droplets flying.

"I hope this is going to be worth it," he continued in a peevish manner.

"Angus," I explained, "this is a puzzle. My job is to fit all the pieces together, to solve it."

"It's your mission, you mean."

"Don't split hairs, it's the same thing. Just let me tune in."

His eyes widened. "You really think Moira might still be here?"

"What might be left is a trace of her emotions, her thoughts and her feelings. They're energy too and energy takes time to dissipate."

"It's been nearly eight years!"

"A long time, I agree. And yet, in some respects, it's no time at all. Angus, please, I need to concentrate."

Still sullen, he fell silent. Immediately, I closed my eyes, breathed deeply and imagined the light, and the protection it would give me.

Moira, are you here? You don't know me, but I know of you – what a lovely, young, spirited girl you were in life and that towards the end of that life you were troubled. What was it that upset you? Was it enough for you to take your own life? I'm here to help, Moira, not just you, but also others on the island who are living still, and who may be suffering as you once did. If you're here, come forward and let me know.

As I've said, I wanted Moira to have passed, I'd be glad if she'd escaped her torment, but I was also desperate for some answers. The cottage, however, was benign enough, even in the failing light, no residue tinged with darkness, not downstairs at least. And not upstairs either, I discovered, although in her bedroom my emotional state became somewhat altered: I felt sad, tearful, bewildered and angry, emotions I was familiar with, but which this time weren't mine.

Did you see something at the lighthouse, Moira? Visions.

And if she had, had they driven her out of her house, to the cliff tops, over the grassy edge and into the sea below – where the storm kelpies were waiting oh so patiently?

I turned to Angus. "Show me where she died."

"I'll take you as close as I dare, but please, listen to me when I say to go no further."

I nodded in agreement. I knew about spiritual perils, he knew about the perils of his home turf – I respected that.

Leaving the cottage behind, Angus securing the door as best he could, we battled our way forwards yet again, heads down, hands in pockets, struggling but determined – at least I was. I could feel it. The closer I got to the cliff's edge, the more intense it became – a battle of another kind: Moira's against whatever it was that had launched an attack. Because that's what it had done, as it had with me and with Ally too. As I'd suspected, she'd opened the door in her mind a little too wide. Her dabbling with LSD had left her vulnerable and this thing liked vulnerable, it *fed* on vulnerable.

Another vision came to mind – Moira rushing as we were rushing. She was alongside us, a pale image, her shoulders hunched as ours were hunched, her sobs choking

THIRTEEN

her.

Oh, Moira!

I wanted to reach out and hug this tortured young woman, but she was no more than a wisp, a mere memory caught on the breeze.

I'm so sorry for what happened to you.

Tears stung my eyes just as the rain did.

"This is as far as it's safe to go." Angus's voice startled me. For a moment I'd forgotten he was there. "Unless that is, you want to end up like Moira."

I shook my head. "I don't."

Standing still, I forced myself to watch what transpired next, heard the words she was screaming in her head. *No! No! No! I won't do it, I won't. You can't make me. You can't.*

Do what?

"Moira!" I yelled, but it wasn't her, it was a shade rushing ever onwards, no stopping, no stumbling, with no hesitation at all.

Angus grabbed me by the shoulders, his expression pained too. "Is she here? Is Moira still here?"

"No, Angus, she's gone. Just be thankful she has."

Chapter Thirteen…

Chapter Fourteen

WAS death the only way to stop these attacks? If so, Ally and her parents were in more danger than I thought, with that danger increasing by the day. Back at Angus's house, both the night and the storm were in full bloom as we gathered round the dining table, Eilidh serving dinner, whilst I discussed with them the significance of the number thirteen.

"I think it stems back to the last supper," Eilidh said, ladling a generous serving of macaroni cheese onto my plate. "There's some honeyed neeps to go with it too. Dig in."

"Do you mean Jesus and his disciples?" asked Angus, also digging in. "Twelve disciples plus Jesus sitting down to eat for the last time, equals unlucky."

Eilidh took her seat too. "Well, it was, wasn't it? Judas was the thirteenth member of the party to arrive and because of him Jesus was crucified."

We both nodded, unable to argue with that.

"But actually, the number thirteen is significant throughout the Bible," she stated. "I can't remember everything I've ever heard, who can? But, Angus, I discussed this very topic with your father once, way before the game started at the lighthouse." Having finished a mouthful of food, she looked at me. "Kenneth was very knowledgeable, he used to spend a lot of time reading. I think it's lovely when a man reads. I wish our son took after him a bit more in that respect."

"Och," Angus dismissed. "I read enough."

"You do not, and that's a fact," retorted Eilidh, but it was a good-natured jibe. "According to Kenneth, there were thirteen famines in the bible, and in one of the gospels, Jesus mentions thirteen things that defile a person, the evil eye being one of them! Can you imagine? What else did he say? Erm… something about the Book of Revelation, that its thirteenth chapter is reserved for Satan." She shrugged, nonchalantly I thought considering the subject. "So you see, just like 666, thirteen has its connotations."

She was right and it was in that very chapter that God had indeed numbered the beast 666. In contrast, seven was the number of perfection, re-emphasising the former as something flawed or incomplete – to the power of three.

"Then there's King Arthur," Eilidh informed us. "He fought twelve battles successfully, but during the thirteenth was mortally wounded. As for Merlin, he spent years searching for the Thirteen Treasures of Britain. Meant to be wielded by the righteous and the brave, woe betide they should fall into the wrong hands, which of course they did.'

As she spoke, my frustration grew. Numerology was a vast and complex subject, it'd take years of study to understand more than the basics.

"Have you got a library on Skye?" I asked, wondering if I could at least get started.

"A mobile one," answered Eilidh, "it's not due for a couple more weeks though."

Silently I cursed. The basics would have to do.

"You know I've heard tell," Eilidh had got the bit between the teeth, "that in some hotels there's no thirteenth floor, not officially anyway, they go straight from twelve to fourteen. Silly if you ask me, if it's there, what's the point in pretending?" She sipped some water. "Also, some streets don't have a number thirteen either. As for Friday the thirteenth…"

"Of course!" I reply. "Friday the thirteenth, they've even made slasher films about it, reinforcing the taboo."

"Have you seen those films, Ness?" Angus asked. "They're pretty good."

"No, I haven't. They really don't appeal."

"Michael Myers a bit much for you, is he?"

"Get your films right, Angus. Michael Myers was in *Halloween*."

"Oh damn, was he?"

"He is, but then… Halloween falls on the 31st October. That's thirteen backwards."

"So it is," Angus said, almost in wonder. "I'd never considered that. And in a witches' coven, there's always thirteen, isn't there?" The expression on my face clearly gave him cause for concern. "It's a rhetorical question," he added. "I'm not asking *you* specifically." Before I could smile to show I'd been joking, he rushed on. "I'll tell you something else, something I learnt in school. You think there are twelve signs of the zodiac, don't you?"

I was confused. "That's because there are."

"Aye, but there are *thirteen* constellations. One got ditched – Ophiuchus – because when the Babylonians invented the calendar over three thousand years ago, they based it on twelve months only. Perhaps they were suspicious about the number thirteen too?"

I shook my head, also in wonder: I hadn't been taught anything that cool in school.

"'I worked out once upon a time," Angus continued, "that if we had thirteen months as the zodiac suggests, we'd end up with a perfect twenty-eight day month, every month. Mind you, having a birthday in the thirteenth month, I'm not actually sure I'd fancy it."

Lucky for some, it was unlucky for others – myself included once upon a time.

We'd finished eating, but Eilidh still looked thoughtful. I gazed at her curiously, trying to catch what was on her mind. Sometimes I could do that, read thoughts, but it was a developing skill, and one I hadn't quite got to grips with yet. I took the easy route, and asked her outright instead. "Eilidh, has something else occurred to you?"

"Aye, something that Kenneth and I mused upon if you like, when we first found out the kids were playing that game at the lighthouse. He was very protective was Kenneth, Angus is our only son and we waited a long time for him." At this she smiled indulgently, which he, like only the very loved can, rolled his eyes at. "He never liked them doing it," she confided, "used to get agitated, whereas I said it was just a bit of harmless fun. More fool me. I'm not sure who liked to think they invented the game, do you, Angus?"

"No idea. It was just something that… came into being."

"Well, whoever it was, maybe they knew about One Hundred Ghost Stories, which is a centuries old Japanese tradition."

"One hundred ghost stories?" Angus spluttered. "That'd take forever! Thirteen was sometimes bad enough, especially whenever Maire MacTavish was involved. I've told you about her, haven't I, Ness, the romance writer, the one that went on and on?"

"Yes, you have," I answered, before turning to Eilidh. "What's this tradition? I'd love to hear about it."

"A group of people sit in a circle, up to one hundred in number, a candle placed before them. It's not a game, but a ritual. I can't remember the Japanese name for it, but Kenneth would. They'd tell a story, blow out the candle, counting all the way to one hundred. Once it's done, and they're in complete darkness, a ghost is supposed to appear in the middle of the circle. See? It's just the same really. The same principle anyway."

"Know any horror stories attached to that particular practice?" Angus asked his mother.

"No, laddie, of course I don't. Why would I? I just know of it, that's all, thanks to your very well read dad. What I was wondering is, if whoever started the game at the lighthouse knew of the ritual, if it was their inspiration?"

Whether they did or not maybe didn't matter. What mattered was that the game had history, and more than that, an *expectation* attached – one that was supernatural. As I've said before, some games shouldn't be played; they should be left well alone.

I came to a decision. "Eilidh, once Angus and I have cleared the dishes, would you mind if we went out again?"

It was Angus who replied. "Where are we going, back to the lighthouse?"

"No. When we go there again, it'll be in daylight. I want to speak to Liam's father and from what you've told me about him, I'm guessing where he'll be."

"At the pub."

I winked cheekily at him. "If you drive me I'll buy you a lemonade."

* * *

Waiting in the hallway for Angus, who'd quickly visited the bathroom, Eilidh came to stand beside me. "You put a spring in his step, so you do."

"Who? Angus?"

"Aye, and little wonder, you're a bonny lass."

Embarrassed, I lifted one hand to push at my hair. "Thank you, but I'm really not."

My protestation surprised her. "Why are you so quick to disagree? Surely your mother's told you countless times how bonny you are?"

"My mother?" I almost choked on the words. "Sorry, I'm so sorry," I said, realising how bad that must have looked. "Erm… no, she didn't actually, not often." Not *ever* more like.

Reaching out, Eilidh took my arm. "Then more fool her. She *should* have told you."

A brief moment of silence hung between us, during which I attempted to change the subject. "I hope the pub isn't too far."

It didn't work.

"I'm glad you came to Skye," she continued, "and I'm grateful for your help. We need it. Like you, I don't think the situation's going to get any better or go away on its own." I looked at her, stunned. At no point had I shared that point of view with her, and yet still she'd picked up on it. "The thing is, Ness, you have to believe in yourself. You're a special person. You're kind, you're beautiful and you're talented. But if you don't think you are, if you keep denying it, then what good is any of it? Whatever we're facing, you're its equal. I believe in you and I'll help too, in any way I can. There are a lot of us that will, we won't question what you do. You're not something outlandish here, you're a hero."

There was no way I could answer, not when a sob had lodged in my throat. Thankfully I didn't have to. Angus appeared, all brisk efficiency, rubbing his hands together as though in excited anticipation before shooing me out the door. It took the entire twenty-minute car journey for me to regain composure after what Eilidh had said, my head turned from Angus all the while, as I stared into the stormy darkness, seeing nothing but my own pitiful reflection staring back. It was so white against the night, so small and insignificant. A hero she'd called me, riding up here on a plane instead of a charger, ready to tackle what had been causing trouble. Was I such? No. A hero wouldn't have done as I'd done in the past.

"Here we are, at the oldest pub on Skye."

I shook my head in surprise. "Already?"

"We are indeed. Were you asleep by the way, you were awful quiet."

"I... erm... might have dozed off for a minute or two," I lied, having to lean forward so that I could see the whitewashed building we were slowly passing, one that ran the length of several houses. On it were words picked out in black: The Stein Inn. "How old is it?" I asked.

"Dates back to 1790 according to a plaque at the entrance. Supposed to be haunted too, be interesting to see if you think so."

"I hope not. There's no time to get side-tracked."

"Aye, well, the only spirits I've ever seen in there are from the local distillery."

As we hurried back towards the pub from the car park, the rain having eased slightly, though the wind was still fierce, Angus told me there was a loch to our left. I looked over, but I have to say, I'd never have guessed, the clouds once again having erected a wall.

We reached the porch and stopped to catch our breaths.

"It's beautiful here on a summer's day," he continued when he was able. "The loch's as still as anything."

"Being the oldest pub on Skye, it must get besieged with tourists."

"Tourists? I should think most of them opt for far sunnier climes than this. No, it's peaceful on the whole, one of my favourite locations. Sitting with a pint, staring out over the water, there's a healing quality to it. You should try it sometime."

Anger flared. "Sorry? What do you mean by that?"

"What? Nothing, I…"

"First your mother and now you."

"My mother…?"

"There's nothing wrong with me!"

"I'm sorry, I really don't—"

"I don't need your pity. I don't want it!"

"Ness, will you calm down, I was just saying, that's all."

"But that whole healing thing…"

"Aye, it is, it's exactly that, it's special. But I wasn't implying *you* needed healing."

"It's just…" Again, my voice trailed off.

"Although to be honest, doesn't everyone, to some degree or other? Life can deliver some hard knocks."

I lowered my head – all fight gone. "Life is what it is, it's a learning curve."

He leant a little closer to me – as close as he dared I suppose. "Ness, what's happening here, if it's putting you under too much pressure—"

"It's not, I'm trying to understand it, that's all."

"Everyone affected is. You're not alone."

Then how come I felt it, especially at this moment, standing in the wind-blown porch of an ancient pub in one of the United Kingdom's most far-flung places? How come I felt more alone than ever? I blinked heavily. "I'm tired, I think. It's been another long day."

"It has. Are you sure you want to go in, or shall we just go home and get some rest?"

"We're here now."

"Come on, then, let's get it over and done with. If he's here, I don't know what state he's going to be in. Sometimes he has to be carried back to his bed."

"We'll soon find out, I guess."

Entering the pub, a welcome blast of heat hit us courtesy of a fire that was devouring logs a few feet away. Also in close proximity was a man sitting on a stool at the bar; he had very red cheeks, a mop of white hair and a stomach to rival that of Father Christmas.

"Ron, how are you?" Angus greeted. "This is Ness, a friend of mine. Ness, this is Ron."

Ron's eyes were already glazed with a somewhat rheumy quality to them, his nose large and rounded, reminded me of a chunk of cheese. One hand gripped his pint, as though hanging on to it for dear life, the other he extended towards me. I noticed it was shaking slightly. "Pleased to meet you. It's a wild night you've come out on."

"Needs must," answered Angus. "Now, Ness, what are you having?"

"Erm… coke will be fine."

"Nothing harder?"

"No thanks." Seeing how the hard stuff affected Ron had had an off-putting effect.

"No problem," he replied amiably, "and I guess it's a lemonade for me."

I tore my gaze away briefly from Ron to smile at him.

"So," Ron continued. "You're English."

"For my sins, yes."

"My lad's just gone over the border to Carlisle, he's working in a boatyard there."

"Liam?"

Ron looked astonished. "Aye. You know him, do you?"

Angus answered before I could, handing me my drink at the same time. "No, she doesn't, but Liam's who we've come to talk to you about."

Ron's whole demeanour changed, he sat further upright, suspicion sharpening his gaze. "And why is that, may I ask?"

"Erm…" I stuttered. For the second time, I wished Angus wouldn't just steam in like that, that he'd take things a bit slower. Next thing he'd be telling Ron I was a psychic.

"She's a psychic you see, investigating what happened at the lighthouse, like a detective almost. In fact, she works for the police too, and the council, don't you, Ness?"

I could have kicked him – right there and then in that genteel pub that was thankfully empty, apart from Ron and a barmaid who had since disappeared.

"Angus—" I began, intending to have another go at him, but Ron cut me off.

"Liam's stint at the lighthouse, it's over and done with. He's moved on."

Before I could reply, he reached for his glass and drank from it, several long draughts that rendered it dry. I couldn't help but be impressed and Angus too by the looks of him.

Belching, he then yelled for the barmaid. "Jan, where are you? Get me another."

Jan appeared – world-weary Jan; a Jan who looked far from impressed with Ron's behaviour, who'd seen it all before, many times no doubt.

"We're going to call it a night soon," she warned, taking his glass from him and duly refilling it. "No one's coming out, not in this weather, no one in their right mind anyway." Glancing at us, she shrugged as if she couldn't care less if her words caused offence. Handing him his glass, she added, "You've ten minutes, fifteen at the most."

Whilst she did another disappearing act, Ron drank again, but managed to stop about a third of the way through this time.

"Look," I said, having waited patiently, "Angus's uncle wanted me to come here, after… well, after what happened with Ally Dunn. I presume you know about that?"

"Aye I do, I keep my ear to the ground. But what's it got to do with Liam?"

"I'm wondering if what happened with Ally is linked in any way with the Camerons' sudden disappearance."

"Something supernatural, you mean?" Yet again his hand gripped his pint, but he didn't raise it to his lips, he continued staring at me.

I swallowed. "Yes. Exactly that."

"You know about the girl who threw herself off the cliffs?"

I heard Angus breathe inwards, but I simply nodded. "Moira? Yes I do."

"Think it's linked with her too, do you?"

"It could be."

Silence descended, not companionable, it felt explosive. Was Ron going to start yelling at me to get out of his favourite watering hole, and take my witchy ways with me? I always half-expected that reaction. He did no such thing. When he started speaking again, his voice was low, ominous even.

"They weren't right, the Camerons. They came from an island more remote than this one. Barra, do you know it? Less than a thousand people live there. Island people – *remote* island people – I'm wary of them sometimes. The Camerons came to man that lighthouse and largely they kept themselves to themselves. Even home schooled their young 'uns, well Mrs Cameron did, didn't want them mixing, picking up funny ways." He bellowed with laughter at that, causing a dog to howl, one I hadn't noticed before, lounging behind the other side of the bar – Jan's dog, it must be. "Ironic, isn't it, that they should be the ones worried about funny ways."

I didn't know whether his prejudice was widespread or peculiar to him, but I listened carefully nonetheless, desperate for more clues.

"Liam never liked working there, truth be told, much less living in that cabin. It's a bleak place, awful. *Da,* he said, *it's like living at the end of the world.* I sympathised, I did, but a job's a job and on Skye, you cannae afford to be fussy. He grew fond of the kids well enough, Caitir and Niall, playing games with them when their parents were out of earshot, having a bit of a laugh. Ach, Liam was just a big kid himself in many ways. Once the parents found out though, they put to a stop to it, told him to do his job and nothing more, that he wasn't to 'interfere'. He was there a year before Cameron insisted he wasn't needed anymore. He had to pack his bags and go. Liam was glad of it though. He said that during the last few months they'd grown even stranger, the kids too, although to be fair, he hadn't seen the youngsters in a while, they barely ever roamed the hillsides, were always kept inside. Terrible that is, to keep kids inside, they need fresh air to fill their lungs, to make them proper Highlanders. I went to pick Liam up and sought out Cameron, if only to shake his hand, to thank him for giving my lad a job in the first place, no hard feelings, like. Despite everything, the job would look good on his CV; it'd help him to go on to better things. So I went looking for him, as I said, and found him at the top of the tower, just staring at the sea. Big man he was, built like a brick shithouse. I said my piece, I thanked him and he ignored me. Can you believe it? He stood there, as still as a statue, with his back to me, as if in a trance. I went back down, passed the house on my way to the car, and noticed for the first time that the curtains were closed, despite it being such a bonny day. I no longer wanted to thank him, I can tell you. I just wanted to get away. I had a sense – a *strong* sense – that we'd made a lucky escape; that Liam had got out in the nick of time. I felt guilty too, that he'd even been there in the first place. A job's a job, I'd said that, but that place, on that day…" He shook his head. "No one's ever that desperate. Soon after that the Camerons upped and left, and good riddance to them."

Having delivered this spiel, he at last finished the other half of his pint. As soon as that glass was empty, Jan reappeared, a troubled look on her face. Had she been listening to Ron, I wondered?

"Come on," she said, "away with you all. I've had enough."

We quickly finished our drinks as Ron eased himself off his stool. As we made our way to the door, he staggered a little and I reached out a hand to steady him.

"So you're a psychic, are you?"

"I… I have a sixth sense, yes."

"A miracle worker too?"

I frowned. "A miracle worker? No. I'm just trying to help."

"I don't want you to contact Liam, I want him left alone. He's happy now, he's settled, out of harm's way."

I stood my ground. "What about those who remain in harm's way? What about Ally?"

"Stupid kids shouldn't have gone to the lighthouse in the first place."

"But they did."

He looked at me for a moment and then relented. "Aye, they did."

Angus held the door open and we stood in the porch once more, whilst Jan slid the bolts home on the other side, making a point. Ron stood swaying in between us. "I see things sometimes," he said, his manner conspiratorial. "When I've had one too many, but that doesn't mean to say they're not there. The drink, it does something."

"It opens you up," I said, thinking about Moira and the

LSD.

He nodded. "Aye, that it does. Please, lass, I'm asking you, don't get Liam involved. He's a good lad, a conscientious lad. If you contact him, he'll come back, won't even think twice about it. He's like you, not psychic, I don't mean that, but he likes to help."

"We can't get in touch if you don't give us his details," I reminded him.

"Well, I'm not going to, not right now."

"Fair enough," I said, disappointed in his decision.

Staring wistfully outwards, he staggered again. This time Angus caught him. "Will I give you a lift home, Ron?" he asked.

"Away with you!" Ron waved a hand at him. "I can walk. The fresh air will do me good."

Although not convinced, Angus didn't object. "We'd best away ourselves then."

All three of us started walking, Ron veering off to the right. As I watched him go, I considered what we'd learnt – something – but not enough. I was still confused. If only we could speak to Liam, it would help further, but we also had to respect his father's wishes.

Heads down again, slightly despondent, we marched onwards. Because of my stance, I didn't realise Ron was making his way back towards us until Angus nudged me.

Coming to a standstill in front of us, it was me the old man focused on. "I've no wish to put you in harm's way. Look at you, you're no more than a wee slip of a girl."

"I'm stronger than I look."

"It might be nothing…"

"Ron, please. If Moira is connected to this, there's already been one death that we know about. Ally Dunn…

I'm concerned for her too. Do I…" I hesitated. "Do I need to go to Barra? Perhaps the Camerons have gone back there?"

"Barra?" He spat the word at me. "You'll not get to Barra in this weather. You'll not get there 'til the springtime."

"Damn!" I said under my breath. Could this case wait that long? I honestly didn't think so. "Angus?" I questioned.

"He's right. There's no way. Not in this."

Ron noticed how stricken I looked. "Don't take on, lass, it's not there you need to go anyway."

"Oh? Where then?" I asked, doubly confused.

"It's your namesake, Loch Ness. On the banks, overlooking the waters, there's a house, Balskeyne. One with a reputation."

"What kind of reputation?"

"A bad one." As he said it, a gust of wind blew him backwards. Quickly he fought against it and straightened up. "Liam heard Cameron talk about Balskeyne once, to his wife. And in the last few months he was at Minch, there used to come a visitor there, when none had been before. It was a man Liam didn't like the look of; he told me there was something about him… something *unclean*. That's when the Camerons changed, when this man started up his visits. Never friendly, they went to being downright odd."

"Balskeyne?" I turned to Angus. "Have you heard of this house?"

"Oh, aye, I've heard of it. But under the circumstances, Ness, I wish to God I hadn't."

Chapter Fifteen

"WE can't do it, we can't go there. I'd rather take my chances with going to Barra."

"Why can't we go there? What's wrong with it, tell me."

Ron had finally left us and we were in Angus's car again, just sitting there, in an empty car park, the wind and the rain as relentless as ever.

"It's just… It can't have anything to do with the lighthouse, it can't have."

"Angus! Will you just tell me what you know?"

"It's… Well… It all goes back to the sixties; a man came to live there – Isaac Leonard." He laughed. "Harmless enough name, isn't it, but apparently he was far from that."

"What was he?"

"I'll tell you what he was rumoured to be: a Black Magician. Have you not heard of him, Ness?"

"I've heard of a few, but not him, no." Inside, my gut was churning. Magic of a warped kind was exactly what I'd feared.

"He bought the house for the purpose of a ritual he wanted to carry out there, one he'd studied in an ancient text apparently, dating back to the Middle Ages. There was a list of rules in preparation for this ritual. You had to abstain from alcohol, remain celibate, and meditate – a lot. The house itself played a role too. It had to be in a secluded location, more or less, with a door opening to the west, in front of which was a gravel or sand path. At the end of this path, there needed to be a lodge of some sort. That's supposed to be where the spirits congregate. The purpose of it all was—"

"To invoke your Guardian Angel," I finished.

"So you *have* heard of Leonard?"

"Just the ritual, it's one that several, perhaps more notable, Black Magicians have followed, I'm not sure how successfully. It's from *The Book of Abramelin*, which, as you say, is a medieval grimoire, one that surged in popularity during this century and the last. I'm no expert regarding it, but yes, I've heard of that at least. This Guardian Angel, as they call it, was supposed to impart magical wisdom, which the recipient could then use for good or bad purposes. The trouble is, it's usually the latter, being as this sort of thing appeals to the megalomaniacs amongst us."

"Megalomaniacs? So, you've never been tempted then?"

"Angus! I may be many things, but hopefully not that!"

He grinned. "No, I have to admit, you don't strike me as such."

"Good," I answered, just as he sighed. All joking aside, I reached out. "You okay?" He was concerned earlier that this task might be having an effect on me, but what about him?

"I'm fine," he assured me. "It's odd, that's all, sitting in a pub car park, late at night, talking about Black Magic of all things."

I agreed. "It is odd, but we're doing it for a reason."

"Aye, I know… to help."

"Unless, it's too much—"

"It's not. Not with you by my side."

I smiled. Like his mother; he had such faith in me. "So, Leonard carried out this ritual at this house on the banks of Loch Ness. What's the consensus? Did he succeed?"

"He may have done, certainly that's what people around here like to think."

"But no one knows for sure."

"They know it's got a bad atmosphere. *I* know it's got a bad atmosphere."

"You?" I was confused and then the penny dropped. "Ah, I see, it was another place you went to as a kid, looking for thrills."

He shrugged. "I've told you, there's not much to do around here."

"Except get involved in a bit of Satanism."

"Aye, well it's something, isn't it?"

I looked at him, he looked at me, and together we burst out laughing. It felt good, so good. I hadn't laughed like that in… well, I couldn't remember the last time.

"Honestly though," he continued, wiping at his eyes, "it's some place, a big old manor house, owned by a rock star after Leonard, although we'd no idea who it was back then."

"Do you know now?"

"Oh aye, it was Robbie Nelson from the band, The Ridge. He was interested in its history, you see, all that occult stuff. The thing is, he never stayed there, not really. An interest is one thing, but the chance to experience it, or at least the aftermath of it, I suppose that's quite another."

"So what year was it when you went there?"

"It must have been around '75, perhaps early in '76, I was twelve, nearly thirteen."

"Wow, that young?"

"Aye, I was the youngest that night, by a fair bit actually."

"I'm surprised your parents let you."

"They never knew," Angus confessed. "As far as they were concerned I was at a sleepover at one of the other lads' houses."

"Ah, I see, that old chestnut."

"It came in handy a fair few times."

"So it was well before Moira?"

"Oh aye, it was before she… you know. Anyway, Nelson had moved out by then, and it was empty for a while. Whoa!" He ran his hands through his hair as he began his troubled journey down memory lane. "It's not as if we went inside the house or anything, we didn't want to break in, get into trouble with the law, but the grounds and the lodge at the bottom of the garden, were bad enough. There were five of us: three lads and two lasses, and as I say I was the youngest of the lot, Will, was the eldest at eighteen. I'm telling you, all of us had goose bumps the minute we set foot on that land. The only way I can describe it is, it was like a thousand eyes were watching us, hiding in the trees that surrounded the place, eyes that didn't belong to anything of this world; they belonged to monsters instead. And that's not my youth and immaturity talking – we *all* felt that way, even Will. We tried to nudge each other on, you know, be brave, but when we got to the house and started peering in through the windows, one of the girls – Lottie – started to scream blue murder. She thought she saw a figure in there, one that was impossibly tall, blacker than black, and who was glaring at her. It was the eyes that did it; they were glowing, she said, neon yellow or something. As she stared, transfixed, the figure lifted its hand to point."

"What happened then?" I asked, able to vividly imagine it all.

"We ran, as fast as our legs could take us. We got out of there. Will had his dad's car, so we piled into that and drove back to the Kyle of Lochalsh. We slept all night in his car, well, what few hours were left, and then we caught the first ferry the next morning. A cousin of mine ran the ferry at the time, so it's not as if we had to pay. But I'll tell you, none of us returned, not as far as I know."

"It could all have been imagination though, preconceptions kicking in?"

He denied it. "Something was wrong there, very wrong."

Perhaps. Just as something was wrong here.

I thought about what I'd learnt. "So, Leonard was at Balskeyne in the sixties, but by the early seventies it belonged to a rock star?"

"Aye, and later on, in '76, it was turned into a guesthouse. Can you credit it? I mean, really? Who'd want to stay there knowing who it had once belonged to?"

"But that's the thing, people don't *always* know. Do you research the history of every house or hotel you've ever stayed at?"

"I've only ever stayed at a handful," he admitted.

"Even so, have you?"

"No, of course not."

"There you go then."

"Yeah, but when it's got a notorious history?"

"I've never heard of Isaac Leonard or Balskeyne. There'd be many who haven't or, if they have, who'd dismiss it as nonsense. Is the house still being run as a guesthouse?"

"Och, I've no idea. There are two roads that skirt Loch Ness, the main road and the back road – Balskeyne's on the banks of the back road. I never tend to go that way, it's too, you know… twisty turny."

"Twisty turny? That's a novel way of putting it."

"But you get my meaning?"

"Aye, I do."

He raised an eyebrow at my impression of him, seemed to find it amusing enough.

"What I don't get," I continued, "is the timing. It's all off."

"How'd you mean?"

"Leonard lived at Balskeyne in the sixties, but by the seventies, the time that the Camerons moved into the lighthouse, a rock star had bought it, one who hardly ever stayed there apparently, and after he sold it, it was turned into a guesthouse. So how's it all connected, *if* it is connected? Do you know what happened to Isaac Leonard?"

"What happened to him and whether he's still alive or dead, I don't know."

"It's something we need to find out."

He cocked his head to the side. "Oh, and how do you propose we do that?"

"You can take me there tomorrow and we can ask whoever's living there now."

"Do I get another lemonade for my efforts?"

"If you let me drive I'll make it a wee dram instead."

"Ness Patterson, you've just got yourself a deal."

Feeling perhaps lighter-hearted than we should, we made our way back home.

* * *

Ness, you're dreaming again.

It was little solace. Not when the dream was this bad.

I'm at my desk, writing, as one of the teenagers had written, scribing the number thirteen, over and over.

Why thirteen?

Because it's a powerful number or at least that's what people think. Certainly it has a hold on me. I can't stop myself, the paper beneath my marker beginning to tear with the pressure I'm exerting. When it runs out, I start on the walls, determined to fill every inch.

What does it mean? What does it all mean?

There's someone in the room with me, laughing. Who could it be? Angus?

I shake my head. No. He doesn't laugh like that. His is a sweet laugh.

You like him don't you, Ness?

No… yes… not in that way… as a friend.

You want him?

It's not me talking to myself anymore, someone else is asking the question.

I swing round, holding the marker as though it were a dagger.

"Who's there?" I can't see whoever's with me. They're hiding in the shadows, but I can feel their gaze, imagine well enough the colour of their eyes – yellow like pus.

I face the wall again. Whatever's in the shadows can stay there. I don't want to know.

13. 13. 13.

It's such a bold number, a number that screams at you.

Just like the figure in the shadows is screaming. No longer laughing, there are words tumbling from its mouth instead, not all of them intelligible. Although some are.

You. Want. No one.

I ignore it.

13. 13. 13.

I'm stabbing at the wall, unable to stop myself, big chunks of masonry tumbling too.

Remember, Ness?

Stabbing, stabbing, stabbing, obliterating what's in front of me; that damned number.

What you did to me?

My hand clenches tight around the marker.

What you did to yourself?

My nails dig into the palm of my hand.

Blood. Why is there always so much blood?

What you did to all of us. When you were thirteen, Ness. When you were thirteen.

Chapter Sixteen

INCREDIBLY the sun was shining the next day, although it was still bitterly cold. After more scrambled eggs on toast – and this time I managed a strip of bacon too – Angus and I journeyed towards Kyleakin, for the short journey across the water to the mainland. The scenery was so breath-taking it took my mind off the restless night I'd had and the dream. Instead of fretting about it, I immersed myself in the might of nature instead, the Cuillin Mountains once more the star of the show, so black against the blue sky, like sentinels standing guard. As I gazed at them, Angus told me about the fairy pools that were hidden amongst them, named for the belief that the fairies, or the little people as they were known hereabouts, bathed in them by starlight.

"And some big people do too," he added.

"Don't tell me, you included."

He laughed. "You're getting to know me very well. Although I've not gone for a dip by starlight, I'm not that daft – the water's freezing enough by day. Another place I'll have to take you, if we have the time, is the fairy glen. Aye, that's worth a trip, if just to admire the strange landscape. It's full of green knolls that tower upwards."

"Where is it?" I asked.

"Up near Uig."

"Uig? Okay, sounds good, I'd love to go." I'd scheduled in a week for this trip and a good portion of that had gone already – another three or four days, that's all I could really spare. Hopefully, that'd be enough. If it was, and if there was time for a little sightseeing as Angus suggested, all well and good. Although I was my own boss to a large extent, I'd said to Angus that I had other projects in the pipeline, plus I missed my flat, my own space. As lovely and as hospitable as Eilidh and Angus were, I needed time to myself. I always had.

The mainland was just as lovely as Skye, so easy to fall in love with. I'd never been to Scotland before and I was amazed at how different it was to where I lived in Lewes, the historic county town of East Sussex. There we were surrounded by gently rolling hills, described by Rudyard Kipling as *'Our blunt, bow-headed, whale-backed Downs'* – beautiful in their own right, but not rugged, not mighty, not like anything I was encountering here.

Angus had driven, despite me offering once again. 'You look tired,' he'd said. 'If we stop for a drink later, maybe you can take over, but otherwise, I'm more than happy to take the wheel.'

He was right; I *was* tired. Even my bones felt heavy. Despite the dazzling views, I yawned. "How far is it to Balskeyne?"

"Not long now, we'll be there within the hour. Nice weather for a visit, don't you think?"

"Yeah, yeah, it is. The weather's wonderful."

"Such a shame we're not heading for the beach. That's another thing that Skye's got, the most amazing beaches.

THIRTEEN

Just north of Dunvegan is a place called Coral Beach, named after the crushed white coral that's there, it makes the sea look really blue."

Immediately, guilt seized me. "I'm sorry to take you away from enjoying whatever free time you have." I bit my lip. "Maybe I should have driven up, it would have been handy to have had my own car. Actually, is there anywhere I can rent one?"

Angus flapped a hand in the air at me. "Och, I'll not hear of it. I like being with you. I find what you do… interesting."

"Thanks. You're fun to be with too."

My words surprised me. I don't normally tend to say stuff like that, but where was the harm in it? He *was* fun. I really ought to loosen up a little.

The journey – and it had been a long one, three hours door to door – at last came to an end. Balskeyne was close to Fort Augustus, as opposed to Inverness, and not visible from the road, due to a bank of trees that stood like custodians.

"Where do we park?" I asked.

"Just here, on the main road. If we tuck ourselves in, it'll be okay."

As we crossed the road, and skirted round to a gravel path that led upwards, the clouds must have covered the sun, for suddenly the day got darker.

Angus noticed it too. "I hope it's not an omen."

So did I. "Are you… erm… nervous about coming here again after so long?"

"A bit," he admitted. "What about you? Are you nervous?"

"I'm trying not to be. I wonder who lives here now."

"I've not a clue, so we'd best be careful, we don't want to be shot for trespassing."

"Shot?" I repeated, somewhat aghast.

"Relax, I'm joking," he replied, but I could tell from his voice he wasn't convincing himself either. My mind started to work overtime.

"I'll say I thought it was still a guesthouse," I suggested, "that I'd stayed here when it was, years ago, as a kid. I could even ask if there's a room available."

"For the both of us?"

"Well… yeah."

"Who shall we say we are," asked Angus. "Mr and Mrs Smith?"

"Mr and Mrs…? Don't push it, Angus."

He laughed. "Sorry, I really wasn't. But your ploy, it might work."

"I hope so. If I can find out anything about the house, it'll be a bonus. I might even be able to tune into something."

"And that'd be a bonus too, do you think?"

I grimaced. "Hmm, maybe not."

We continued up the path, our feet kicking at stones. It had to be secluded for the sake of the ritual, and secluded it was. Where was the house for goodness' sake? Rounding a corner, I held my breath – soon I'd be able to see it, in all its murky glory.

"Bloody hell!" Angus exclaimed.

"Christ!" I added.

There was nothing glorious about what was in front of us; it was a hollow, burnt out wreck.

"What's happened?" I said, at the same time as Angus pointed out the obvious: "There's been a fire!"

THIRTEEN

Dragging my eyes away, I turned to him. "Didn't you realise?"

"I've told you I haven't been here since."

We heard a voice behind us. "Hey there! Who are you? You're on private land."

We turned to see a woman hurrying towards us; she had to be in her late forties or even early fifties, with dark brown hair in a bun, although several strands had escaped, and wearing corduroy trousers and a zip-up fleece. As she drew nearer, I could see fury had caused her complexion to redden, and that she was doing her utmost to contain it.

I held my hands up. "I'm sorry, so sorry. It's just I was here as a kid and—"

"Rubbish! If you'd visited as a child, there's no way you'd come back, not unless you were a stupid child and an even stupider adult. You're another voyeur, wanting to see what all the fuss is about, but there's nothing to see here, not anymore. Please go."

I was stunned, so was Angus. We just stood there, staring at her, as she'd said – stupidly.

Angus recovered first. "You're right, that's a pack of lies. We have come to see what all the fuss is about, but for a good reason, the best of reasons actually. My name is Angus Macbrae and this is Ness Patterson, I'm from Skye, Ness is from Lewes, not the island—"

"I know where Lewes is," she barked.

"Oh, right," Angus dared to speak again. "I can tell from your accent you're not local."

"I'm from London," she said. "West Ken. I live here now though, this is my property."

He inclined his head to the ruin. "But there is no property."

"There's a lodge. I'm comfortable enough in it."

"The lodge," he repeated. "Where the spirits could gather."

Her fury erupted. "That's it, get off my land. Idiots! Utter idiots! You don't know what you're dealing with. I'm warning you, if you don't go, I'll call the police."

"Please," I said, taking my turn at trying to appease her, "just listen to us, hear us out. It's as my friend says, we've come for the best of reasons, although…" I hesitated, "the worst of reasons too. What happened here, it may be happening again, over on Skye—"

"Don't pretend you know what you're talking about."

"I do though, I honestly do. I'm a psychic."

That surprised her. "A psychic? Prove it."

My heart sank. Prove it? How could I do that? It wasn't as if there was a convenient spirit hovering close by, either good or bad. *You can sometimes catch thoughts.* True, but it wasn't all the time, it was more random than by design. Even so, if I could catch what was on her mind, even just a word or two, it'd be something in our favour.

"If you could formulate a thought," I said, "I'll try and see what it is. I know that's not necessarily proving I'm a psychic, but what it will do is prove I have extra-sensory skills."

"You want me to think something?"

"Besides us being stupid," I added, chancing a smile.

"That would be too easy I suppose." Was that a hint of a smile on her face too?

"Just… pluck something out of the blue," I advised.

"Okay, I will."

She closed her eyes and raised her head a little, as if in salute to the sun.

I was grateful; it allowed me to stare at her unhindered, to focus. What was she thinking? What could she possibly be thinking? I continued to stare, biting at my lip – what the hell was it? Panic set in. Thoughts were easier to detect if the other person was psychic too, or had a degree of psychic ability; with non-psychics it was so much harder. *Oh, please, please, let me get something – a word, two words, a few even.*

If I failed, she was going to run us off her land, and there'd be nothing we could do about it. I doubted severely if my connections with the Sussex police would count for anything – we had to get her permission to look around, we had to. *Come on, please, pick up a word, just a word, anything. Ness, come on!*

Don't try so hard. Those were the words that eventually appeared – all four of them in my mind, perfectly scribed. Was it self-administered advice or could it possibly be…

"Don't try so hard!" I whispered the words in the vain hope I was right.

She opened her eyes and fixed them on me, another slow smile developing. "You know, it really is so much easier if you just allow your gift to flow."

I smiled too, partly in wonder. "You believe me then?"

She nodded.

"And you're psychic too?"

"I'm intuitive. Let's leave it at that. Tell me the truth about why you're here."

As she asked the heavens opened.

"Come on," she said, her back hunched against the sudden downpour, "come to the lodge house. If you're brave enough, that is."

She started running, and without hesitation Angus and I

followed her, reaching the door of the tiny structure that stood just a few metres from what remained of Balskeyne.

Disappearing into the bathroom whilst we stood inside the doorway, she returned with towels for us to dry our hair, waiting patiently for us to perform the deed before taking them from us and dropping them back in the bathroom. We were then ushered into a small living room, where a log fire remained unlit and books crowded every surface.

"You like to read?" I said, picking up one book. Not a work of fiction, it was called *Symbols of Eternity*. I quickly scanned the titles of the other books I could see. They were all non-fiction, all dealing with esoteric subjects.

"Take a seat," she said, offering us neither coffee nor tea.

We did, Angus opting for the sofa and having to shift several books aside. I took the armchair that was opposite her, looking longingly at the fire, wishing it were lit.

"What's been happening on Skye?" she said. Regarding bluntness, I'd met my match.

As succinctly as I could I explained, noticing that when I told her about the visions she started to pick at her nails.

"I see," she said, when I'd finished. "So that's the link, the fact that the lighthouse keeper was overheard mentioning Balskeyne."

"And there was the visitor to the lighthouse, someone Liam didn't recognise, someone he didn't like the look of. It was after those visits that Mr Cameron changed."

"It could be something and nothing," she said, leaning into her chair

"But what if it's something?" Angus asked, both of us turning to look at him. "Just saying," he shrugged, going slightly red again.

THIRTEEN

I returned my gaze to the woman. "Erm… sorry, I don't even know your name…"

"Shelley Cooper-Brown," she replied curtly.

"Shelley, we were… erm… quite shocked to see that the house had burnt down. Did that happen recently?"

"Yes."

"No one was hurt?"

"No one."

I don't know where I got the courage from, but I had to ask. "Did you do it?"

She stared at me for so long that I grew hot and sweaty under her gaze, any chill I'd felt before, forgotten. And then to my relief, she laughed, a deep, throaty sound. We waited patiently until she stopped, until she spoke again.

"I admire your cheek," she said eventually. "In answer to your question, no, I didn't do it. It was an accident, a kitchen fire that got out of hand. I wasn't here you see, I was stocking up on groceries in Inverness. By the time I got back, it was raging. And I let it rage. Everything happens for a reason, and fire can be so wonderfully cleansing."

"Perhaps the lighthouse should go the same way?" I suggested, even more boldly.

"You're an arsonist now as well as a psychic?"

I hung my head. "No. No, I'm not."

"Didn't think so," she said. "There's actually no need to go to such lengths. It's enough if there's an overseer. That's what I am, an overseer, I keep things in check."

"There are plans for the lighthouse to be made into a guesthouse. Angus is going to manage it."

She turned towards him. "You'll be an overseer too."

Angus paled slightly. "I'm not sure I'm up to that," he

cried.

"Believe it and you will be," Shelley answered.

"So," I said, "this place, Balskeyne, does it live up to its reputation?"

"Concerning Isaac Leonard? Perhaps. You've told me you know something of the ritual he performed here, one that took many months, much patience, and meticulous planning. He may have been successful to a degree, but that's because he really had chosen the ideal place – this land is drenched in negative energy – long before the house was built."

"Oh?" I said, curious.

"In the twelfth century, there was a kirk here, a church in other words. No one knows for sure why, but one day, during a service, a fire broke out, right at the entrance to the church. There were a lot of people in attendance and none escaped. After that, in the 1760s, Balskeyne was built as a hunting lodge. The owner, Colonel Aleister Fraser, was involved in a duel thereafter and shot dead just feet from his own front door, his blood soaking the land. When Leonard lived here, doing whatever he was doing, a lot of strange goings-on were reported by people hereabouts. There were tales of people dying or mysteriously disappearing, even a butcher who chopped his hand off after receiving a meat order from the house. Part of the ritual involved summoning a number of demons, all harbingers of negative energy; it could have been these who ran amok locally, causing havoc. Or..." she paused to take a breath, to look at both of us in turn, "... it could all be imagination, which in itself is powerful. People *believed* this place was cursed. Through the centuries they believed that. And so it came to pass. Who knows? I don't. Not really."

"So what are you doing here?" asked Angus. "What are the duties of an overseer?"

"To restore balance."

Angus looked at me. "It really is as simple as that?" he queried. "Don't you get scared? I mean alone here, at night."

"No, I don't. I keep my imagination in check."

"But what if there really are demons?" he persisted.

"Not within me there aren't. I purged my demons a long time ago. And that's why I'm not scared. They've nothing to seize hold of." Shelley then did what I feared she was going to do; she focused solely on me. "If there is something at the lighthouse, if it's something similar to what was once rife here, you need to tread carefully."

I nodded slowly, wondering if the demons in me were really that easy to see. "The man that used to visit Mr Cameron, could it have been Isaac Leonard himself?"

"In the seventies? No."

"Why not?"

"Because Leonard left Scotland in '67 and died a few years later, in Haiti of all places."

"He died?"

"Yes, his death is well documented, in certain circles anyway. He was dabbling in voodoo by then, no doubt trying to master it as he once attempted to master the dark side here, and being driven insane for his troubles. But I have a theory about that."

"Which is?"

"That he was mad anyway."

I couldn't help but feel the same. "If it wasn't him, then who could it be?"

"No telling, is there? But after it had lain empty for a while, an American couple bought Balskeyne, no doubt thrilled by its bargain price if nothing else, and ran it as a guesthouse until 1980, and if there were any repeat visitors, I'd have to question why."

"Because of the bad vibes?" said Angus.

"Of course," Shelley answered.

"That couple, didn't they feel those vibes too?"

"Maybe they did, maybe they didn't – children are far more sensitive than adults, which is why I knew you were lying instantly when I first met you – there's no way you'd have come back if you'd stayed here when you were younger. On the other hand, it's amazing how oblivious adults can be. One thing I do know is that Leonard still has many devotees, people who make a pilgrimage here. That's why I have to be careful you see. Why I have to run at you, shouting and threatening the odds with the police. I can't let just anyone roam these grounds. It's all about the balance. As long as it exists, I'm safe."

"But at Minch Point, it could be unbalanced?" I said.

"I'm afraid so. And the game you mentioned, Thirteen Ghost Stories, that could have unsettled matters further."

And now, as the property lay empty, that negativity was growing in strength. There was no one to challenge it, if anything it had been encouraged, no matter how unwittingly.

Quickly I came to a decision. "I'm going back there. Tomorrow."

"Are we?" Angus muttered. "I suppose it's about time."

I ignored him, staring at Shelley as she was staring at me – her dark eyes just as penetrating as Eilidh's.

Finally she spoke. "I don't think you're the person for

the job."

"Because of my demons?" I said boldly.

"In a way, yes."

"I'm going anyway."

"Can't you come with us?" Angus asked Shelley.

She shook her head. "My place is here."

"Then what's your advice?" I said. "Give us that at least."

"The only advice I can give you is what I suspect you know already. Give what's there nothing to feed on. Because if there is something, if there is a weakness, it will find it."

"*Everyone* has a weakness," I insisted.

"But it's about degrees of weakness. Some of us happen to be content. If you really want my advice, then it's leave, go home! Like I said, you're not the person for the job."

Chapter Seventeen

"HOW dare she! She knows nothing about me."

"She said she's intuitive."

I glared at Angus as I yanked his car door open. "She's presumptuous, that's what she is. I'm not going home, not yet. Just because *she* thinks it's for the best."

"There's no need to get narky with me, Ness. I'm glad you're staying."

My breathing was heavy as Angus turned the engine over. "We need to find out what happened to the Camerons," I muttered, as much to myself as him. "They disappeared, but not into thin air, they went somewhere." I looked up. "I need to get to a phone."

"Why?"

"I want to phone one of my police contacts, see if they can run a search on the Camerons for me."

"You think something bad might have happened to them?"

"It'd be handy to know, one way or the other."

"Okay," Angus replied, nodding. "I'll also ask around, see what I can dig up." He smiled ruefully. "Actually, perhaps that's a poor choice of phrase, considering."

My smile was somewhat rueful too. "I can do this you

know."

He held his hands up. "I'm not the one saying you can't, remember?"

That was true, neither him nor his mother. But Shelley… My throat constricted again. She wanted me to give up, because I wasn't at peace with myself as much as she was. Maybe I wasn't, but one thing I had was determination. I'd make sure my efforts paid off.

After she'd 'denounced' me, as I'd interpreted it, Shelley asked if we'd like to take a walk through the grounds.

"Don't expect to sense much though," she'd warned. "I run a tight ship here."

And it was true, I hadn't sensed much at all, a simmering perhaps, a skulking even, something hiding in a corner, plotting and planning, but those plans coming to nothing. I was awed with what she'd achieved, and that annoyed me further.

Before we'd departed, she'd said to me. "You know about white light?"

"Of course," I answered.

"Good intent?"

"Yes, I'll go to the lighthouse with nothing but good intent."

She nodded. "Because even evil needs to be understood."

I remained mute. Was she trying to get at me again?

"You have obsidian in your pocket?"

I gasped. How did she know? Intuitive, that's how. She was damned intuitive.

"Cleanse it regularly," she continued, "by moonlight is best, otherwise in bright sunlight. Prevent any negativity from clinging to it."

"I know, I do." God, I sounded like a petulant child.

"Good."

On the drive back to Skye, the sun re-emerged, but it was nowhere near as bright as before. Even so, the light was still beautiful, hazy almost. As I stared out of the passenger window again, I had to admit, despite how irked I was, that the balance Shelley was talking about made perfect sense and how easily it could be tipped one way or the other. If it could be maintained, then both sides could co-exist, in harmony almost, like night and day – the two opposites, the yin and the yang. It was an intriguing concept, one that consumed me so much I had no idea we'd reached the Kyle until Angus announced it.

"We've a bit of time to kill before the ferry gets here," he continued, "so let's head to the pub, and get that drink we'd promised ourselves. And don't worry; I'm fine with lemonade. Something tells me it's wise to keep a clear head at the moment."

It was – very wise.

"There'll be a phone in the pub too," he added. "If you want to phone that contact of yours."

As soon as we were inside, I did just that, the response I got from my contact being what I'd expected; he'd try and find out about the Camerons, but couldn't promise anything. As he pointed out, some people just didn't want to be found. I was grateful for any help though and, after ringing off, went to buy Angus his drink.

Later, back on Skye, Eilidh had prepared a one-pot vegetable stew complete with dumplings that I realised I was ravenous for, devouring two sizeable helpings. Both Angus and I explained what had happened that day, and I announced my intention to go back to the lighthouse in the morning, breaking it to Angus that I wanted to go alone.

"But—"

"Please," I said, interrupting him. "If I'm alone, it's easier to focus."

"What about the visions? What if you get them again?"

I took a deep breath. "I'll deal with them."

"Really?"

It wasn't just him who raised an eyebrow this time. Eilidh did too.

"I think you should take Angus with you," she said, "as back-up if nothing else."

The irritation I'd felt earlier hadn't quite died down. I had to fight to keep my voice steady. "I thought you both believed in me?"

"We do," they replied, almost in unison.

"Then please, can you trust me on this?"

A moment of silence stretched on and on.

Eilidh eventually spoke. "We trust you."

I exhaled heavily, not realising quite how much I'd needed to hear that.

"You'll be wanting to borrow my car?" Angus asked.

"Yes please, I'll get up early, and go first thing. It's a cleansing I want to perform tomorrow. I'm learning Reiki, so I'll be incorporating that, trying to balance the energy, as Shelley recommended, as well as using psychic persuasion if it's needed."

"You think that's enough?" Eilidh was frowning slightly.

"I think it's a good start. When it's up and running as a guesthouse, that'll be even better. Angus, if you're in charge, it'll be a happy place to visit."

He flashed a shy smile at me. "I hope so."

So did I. Balskeyne had been run as a guesthouse for a period of time too, but what was there, what had been conjured by a man if not mad at the time, certainly on the brink of madness, still remained, although in a much subdued form, Shelley the overseer, the keeper, the guardian making sure it stayed that way. I looked at Angus, still with that shy smile on his face, his red hair as scruffy as ever, and placed my trust in him too.

* * *

I was thankful for a good night's rest, with no dreams – or none that I could remember. It wasn't the lighthouse I drove to first; it was Moira's house, even though all that I'd sensed there, and the image I'd seen rushing headlong towards the cliff, was residual. Moira may be at peace, but the negative energy she'd left behind needed cleansing too. The weather was on my side this time, and the sun was shining again. It's amazing what a blue sky can do; it can lift even the dullest of hearts, inspire confidence even. Certainly I felt confident today, despite Shelley, or perhaps *in spite* of her.

Good thoughts form the backbone of good intent, Ness.

I ought to listen to myself and cleanse my mind too, not contribute to any negativity.

Moira's house was easy enough to get into. Angus had secured the door he'd shoved in with his shoulder, but actually it was slightly ajar when I reached it. I was hesitant for a few seconds and shouted, "Hello, hello," as I entered, just in case someone was in there – and it could be anyone: an estate agent perhaps, come to value it at last; a farmer checking one of his flock hadn't raced in here for shelter during the storm and then found it couldn't escape when the more clement weather came. No one answered, and there were few places to hide. Checking upstairs was empty too, I returned to the living room and set to work, calling on all four elements – Earth, Air, Fire and Water – to heal and to balance the house. As I'd found before, sadness was the dominant emotion, in the wake of Moira's suicide – I had to fight hard to stop it from overwhelming me again. Afterwards, I sat in Angus's car, in the driver's seat, gripping the steering wheel, just staring out at the cliff top, wondering if I'd see her, the shade of Moira, in perpetual flight. But all there was on the horizon was a flock of sea birds that swooped and soared, freer than I'd ever be, as free as the dead, hopefully.

At last, I put the car into gear and drove to Minch Point Lighthouse, occupying the same parking space that Angus had when we'd visited before. Making my way to the cabin, I stopped briefly to admire a view that I hadn't had the pleasure of seeing previously, thanks to the darkness and the weather. The sea was calm, glittering in the sunlight, and beyond it, there were silhouettes of yet more islands, Lewis and Harris, the Western Isles – their presence on the horizon mythical almost. It was so hard to believe that anything bad could taint such a hallowed spot, but looking at the cabin in front of me, and the lighthouse tower and the keeper's quarter slightly higher on the hill, I'd better believe it, not allow myself to be fooled or sucked in.

The cabin was in worse shape than I'd realised. Its rough rendered walls had big chunks missing, and guttering hung precariously from the roof. All the windows were smashed, as if someone had diligently sat and thrown pebbles at each and every pane. It was hard to swap the majesty of the outside to venture back in there, but that's exactly what I had to do – lay down the foundations for change.

As it was such a tiny dwelling, at least I wasn't in the cabin for long, half an hour at most, after which I made my way up the gravel path to the main house. Like the cabin, it was painted in white with a buff trim, but coated in the grime of years, the tower that stood beside it a classic piece of maritime architecture. Again I stopped to admire it, almost defiantly this time. Built to be a guiding light, shining brighter than stars in the darkness, how could it have ever failed? It was lonely, a doomed romantic hero mourning the loss of its *raison d'etre*. I felt sad, sadder even than when I'd been in Moira's bedroom. To witness such silent doom was terrible. There was no sound, nothing at all, not the crashing of the waves, or the birds as they'd screeched on that stormy night.

At the front door to where the Camerons had lived, I took all the time I needed to feel grounded, hugging my chunk of obsidian close to my heart. I was about to take a step forward when I thought I did hear something: a shuffling.

It's probably just an animal, darting for cover.

The last thing I needed to do was let my imagination get the better of me – in this scenario it was a weapon too. There'd be some who'd argue that what was happening at the lighthouse was in fact solely the product of overimaginative minds. I envied that view. If you held no belief in the spiritual world, could it ever harm you? The American couple that had run Balskeyne as a guesthouse might well have been protected, purely because of their disbelief. On the other hand, if you did believe, if you *knew…*

Deciding to stop philosophising and get on with the job, I entered the main building. All was still inside. The first thing I did was cross over to the windows, pulling aside or yanking down what curtains remained. The difference was immediate – the gloom losing some of its opaqueness. I tried to open the windows next, but they were all stuck and, unlike at the cabin, the glass panes were intact. Deciding to rectify that, I picked up a stool and, utilising one of its wooden legs, took great delight in smashing a few. I really wouldn't consider myself a vandal, but there's a saying: needs must when the devil drives. It was essential to change the air inside this place, not let it fester any longer.

Having done all this, it was time to begin the ritual cleansing, again harnessing the power of the natural elements, which were so abundant on Skye. Kicking a tide of debris out of my way as I walked, I was surprised not just how calm I was, but at how calm it was in the lodgings too. Things were different in daylight; I knew that, but *so* different?

Visualising myself as well as this entire structure at Minch Point blanketed in a white glow, I practised the symbol of *Cho Ku Rei,* enticing the power of the universe to enter this domain, to reside here, and for balance to be restored. Throughout the entire area downstairs I practised this symbol, feeling the power of my energy, and how it flowed, creating another shield against the threat of attack. Having finished downstairs, I climbed the stairs, any trepidation I harboured successfully packaged up and stowed away. I repeated the process in the main bedroom, Niall's bedroom, and finally headed to Caitir's bedroom.

My breathing still deep and even, I pushed the door wider, *Cho Ku Rei, Cho Ku Rei* repeating in a loop in my mind. It was so quiet inside, the curtains closed at the window, which I opened straightaway. Rather than break another windowpane, I struggled with the sash. Eventually I managed to open it an inch or two, imagining fresh air like a Pac-Man, rushing in, and devouring all that was stale. I turned around and walked to the centre of the room. There were several candle stubs on the floor, along with glass jars that had once housed them, most broken, but some intact. There was general litter too, left behind from many teenage gatherings, even an item of clothing – a girl's red cardigan – which I picked up and handled, checking for any vibes that might still cling to it. There were none and so I dropped it.

Benign; it was all quite benign.

Chanting out loud, I called on the universe to work with me, not against me. If black magic had been practised here, then white magic was going to cancel it out.

"And soon there'll be life here again, lots of energy, love and laughter. Because of that, any negativity will diminish, become insubstantial. Whatever you are, I'm not afraid of you, I'm the *antithesis* of you, and my word is true. You do not belong here in any significance. If you've been conjured by vain, inglorious men, I'm sorry for that. But you cannot stay."

Resolutely, I stood there – a lone challenger. If it attacked, if it tried to force-feed me a diet of terrible visions designed to bring me to knees, it wouldn't work. Last time I hadn't known that would happen. This time I'd closed my mind against such infiltration. My lack of fear would be the thing that would frustrate it, that and my belief in myself. I *could* do this. That was the entire reason I possessed this gift – to help. If I could help, it made sense of it; it helped me to cope with how different I was.

Different?

Ness, shut up, don't think anymore...

It *had* to be the reason – if not, then why? So much persecution it had cost me, by strangers as well as those that were supposed to love me, my family...

Ness!

But it was true; I *had* been persecuted. Only now, in my mid-twenties, was I coming into my own, doing things like this, standing in an abandoned house, one that was reputedly haunted, the smell of something sickly sweet in the air, the haven of mice, rats, spiders – and me. It was laughable, so damned funny, so why wasn't I smiling?

You'd think I'd be smiling.

NESS!

I blinked, came to, shaking my head vigorously. What had just happened to me? I'd gone into a reverie of some kind, negative thoughts doing their utmost to entrap me.

Breathing slowly in and out, I clenched and unclenched my fists. This thing, it was clever, I'd give it that. It was canny.

"Even so, I'm not frightened of you," I reiterated, "or the games that you play, because that's all they are. And all games must come to an end."

Laughter! I definitely heard laughter. Was someone here after all?

I darted forward in the direction I'd heard it – the hallway – and looked from side to side.

Breathe, Ness. Keep your cool.

In case someone was hiding – someone living that is – I

called out, just as I'd done in Moira's house. "Is there anyone here?"

No reply, but my sense that someone was spying on me intensified.

"If there is, show yourself!"

And have a good laugh at my expense. How can I blame you? Look how stupid I am, an idiot, trying to face a demon on my own, to fight it. How can I ever hope to succeed, when I'm just as bad? When I'm a demon too? I'd have to be to do what I did, to cause so much shame, more than I'd caused already. Officially mad, that's what I was. How can I continue to deny it? I'm not worthy. I'm a freak. I'm the one who should be banished.

As though I'd received a blow to the stomach, I doubled over, the bitterness of bile scorching my throat. I hadn't been physically attacked, but I almost wished I had, it would be far easier to bear. Those thoughts, they weren't mine, surely they weren't. They'd simply formed in my head, sentences running on and on, crashing into one another. I had to get out. There was nothing benign about this place, or what was in it.

Oh, look, poor me, feeling sorry for myself, I can't seem to stop. I'm always feeling sorry for myself, I'm such a victim, such a martyr, a curse, and an abomination. I can't even bear to think of what I did, to acknowledge it. And at such a young age too. Thirteen, only thirteen. Of course it would have to be: a cursed age for a cursed child.

Doing my utmost to straighten up, I ran for the stairs, practically blind with tears. I only wished I could shut off my hearing too, silence that laughter, which wasn't mine, but was so like mine. I could hear it still and knew without doubt it would soon turn to wailing – something I couldn't bear to hear, not again, not after I'd tried for so long to shut it out.

"You're dead," I hissed, "you and mum both."

At the top of the stairs I hesitated. Was there someone at the bottom, a crone-like figure, staring up at me? I wiped at my eyes. Although I'd torn the curtains down, although it was barely noon, there was so much darkness – obscuring the figure, or hiding it. One minute it was there, the next it wasn't. Would it reappear when I got halfway? Would it fly at me, and smother me with the weight of hell as I lay screaming?

I had to control my imagination. There's nothing there, nothing!

Why am I denying it? Why am I pretending? For so long, I used to say the same thing: there's nothing there, nothing. Try and convince myself. But there always was. Always. 'Only a witch can see what you can see, an evil, stinking witch.' That's what she told me once, that bitch of a mother, that crone. 'And you know what happens to witches, don't you? No? Well you should. We rid the world of them. We don't want them.'

"For God's sake, stop this," I cry, feeling in the grip of madness more than I ever had. The laughter was changing, just as it had done in my dream last night, no longer soft and sweet, it was becoming more stilted, a sob creeping in, becoming more pronounced.

If I stayed here…

I couldn't. It knew my weakness too well.

Having checked the bottom of the stairs again, that there was no one lurking, I practically threw myself down the steps, praying I wouldn't fall, land in a heap and injure myself. If I did, I really would be at the mercy of what was here. It could toy with me further, take its time, and really enjoy the game. Thankfully, I reached the bottom in one piece, refusing to look anywhere but ahead, hurtling myself forward as the wailing began.

Pain shot through my fragile heart.

At the front door, I grabbed the handle and yanked it open. Again, I couldn't believe what I was seeing: the weather, so beautiful before, had turned – either mourning alongside me or mocking me. Such hard rain they have in Scotland, the clouds closing in, encircling me – a shield wall, so much more effective than the one I'd built.

The car, I had to find it, get out of here, and not be stranded. The thought of being stranded…

Coward. I can add that to my list of glowing attributes. I'm a born coward.

I wouldn't listen anymore, I refused to – those were not my thoughts, they were being planted in my head. Or were they? Because I *had* thought along those lines before, many times, thoughts like that had once plagued me. I pressed forwards through the rain, my eyes peeled for the car. Where the heck was it? A little green Fiesta, not new, but as scruffy as anything, as its owner. Would Angus be safe here in the future, the guardian of Minch Point Lighthouse? Would anyone? There it was! The car hadn't been spirited away as I'd half-expected, it was where I'd left it. I felt in my pocket for the key, found the chunk of obsidian, retrieved it and held it to my chest again, drawing what comfort I could, but it was the key I needed. That was in the other pocket. Thank God.

In the car, it took several attempts to insert the key into the ignition, my hands were shaking so much, but finally I succeeded. Quickly putting it into reverse, I pressed my foot to the floor, the tyres screeching. Back on the road, I drove away, taking bends and corners at the speed only a native would. As I drove, another thought occurred, this one very much my own: the cabin, the gravel path leading up to the house, the *west-facing* house, and the isolated location: it had exactly the same qualities as Balskeyne.

Chapter Eighteen

IF I'd hoped to find respite at Eilidh's house, I was wrong. As soon as I entered the front door, I sensed commotion, even a non-psychic would have been able to – the atmosphere so tense you could slice through it with a knife. Hurrying up the hallway, I heard voices coming from the dining room, several of them, speaking in hushed but agitated tones. Sure enough, when I stood at the threshold, I found not just Eilidh and Angus in situ; Craig's father, Mr Ludmore, was also present and another man, that I hadn't yet met.

Seeing me, Angus shot to his feet. "Ness! You're all right! I was about to borrow Ben's car and drive out to the lighthouse to look for you."

"I… erm… who's Ben?" I asked.

The man who was a stranger to me stood too. "That's me, Ben Mowbray, I'm Amy's father, one of the teenagers who was at the lighthouse the night something happened to Ally, happened to them all. The thing is, Ally's taken a turn for the worse. She and her parents are at the medical centre in Broadford, waiting to be taken to Raigmore on the mainland. That's when they can move Ally that is."

"When? Why? How has she got worse?" My own

predicament shelved, I wanted to know as much as possible. "When did she deteriorate?"

"Sit down, lass." It was Eilidh. "You looked flummoxed enough when you entered the room, let alone after. We'll tell you everything and then… we'll decide what to do about it."

What had happened was even worse than I thought. Molly had heard banging and crashing coming from Ally's room, not an unusual occurrence – she'd already told us that Ally was sometimes given to fits of rage – but this time it was accompanied with the most terrible screaming. Her husband was at home too and both of them rushed upstairs to find out what was happening. Ally hadn't barricaded herself in this time; on the contrary, she'd left the door open. They rushed inside and that's when Ally attacked them. She had a knife, which she managed to stab her mother with before her father got her under control.

"She stabbed her mother?" I gasped. "How badly is she hurt?"

"Not badly, thank goodness," Ben replied. "It's an arm wound, but she'll be going to Raigmore for treatment nonetheless. I live along the road from them; I was passing, on my way to the village, when I heard the commotion. After having to bash the front door down, I raced up the stairs, made my way to where all the noise was coming from and I'll tell you, the sight that met me… All I could do for a few seconds was stand and stare." He shook his head, clearly still in shock. "They were always such a normal family, the Dunns, a *nice* family, you know? What's happened to them, to all of our kids? I don't understand it. In Ally's room, the walls were covered in the number thirteen. She'd written it everywhere. I've heard that some of the others have done that too, och, not on the walls or anything, but on paper. They sit there and they write it over and over. It's like they're obsessed."

As I'd been in my dream – obsessed or possessed – what was the difference?

Mr Mowbray continued to speak. "John was struggling with Ally, I mean really struggling. It was wrong, all wrong, he's a big bloke, and she's just a wee thing. He yelled at me to call an ambulance, so I had to leave them and rush back downstairs, but I could hear Ally screaming all the while, and not just screaming, she was saying stuff too."

My breathing becoming more rapid, I was unable to calm it; I didn't even bother to try this time. "What was she saying?"

"Something along the lines of *'It's won. We played the game and it's won.'* What could she mean by that? What on earth could she mean? I'm telling you that girl was bucking and kicking, she was foaming at the mouth. And when I got home, Amy, my own kid, had locked herself in her room too, as if she knew what had happened, although I hadn't yet told anyone. She was crying, inconsolably. My wife and I, we tried our best with her, even our dog, Smokie, sat by her door, howling away as if pleading to be let in, but she just kept on crying. And then she stopped and said something, something which raised the hairs on my arms." He paused again, looking as if he was about to start crying himself. Instead he clamped his lips into a tight white line before continuing. "She also said 'It's won'. The same words Ally used. *Who's* won? What's going on? I came here because I'd heard you were investigating the case, that you're a psychic. I need to know what's going on!"

"I don't know the full picture," I admitted, "not yet. But it's far from good."

His complexion was grey almost. "Don't tell me they've summoned the devil?"

I was eager to dispel that notion. "I think it's more likely they've tuned into negative energy of some description, and it's… erm… a force to be reckoned with."

"I told Amy not to go to the lighthouse," he said, such despair in his voice, "to stay away. But would she listen? Do teenagers *ever* listen? And that game, that stupid game… Why do they do that, try and spook themselves? How can we put an end to this… I don't know… spell that they're under? How do we reverse it? Play the game again?"

About to say no, I stopped. What he'd suggested made a dreadful kind of sense.

Looking at each of them in turn, noting the fear and confusion that had begun to haunt them, I finally gave an answer. "I think we should do exactly that; beat it at its own game."

Chapter Nineteen

ANGUS had grown pale, and Eilidh was clutching at the collar of the dress she wore. My agreement with Ben had shocked them, but Ben – a parent of one of the teenagers afflicted, a girl who was barely sixteen – looked hopeful, and that spurred me on.

"We'd have to exercise the utmost care," I explained, "perform some rituals of our own before we enter the lighthouse en masse again. I don't want you to be alarmed by that; it's not black magic. It's working with the universe, and drawing on the light to protect us."

"I'm not alarmed," Ben said. "Pardon my language, but I want to beat this fucker at its own game. And believe me, I'll do what it takes."

"But will your daughter?" I asked, wary of putting traumatised kids under more pressure.

"We need to hold a meeting," Eilidh declared, "with all those who've been involved. See who's willing to help and who isn't. And if they're not…"

"If they're not, some of us will take their place," Angus insisted. "In memory of Moira."

I smiled at him. "In memory of Moira."

Eilidh stood, brushed the front of her dress down and

then clasped her hands in front of her. "There's a community hall near Dunvegan, that's central enough for everyone I think. Angus and Ben, can you see who's willing to come to the meeting?" She checked her watch. "It's nearing two, we need to get on. How about we set a time of five o' clock?"

"It's doable," Angus said, "if Ben and I leave now. There are eleven families other than the Dunns to speak to, we could divide them between us, Ben?"

"Aye, that's fine, everyone needs to know what's happened to Ally."

"Ben," I reiterated, "it's imperative that no one goes to the lighthouse under duress, only those that are reasonably confident. If they all decline, fair enough, I'll find another way."

"If they all decline?" Ben repeated and then he laughed, a booming sound that startled all of us. "You're in the Highlands, lassie, we don't breed wimps up here. There'll be very few that decline, you'll see. You cannae play Thirteen Ghost Stories on your own."

A short while later, with Angus and Ben dispatched, I was ruminating on that thought. Could I ensure the safety of those who chose to go back to Minch Point? Was it reckless of me to even think so? What if it put them all in the line of danger? More danger, that is, than they were already in. After all, if Ally had worsened, so could the others. No one was safe, not really, no matter where they were – at home or at the lighthouse.

Eilidh came up behind me. "It's a heavy load, isn't it?"

"What? Erm… I suppose. Oh, what the hell… Yes, yes it is. To tell you the truth, Eilidh, I don't know what to do for the best."

Pulling up a chair so that she could sit beside me, she took my hands in hers, her skin felt like velvet, but despite that, her grip was firm. "Ben's right in what he says, we're a hardy lot that live here, but for all that, we're spiritual too, you can't help but be."

"Angus said something similar," I replied. "He called this God's own country."

She nodded. "Aye, and it is, but if we're close to God, maybe the devil's close too."

"It's so hard to believe, isn't it? It's so beautiful here."

"But it's wrathful too, when the weather sets in."

Remembering what had happened at the lighthouse, I agreed. "It can certainly turn on a sixpence. One minute the sun's shining, the next there's another storm on the horizon."

"Four seasons in one day, that's how it goes on Skye. Look," – releasing a soft breath, she leant forward – "something's happening here, we can't deny it, try as we might. We can't hide from it either. And so what choice is there, but to face it head on?"

"But I'm worried about people getting hurt… more people that is. Ally stabbed her mum for goodness' sake, she could have killed her, or turned the knife on herself."

"I know, I know. I don't think any of us are going to take this lightly, dear, believe me."

"I know that. You're good people, all of you."

She smiled. "Surely that's something in our favour?"

I smiled too. "I just… Like you said, it's a lot of responsibility. If it goes wrong, and I can't guarantee that it won't, the buck stops with me."

"I'll not blame you, lass, or Angus, or any of the folks that I know." She released my hand and sat back. "Och,

THIRTEEN

but I bet you wish there were two of you sometimes, don't you?"

For a brief moment I could only stare at her. "What did you say?"

The phone rang, a shrill sound that startled me again.

Still smiling, Eilidh eased herself out of her chair. "I'd best answer that," she said, leaving the dining room and heading into the hallway.

I barely had time to think before she was back. "It's for you. It's the police."

"The police? Oh, it must be Dan; he's with the Sussex Police. I asked him to run a trace on the Camerons. Sorry, I gave him this number to contact me, I hope that's okay."

"Of course it's okay. Come on, don't keep him waiting."

I hurried into the hallway, eager to hear what Dan had to say. When I returned to the dining room, Eilidh was looking as grave as I felt.

"It's bad news, is it?"

"The worst," I answered.

The Camerons were dead, all four of them. Mr Cameron had shot his family and then himself eight years ago, on another remote island, this one off the coast of Ireland.

* * *

Despite Ben and Eilidh assuring me there'd be a big turnout at the community hall, there wasn't. There was Mr and Mrs Ludmore and their son Craig, Ben of course, with his wife, Caroline, and their daughter, Amy. Also in attendance were Isabel and her parents, Grant and his parents, a young lad known as Denny with his mother and father, and another girl, called Elaine or Lainey, as she preferred. She was there with her mother, Diane. Other parents had been talked to, but declined getting involved further, as had their teenage offspring. I guess there are some things even the hardiest of folks can't face. I could sympathise with that. Ben started to apologise for the turnout, but I stopped him.

"There's enough for us to do what we have to."

And we did *have* to, I saw that now, the deaths of the Camerons had clarified that for me. I was still reeling from the information that Dan had imparted. Mr Cameron had shot his entire family and then turned the gun on himself? For no obvious reason? Where they'd been living, Arranmore, with a population of roughly around five hundred according to Dan, and in a cottage, not a lighthouse, they'd done more or less what they'd done on Skye, and kept themselves to themselves, not mixed at all. "The fella I talked to that dealt with the case told me that fellow islanders described the family as weird," Dan had said. "The general consensus amongst them was that Cameron wasn't a man to be messed with, that he only had to look at you and you'd start shaking. The .22 rifle he used was registered to him."

I'd asked Dan about the kids, Caitir and Niall, and whether that same man had said anything about them.

"Only that they were a pitiful sight, in death I mean. They looked half-starved, as did their mother. Not him though, he was a big man, he obviously ate well enough."

"Poor kids," I'd responded, "his poor wife." I'd never known them, I'd only ever heard of them, but that didn't stop my heart aching for them. They were victims in more ways than one. Even though the news was gruesome, it didn't make me want to run away and take the next train headed south, removing myself from this lonely land and what dwelt in it. My *friends* also dwelt here. That's how I'd come to think of Eilidh and Angus. Together, we had to try and finish what had been started so many years before.

In the hall, it was Ben who kicked off proceedings, explaining who I was to those who hadn't yet met me, and also what we intended to do.

"There's no pressure on anyone to go back to the lighthouse," he said. "We've been quite clear about that, but we also think it's the only way to eradicate this thing."

"And if not eradicate it," I added a touch more cautiously, "to subdue it."

The usual questions were asked. 'Is it the devil?' 'Are you really psychic?' 'What if we play and it wins again, if, like Ally, we end up losing our minds?'

"We'll win this time," I said in response to such questions. "And when we do, that will help Ally too; it will tame whatever's in her. An important thing to remember is that we're going in fully prepared, we're not blind anymore. Our *expectation* is to win. Believe it."

"It can't be that simple," someone said, Denny's father I think.

I inclined my head towards him. "You think it's that simple, do you, to believe in yourself? It isn't. Sometimes, it's the hardest thing of all."

He pondered that, opened his mouth to respond, but clearly decided against it.

"You mentioned something about protection procedures," Ben reminded me. "What did you mean?"

"More magic?" someone else muttered before I could respond.

"It's not magic," I said, reiterating what I'd said to Ben earlier today. "It's working in harmony with the earth's natural energies, an holistic practice if you like, and partly rooted in an ancient practice called Reiki, which I'm learning at the moment."

"Learning?" It was Lainey's mother who questioned this. "You're not an expert?"

Eilidh stepped in. "Diane, there are some things that take a lifetime to learn. I can vouch for Ness, she does have psychic ability, but more than that, she has a good heart. That's what really matters when you're dealing with something like this."

I was grateful for the support. "Eilidh's right, but drawing on universal energy does help, and we all need to do that. Imagine the purest white light you can, coming straight at you from source, and wrapping itself around you. This is your armour – keep it in place. We also need to go in with good intent. Whatever's there, however dark it is, it's to be pitied, rather than feared." Drawing on what Shelley had said, I added, "We can't rid ourselves of negative energy entirely, it's unrealistic to think that, but what we can do is restore balance. The plans that Angus's uncle has for the lighthouse are a good thing – they'll help to *maintain* balance. When we're done, when the builders have moved in, when there's life at the lighthouse once again, it'll be a good place to visit; one where happy memories are forged, where there's conversation and laughter. All that will help."

"So why are we doing anything?" asked Mrs Ludmore. "Why don't we just encourage Angus's uncle to get started as soon as he can?"

"Because of Ally," Angus said. "This thing is becoming

more powerful, so we have to try and break it while we can, not wait for sales negotiations to be completed."

"But why Ally? Why did it pick on her so bad?"

Craig had posed the question, but it was Isabel who answered. "Maybe it was because she'd just found out she was adopted."

There was a sharp intake of breath in the room, and a few people looked at each other; their eyes wide with surprise. "Was she?" asked one.

"Aye," Isabel continued, "and she found out by accident. She was looking for something and came across the papers. They were going to tell her at some point, but I think it was her mam who kept putting it off. She told Ally that it didn't matter, she was their child, and they were her parents, in all the ways that mattered. There was a big hoo-ha and Ally was distraught, but I thought they'd sorted it out. What happened at the lighthouse, it wasn't long after that, and Ally had been drinking – a lot. She never usually drinks." Isabel looked at her parents, "And neither do I by the way, before you start."

But no one started. If anything, everyone appeared dumbstruck.

"I'd never have guessed," said Ben finally. "She actually looks like them."

"Och, away with you," his wife replied. "As Molly said, she's theirs, in all the ways that count. I can understand it's difficult to break the news, why you'd keep putting it off. You don't want your child to love you any the less, do you, just because of biology, or rather the lack of it?"

Various murmurs of agreement floated around the room.

"Look," I said, "I haven't got all the answers to the

situation we've found ourselves in, but Angus is right when he says that what's there is gaining in power. I went to the lighthouse today to perform a basic cleansing, and, well, let's just say, it's clever, this thing and what it can do – it has intelligence, no matter how basic. From what I understand, especially in the light of what I've just learnt about Ally, it plays on your weaknesses, your sorrows, and your fears, it unearths them. If any of you feel vulnerable in any way, then please don't come. If you're going to do this, you have to do it in the right frame of mind."

"What happens if we don't come with you?" Again it was Diane who asked.

"Then I go alone."

"Erm… hang on a minute, you don't get rid of me that easy," Angus looked as if he was going to breathe fire through his nostrils. "I'm coming too. I've told you."

"Thanks." It was all I could say. I *would* go back to the lighthouse alone, but the truth is I didn't want to. As thirteen had proved, there's strength in numbers.

"Well… in that case, Lainey," said Dianne, "what do you think? It's entirely up to you."

Lainey was a pretty girl, as dark-haired as myself, her skin just as white. She hesitated, but not for long. "I'm going back, Mum. If there's a chance we can stop this, then I'm taking it. It is getting worse, that lady's right. And lately, there've been visions."

"And urges." It was Grant speaking, a boy with hair as red as Angus's. "That's recent too. I've the urge to hurt someone." He shook his head. "The hours I spend in my bedroom, sitting on my hands, trying to stop that urge. Mum, Dad, I'm scared for us. Ally's a great girl, as gentle as they come, the fact that she attacked her parents…" He paused, as if trying to understand such a heinous fact. "Even despite what she'd just found out, she wouldn't do stuff like that, not normally. But there's this voice, it whispers in your ear, it tells you to hurt as many people as you can, and it's getting louder. Just lately it's not a whisper anymore, it's more like a command." Suddenly he lunged himself into his mother's arms, who was sitting right beside him. "I'd never do what Ally did, Mum, Dad. I'd never hurt you. I love you. I'm sorry. I don't want to think this way, but it's making me."

His mother didn't even hesitate; immediately she comforted him, told him that she loved him too, more than anything. His father joined in, all of them hugging, clinging on to each other as if their lives depended on it. Seeing such a display of emotion, other teenagers in the room turned to their parents too, their parents reaching out just as readily to them. It was something wonderful to see – the love that they all had for each other and once again I was filled with hope. Love was stronger than hate. Love got things done.

But hate's powerful too, Ness. Whoever loved you like that?

The thought formed before I could stop it, but I couldn't disagree with it, not when it was true. Before I could think any further, Eilidh stood up and made her way towards me.

"Eilidh?" I questioned.

She didn't answer, she simply stopped in front of me and held out her arms. I felt awkward, unsure how to respond.

"Go on," Angus nudged me. "She wants a hug. And afterwards, so do I."

I stared at him too, somewhat aghast.

"Go on," he said again.

Still feeling awkward, I stood up, a hesitant smile on my face. It was Eilidh who closed the gap between us, enfolding me in her arms. Again, there was such strength in her embrace. At once the tears started, I couldn't stop them. How awful to cry like this, in a room full of people. But it was also cathartic. She was giving me something I'd craved all my life – acceptance and love: *motherly* love.

"This is something your mother should have done too," she whispered in my ear. "If I'd had the privilege of being your mother, I know I would have."

And there it was – *if* she'd been my mother. Sometimes we luck out. Sometimes we don't. Is it right to think you're unlovable because of an accident of birth? I wondered. Was it time, aged twenty-five, to put all that had happened behind me? God knows I'd tried.

Luckily everyone else around the room seemed preoccupied with each other, no one noticed what was happening with me, except Angus. He stood too and hugged me and then all three of us hugged together.

"You can do this," Eilidh said.

"Try telling that to Shelley," I replied, looking wryly at Angus, but he was looking elsewhere, towards the entrance of the hall. As he pulled away, I frowned.

"You can tell her yourself," he said.

Chapter Twenty

I swung round. Shelley stood at the hall entrance, dressed in identical clothing to yesterday, surveying the scene before her. Slowly, leisurely, her gaze travelled towards me. There was something in her eyes, what was it? Approval? Dared I even think it?

Angus hurried over to stand by her side. A few others had noticed she was there and were nudging each other, whispering.

"This is Shelley," Angus announced. "I asked her if she'd come today and, well, I'm grateful that she has."

I looked at Angus stunned, when had he taken her telephone number? I hadn't even thought to do that.

"Shelley's the overseer at Balskeyne," he continued, "which, as some of you know, is a house on the banks of Loch Ness, the one that used to belong to the Black Magician, Isaac Leonard."

"And Robbie Nelson," Craig piped up. "Such a great band, The Ridge."

"Overseer?" His father questioned. "The caretaker you mean?"

"He means exactly that," Shelley announced, her imperious tone holding everybody's attention. "The house burnt down last year, a kitchen fire. I don't know if any of you were aware of that?" Several shakes of the head confirmed that people hadn't been. "There's no reason why you should, really," Shelley continued. "I'm glad none of you have a lingering interest in the house, except of course," and here she smiled at Craig, "as the former dwelling of a rock star. Angus tells me you're all planning on going back to the lighthouse, to play Thirteen Ghost Stories, to beat the negative energy that's in residence at its own game. I have to admit there's logic in that." Eyeing me, she added, "An *impressive* logic. Even so, I was concerned, and that's why I came tonight, to see how people felt about this. I walk in and… you're all hugging. That's good, very good. Who's going back?"

"Me!"

"We are."

"All of us I think."

The answers came thick and fast.

"And you're all going with the intention of helping each other as well as yourselves?" Shelley asked. "Ally Dunn in particular?"

"Aye."

"Yes."

"Of course."

Again, there was a barrage of answers.

"Because it's real what you're up against," she warned. "But it's not invincible. There are some in this world that will have you think otherwise, but they'd be trying to frighten you. The dark is not as strong as the light. Light has the upper hand."

There were several nods of agreement.

She gestured to me, putting my nerves on edge a little. I

agreed with all she'd said so far, but what was she intending to say about me? Keeping my gaze steady, I bit on my lip as she spoke. "Leading you all is this young woman. I want you to listen to her, to do as she says, because she's the real deal, she knows what she's talking about."

Whilst I gazed at her in wonder, she added, "If you don't mind, everyone, I'd like to have a private word with Ness and then I'll be on my way. Good luck to you all."

"Why can't you come?" Isabel's father seemed as awestruck by her presence as I was.

"Because my place is at Balskeyne," she explained. "I can't stay away for too long. And also because," she inclined her head towards me, "Ness is more than capable."

As she approached me, I was battling confusion. Yesterday she'd said one thing and now – in Dunvegan's community hall – she was saying quite another.

Before I could question her about this, she leant into me, her voice low, conspiratorial, "Ever heard of reverse psychology?"

"Reverse…? I'm not sure I know what you mean."

"If someone says you can't do something, it only serves to make you want to do it more. Some people anyway. There are those that will take heed of what you say, will see it as a get out clause, seize the opportunity and run."

"So it was a test?" I said, slightly annoyed.

"Which you passed with flying colours."

"You really are blunt."

"I see no harm in that. Not in these circumstances."

My annoyance faded. "Fair point."

All around us, people were huddled together in small

groups, although a few kept glancing over to where I stood with Shelley, especially Angus, who looked as if he was going to burst with curiosity. Some were pulling their coats on, or tightening scarves, and I realised something: we couldn't delay any longer; we had to go tonight, whilst morale was high. If we put it off, perhaps waited until the next day, it would give fear a chance to creep back in, to find the cracks in these people, and strangle their hearts and minds.

"That's right," Shelley said, "seize the moment. Tonight is best."

I stared at her. "Intuition, right?"

"If I'm honest with you, Ness, it doesn't take a genius to work out the way your thoughts are running. I can read your intentions well enough in your eyes, and by the expression on your face. But listen, I've more information for you that may prove vital. The person who used to come and visit Cameron, he was, as I thought, and as you suspected, a devotee of Isaac Leonard, a disciple if you like."

I inhaled. "How do you know?"

"Because Donder McKendrick told me."

"Donder? I've heard of him before."

"He was the lighthouse keeper before Cameron, he's now a taxi driver, lives close to me, on the banks of Loch Ness. He's an old guy but he's still working. I don't think he'll ever stop. After the isolation of working at Minch Point, he's gone the other way; loves the company of people. In many ways, although he doesn't acknowledge it, not consciously anyway, he's an overseer too, or at least he was. He kept balance at the lighthouse, kept the darkness at bay, in a literal sense and just by being who he was, a good man, a kind man, always with the welfare of others at

THIRTEEN

the heart of everything he did. You see, Minch Point, it's not too dissimilar to Balskeyne—"

"It has the same dimensions," I blurted out, "as Balskeyne I mean, those that were needed for the spell."

"Does it?" She asked the question, but there was no surprise in it. "I've not been so I wouldn't know, but it fits with what I'm about to tell you. The land that Minch Point is built on is drenched in blood too. The ship that was wrecked there, in 1909, just after the lighthouse was built, claimed the lives of so many innocents, just as the fire in the church did at Balskeyne, remember?"

I nodded.

"Sometimes, when there's death on that scale, when there's so many emotions involved, all of them steeped in fear, it forms an imprint, an attraction. It serves to *alert* energies that are similar. When Donder handed over the lighthouse to Cameron, he thought him a fine and upstanding man; those are the words he used. He'd come from Barra with his family, no stranger to peace and quiet, not one to be unsettled by it, to be driven mad. On the contrary, he seemed keen to perform his duties; Donder sensed nothing wrong with him at all. Sometime later, he gave a lift to someone who was staying at Balskeyne; he wanted to go all the way to the lighthouse, to speak to the man who runs it. On the way there, he told Donder the purpose of his visit. He had a proposal for the keeper, that's what he said. What that proposal was, he didn't elaborate, and Donder was too polite to ask. But Donder took him several times to the lighthouse after that, over a period of weeks, that's how long he must have stayed at Balskeyne, and on one of those occasions, Cameron came to the car, where Donder would wait to take the man home again, to see his visitor off. He told me he was shocked to see the change in him, he was surly, gruff, barely even acknowledged Donder. In contrast, every time Cameron looked at his visitor, he seemed dazzled, as if he were staring into the face of a God. The fares to the lighthouse eventually ceased and Donder was glad. He never liked his passenger, or his enigmatic conversations. One thing he did though, he asked the man his full name – before that he only knew his forename – and when I spoke to him this morning, he managed to recall it without hesitation: Jonathan Grey. I did some more phoning, some more digging, as there are those in my circles that might know such a name."

"And?"

"And someone did: a woman who lives in the south, close to where you live, in Hastings. She's a talented psychic, so is her daughter, Jessica." She paused. "She explained that Grey was an Occultist, one known to have rented a house on Skye, which is probably why the taxi rides finally came to an end. Donder, knowing Skye so well, as well as everyone on the west coast, knew exactly where it was that he'd stayed. He'd also heard what happened to Moira. When we were discussing it, it became clear that all three houses formed a triangle, with Grey's at the pinnacle."

"A triangle?"

"That's right, for added occult measure. Like the number thirteen, a triangle has significance too, it represents a merging of the spiritual and earthly realms."

"Another reason why Moira was perhaps affected?"

Shelley agreed. "She was implicated without even knowing it."

"Combine that with LSD…"

"And it doesn't bear thinking about."

"I wonder if he was her supplier?"

"Grey?" Shelley questioned. "You'd have to work it out, and see if the dates tally, but you can find a peddler of drugs anywhere in the world, in places even more remote than this. I was in Bornco once, deep in the jungle… " She paused. "But that's a story for another time. Concerning Grey's house, I took a detour there this evening, there's a *For Sale* sign outside it, I don't know how long it's been up for sale, or indeed how long he stayed on Skye, but the sign is as decrepit as the house itself, creaking on its hinges as the wind blows around it. As for its aura, even the most hardened cynic would be able to sense something wrong. I doubt anyone will ever buy it. In fact, I know they won't."

"You know? How?"

"Because on my way back to Balskeyne, I shall visit the house again and set fire to it, thereby breaking the chain. It will help in your endeavour. It will help a lot."

My eyes widened as my mouth dropped. "But what if you get caught?" I whispered. "There's already been a fire at Balskeyne, what if people put two and two together?"

She gestured around her. "These people? You really think they'd turn me in?"

"Erm… no." Of course they wouldn't, not given the circumstances, they'd close the net. As for the people who owned the house, perhaps in some way they'd be glad too. What had been tainted, would be cleansed, and the land more valuable because of it. "Thank you," I added.

"Believe me, the pleasure is all mine."

I thought back to the supposed kitchen fire at Balskeyne. "Is that the fate of the lighthouse too? If all else fails, I burn it to the ground."

"You won't fail, you know what you're up against. As I've said before, this conjuring needs to be subdued, and a guardian set in place."

"Angus. He'll be in place soon."

"A good choice. He's a good lad. Fond of you it seems."

"He's twenty-three!"

"And you're a young head on old shoulders, I get it."

"What happened to Jonathan Grey? Did your contact know? Is he still at large?"

"No. He did leave here at some point, ending up in Brighton. And there he was discovered, in the early eighties, in a grimy little bedsit with his head blown off."

"He was murdered?"

"Like his master, he'd committed suicide. You can't get that close to darkness and remain sane."

I swallowed, digesting this before revealing what else I knew. "The Camerons are all dead too, Mr Cameron shot his wife and kids and then himself. That was in '79."

"It doesn't surprise me."

"So much death," I mutter, swallowing again.

"In the Camerons' case, it might help to think of it as release."

It was certainly a more preferable angle. "And you're certain about this, are you? That Grey ensnared Cameron somehow, that maybe he plied him with promises of magnificent riches if he helped him with his work, with his spell. It does seem to fit, but—"

"I'm certain," she replied. "Call it intuition."

As she smiled so did I, but it was with difficulty, the gravitas of what she'd said – *You can't get that close to darkness and remain sane* – weighed heavily.

Shelley laid her hand on my arm. "You *are* the person for the job."

"Am I?" My voice was nothing but a whisper.

"Yes. But for reasons that I wish weren't so."

I frowned, puzzled by her words, but fearing to ask – and she knew it. Her expression softened as she took pity on me. In many ways she reminded me of Eilidh: such a good person at heart. "All you really need in this situation is love. There's plenty of that here."

She was right, there was.

"And forgiveness," she added. "Forgiveness is good too. If you can, that is…"

Chapter Twenty-One

SHELLEY went her way and the rest of us went ours. I was right: morale was high, everybody piled into their respective cars, not to go to the lighthouse, not initially, but to various houses to collect the equipment that we'd need for the night – torches, plenty of them, candles and tea-lights, thick jumpers and jackets, lots of them too, and bin bags for clearing the rubbish. Everywhere in the lighthouse there were glass bottles and other items that could be used as weapons; we needed them gone, for the space to be as clear as possible. The plan was that whilst Angus and I went up to Caitir's room, with the kids that were willing to accompany us, the parents would remain downstairs, making sure candles stayed lit and continuing the clean-up operation, making a dent in it, a difference.

Eilidh held my hands before being dropped home by one of the parents. "I'm too old for this," she said, somewhat regretfully. "You need strong, young folk, I don't want to be a hindrance." I remonstrated, but she was insistent. "I'll be doing my part from here, don't you worry. I'm going to sit by the fireside and imagine every one of you bathed in light, and plenty of it. And I won't stop, not until you've all returned."

THIRTEEN

Together with Angus and me in his car, there was Mr and Mrs Ludmore and their son Craig, our mood almost buoyant. There's satisfaction in taking action, rather than sitting and waiting for the next attack, we all felt that. It was right what we were doing. It empowered us. I'd even secured Shelley's blessing. In some ways I wished too that she'd been able to come with us. She was such a wise woman, so brave, but I understood where her energies were needed and instead prayed for her safe return via Grey's house.

The drive time whizzed by with no traffic encountered en route, just a steady stream of cars – a convoy – our headlights a blazing trail of defiance.

Parking close to our usual spot, I climbed out of the car, noticing drizzle in the air and a heavy mist starting to swirl.

"The weather's on the change," remarked Angus.

"Let it rain," I said. "Rain is cleansing."

"That's one way of looking at it," Mrs Ludmore commented. "A nice way."

"If that's so," her son quipped, "Skye has to be the cleanest island in the world."

"Not quite," I said, smiling at him. "But soon it will be."

"Good," he answered, serious again. "Because I want things to go back to the way they were, you know with Ally, with all of us."

"They will," Angus ruffled Craig's hair. "Believe it."

That also made me smile, Angus buying into what I'd said, what Shelley had said too. Love. Belief. Forgiveness. I had two in the bag at least.

We convened with the others on the gravel path that led to the lighthouse, our various torches shining, bringing light to where light had been absent for so long.

Looking around I noticed one of our number missing.

"Where's Grant?" I asked.

The silence seemed guilt-ridden for a moment, and then Lainey's mother spoke up. "His parents, they changed their minds, they didn't want him to come."

"Cowards," someone mumbled, but I disagreed.

"If they thought their child might be vulnerable in some way then they're far from that. But those who have come, thank you, thank you so much."

Again there was silence, followed by another comment on the weather.

"Shouldn't be surprised if the rain turns to snow soon, it's so cold."

"Aye, right time of year for it, and if it does, it'll last 'til Christmas and beyond."

I marvelled at that. A white Christmas on Skye, that'd be something to see.

Another parent stamped his feet. It was Ben. "Tell you what, wish I'd bought a flask of whisky too, for medicinal purposes you understand."

Everyone laughed before Mr Ludmore replied, "Let's deal with this first, then there'll be all the time in the world to celebrate."

I hoped so: that life could go back to how it was for these people, as Craig, and as all of them so desperately wanted, with its ups and downs for sure, but nothing extreme, nothing to tip it into the abyss. A steady life, *normality* – it was a gift we often took for granted.

As we made our way to the house, I looked up at the tower, the top of which was lost in cloud, as though a shroud had been thrown over it – a natural occurrence, but

I knew it to be something else too: a mockery, a challenge even. I tore my gaze away.

At the door, we waited; every one of us steeling ourselves for what lay beyond. I hoped that by assigning the parents practical tasks, it would keep their hands and minds occupied downstairs, allowing me to address more spiritual matters upstairs without interference. Again, I looked upwards, this time at the window of the bedroom that Caitir had once occupied. Poor, terrified Caitir. What easy prey her father had been, and what terrible consequences it had had for them all.

That's what we refused to be: prey. Not anymore.

"Are you ready?" I said, turning to those gathered beside me.

The response, as ever, was positive.

"Remember what I said earlier, everyone has weaknesses, God knows I do, but we put them aside, we don't take them in there with us. We're here, we're together and we're strong. We can do this. We can restore balance, at the lighthouse and in our lives. We're doing this for Ally and for Moira, for all those who lost their lives here when that ship floundered on the rocks below, and for the Camerons too, who were as much victims as anyone else, especially their children, Caitir and Niall. We're doing it for every one of us."

"When good men do nothing," Angus muttered.

"Sorry?" Diane questioned. "Did you say something?"

"Och, it's just a saying," Angus told her, "a famous one. *The only thing necessary for the triumph of evil is for good men to do nothing.*"

"Oh," Diane said, but unless I was mistaken her eyes seemed to mist, as if she found such a quote incredibly touching. I know I did.

"Amen," said Ben and then began to clap. Slowly the others joined in and I did too. Who were we clapping? Ourselves, I suppose, and why not? Why shouldn't we give ourselves the biggest round of applause ever? These people deserved it.

Bolstered further, we pushed the door open and, single file, trooped inside.

"Keep your torches switched on and light as many tea-lights as possible. At no point let the lights go out completely, that's imperative."

I apologised about the rubbish clearing. "I know it seems a menial task, but it isn't, it heralds change. This is no longer a dumping ground where things that are rotten can thrive. It will soon become a guesthouse, and there are plans for more buildings to be added, so the whole feel of it, the energy, will become more dynamic. It'll attract people, not those looking for cheap thrills, sorry kids, I don't mean any disrespect by that, but it's true. Those who come here in future will be those in search of beauty, who want to immerse themselves in God's Own Country as Angus once called it, and, of course, to enjoy his very own brand of hospitality, which I can highly recommend."

"Aye," Angus said amidst more laughter, "there'll be a roaring log fire, and a good choice of whisky to hand."

"That's right," I said, "keep the home fires burning. Always."

While everyone made themselves busy, Angus, five teenagers instead of six – Craig, Amy, Isabel, Denny and Lainey – and I went upstairs. A total of seven. A good number, I decided, the number of perfection. Perhaps it was providence Grant hadn't come. We all carried torches, back-up torches and had a bagful of tea-lights between us, some of which, even now were being burned downstairs, each tiny flame a protest.

Understandably, the parents were nervous at letting their offspring out of their sight, but at least they weren't far away. I'd already agreed with them to only come running if they heard me shouting the word 'help'. Otherwise, they were to expect some noise, some banging, and crashing, as the conjuring railed against its suppression.

Climbing higher, I was assaulted with a vision – Caitir and Niall and their terrible demise. I expected the assault, but for the subjects to be strangers, not them. It shook me, but quickly I sideswiped the image. Later I'd spend time with their memory, imagining sweet smiles on their faces, their childish wonder at simple things: a favourite meal perhaps, or a walk in the open air. I wasn't like this thing; I wouldn't dwell on the negative.

We reached Caitir's room, it wasn't an attack this time, but I could see her clearly. She was lying on the bed, or at least the residue of her. She was reading a book, trying to lose herself in a story, anything to take her mind off the increasing madness she was being subjected to in her own home. Her parents were arguing below, their voices so loud she could hear every word. In subsequent months, her mother would no longer argue, she'd be afraid to – and the silence that ensued, especially at night, was far worse, because in it you could hear other things: whispers, a sudden peal of laughter, a low scream, none of it from the people inside. Finally, the shade that was Caitir threw the book across the room – frustrated, frightened, and angry too – you couldn't help but be angry here, you fed on it as much as it fed on you. Such a young child and so bewildered, resident in a home that had once been ordinary, but was now filled wall to wall with terror. As for Niall, he barely spoke, barely left his room and no one cared, no one gave a damn.

"Ness, are you okay?"

Angus broke the connection. What I'd seen had taken mere seconds, but the depth of emotion would leave a permanent scar. Her fear and her loneliness, I understood it. There were other children in the room, however, *living* children, I mustn't let the dead consume me. I could help them whereas I couldn't help Caitir. I had to fill my mind with practical tasks too, lest it start to wander again…

"Clear the room," I instructed. "You've each got a bin bag, fill it to the brim."

Torchlight bouncing haphazardly off the walls, we set about our first task. We'd thought to pack latex gloves courtesy of Diane, who worked on reception at a doctor's surgery and had a bundle in her house already. "You never know when they might come in handy," she'd said enigmatically. They were certainly coming in handy now. I don't suppose anyone in the house actually wanted to touch anything that was here, covered as it was in a layer of filth, but there was glass too, some of it broken, and glass could cut.

Whilst we were working diligently, it was Denny who screamed.

"What is it?" I said, straightening up. "What's the matter?"

"Oh nothing." He seemed embarrassed by his actions. "A rat or something."

"A rat?" Lainey sneered. "You sissy."

"It was a big rat!" he retaliated.

THIRTEEN

"Where's it gone?" asked Craig.

"I hate rats!" declared Isabel.

"Hey, hey, hey," Angus calmed them down. "Think of it as a giant mouse, and mice are cute, aren't they?"

"Well, yeah," Isabel admitted.

"And it's gone now, more scared of us than we are of it."

"Just like the other thing will be," Craig said boldly.

"That's right," I said, encouraging that boldness.

When the room was cleared, I took something else out of the carrier bag we'd brought – salt – and made a large circle with it.

"That's where you sit," I told the group, "inside the circle."

"Because in ritual magic, salt forms a protective circle, one in which summoned energy cannot encroach."

It was Amy who'd recited those words – almost exactly as I'd said them in the hall.

I smiled at the spiritualist in the making. "Whatever happens," I added, "stay inside the circle. In it you'll be safe. If you'd like to take your seats…"

"What about you, Miss, are you sitting in the circle too?"

His somewhat schoolboy address amused me. "Yes, Craig, and so is Angus."

"Good job it's a big salt ring you've drawn then," Angus said, smiling too.

Once seated with our legs crossed in front of us, I suggested we place our torches on the ground. I had one, but the kids and Angus had two, one for each story they were going to tell – and that we hold hands. "Feel the energy that exists between us," I instructed further, "how powerful we are when we stand together. We need to draw on that power, on the positive in each of us, *feed* on it, as this thing has fed on us. You know what, you can feast as much as you like, fill your boots, as long as it's the good stuff. If any negative thoughts creep in, shut the door on them and turn the key."

"It's like witchcraft," giggled Isabel, a little nervously.

"If it is, it's the white variety," I answered. "Remember what I said about the light too, to keep it ever present in your mind, as though it's surrounding us in a bubble."

"And the torches?" asked Amy, more serious than Isabel.

"We turn them off, all except one. Angus, you said you'd tell your ghost story first, so keep yours on. Next up is Craig, then Amy, and so on, remember the rota?"

All nodded.

"When it comes to your turn, switch the first of your torches on, switch the second on when you tell your second story. If either torch should fail, light a tea-light, and if that blows out, light another and another, keep going. There's no shortage, we've plenty with us. That's how we play the game this time, in reverse, instead of lights going off, we keep them coming on. At the end, when they're all fully ablaze, we blast this thing into oblivion."

As torches were turned off, the darkness crept closer, I could hear several sharp intakes of breath, and the hands that were holding mine, tightened their grip.

"Are you ready?"

"We're ready," everyone replied in chorus.

"Then let's begin."

Chapter Twenty-Two

"IT was a wild and stormy night…"

Angus's opening line – the same that he'd used with me when we'd first visited the lighthouse – drew giggles from several of us, including me. That was good, that was what was intended. Laughter was the best kind of energy. To his credit, he didn't falter, but carried on. We'd agreed a maximum of five minutes per story, shorter if possible and I was to oversee, making sure that no one ran over their allotted time, encouraging the next person, watching for subtle changes in behaviour, and dealing with them. We'd also agreed to make each ghost story end on a high note. 'They don't need to be dark, or frightening, they can be heart-warming instead, a spirit is united with the light for example, or gets a message across that he or she hadn't been able to do in life. They might help to solve a mystery. Use your imagination, but use it for the good.' After all, the last thing I wanted was fear to get a stronghold, not when we'd only just managed to kick it to the curb.

Angus's story continued, concerning the ghost of a highwayman parted from his head during an execution, but managing to find it at last, although preferring to carry it under his arm rather than stick it on his neck – the view was better apparently! It was a good story, a classic story – one that made us all smile because of its familiarity.

Craig was next, his story containing a small amount of gore and more sci-fi than horror, with Artificial Intelligence at its heart, but we could forgive him that. It was thrilling in parts, amusing in others, making us wince only slightly. As soon as he'd uttered the last sentence, he switched his torch on too, chasing away more of the darkness.

Amy's story erred towards the sentimental, centring round a lost child reunited with his mother. As soon as she finished, she switched her torch on – a third light joining the rest.

Isabel told the fourth, Denny the fifth – it was all going so well, and then Lainey started. It was nothing to do with the tale she told, which was harmless enough – it was the energy here, besides ours, fighting back, making her torchlight flicker.

"Damn," she muttered. "I put new batteries in as well."

"Let's just carry on," I said. "Angus, it's your turn again. Limit it to three minutes I think."

He eyed me warily. "Is that necessary?"

"It is."

"Ah, that's a shame, it's a belter this one, but I'll do as you say."

It was another humorous story – this time about the ghost of a cheeky monkey. He had us all in stitches by the end of it, although my laughter was forced. It had grown so much colder in here, the temperature dropping several degrees – had no one else noticed?

When Craig had finished his turn, he picked up the second of his torches and switched that on. It refused to work at all.

"Light a candle," I instructed.

Immediately obeying, he leant across to a selection of tea-lights closest to him, grabbed one of several boxes of matches and lit the flame. It took a few attempts, and a fair bit of swearing as he burnt his fingers, but eventually the candle burst into life, and was a wonderful sight to see – small but perfectly formed. I willed it to stay put, to do its job.

Amy picked up the second of her torches, ready to start her tale, and as she did, she screamed. "Look! There's a spider! Just outside the circle. Oh my God, it's huge! It's close, really close. I can't sit here with that thing next to me."

I looked to where she was pointing and could see nothing but empty space. "Amy, there's no spider."

"There is! There is!"

I sensed panic on the rise, not just in her, but in some of the others too. If I didn't do something, if the spider she thought she was seeing edged closer, she'd bolt, and the others would follow suit. I sighed with exasperation, couldn't help it. A spider – that's all this entity had to do, conjure a spider and the circle would be broken. It was so simple, yet so damned effective; some might even call it genius.

"Amy, look at me. Amy, please. Take your eyes off what you think you can see and look *only* at me."

"I… I…" Despite the preternatural cold, I'd bet she was sweating.

"AMY!" I shouted this time. "Look at me! Every one of you do the same. There is no spider. This thing that we're dealing with, that we're trying to beat, it plays havoc with your imagination, you know that, I've told you that. It'll worm its way into your psyche and it'll dig out your fears, and your phobias, all the stuff that makes you question yourself. Slam the door on it, Amy. Bolt it in place. You have to lock away your fears, just for tonight. There's no way we can break the circle, not until all the lights are shining."

"Is it scared too, Miss?" Craig asked. "Because it knows that we're winning?"

His words were such a relief. "Yes, Craig, it's scared too, very scared. I'm so glad you understand that. We've got Amy's story to go, then Isabel's, Denny's and Lainey's. It's not long now 'til we blast this sucker to kingdom come."

Clearly he approved of my use of language. Turning to Amy, he said, "Listen to her. There's no spider. Get on with your story."

Amy was still rigid, but she relaxed slightly as she moved her gaze from the corner to the centre of the circle again. "It's gone," she said. "It must have crawled off somewhere."

"Amy," Angus echoed, "listen to Ness. It was never there."

"But what if it returns?"

"Then… I don't know, I'll try and catch it, although what I'll be grasping at is thin air. Honestly, don't give it another thought. Tell your story, we all want to hear it."

She gave a timid laugh. "It doesn't involve spiders."

"Just as well," Angus said, smiling back at her.

She not only obeyed, she did incredibly well under the circumstances, her voice shaking only slightly here and there as her eyes left mine and roamed elsewhere. When she did this, I had to interrupt. "Look at me, Amy, only me."

Finishing, she picked up the second torch – it came on, but hers, like Lainey's was flickering, growing weaker as she fiddled with it.

"You know what to do," I said. "If it goes out, you light a candle."

She swallowed audibly. "I keep thinking something's crawling on my back," she said, "I know there isn't, but…"

"There really isn't," I said. "We cleared this room, remember? There were no spiders then and there are none now."

She nodded, but her breathing was heavier too.

"Isabel…" I prompted. "It's your second turn."

"I'm not scared of spiders," she answered.

"Let's not talk about spiders."

"But I don't like rats, or snakes. There won't be any snakes manifesting, will there?"

"Not if you close a door on that fear."

"My story is about monsters though," she continued, "not scary monsters, they're cute actually. They turn out to be the good guys in the end. I based it on *Beauty and the Beast*. This situation, and you, it sort of inspired it."

As flattered as I was, this was no fairy-tale.

"Denny," she said suddenly, "will you stop doing that, shining your light in my eyes?"

"What?" Denny sounded surprised. "I wasn't. I'm pointing it straight ahead."

"No you weren't, you were shining it at me, blinding me. Turn it away."

"You don't know what you're talking about," Denny continued to object. "I'm not!"

"Denny—"

"Stop!" I commanded. "No arguing. That's one of our rules, isn't it? We keep calm, we even have a bit of fun, and we shine the lights."

"Some fun this is," whispered one of them, Lainey I think, immediately inciting anger. *How dare she say that! Who does she think she is? Stupid fucking bitch!*

The force of my thoughts shocked me. They made me want to reach out and grab Lainey by the throat, shake her until she was as limp as a rag doll, tear her limbs apart.

"Light another candle," I said, a desperation in my voice that Angus responded to straightway.

"Light a few of them," he added.

We needed the light and I needed to keep calm, close a door on my weakness too – my anger. But it's not easy; it's not bloody easy… "Isabel, please, just tell your story."

She did and it was a good one, as light as I'd hoped, as funny as I'd wished for. Her torch also worked perfectly, and because of that we seemed to settle again.

"Breathe, kids," I reminded them. "Slowly and deeply."

"It's impossible to panic when you breathe like that," Isabel piped up.

"That's the intention," Angus answered for me.

"Denny, yours is the eleventh story," I said. "Almost there. We're almost there."

Denny began his story but he kept faltering… his gaze constantly drawn to another corner of the room, the one behind me. I wanted to look round, to try and see what had captured his attention, but I refrained. If I did, I'd give it validation, and so I kept gently prompting him instead. "Just another minute or so, Denny, and then it's over."

"I… I… Sorry, I can't. I keep forgetting the words."

"Then wrap it up," I suggested. "Any way will do. Give

it some kind of ending."

"It's just he keeps laughing at me, that's all."

"No one's laughing at you, Denny."

"There is, it's that man in the corner. He… he… keeps looking at me and laughing."

Denny was a sweet kid, a *brave* kid – he was here after all, when others wouldn't come near – but he was also very overweight with a mop of dark hair that was even more unruly than Angus's. The man he insisted was laughing at him, I think I knew where that was coming from – people *did* laugh at him, his friends, his friends mates, maybe even total strangers. They'd look and they'd laugh at the fat kid. And it hurt. It really hurt. And this thing that was with us, it knew how much its laughter also hurt the boy.

"It's just the seven of us in this room, Denny, that's all."

Denny paused, his expression turning slightly sour. "He's laughing at you too, Miss."

"Then let him," I replied. "I'll tell you what, why don't we laugh along with him, let him know that we find him just as funny."

That horrified Denny. "No, no, please don't do that, it'll make him angry." He hung his head in fear and sadness. "Let's just… ignore him. I can do that, honestly I can."

"He isn't there," I repeated, glancing at Angus who couldn't resist turning his head to see what had transfixed Denny. Having done so, he looked at me and gave a slight shake of the head. A manifestation unique to Denny, as the spider had been for Amy, I only hoped it would fade soon. "Denny, bring the story to an end, then turn on your torch."

He managed to do as I asked, but I could tell he was

struggling. His torch came on, but the light was weak. "Can I light a candle too, Miss?" There was a quiver in his voice.

"Light as many as you want." I was glad to give him something else to focus on.

There was silence again, a few sounds from downstairs managed to pervade, but they sounded so far away, as if at the end of a long, long tunnel. It was isolated on this part of the island, but in this room I felt more isolated still. We all did I think, cut off from the rest of the world, from reality even – playing a game that had serious consequences.

The time for the twelfth story had come – Lainey's second turn. Not all but some torches at least, shone around us, the light confined to the circle that we were sitting in. The candles glowed too, but some had already gone out. No matter, Denny was continuing to light the ones he could, pushing those that remained lit away from him, making room for more. There was an obsessive quality to his behaviour, and the others, plus Angus, noticed. The game had to come to a head soon – one way or another.

"Lainey, can you please take your turn?"

The girl tore her gaze from Denny to stare at me. Was I mistaken or had her expression changed? There wasn't fear in it, or worry, not any more. She looked... *amused*.

"Lainey, are you okay?"

"I'm fine," she insisted.

"Keep your story short, two or three minutes is fine, then Angus can finish the game. The light is so much stronger than the dark, and we are so much stronger if we work together. And that's what we're doing; we've got each other's backs. I'm proud of you, Lainey, I'm so damned proud. I'm proud of all of you. What a great team we are."

Her expression was beginning to return to normal, just as another torch went out.

"I'm scared." It was Amy, her eyes darting furiously around again.

"I know you are–" I began, but Angus interrupted me.

"Amy, Lainey, all of you, we fight this thing or it wins. We've come so far, do you really want to give up now?"

"Lainey, come on," urged Craig.

"Okay, okay," she responded, no hint of amusement in her voice at least, she sounded defiant instead – whether that was in our favour or not, I couldn't tell.

Taking a deep breath, looking at each of us in turn, her gaze finally came to rest on me. In the glare of the torchlight, with the darkness at her back, she *had* altered. She seemed bigger than she was before, and she had a yellowish cast to her eyes. Was it because of the flames spluttering at her feet? Not a cheerful yellow, it was dirty instead…

As she opened her mouth, I braced myself.

"Once upon a time there was a girl, a lonely girl, a girl who was misunderstood."

Don't rise to it, I told myself. *This may have nothing to do with you.*

"She had hair as dark as mine, and lived in a big house with her mummy and daddy, and her brothers and sisters."

The skin on the back of my neck began to tingle.

"Her bedroom was tiny, the smallest of all the bedrooms, but in it she would hide from the world. And not just the world, but those who were from other worlds too."

Should I interrupt? I couldn't, the twelfth story had to be told. It would be all right if I just didn't take the bait.

"One of those that she hid from was her twin, her *dead*

twin. Even though the twin was nice to her, *needed* her, this girl wasn't nice back, she was mean to her poor dead twin, nasty, and she was that way because she'd learnt to be. Her mother had taught her well."

I couldn't do it, just sit there and listen, I tried, but words tumbled out of my mouth. "Lainey, if you don't feel well, if something's wrong—"

"Let me speak!" she hissed and not only me, all of us flinched. Reminding myself that this was someone's child, not something terrible, I tried again to reach her.

"Lainey—"

"Oh this mother of hers, she taught her hatred, anger and fear, and all of this the girl practised on her twin, someone who'd suffered enough, who was dead for Christ's sake! She'd killed her in the womb; sucked the life from her. That's why her mother felt the way she did, that's the true reason. Her mother knew the twin that lived was evil."

"STOP IT!" I shouted. "STOP IT NOW, LAINEY!"

As Angus looked at me in both shock and bewilderment, as the teenagers looked at me in that way too, Lainey began to snarl. "The twin that lived then decided to hurt her family more, to bring great shame on them and herself. She hurt her twin too, the twin who'd always tried to help her, to comfort her, the twin who'd forgiven her for the life that she'd stolen. But the living twin couldn't forgive, her soul was black, and her heart was twisted."

"Lainey…" My voice seemed to have lost its strength as sobs threatened to choke me.

"Go on, Ness, tell them what you did, to your twin, to your family, and to yourself. Tell them about the madness that runs thick in your veins…"

THIRTEEN

"I'm not mad," I denied as the lights flickered, but again my voice was weak.

"The psychiatrists said you were."

"I'd been *driven* mad," I countered, so many shocked pairs of eyes on me, "but it was only temporarily. I swear I'm *not* mad."

"You are," Lainey insisted, "and yet here we sit, listening to you." She shrugged. "Perhaps we're mad too."

"Ness… Lainey…" Angus didn't know which one of us to address first.

"Tell us what you did," Lainey took no notice of him at all, her gaze, that filthy yellow gaze, fixed solely on me, "when you were thirteen."

"No," my voice was a mere whisper, "I can't." I was drenched in shame all over again. Why couldn't I close the door on what had happened, why had I never been able to do that? How ironic, that of all of us here, I was the weakest link. "We need to end this game."

"We can't," Lainey replied, "not until the thirteenth ghost story's been told. And it's your turn, Ness. It's your story that completes the game."

Chapter Twenty-Three

1975

HAPPY thirteenth birthday!

The card I held in my hand, the cheery greeting printed in large red letters against a backdrop of a girl on a scooter, felt flimsy. The words, the girl, equally as cheery, seemed to mock me. Happy was the very opposite of what I was feeling as I sat at the table in our dining room, my brothers and sisters around me, chatting with each other, but rarely with me – even though this was all supposedly in my honour. Dad was trying at least. At the head of the table, he smiled in my direction, even raised his eyebrows a couple of times as if issuing some sort of apology. As for Mum, she was in the kitchen – spending as much time as possible in there, an avoidance tactic. I knew it, and so did everyone else.

Since the miscarriage last year she'd been even more distant with me. Whenever I did catch her glancing my way, the look in her eyes was almost more than I could bear. I'd stopped looking lately, stopped seeking any kind of acceptance. I wasn't as young, as naive, or as hopeful as I used to be, I knew when I was on a highway to nowhere.

THIRTEEN

As I sat there, toying with my birthday meal – hamburger and chips, my favourite, or at least it used to be, nothing seemed to taste good lately – I furtively glanced around the room. It wasn't just my birthday, it was hers too – my twin's. She hadn't shown herself since this morning, when she'd dragged me from sleep, excited about the day ahead.

We're thirteen! We're thirteen!

She kept saying it, over and over again, the shape of her more substantial than it had ever been. Her hair, her clothes, the heart shape of her face, it was all mine, but my eyes, I swear they were emptier than hers.

I'd had to go to school – no day off for the birthday girl, not if my mother could help it. The teacher had made a bit of fuss over me, got the other kids to sing *Happy Birthday,* but few, if any, had done so with enthusiasm. I wanted them to stop. I wanted to get to my feet and yell at them to shut up. So what if it *was* my birthday? But I sat there and endured it, my hands clasped under my desk, my nails digging deep into the palm of my hands.

And then the bell had rung and I walked home alone, to this: a birthday tea, a family gathering, the only presents given to me 'serviceable' ones: a flannelette nightdress to replace my old one, socks, a winter scarf, and vests. Nothing frivolous, nothing fun, no make-up, not even a new book – how I'd wished for another Brontë book, *Wuthering Heights* this time. Perhaps they'd have it in the library, I could always borrow it from there.

Having finished their meal, two of my sisters started complaining.

"Where's Mum? Me and Suzy want to go out tonight, we can't hang around for long."

"And I've got homework," said Paul, "I need to get on with it really."

They were itching to leave the dining table. Dad too, he kept glancing at his watch and then at the TV – clearly worried about missing something, the news probably.

"Love," he called through to the kitchen. "How long will you be?"

"Not long," came the irritated reply. "Just give me a minute, will you?"

To do what, I thought? Brace yourself to face me again, your demon daughter.

Eventually she left the kitchen and entered the room, a cake in her hands, one that, to my amazement, looked homemade. I'd *never* had a homemade cake before.

"Get the lights!" my father said, nodding at Ollie. "Quick!"

In the darkness, the cake, with its white icing and jammy middle was remarkably pretty, with not just one or two candles, but thirteen, blazing merrily away.

A voice interrupted my wonder. *Ness, look at our cake!*

It's my cake. Straightaway, I shot the thought back. *Just mine!*

But Ness, it's our birthday, both of us.

That cake is mine!

As the second chorus of *Happy Birthday* began, I tried to ignore just how mean I was being, didn't truly understand the reason why – my moods had been up and down a lot lately, more down than up if I'm honest. Maybe it was the number of candles that did it. As far as I could remember there'd only ever been two or three in the past, and not just on my cake, but all my siblings' cakes. 'Candles are an unnecessary expense,' Mum would say, if someone happened to complain. 'We're not made of money.' But today I'd got the correct number *and* a cake she'd baked herself, not something shop bought. She'd made an effort – a *huge* effort – and my eyes watered to see it. Perhaps I wasn't so hardened after all; perhaps I did care. And wonder of wonders, perhaps she did as well.

As the cake was set before me, I leant forward to blow the candles out.

Let's blow them out together.

Still my twin was insisting. Forgetting myself, I turned my head to the side and glared at her. *No!*

"Ness," my mother's voice contained its usual curtness. "Will you hurry up? I don't want wax dripping all over that cake."

"Sorry," I muttered, chancing a smile at her. She didn't return the gesture.

Drawing in another deep breath, I warned my twin again. *Just stay back.*

Maybe it was this way even when you had a living twin. Sometimes, just sometimes, you wanted your own space, a bit of individuality, and a fuss made of you and you alone.

As I went to exhale, she beat me to it – the candles spluttered for a moment, as if on my side, as if protesting, but finally giving in. I stood there, staring at the extinguished candles, at the smoke trails, stunned. How was she able to do that? She'd already used a fair amount of energy this morning, materialising to such an extent. She'd need time to recharge before interacting on this scale, a day or two, a week – not mere hours.

Something inside me – brittle for so long – snapped. Without thinking of the consequences, I lunged forward, one hand connecting with the cake and swiping it off the table, knocking it flying across the room, all the while screaming in my head, *NO! NO! NO!*

It wasn't just in my head I realised, I was screaming out loud too, and not just those words but far more. "You're always here, you're always interfering. I don't want you anymore, don't you realise? I want you to leave me alone. You didn't have a birthday. Not really. Only I did. This is *my* birthday, and *my* cake, and those were *my* candles."

Too late, I realised the horror on the faces that surrounded me, my twin's included. And then as always, from those who were living anyway, came the suppressed humour, the tired sighs, the eye rolling, and my mother's terrible ire.

"Look what you've done!" she screamed. "You… You… I don't know what you are!" There seemed to be genuine confusion in that last cry. My mother honestly didn't know what she'd spawned. "That's it, your birthday's over. Go to your room. Get out of my sight!"

In just as much shock as she was, I forced my legs to move, my feet connecting with the goo of the cake that lay splattered on the floor, slipping and sliding momentarily, causing even more merriment amongst some of my siblings. Once in my room, as much a sanctuary for me as the kitchen had been for my mother, I slammed the door shut, threw myself on my bed and prepared for the sobs that would surely wrack my body. It surprised me when they didn't come, when my eyes remained stubbornly dry.

Pushing myself up, I shunted along to the edge of my bed and sat there instead. How long for I don't know. Time had ground to a halt. Eventually I could hear activity on the landing – my brothers and sisters, my parents, preparing for bed, passing my room but not bothering to call out to the occupant inside. Silence descended. My twin was close by, I could feel her, but she had the good sense to keep her distance.

At some point I rose from my bed with the intention of going downstairs to the kitchen. Before I did, however, I walked across to the mirror that hung on the far wall and stared at my reflection. I hated what I saw – the monster that faced me.

Gently easing open the bedroom door, managing to avoid all the creaking floorboards, I padded downstairs, carpeted floor soon giving way to cold tiles. In the kitchen, I didn't bother to turn the light on. The darkness suited my purpose. I welcomed it, wondering just how dark it was going to get; not on this side, the other side – the darkness in which things existed.

Ness, don't.

Finally, my twin had dared to materialise, but I ignored her. Instead, I reached for the wooden block just behind the toaster and chose what I hoped was the sharpest knife.

I'm sorry. It was mean of me to blow out the candles, you're right, but I couldn't help myself.

Calmly I turned towards her – not substantial, not anymore, she was barely a shade.

"That's because you're a monster too," I said.

She seemed to fade a little more at that.

The knife in my hand, I stared at the blade, not gleaming, not in the darkness, but dull.

If you do that, I'll tell Mum. I'll race upstairs and tell her.

I shrugged. "She can't see you."

You know that she can.

"She'll never admit it. Besides," I lifted my head to stare at her again, "I thought you'd be glad. I'll be dead like you soon."

She shook her head – a fractured gesture. *I want you to live, for both of us.*

I think I actually snarled as I lifted my left arm, palm side up.

I'll tell Mum! Her voice was a screech that rattled inside my head.

"Tell her," I said, "and tell her this if she's listening, she's a monster too, and I will never forgive her for denying what I am, when she's the one I must have inherited it from. And there's something else – I blame you just as much. Both of you have driven me to this."

Were those sobbing sounds she was making? My dead twin reduced to tears? If she expected sympathy, she'd be disappointed. I had nothing more to give.

Ness, I love you. I've always loved you.

The knife biting into my flesh, I felt no pain, it was as though I'd gone completely numb. Leaning forward slightly, my face close to hers, I whispered more words – her sobs becoming wails on hearing them, on seeing the knife turn crimson.

Chapter Twenty-Four

AS I finished my story, I raised my head to find several pairs of eyes staring back at me. I'd never talked about what had happened to me at thirteen. For twelve years, I'd kept the shame of it locked inside, burning, always burning. Obviously, I hadn't bled out. My mother had found me, my father dialled for an ambulance, doing their duty, as parents should. I'd never talked about the aftermath either – the psychiatric care I'd received – *enforced* care – the lies I'd had to tell in order to escape its clutches: 'No, I can't see spirits. Yes, I made it all up.' Was it to seek attention, they'd asked? After all, I came from a big family, trying to get noticed must be hard at times. I'd nodded at that, 'Yes, it was all to seek attention.'

Such answers kept the doctors satisfied.

"Miss?" It was Craig with his typical schoolboy address. "What happened to your twin? Have you seen her since?"

It was my twin who'd captured his imagination, not the way my family had treated me, or my suicide attempt. Somehow there was comfort in that.

"Miss?"

"No," I replied, "I haven't seen her."

Another voice piped up: Isabel's. "What happens now?"

Now? Angus's gaze was questioning too.

"Erm…"

"Miss." Not Craig, it was Lainey, her eyes had returned to normal, but something in her voice unnerved me still. "You haven't turned on your torch."

"My torch?" I looked down at what lay in my hands, at the slim metal casing – the torch! How had I forgotten it? It was the whole point of the game!

"And your story," Lainey continued with a sneer, "it wasn't exactly uplifting, was it?"

"Just switch on the torch, Ness," Angus instructed.

I did my utmost to obey, but my hands had started to shake.

"It's cold in here, Miss, really cold," Craig said.

"I know, I know," I said. Where was the bloody switch?

"Ness, give it to me." Still Angus sounded calm

"Haven't you noticed how cold it is?" I whispered to him. "Surely you've noticed?"

"Give me the torch."

"No, it has to be me who switches it on, it has to be."

There! My fingers had found the switch. I pressed down. Nothing happened. I pressed again. Still it refused to comply. I jabbed and jabbed, but no matter how hard I tried, there was no thirteenth light. Damn it, it had to come on. It had to! I *willed* it to come on.

"MISS!"

It was Craig, screaming as all the lights went out, just as they'd done on my thirteenth birthday, all the torches and all the candles, plunging us into darkness so intensely that for a moment I doubted my own existence within it. *What you can't see…* But I *did* exist, as did the thing that resided in such darkness – it was here in this room, still intent on playing.

The scrape of boots on the floor indicated that people were scattering.

"Don't break the circle!" I shouted, but it was in vain. With no protection, and no light, the darkness was winning. Amy's cries confirmed that.

"The spider! It's back. It's on me, I can feel it." So fast she'd descended into panic, providing fuel for the fire. "There's more than one, there's loads of them. They're huge!"

I shouted for Angus. "Will you see to her?"

"Aye, leave it to me. Amy, where are you? Where the hell are you?"

It wasn't a large room, so he should have no problem in finding her, she should be at arm's length. Except she wasn't. No one was. The room had become vast, a cavern, one that was filled with more cries and more screams. "Miss! Miss! Where are you?"

"Craig, I'm here. Make your way to the door!"

"I don't know where the door is!"

"It's... It's..." He was right, where was it? I spun round and round, completely disorientated.

"Stop shining that light in my eyes!" It was Isabel, scolding Denny.

"Isabel," I shouted, "Denny's not doing anything. There *is* no light, remember?"

"He is, he's blinding me," she continued, and then her voice faltered, became more wary. "But... it's a strange kind of light, it's... it's... *dirty*."

"Isabel, where are you?" I shouted.

"I'm here. Where are you? I can't see anything, because of Denny, because of this... horrible, horrible light.

DENNY, WILL YOU STOP IT!"

She began to cry, and at that moment Denny screamed too. "That man, the one laughing at me, he's coming over. Look! He's as clear as anything. He's going to get me!"

"There's no man, Denny," I answered. "Shut your eyes if that helps, but he's honestly not there. Angus, Angus, where are you?"

Gradually, I became aware of other voices, those belonging to the terrified parents gathered at the door to Caitir's room, a door that was so far away, in another time, another realm almost. I hadn't called for backup, or yelled out 'help', but we needed them and the light that they could bring more than ever. We needed to up our game, not panic further.

"Ben, Mrs Ludmore," I responded, striding across the room to where I thought the door might be. I took so many strides, an impossible amount given the room's size. I tried shouting too, wondering if my voice might sound as far away as theirs, if they'd be able to hear me at all. "All of you, force the door open if you can. We can't seem to find it and all the lights have gone out. We need you in here. We need you now!"

"You're not going anywhere." It was Lainey. In the darkness she'd found me, her voice with that strange slithering quality, her eyes the only thing visible… and yellow.

"You don't frighten me," I said, straightening my spine and preparing for battle.

"Filthy bitch," she continued, as if she hadn't heard my forced words of bravado. "What a burden you were for your family to carry. Such shame you brought on them."

I swallowed and the cries around me – all of them –

began to fade, even Isabel's shrill insistence that there were snakes in the room now as well as spiders, as she began to retch with horror. "I've confessed to that shame," I said, "right here in this room, in front of all of you. It's no secret anymore."

The thing that was Lainey but wasn't, that was *masquerading* as Lainey, pushed its face into mine. "You think that words absolve you?"

I stood my ground "Why shouldn't they? Words are powerful."

"You feel cleansed?"

In a way I did, of that sin at least. A secret that's been told loses its power.

It picked up on my thoughts.

"But what about the other words you said?"

"The other words?" *Don't think about it, Ness. Don't let it trick you.*

"The worst words. You haven't confessed to them yet have you?"

"Get out of my way. I'm going to find the door."

She laughed – a hateful sound. "There's no escape from here."

"There's always a way out."

"That's just it, sometimes there isn't."

As I stared at her, Lainey grew more visible, the darkness around her seeming to shrink back. A girl of average height, she was becoming smaller, withered almost… and familiar too. Opening her mouth, she began to speak – her voice so much like mine.

"Why'd you do it? I said I was sorry."

I tried to retreat, to turn even, but I was rigid, my feet glued to the floorboards. Around me, all sounds had faded entirely. There was just me in the room… me and my twin.

"Y…you're not her," I stuttered. "You're pretending to be."

"You're denying what you see?"

"You're. Not. Her." It couldn't be, not this withered, shrivelled thing, this husk.

"After what you said, Ness, a husk is what I became."

Wildly, I shook my head. "I won't be fooled."

"I told you I was scared of the dark, didn't I? I told you that there were things in it… *waiting*. Bad things, evil, vampiric. I told you all of that and still you banished me."

I lifted my hand and rubbed at my eyes. "No… This isn't… I didn't…"

"YOU DID! YOU BANISHED ME!"

"I… Because…"

"And all because of something I did when I was a child."

"You're not real!"

"I'm your twin, I'm part of you."

"You're dead."

"Because you sucked the life from me, and then you left me in the dark to fend for myself. Mum was right about you all along. You're the demon that walks amongst us."

Tears! Damn them for falling, but they were, gushing from my eyes as blood had once gushed from my wrists. What she'd done, my birthday cake, it had been the final straw, but she was right, we *were* kids, both of us – only thirteen. *Ness, I love you. I've always loved you.* Those were her last words to me. But my last words to her… what had they been?

"I never want to see you again, not even in death." Lainey – no, my twin – was repeating them pitch perfect.

THIRTEEN

"If you break that rule, if you try and contact me, if you plead, if you cry, even if you beg, I will ignore you. I will never, *ever* acknowledge you again. That's what you said, Ness. To me, the one who loved you. The only one who ever loved you!"

And I'd hated her for that too. I'd blamed her for all those that didn't.

I couldn't stand it any longer, the weight of all that hate too heavy to bear. As I fell to my knees, the husk became the victor.

"That's right." There was another voice in my ear. Again it was familiar. "We've won."

It was Mum, gloating. Whether she was a conjuring or not didn't matter – she was here, in my head. She was *always* in my head.

Ness! Ness! My twin's voice had changed – it wasn't as scathing as before. Despite that, I didn't look up, didn't want to see again what she'd become, because of me.

Ness! Look at me. Please!

"Stay on your knees, girl." It was Mum again. "It's where you belong, in the gutter, crawling alongside other vile things. A witch, a mad witch. We should have let you bleed."

Ness, quick! You have to be quick! Ness, listen to me. Look at me.

How I wanted to curl in a ball, and go quietly mad once more. My head was pounding, my heart beating as frantically as the wings of a caged bird. When was enough enough? Why wouldn't my heart just stop? Release, Shelley had called it. If I had a knife…

You knew. I aimed the words at my mother but only in thought. *You kept saying I was a liar, over and over, and yet you knew. That's why I didn't bleed out, why you found me so quickly that night, because she did what she'd said she'd do. She saved me.*

My twin.

Ness!

Still she was calling.

Please!

I couldn't lift my head; all strength had deserted me.

"Ness!"

Go away.

"Ness!"

"Just go away," I repeated, able to speak out loud this time.

"Go away? Are you joking? I'm not going anywhere. It's taken me ages to find you in the first place. I thought I never would. Come on, soldier, up you get, on your feet."

Strong hands lifted me. Was this a trick again, another act of cruelty?

"Angus?" I said. "Is it you?"

"Who else?" he said, and I remembered his cheeky grin, his eyes always so enlivened. What would this do to him, this experience at the lighthouse? How would it taint him?

"Oh, Angus." How many tears could I cry this night? There was a reservoir inside me whose dam had burst. "I was wrong. I'm so sorry. We've lost the game."

"Lost? I don't think so."

Barely registering his denial, I rushed onwards. "I've put you in danger, all of you. I was mad to bring you all back here. I *am* mad. Officially. You know that now."

"You're a little quirky at times, I'll admit. But… I kind of like that in a girl."

"Angus!" I shouted. "Listen to me!"

THIRTEEN

It was what my twin had shouted – mere seconds before – and I'd ignored her. Would he do the same?

It seemed not. Grabbing my face between his hands, he brought it closer to his.

"We haven't lost. I found you, in this… whatever this is. It didn't want us to find each other, I know it didn't, but we did anyway, thank Christ! Isn't that some kind of triumph?"

A triumph? We were standing in this wretched room, on a remote spot on a remote island, at the mercy of something terrible, something evil, and he was talking about triumphs? I was about to retaliate, to try again to get him to listen to me, to beat against his chest if that's what it took, my fists pummelling, as the fury inside sought release too, but then I stopped. This thing *had* tried to separate us; we're all so much easier to attack that way. Standing here, with Angus, I still felt scared, ashamed and angry. Such strong emotions couldn't disappear in an instant, but one thing I didn't feel was vulnerable, not anymore, not with him by my side. Perhaps he was right. It was a triumph after all.

"Angus…" I began, but he silenced me, bringing me closer to him and placing his lips on mine – *kissing* me.

As he did, light flooded the room – not just the dim glow of tea-lights, of torches, all of them struggling. It was a massive flood of light, blinding in its intensity.

Angus pulled away.

"What the…?" I said. Had we died? That thought honestly crossed my mind.

I could see Angus's face clearly, his *smiling* face.

"Good old Ron," he said. "He must have asked for Liam's help after all."

Chapter Twenty-Five

"LIAM'S here?" I quizzed. Around me, I could see the others – Craig, Amy, Isabel, Denny and Lainey – and they were looking as bewildered as I'm sure I was. Lainey in particular, kept staring at the light and blinking, recovering with every passing second.

Angus nodded in reply. "He is. And just in the nick of time if you ask me."

"The light, where's it coming from?"

"Where'd you think it's coming from?"

"I…"

His eyes widened with amusement. "It's not a heavenly light, if that's what you're thinking, although… in a way perhaps it is."

Like Lainey I blinked. It was the closest thing to a heavenly light I'd ever seen.

The door swung wide, the parents almost falling over themselves with the effort of getting it to open. Looking wildly around, they quickly located their various offspring, running to them and enfolding them in their arms just as they'd done before the event.

"Thank God you're all right," I heard Diane say to Lainey.

"I… I think I'm all right," she replied.

"What happened?" her mother continued. "There was so much noise and commotion coming from in here, we raced up the stairs, but the door was stuck. We tried so hard to get it open, but it wouldn't budge. Can you believe it? An old door like that? We were going frantic out there, all of us. It was awful, we felt so helpless. Oh, Lainey," she cried, throwing her arms around her daughter again. "I'm so relieved you're okay. We wouldn't have given up; we would have broken that damned door down to get in. No devil's going to keep me from my child." The outpouring of emotion over, she started to squint. "Where *is* that light coming from? Not the tower, surely? The lens hasn't worked in years."

Before anyone could approach me, I made for the door too, leaving the room in as much of a hurry as they'd entered it.

"What you doing? Where you going?" Angus fell into step beside me.

"To the tower," I said. "I need to be as close to the source of the light as possible."

"Why?"

Before heading down the staircase, I stopped briefly to answer him, noting the baffled look on his face. "For good reasons, Angus, *personal* reasons. You said Liam is here. How come? When we spoke to Ron, he specifically said he didn't want us to involve him."

"Aye, but I spoke to Ron again."

"When?"

"His was the phone call after Shelley. I explained what had happened to Ally, and then I left it with him to decide what to do for the best. I… erm… I trowelled it on thick."

I couldn't help but smile at that. "Trowelled it on thick? As if there was a need for that."

"Aye, well, you know how the saying goes, things could always be worse. His conscience must have got the better of him, and he decided to contact Liam after all. It's a fair drive from Carlisle to Skye, but Liam, God bless him, obviously made it. No one else around here knows how to operate the lens." He cocked his head to the side, his face youthful, but his eyes wise. "I thought it'd help, you know, it being the mother of all lights."

"It's not quite," I said, "but thank you. It does help. It helps a lot. Thanks for the kiss too."

He reared back slightly, a big grin on his face. "I don't think I've ever been formally thanked for kissing someone before."

"It's like you said, I'm quirky."

"That you are, Ness, that you are."

As touching as this exchange was, the night wasn't over – not yet. Whatever was here was still at my heels.

With Angus following, I flew down the stairs faster than I'd ever done before. Below, the living room was largely clear of the debris that had carpeted it – the parents had done a great job. Barely any candles remained lit, but those that were flickered valiantly, as impressive in their own way as anything bigger. Making my way to the front door, I pulled it open and stared outwards – the rain had turned to sleet, the clouds as low as ever. The wind was picking up too, and blowing my hair across my face.

"Where's the service room?" I asked Angus.

"It's beside the tower, follow me."

With the gravel beneath our feet, we did as we'd done so often these last few days; we put our heads down and

THIRTEEN

forged ahead. Sure enough, in a small room to the side of the tower, one that had had its door wrecked, probably years before, stood Ron McCarron and a man younger than him but who shared the same stocky build.

"Ron!" I had to shout over the wind. "Thank you, thank you so much. And you're Liam?"

"Aye, I am," the younger man shouted back. "I hope we've been able to help. We went to Angus's house first, and it was Eilidh who told us that you'd all come here." He glanced in the direction of the light that blazed. "I didn't think I had a hope of getting the stand-by generator to work, not after all this time. This salty air, it rusts stuff to buggery. But between Dad and me we managed it. We only bloody managed it!" He laughed. "Don't ask me how though, I don't know, but it wasn't as hard as I thought. In fact," he stopped laughing and looked genuinely perplexed, "it wasn't hard at all. It shouldn't even be possible. Anyway, it's a light! It's static though, it won't sweep. I hope that's okay?"

"Okay? It's brilliant, in every sense of the word. How did you know we needed it?"

He shrugged, a grin as wide as any that Angus could muster on his face. "How?"

I nodded.

"What else are you supposed to fight the forces of darkness with?"

I think it's safe to say I'm not particularly demonstrative, I've never been encouraged in that respect, but I practically threw myself into Liam's arms. "Thank you, thank you so much." Extricating myself from him I then hugged Ron. "You're a good man," I said.

"And you're a good lass," he returned. "We both have

demons to fight, but we can do it. We're capable."

"We just have to believe it?"

"Aye, it's as hard and as simple as that."

"It's what we make it, I suppose."

He nodded. "It is. Now away, lass, get on with whatever it is you have to do. We have no idea if and when the generator will fail. Like Liam said, it shouldn't have worked at all."

I did as he instructed, leaving the service room and drawing closer to the tower as lightning pierced the clouds. I looked upwards. *Oh no, you don't, the elements are on our side, not yours.* I was no expert at Reiki, I've mentioned that, but, making the symbol for *Cho Ku Rei* again, I mentally called on Earth, Wind, Air and Fire to assist us and us alone – utilising natural elements for natural purposes only. Certainly, if Shelley had done what she'd promised to do, one of those elements – fire – was right now engulfing Grey's former home, breaking the chain, as she put it. Keeping the Reiki mantra at the forefront of my mind, I carried on walking – deep rolling thunder accompanying me.

Angus was once more by my side, but at the door to the tower I stopped him.

"I have to do this alone," I said.

Worry darkened his features. "But what if you need me?"

"Angus, I *do* need you, I couldn't have done any of this without you, but it's as I said, this next step is personal."

His eyes flickered towards the main building. "It's not a good idea to go up there alone."

"Because I'm weak?" I said, understanding his gesture.

He started to object, but I held up my hand, not quite

finished.

"Not all the time, I'm not saying that, but on occasions I *am* weak. I let negativity swamp me. I don't have the strength to fight it all the time, and maybe I never will. But that's because I'm human, I'm flawed, and sometimes I can only take so much."

Reaching out, he took my hands, his thumbs pushing back the sleeves of the coat I wore. I knew what he wanted: to see for himself the damage I'd once inflicted.

"There's strength in admitting that," he said, his thumbs gently rubbing the scarred tissue. "Great strength." Dragging his gaze from my wrists, he stared into my eyes. "I'll be here when you've finished whatever it is you have to do up there. I'll be waiting."

Knowing that, lent me strength too.

* * *

I took the cast iron stairs two at a time in places, more thunder drowning out the clatter of my shoes against the treads that spiralled upwards.

It wasn't a tall tower, but I was breathless by the time I reached the top. To access the outside gallery, I pushed open an iron door, praying that it wasn't rusted and would give way. I was so relieved when it did. Poking my head through, I was instantly hit by a blast of air; sleet coating my cheeks, to lie frozen there. Quickly, I had to shield my eyes. Being so close to source could cause permanent damage; my daring might cost me like it did Icarus from Greek mythology, but I wouldn't stay for long, just until, as Ron had said, I'd done what I needed to do.

Still hardly daring to open my eyes, I eased out onto the

gallery. The exposed balcony ran all the way around the underside of the lantern room, which itself was enclosed by glass windows, storm panes I think they're called, able to withstand 'the fine Scottish weather' as Eilidh once termed it. The railing was at waist height and I had to grab hold of it in order to steady myself, for the wind was capable of knocking me off my feet, which might send me plummeting below.

Madness, that's what this was, sheer madness to be up here when the lens was on, in the midst of a storm. But so what? I'd been mad before. Rather than fear it, I'd embrace the extreme weather, the curious mixture of heat from the lens and cold from the air somehow managing to negate each other. I'd throw my head back in the wind, I'd listen as the sea smashed against the rocks, imagining the blue men, the storm kelpies, watching and waiting. I'd marvel too as the lightning kept chasing the darkness. And I'd roar – louder than a lion.

Taking a deep breath, I opened my mouth as wide as I could and, with one giant exhalation I screamed for all the hurt and the agony I'd ever endured; for all the sorrow, the blame and the guilt that had marked me from the day I'd come into this world kicking and crying; for the baby born just minutes after me who'd never cried at all. I screamed for all the hurt that I'd caused, the blame that I'd so wrongly apportioned; for my immaturity, my jealousies, my pettiness, my refusal to accept love when love was offered; for my insistence on embracing hatred instead, and becoming something hateful too. I screamed because of my gift that so often seemed like a curse, it was such a burden to bear. I screamed for my desire to be normal when normal I'd never be. I screamed at injustice and prejudice;

for those who felt the need to hit out at what they couldn't understand; for my mother's denial and the loathing in her eyes whenever she looked at me; for the weakness in my father, and the indifference of my brothers and sisters. I howled at the psychiatrists who only ever believed me when I lied. I cried for what I'd done, not just to myself, but also to my twin; for being her shadow side, the darkness to her light; for the irony of that. And I screamed because of how weak I was... still. I might crave forgiveness from my twin, but I couldn't dredge up forgiveness for my mother, not after all that she'd done. There was strength in honesty – Angus had said that. Was it true? Could it really be true?

My voice hoarse, I continued to scream, to let go what I could, to accept what I couldn't, the expulsion as dark as anything we'd encountered in Caitir's bedroom, joining forces with it no doubt, as like called to like. With my back to the lens I stared into the abyss and remembered what she'd said: *My dark isn't like your dark. There are things in it.*

"I'm sorry," I shouted, my raw throat not the only thing responsible for the cracking of my voice, "for all of it. The husk that was pretending to be you in Caitir's room, its voice changed, right at the end. Was that you then? Truly you? You asked me to look, to listen, and to be quick about it. I didn't realise... It's only just occurred to me that it was the real you. I ignored you, but I didn't mean to, not that time. Are you here? Are you anywhere?"

As my eyes strained to see, I could tell she'd been right; there *were* things in the darkness. I could see them, so many things, innumerable, twisting and writhing, agonised things that wanted to crawl towards me, and drag me into the darkness with them, but they couldn't. The light that I was at the centre of was just too bright. It would obliterate them if they dared, as I had dared – like Grey's house, like Icarus, they'd burn too. One other thing, one *important* thing: they couldn't hurt me any more than I'd been hurt already. *That's* why I was the person for the job, and why Shelley had wished I wasn't.

The things – it wasn't my place to name them – retreated. Not far, never far, but far enough. As long as there was light at the lighthouse, and a lightness of being too, they'd keep their distance.

As I continued to stare, I was grateful: there was no mirror image staring back at me. My twin wasn't part of it.

Chapter Twenty-Six

FROM rain to sleet to snow, there was a heavy and glorious swathe. As awed as I was by what was this time a natural phenomenon, brightening the night further, the people around me took it in their stride, as they took so much. Slowly but steadily we all left Minch Point and made our way back to our respective homes, the lighthouse still miraculously blazing behind us; a beacon in the night, an attraction, for all that was right.

Later, when we were ensconced in Eilidh's living room, with endless cups of tea on the go, and a bottle of Talisker too, Angus wanted to know if the darkness had gone forever.

"It's always there," I explained, "in some propensity, but give it nothing to feed on and its strength will continue to deplete."

"This is good news for your Uncle Glenn too, Angus," Eilidh said. "He'll be pleased."

"Are you looking forward to taking over?" I asked and he nodded. "You'll make a brilliant manager," I added. "There's no doubt about it, you're the man for the job."

"Will you come and visit when it's up and running as a guesthouse?" I picked up the plea in his voice, as did

Eilidh, who lowered her eyes to stare at her hands.

"Of course I will," I answered. "In time."

We'd both have to be content with that.

The snow prevented any thoughts of an immediate departure and so I stayed for a few more days, just relaxing, doing nothing more than that, enjoying short walks with Angus in the snow, even having a snowball fight – several of them, collapsing in a heap of giggles at the end of every one. I was finally allowing myself to play, but, oh, how I missed the one who'd wanted to play first. We'd also rung Raigmore to find out about Ally. She'd much improved, according to her mother, who came to the phone to speak to us.

"She's like a different girl. It's in her face, you know, it's more relaxed, her skin not as taut. She even smiled today, the old smile, the one that lights up her eyes. Ben told me what you did at the lighthouse, what you all did. Is it over? Please tell me it's over."

I assured her it was, and stressed the importance of keeping Ally's world calm, ordered and familiar in the coming months, as she'd need time to recover completely.

"I know we shouldn't have kept putting off telling her that she was adopted," Molly continued. "I understand that withholding that information made her susceptible in more ways than one. We just… We didn't want to upset her. We love her so much, you see. In all honesty, we forget that she's not ours biologically, that we're not a proper family—"

"You *are* a proper family. You're the real deal. Ally's a very lucky girl."

"I just want to make her life as amazing as it can possibly be."

THIRTEEN

"Don't try so hard." It's what Shelley had said to me. "There's great value in just letting things flow naturally."

"I… Maybe you're right. I want to put it all behind us and start afresh. Once again thank you for all you've done. I hear Angus's uncle's offer has been accepted, that it's all going through. Will he be starting work quite soon at the lighthouse?"

"Yes." And in the meantime the parents had drawn up a rota of daily visits and tasks to be performed, including the removal of more debris, a bit of scrubbing and cleaning, the liberal use of bleach… all with Uncle Glenn's delight and approval, who'd promised them the party of the year to look forward to on opening night.

The tower light couldn't stay on indefinitely, in fact, when Liam had tried to get it going the night after it wouldn't even flicker. No matter; it had done its job, as had he. The parents promised to leave a light of some description blazing come nightfall – it would never be allowed to reside in darkness again. Guardians of the lighthouse – they all were, more than thirteen in number, an army, and with Angus at the helm.

* * *

November had given way to December as I made my way to a remote woodland spot in the depths of East Sussex. The air was crisp, not bitter as it had been on Skye, dark clouds gathering above me and threatening yet another onslaught of rain. Parking my car where I'd parked it so often during the police investigation, I was relieved to see no one else mad enough to walk here on a day like today – only me. To be honest, I'm sure the fact that there was no one here had nothing to do with the weather, but everything to do with the girls who'd died, who'd been murdered here – the spirit of one still so traumatised that she lingered still, hiding behind a veil of mists that only she – and sometimes I – could see. Claire was her name, and, walking to where X no longer marked the spot, I called out.

"Claire, do you remember me? My name's Ness, I've been here several times before, to try and speak to you, to get you to come out of hiding. Claire," I continued, "you've nothing to fear from me. I've come here to help you leave this place behind and all the pain, and terror that you suffered here too. Your friend has left, and now it's your turn. Don't stay anymore, it's lonely here, go to where those who love you are waiting."

It was as I expected: no answer.

The man who did this to her, who trapped her in more ways than one, I was having trouble forgiving him too. How could he do this? How could anyone hurt a child? But people could, I knew that. I'd *seen* what they could do. There were plenty capable of committing such a heinous deed. Maybe they'd had terrible childhoods themselves, but even as I thought it, I dismissed it. There was no excuse. None. Everyone has a choice, two paths to follow. If you start walking down the wrong one...

"Claire, I'm not going to give up on you. I want to be clear about that. There's a light that shines, and I want you to go towards it; that's your home, where you belong. You'll be happier there, much happier, please believe me. I have a sense about that too."

A noise broke the silence – not a bird cawing, so few birds sing here, but the snap of a twig. I turned my head towards it, my eyes searching. Nothing. No one. Perhaps it was a rabbit or a fox or whatever animal calls the woods home, but in their case, quite rightly.

Hunkering down, I rubbed my hands over the ground, which is covered in leaves, small stones and clumps of mud. At once an earthy smell drifted upwards and I inhaled deeply. It smelled so good, so natural, no trace of the bodies that had once festered there. In spite of what happened, the seasons still change, the wind still blows, and the world still turns – life carries on. But I won't forget the dead. I'll be their champion. I'm on their side.

"Claire, I'm going to keep this simple. I'll come here on a regular basis, as often as I can. I won't force you to come forward, I can't. I don't have that power. Sometimes I'll sit and chat and you can perhaps listen. Other times I'll only spend a few minutes before I have to go. Take all the time you need. When you're ready, step forward and show yourself. That light I was talking about? I'll walk with you towards it; I'll go as far as I can with you. I hope that's sooner rather than later. You see, it's not good to be alone. It can make you... susceptible. I hope with me visiting regularly, you won't feel that way, you'll feel stronger. I'll say goodbye, Claire, for now."

I waited several more seconds, just in case, and then I retraced my footsteps, back to where I'd left my car. Closer to it, I heard another movement behind me, and turned.

"Claire?"

And if not her, could it be someone else, someone I longed to see – my mirror image? My heart raced at the thought.

"Is it you? Have you come back?"

If she had, she was silent too.

"I'm not ignoring you, not anymore. Why do you insist on ignoring me?"

She got her stubborn streak from Mum, I was sure of it. Maybe I had too.

"You wanted me to live for both of us, and I've been trying to do that, you know, getting out a bit more, having fun. I've been to the cinema a couple of times, to pubs and even a restaurant. My work's busy too – I've got a few more private cases in lately."

If she was there, she was giving as good as she'd got, by dishing up a bit of karma, but I wouldn't get angry with her – those days were gone.

"The thing is, despite all that, it's you I miss. It's been twelve years."

Still there was nothing.

"Okay, all right," I said, digging in my coat pocket for my car key and withdrawing it. As I did, I sighed. "Have it your way, but you can't sulk forever. And do you know why?"

Deliberately I paused, to let the atmosphere build, to let the mystery that would reel her in – *eventually* – deepen.

She always loved to play games, so where was the harm in playing one now?

"Because I know your name," I said. "I finally managed to find it out."

The End

Psychic Surveys Companion Novel
Book Three

ROSAMUND

Prologue

1889

THIS is why I do it. Why I write.

It is not comfortable where I am sitting. It is a small space, cramped. In front of me is a child's desk, and barely any light to see by, just a pale shaft that shines through a small oval window. How valiant that light is; how it tries so hard to pierce the gloom. My hands, oh my hands! They shake as I scribe, guilty of knocking over the inkpot on several occasions. Not that it matters about the spillage. Not here, in the attic. He will not see it. He refuses to venture in here. As to why, I have no clue. Perhaps he is afraid, although it holds far less to be frightened of than what dwells in his mind. There *are* things to be frightened of, however… strange things…

I do not have long. The day is beginning to wane and soon I will not be able to see to write – not anymore. My hands shaking worse than ever, I add to the quantity of paper already filled. I outline; I describe. Sometimes in fleeting detail, at other times so much more than that, even though my heart threatens to burst from my chest because of it and my head screams: *'Try and forget. It is best to forget!'*

There will come a time to forget.

These dark details are not being compiled for the sake of it; they are to let her know she is not alone. For she will have to bear the burden of what is to come.

My darling girl, my angel – for that is what she is, despite being born into such hell: his land; his house; a marriage forced upon me. One child, but there will be no more. His hand will never touch me in that way again, I will make sure of it. If only I were stronger; if only I could bear this burden instead of she – but it is not to be.

There are things one should never see, not here, not in this realm; that should never be allowed to cross the great divide. But they *will* cross, if you goad them, if you taunt them, if, above all you offer them sanctuary. A devout Christian is how he portrays himself, and how he fools those around him with his supposedly pious ways. Such a pillar of the community! So benevolent! But he has never fooled me. I could see the darkness in him from our very first meeting and I shrank back because of it. He saw something in me too – not a shining heart, a girl to love, not even innocence, for in so many ways this gift erodes that. What he saw was someone he thought he could mould, and so he pursued me, he *hounded* me – his supposed wealth and power blinding my otherwise loving parents. I was handed over as a prized animal might be handed over: to the slaughter.

And now I am a mother…

I look up. The door is rattling, the handle turning, first one way, and then the other; not a frenzied action, not yet, but soon it will be. It is not him, nor the maid or the housekeeper, for they will not venture into the attic either. They have no need.

It is one of *them*, seeking to stop me; desperate to do so. Ignorance is such a powerful thing; it gives the idle an excuse to follow, to bend the knee, to be led. It is the ignorant who will summon those from across the gulf that exists to divide us. If only they realised more fully what they were doing; what it is that they unleash.

I am not ignorant. I do know. And what is on the other side of the door *hates* that I do. These things – for I refuse to name them – are the very embodiment of hate.

But they will not enter either. In here I have spun a light, one that has nothing to do with the sun or the moon and that will never fade. I have built a wall so high I can no longer see over the top. It protects me, but more than that, it protects what is now written. It will hide these pages should they ever manage to enter. It will block them.

In the end it will block everything.

Such is the price I must pay.

Darling Rosamund, my greatest wish is that you – and only you – unearth what lies buried, and when you do, may it help you to find a way through hell.

Do not despair. Be strong, far stronger than I have been.

I am sorry at having borne you into this. At least I will not bear another.

This is why I write. Not to save myself, but to save you.

Chapter One

Fourteen Years Later

"ROSAMUND! Rosamund! Where are you?"

With the tiled floor cold against my stockinged feet, I flew down the length of the corridor as far from that voice as possible. The narrow walls on either side of me were covered in floral wallpaper, not bright in colour, and not cheerful either, rather it looked as if a thousand tiny flowers were caught in various stages of decay. It was only I that ever used this corridor, although it was one of many in this house, which, beside myself, only my father, a housekeeper and a maid occupied. A house set miles from towns and villages, from *life*, concealed deep in the countryside.

Father was not always in residence, spending a great deal of his time in London, mixing no doubt with other eminent landowners born into riches. I was glad he was rarely home. My father and I were not close; I make this known from the outset. There was *no one* in the house to whom I was close. The new maid, Josie, was proving to be an elusive creature, and Miss Tiggs, the housekeeper, who seemed to have been here forever, certainly since my birth, disliked me as much as I disliked her. There did not appear to be a particular reason for our mutual dislike but for my part, I found her… peculiar, keeping to the kitchens as she did, her domain, as I have always thought of it. I once had a governess, but I had not seen her in months and no one thought this odd, least of all my father, who, when I saw fit to remark upon her absence, shut me up with a stern 'Can you not see I'm busy? I am reading.'

When home, when not in search of me, he usually locked himself away in his study, on which occasions I could imagine well enough the concentration on his foxlike face as he waded through the tomes that lined the shelves there. When he grew weary of the books, however, he would demand I sit with him, his whisky-soured breath potent as he asked me the same question over and over. *What do you see?*

I did not wish to play such a tiresome game today; to gaze deep into his eyes, as dark as mine, as they continued to narrow and hunt for any information I might be able to impart. The moment I heard him roar, I glanced towards the clock on the mantelpiece of my bedroom. It was early; barely midday. Surely he was not imbibing already? Frightened that his summons meant something; that he was angry in some way, distressed or disturbed, I tore myself from my book – for I loved to read too – and picked up my skirts and ran, through labyrinthine corridors, past empty rooms, barely glancing at the rain-drenched Sussex landscape outside.

I had been doing this ever since I could remember: running. Sixteen now and no longer a child, I was practically a young woman, but running seemed to have been as much an integral part of my life as the mutual dislike between myself and Miss Tiggs; a simple *fact* of it. Was I indeed frightened when he came for me? Sometimes. At other times I was angered by it – especially if engrossed in a particular passage in a book, or involved in the painting of a watercolour, depicting the misty grounds of the house perhaps, or its rather grand Georgian exterior. Mears House was where I resided. No one had ever explained to me why it was christened as such; whether indeed it was a Mears family that lived there originally, or if it was named for the architect that built it. Certainly, it seemed to have no connection to my family name, that of Howard. I sketched the house quite often: nine windows plus the grand door with a portico dominating the front elevation. I also painted the grounds in which it sits; the grass and the countless trees that form a ring of woodland around the house, in which only I ever seemed to roam. I would draw the path in front of the house, the one that meandered through the landscape, which I longed to run down, away from here and into a world I could only imagine. And, of course, I would draw the roof with only one window at the rear to punctuate the expanse of grey slate – not nearly enough to benefit such an attic. I imagined there should have been more, if only for the sake of symmetry.

The attic was a safe place for me. I had no idea why Father would not venture there. I knew only that once he had taken the right turn at the rear of the house that led to another much narrower flight of stairs, one I always regarded as hidden, he would come to an abrupt halt. Only once had he dared to stand outside the attic door; to touch the handle, tentatively, testing it this way and that, almost pushing it open before deciding against it and retreating. The relief that I had felt!

I held no such reservation and having reached the attic myself, I closed the door behind me, stopping at last to catch my breath from the steep climb. As I have previously noted, it is a vast room, not entirely covering the length and breadth of the house, but within the attic, it did feel so. In many ways it seemed *bigger* than the house. There were discarded boxes everywhere and items of furniture covered in white sheets that, in the gloom from the single distant window, were capable of casting the oddest of shapes, conjuring people with twisted limbs. According to my former governess, I had always had an overactive imagination! The attic was not overly dark as the daylight from that intrepid window filtered well enough through the cobwebs. What would it be like with no sunlight at all, however, and no moon glow either? Perhaps then there would be reason enough to be frightened.

"Rosamund!"

Still I could hear him. No doubt he was at the bottom of those hidden stairs, standing with fists clenched, his lips a thin white line.

As I looked around, I tried to understand: why would he not come up here? What was it that repelled him? I would pay for being disobedient in due course, for not coming to heel as a dog might. If only I could hide in this lofty space forever, but I could not. I would have to resurface. And when I did, he would drag me to his study, push me back into that cracked and worn leather chair that stood across the desk from his, and growl at me until I succumbed; until I gave him at least some semblance of an answer. *What do you see?*

Not wishing to think of my fate, I weaved around the furniture, my tread careful as I made my way to the far end of the room, to where the hazy light shone like candlelight through gossamer, so softly. There was a desk there, positioned in an alcove; a small one, the kind that may have been used in a school I tended to think, although I had never been to one, but I had certainly seen sketches of such institutions in books. Fine places they looked, with so many others just like me – children that may have become friends. How wonderful to have had a friend.

Or a mother.

As I took my seat at the desk; as my shoulders slumped and my head fell forwards in despair, I forced myself to take more deep breaths. I would not cry. I refused to. In my current reading matter – aptly named *Bleak House* by Mr Charles Dickens – was a character described as a 'plucky little thing'. That is what I now aspired to be – plucky. But, oh, how I missed Mother. Strange, considering I had no living memory of her, that in this house there was nothing that even alluded to her. Certainly, Father never mentioned her name; would *never even* have her mentioned.

I remember when I had tried.

"Father, was Mother kind? Was she gentle? Were her eyes as dark as mine? What happened to her, Father? You have never really told me. How did she die?"

Perhaps it had been wrong to act in such a manner, firing question after question at him. Shadows had darkened his face and his nostrils had flared. Could he really be blamed for losing his temper, for shouting at me, for screaming?

"Stop plaguing me, child! I can stand no more of your infernal curiosity. Where is Miss Lyons? Where is she? Why am I paying her such a handsome fee?"

Miss Lyons was the governess, missing as my mother was missing; 'gone home to London' apparently, 'for she's 'ad her fill of you too,' that last tidbit told to me by Miss Tiggs, a cruel smile on her dough-like face as she delivered such harsh words.

On that day my father had wanted to cast me from him, into the hands of Miss Lyons, rather than seeking me out – it was always about extremes with Father.

And now I must hasten to correct myself. I have said that there was no trace of Mother in this house, beside myself, her progeny; but I *had* found something; something that he knew nothing about. And I kept it safe. I kept it here, in the attic.

It was a photograph of her, just her and no one else. In it she wears a dark dress. It is impossible to tell the colour of it, as it simply appears black in the photograph, just as her hair appears black, coiled around her head. Her eyes are dark too, but her skin… it is as pale as milk. The dress is high-collared but around her neck there hangs a necklace, one hand resting below it, her long slim fingers artfully curled, although one, the index finger, is elongated, as though it points to the necklace. She has about her a wistful quality, and behind her is a curious, almost luminous light.

The photograph lay inside the desk. Opening the lid, I retrieved it, moving further into the light in order to study it. It was found in the library, my favourite room in a house I could otherwise not abide. Put there by Mother herself? Did she want someone to find it, and specifically me, her daughter? As I held it in my hand that was the feeling it conveyed, as if her mouth was far from closed but whispering: *Remember me. I did exist.*

The photograph had been guarded between a book by Charlotte Brontë called *Jane Eyre* – a book I adored about another 'plucky' character, Jane herself – and *Songs of Innocence and Experience* by the poet William Blake, that I had yet to read. Had Mother known I would love reading so much? It was not difficult to guess at, I supposed. In this house, so far removed from everything, reading and drawing constituted full-time occupations. When I chose *Jane Eyre* and the photograph fell to the floor, I was amazed. Setting the book down on a nearby table, I studied the picture. The feeling I mentioned earlier – that she wanted to be recognised – engulfed me. Although no name was scribed on the back – although I appeared to look more like my father than her – this was, without doubt, Mother. She had hidden it here; she had wanted me to gaze upon her.

If Father knew what I had in my possession, what it was I *could* see right now... I did not care, for she was the only thing I wanted to see.

*Oh, Mother, I might look like Father, but it is you I take after in all other aspects. Say it is so. Please. I do not want to be like him. He is everything I aspire **not** to be.*

If only she would speak.

A movement a few feet away captured my attention and stopped me from sliding further into melancholy. What was it? A spider? A rat? I hoped it was not the latter as I had a fear of them with their bead-like eyes and their sharp, pointed teeth. I was not so fond of spiders either, especially the big leggy ones that scurried rather than ran along the corridors of Mears House. I stood up and stamped my feet hard against the floorboards, noting a slight loosening of one as I did so, and quickly sidestepping it. If it was a rat, such actions should be enough to deter it from drawing closer.

But still there was movement.

Persistent movement.

A stirring and a rustling.

I braced myself as I continued to stare at the corner where the noise was coming from, remembering my father's words.

What do you see?

Chapter Two

"IT is madness, William! Sheer madness!"

The voice of the friend that had come visiting, unlike Father's quiet, almost whispery conversational voice, was bellowing. It was *his* friend, of course, not mine. As I have stated, I had none. How could I, when I was confined to Mears House? Soon other friends would arrive to gather in his study. They would smoke cigars and drink whisky, venturing further into discussion as I lingered here, at the far end of the corridor, hiding behind a door that led into the drawing room – one of the three reception rooms the house boasted – trying to listen to what it was that they had to say.

Of course they did not limit their assemblies to here, as I was sure they congregated in London too, because that is where most of them hailed from. I knew this because I had overheard them discuss their places of residence on several occasions; suburbs such as Knightsbridge and Hammersmith, Highgate and Chelsea, which I envisaged to be outrageously grand places with buildings that towered over you and a fine assortment of ladies and gentlemen parading on the streets or galloping along in carriages. I was under no illusion London was entirely grand; I understood it had its dark side too – Mr Dickens had made that clear enough. There appeared to be a dark side to everything and perhaps in turn, everyone. When I thought of Mr Dickens' London, I imagined a thick blanket of fog enveloping it – the 'London Particular' as Mr Guppy in *Bleak House* tells Miss Summerson; a real pea souper, worse than anything we have ever had in the countryside. The city I pictured was both a den of magnificence and inequity, smog lending it an otherworldly air, and I longed to visit this mystical and terrible land; to experience it for myself rather than through the eyes of an author.

My father's visitors travelled by horse and carriage to Mears House and were furtively deposited on the gravel path outside, their means of transport quickly disappearing into the distance. Almost always they stayed the night. The moment they retired was when I would stop eavesdropping, pick up my skirts and run once again, this time to my bedroom. Once inside I would push a chest of drawers up against the door, heaving with all my might for it was a solid piece of furniture, just in case one of the gentlemen should decide to go wandering in the night and become disorientated, and I would find the handle of my door turning, always turning…

But for now I listened, filled with curiosity. Just what was 'sheer madness'?

"It's just… There is danger," the friend continued. "What if it should go wrong?"

"You have now changed your mind?" my father questioned.

"For God's sake, William, acknowledge the risks involved at least!"

My father laughed, but I could detect no humour in it. When he spoke again, his voice was so low it forced me to leave my hiding space and creep forward to hear.

"You are aware that there are many, many men that would willingly take your place, who would give their eye teeth for such an opportunity?"

After a moment of silence, Arthur coughed. "I am merely saying—"

"Courage is required, Arthur, not cowardice."

Arthur was clearly considering the warning in Father's voice. "Are you sure she is able to assist us?" he said at last.

I was merely a step or two away from the door now, my hand cupping my ear as I strained to hear. *Who* were they talking of?

"Arthur, I am certain of it."

"There will not be a repeat of what happened previously?"

"You are right, sir, there will not."

Another voice startled me.

"Miss, is there something I can help you with?"

I swung around. In front of me was the maid – not quite so elusive now – her expression perplexed. In my estimation I was younger than Josie by two or three years, but I was the mistress of this house, *her* mistress, and so I straightened my back and my chin too, refusing to be embarrassed at being caught out by a servant.

"Thank you, but I am quite comfortable. Is there anything I can help *you* with?"

She shrugged – an insolent gesture I could not help but think, or was it? Was it that she was just a simple girl, an untroubled girl? For in the few times I had encountered her, not scurrying around the house as I scurried, or as the spiders scurried, but 'drifting' around it, she had looked so serene and contented. Strangely, she had also looked at home. How long had she been with us? A matter of months, replacing Lottie who left to marry a cousin twice removed from the West Country. Time in this house, however, could not be trusted. It was something of an anomaly, either passing by in a moment, or stretching on before you with no end in sight. Josie carried out her various duties in a world seemingly of her own making, often remaining just on the edge of vision; but now she was in full view and staring at me.

The time was three o' clock, the month November. Soon the already weakening light of winter would fade entirely to be replaced by a darkness so complete it would require effort to see your own hands held up in front of your face. I had read that eyes take some minutes to adjust to such intense darkness, but in my experience that was not always true, for the darkness could remain that way – intense – right up until morning. There was much for Josie to do before the arrival of Father's other friends, yet still she gawped at me.

"Josie," I asked, breaking the silence that seemed to have settled so heavily upon us, "is everything well? I asked if there was something I could help you with?"

"Oh no, miss. I don't think so."

Her amusement, or rather *bemusement,* failed to amuse me.

"Everything is prepared for Father's guests? The beds have been turned down?"

"Everything's prepared," she accompanied that statement with an enthusiastic nod, causing wisps of red-tinged hair to fall from under her cap.

"Miss Tiggs has supper ready?"

"Just a light supper's been requested, miss."

Of course it had! They would be light on eating, heavy on drinking.

The way Josie continued to look at me made me feel like some sort of oddity. Perturbed, I had to struggle to retain my composure. Turning my back on her, I retraced my footsteps along the corridor, back to the drawing room.

"The grate in here," I called, intending to lead her to it, "I noticed it still had embers in it earlier. Why is this? It is supposed to be raked out every morning."

I turned my head just enough to see her smile slip.

"I'm sorry, miss, It's just…I've been so busy…"

"Busy staring is what it seems."

I disliked the sound of my own voice, it reminded me too much of Father's, but, as I have pointed out, I was the mistress of this house, despite my tender years. Perhaps this was how I was *required* to sound – not acerbic, not exactly, but authoritative at least. During Father's absence, I was in charge of this… this… mausoleum; it seemed such an apt word to describe it. As Josie's smile had slipped, something inside me followed suit. It was just so dreary in here, so lacklustre, with paint peeling on every ceiling and the wallpaper fading. When rarely the light crept in, it did so half-heartedly.

I faced her fully now. "Why do you stay? Why do you not leave? You have family, so why not return to them?"

Josie's green eyes widened and I understood why. How could I have let such desperate words escape me? But there was such a longing in me to know; a need. "*Do* you have family, Josie? A mother?"

"Everyone has a mother."

About to rebuke her for being so insensitive – surely she was fully aware of my situation – I managed to stop myself. Firstly, I had asked the question and so there must be a reply, and secondly, she was right, everyone did have a mother. *I* had a mother, or rather a photograph of her.

I hung my head, my own hair, brown in colour, not restrained, not today, but falling forwards to frame my face. "Why do you stay?" I asked again.

"I…" she was tentative now, nervous at last. "I like it here."

I was incredulous. "You like it? Why?"

"It's quiet."

"Quiet?"

"On occasion."

Before I could query that too, she continued. "I have my own bed."

"Your own bed?" I seemed doomed to repeat her words.

"At home, there are nine of us, and only two beds."

And that was it, the sole reason. This was a girl whose own bed – her own space I supposed – meant everything. Was it no more complex than that?

From outside there came the crunch of carriage wheels on gravel and, like co-conspirators now, we both took a step towards the window so that we could cautiously peer onto the driveway. There were more guests arriving and no doubt Miss Tiggs would escort them straight to Father's study and wait on them throughout the evening. She was the only female allowed access to the inner-sanctum at these times – Miss Tiggs with her doughface and her cruel smile. We watched them alight. There were two of them, an older man and a younger one with fair hair. The former was quite stooped, the latter straight-backed, handsome even, with a somewhat confident gait. Having deposited them, the carriage turned swiftly around and sped back down the approach, eager as always to put as much distance between it and the house as possible. As I watched it, I recalled snatches of Father and Arthur's conversation.

'Madness, sheer madness' and *'Are you sure she is able to assist us?'*

Once again I wondered, who was this 'she' they talked of?

Chapter Three

FATHER'S associates had returned to London, but surprisingly he had stayed at Mears House. I had not foreseen this, as it was far more usual that he should leave with them, and so I had risen later than normal, shooing Josie away when she appeared at my door to tend to me. I had failed to sleep well the previous night; I never did when Father's gentlemen friends stayed over, and what sleep I had managed was filled with such strangeness, such turmoil, that my eyes frequently snapped open as my mouth gaped, fish-like, for air; and yet, in the cold light of day, I could barely recall the hazy, twisted shapes that had caused such angst. In truth, I had no desire to recall them, but there would be torment ahead for me regardless – that caused by my Father.

Breakfast had already been taken in the dining room, where I had sat alone as usual, staring idly out of the windows at yet another rain-swept day, the colours outside matching the sombreness of those inside. It threatened to be one of those endless days, but at least, besides Miss Tiggs and Josie, I had the house to myself – or so I believed.

"There you are!"

I was passing his study on my way to the drawing room,

intent on doing some reading perhaps beside the fire, or to indulge in a little drawing. Although I was not having any tuition at the time at least my past governesses – for Miss Lyons was only one of them – had taught me sufficiently in both respects.

"Father!" On spotting him, my voice was little more than a croak. "But I thought you had gone." Or rather I had *hoped* he would be gone; that I was rid of him.

"Several times I have called for you," he declared, "in vain, I might add."

"Perhaps I was out walking, Father," I lied. "I do enjoy being outside, even in the rain." Another lie, I was wary of the rain as my chest tended towards weakness.

Father made no reply, he simply stared at me – again he reminded me of a fox with his intent, narrow gaze and features that jutted and jarred. His dark eyes were infinite pools that mesmerised and tethered: I had to fight against this, not look away – Father would deem such an act insufferable rudeness on my part – but not lose myself in them. I cursed that I resembled him; in truth I despaired of it.

"Come to my study," he said at last, not asking but demanding.

My heart plummeted further – why oh why must we do this? What did he want from me? How was I to answer the oddest of questions that fell from his lips? I am just a girl, an ordinary girl – his *daughter* – why did he interrogate me so?

I have mentioned that, besides the library, Father's study harboured books too, many of them lining the length and breadth of three entire walls. As much as I loved books, in Father's room they failed to furnish it;

rather they gave it a closed-in claustrophobic feel and made it so much darker than it already was. They were not storybooks either; Father held no regard for the frivolity of fiction. No, these were books pertaining to lofty scientific subjects such as astronomy, physics and medicine. Some of them had titles and text in Latin, and once, when he had left me alone in his study for a short while, I had made a closer examination of them, running my fingers up and down their crumbling leather spines. And oh, the feelings that had overwhelmed me as I had done so! The visions that had begun to form in my mind...

"Sit down." Again it was a command, thrown at me from over his shoulder as he stalked to his own chair. How I wished I could be 'plucky' and continue to stand, to ask why it was he always commanded, why we could never just converse.

The air reeked of stale whisky and tobacco, one managing to dominate for a few seconds before the other fought to take over. Velvet curtains at the window – burgundy in colour but far from opulent owing to their almost decrepit state – were barely pulled apart, keeping the daylight deliberately at bay. I had to battle to keep my breathing steady as I hated to show Father I was frightened. More than that, I hated to admit it to myself. If only I had the picture of Mother to cling to, but she was in the attic, safe from discovery.

As he sank onto his chair, he leaned back, clasping his hands together and landing them on the deep red leather of his desktop. There were several books within arms' reach, perhaps those that had been referenced recently by himself and his acquaintances. They were not neatly placed, as I tended to place mine on the side table in my room or on the desk in the library, but strewn in a haphazard manner. Also on the desk there was an inkpot, a pen and some notes, illegible perhaps except to the scribe, for certainly the scrawl seemed chaotic as well. All this I took in over the course of seconds, bracing myself; suppressing any rising panic.

Father surprised me with what he said next.

"You need a new wardrobe of clothes."

I inclined my head to the side. "Clothes, Father?"

"Yes," he replied, no smile upon his face, indeed his expression was sombre.

"An assortment of dresses, a new coat and a shawl. Your boots are scuffed. Goodness knows what you kick at all day. You will need to replace them as well."

"Clothes?" I said again, beginning to feel a curious stirring in the pit of my stomach – could it be excitement? "But, Father, where am I to buy such clothes?"

"London."

"London?"

"Of course, where else would one go but London?"

I could barely believe the evidence of my own ears. I had entered Father's study expecting the usual bombardment of questions, but instead was being offered the most incredible of opportunities! I was to leave Mears House – actually *leave* here – and travel to London; witness with my own eyes the carriages that pounded the cobbled streets; the fancy men, women, and children that lived there.

"Am I to go with you, Father?"

"I will accompany you, yes."

"But how will I know where to go, and where shall we stay? It is such a long way, surely we cannot be travelling to and fro on the same day?"

Abruptly, Father stood up, his nostrils flaring. "Questions, questions. You are always so full of questions, Rosamund!"

I took a moment to digest that statement, or rather the irony of it. Was it not always *he* that asked the questions – questions I did not know how to *begin* to answer. *What do you see?* I shall tell you – just as I told him on so many occasions. I saw the world around me, which comprised four crumbling walls and a series of rooms that lay empty, nothing within them but dust motes which performed a frenzied dance in the air should one happen to disturb them. Outside there was endless grass; a sky that tended only towards blue in the summer and a collection of tall trees that encircled us; that formed a barrier almost, only permitting a choice few into its realm, but mostly guilty of keeping others away. That is *exactly* what I saw but soon, if Father was to be believed, I would be seeing something else too.

Determined to hold onto the excitement of the moment rather than give in to intimidation, I took a deep breath and pressed further with my concerns. "Father, I have never been to London before, as you know, and I am certain that Josie—"

"Arthur's daughter has agreed to be your guide."

"Arthur's daughter?" Had he not just heard what I had just said?

"That is correct. Her name escapes me, what is it?" He huffed and puffed for a few seconds before clicking his fingers. "Constance, there it is."

"Arthur is one of the gentlemen that visited yesterday evening?" I knew this to be true, but what Father forgets is that I have never been introduced to any of them.

"Yes, yes," was his reply, and again there was that annoyance; that implication that I had no right to question anything.

As he started to wear the carpet beneath his feet with his constant pacing – Father always did this, as if he could never rest, not for long – I noticed something else, something that perhaps had not fully registered until now. Father was *impeccably* dressed. There was no need for him to be entirely outfitted. His black thigh-length jacket covered a waistcoat and trousers that were cut from the same cloth, the waistcoat boasting ivory buttons, and his white shirt with its tall collar was perfectly starched. On his feet were boots that either Miss Tiggs or Josie had polished so well you could see your own reflection in them. He cut a dapper figure; another word I had learnt courtesy of Mr Dickens. I glanced down at my own attire and realised how much I looked like a poor relation rather than the daughter of a moneyed landowner. The dress I was wearing was slightly too small for me, as all my dresses were, every stitch doing its duty. However, it was not only me that was shabby; something else was too.

I swallowed slightly before taking yet another breath.

"Father, should we… Is it right…?"

Coming to a grinding halt, Father turned his head towards me, such a swift, jagged action that for a moment I was reminded of dreams I would prefer to forget.

"Spit it out, Rosamund," he insisted, although it was he who was guilty of spitting.

"It is just…" Still I struggled to find the right words, but once begun, I had to finish. "If there is money, should we not spend it on the house?"

As soon as my sentence was complete I realised my mistake.

"*If* there is money?" he repeated.

Breathe, Rosamund, continue to breathe.

Pitifully, I gestured around me. "There is a leak in my bedroom ceiling, I noticed it last night. I will have a bucket put in there to catch the drips, but also, in the dining room, there is mould in several corners, and in the drawing room that I frequent—"

He was by my side in an instant, his breath scalding my cheek as he grabbed my shoulders. "Are you questioning my solvency?"

"No… I… The house…"

"The management of my financial affairs has nothing to do with you. Question me again and it will be at your peril."

"Yes, Father. Sorry, Father."

"You will do as you are told."

"Yes."

"As *I* tell you."

"Of course, Father."

"You are to be seen, Rosamund. *Seen!* And look at you! You are no better than an urchin that haunts the dark alleys and streets of the city that we are to visit."

"An urchin? I meant no ill—"

My desperate attempts to appease him fell short. He held me still and, as though I was caught in a vice, there was no escape. Try as I might I could not look away or refuse to stare deeper into those eyes of his – his gaze captured me, it *seared* me. And in it, there was no love, not a hint. Nor was there any mercy.

Chapter Four

THE trip to London was postponed. Further into the day that Father had sprung such glorious news upon me, I had begun to sniffle. By the following day, I had fully developed a head cold. Father acted as if I had become deliberately ill. Quite how he could think so was beyond me as I was *desperate* to escape this house. The very next day, however, he left without even saying goodbye, leaving me with just Miss Tiggs and Josie to nurse me – and of the two, Miss Tiggs kept her distance, as she always did. I presumed he had gone to London, but for how long this time I had no idea. Sometimes it was just days; at other times he would be gone for well over a week, more rarely two. I experienced the usual relief at his departure, but now, for the first time, there was also a touch of dismay. Sincerely, I hoped I had not ruined my chances to accompany him in the future.

London. How I had dreamed of it! How I had wanted to be a part of it! Society: it was such a glorious word, so full of life and magnificence compared to the word I would choose to describe my current circumstance: isolated. As I lay on the sofa in the drawing room, I do not recall ever feeling so adrift. Beside me on a long low table, my books lay untouched; my sketchpad too, a collection of lead pencils looking somewhat forlorn beside it. I had quite a collection of pencils and sketchpads, this being the one avenue in which Father would indulge me, seemingly keen that I should spend my time sketching. Occasionally he took my scribbles from me and kept them in his study. I wished to think it a sign of affection that he should be so interested, but in truth it was merely self-delusion.

Why had Mother loved him so, if she ever really did? Could he have been different as a young man, when she was alive and breathing beside him? Did losing his wife and being left with a baby to tend affect him so deeply that it changed his character? Was he handsome once as she was pretty? Just as there were no photographs of Mother in the house save for the one I had in my possession, there were no photographs of him either, or indeed myself. This house, with its stark walls and its aura of sorrowfulness, was a house held in a moment; that moment being despair.

I sensed someone else in the drawing room beside myself. I turned my head to look, not quickly, but slowly, feeling strangely unnerved.

"Oh, Josie," I said on a release of breath. "It is you!"

"Of course, miss, who else could it be?"

Perhaps because I was feeling so unwell – my chest tight, my head pounding, my nose sore – that I grew instantly irritated. "For goodness sake, must you creep up on me like that? I would prefer that you knocked on the door before entering."

"Oh," Josie replied, looking instantly stricken. How pale she was; such a delicate creature, slighter than myself and I had barely any flesh to boast of. "I'm sorry, miss. I did knock, honest I did. When you didn't answer—"

"You thought you would walk right in."

"I thought it'd be empty, miss. Often it is."

Insolence! She was so insolent!

To my amazement she did not cower further, but continued walking towards me, a bucket in her hand, one that contained more wood for the fire. It looked very heavy to me, but she managed it well enough. She was clearly stronger than her appearance suggested. Dropping to her knees, she placed a fresh log upon the grate, and immediately flames sprang up around it, growing higher and higher.

"It's cold in here," she murmured.

"It is cold in all the rooms," I snapped. "Even in summer there is a chill throughout this house."

"Is that why you're prone to head colds, miss, because it's so chilly?"

"Prone?" I was already wearing a frown but it deepened. "How do you know that I am prone to head colds?" As far as I could recall I had succumbed to only one since Josie's arrival, and it had been far less tiresome than this present one.

There was that shrug again. "I just wondered, that's all."

After placing the bucket by the side of the fire, she stood, smoothing her apron with her now free hands. "Can I get you something to eat, miss? There's a cheese flan in the pantry, I can fetch you a slice if you wish."

"No thank you, I have no appetite."

"Another warm drink?"

Another? I had not yet been offered a first!

"That would be nice."

"Some lemon and honey in water? It'll help to soothe

your throat."

"Yes, thank you, Josie. Ask Miss Tiggs—"

"No need. I'll make it. I know how. I used to make it often enough at home."

Having informed me of this, Josie smiled and again I was startled – it contained such brilliance, such enthusiasm. Any irritation of mine that lingered was wiped away immediately, and despite how wretched I felt, I found myself smiling back at her, although I could not match such brilliance.

Hastening to her task, she turned to go, taking a few steps before coming to a stop. She was gazing at something on the table, my books perhaps? I followed her line of sight and it led not towards the books, but to my sketchpad, which was lying open at a depiction of Mears House, as viewed from the gardens.

"Josie? Is it the drawing you are looking at?"

She nodded rather than answered.

"Do you like to draw too?" I asked.

It was a wry smile that graced her face this time. "I don't have time to draw, miss." Before I could reply further, she shifted her gaze and stared at me instead. "It's a very good drawing," she somewhat grandly informed me. "Interesting."

My tone was irritated again as I leant over and closed the sketchpad. "I am delighted it meets with your approval."

"Is that how you see it, this house?"

My frown returned. "Of course this is how I see it. This is how it is."

"When you're better, I should like to accompany you for a walk in the grounds."

"A walk?" I choked on such an offer, my cough rendering me quite incapable of further speech.

"Yes," she said before taking her leave, "so that we can see the house together."

* * *

It was practically a full week after my conversation with Josie in the drawing room that I felt well enough to take in some fresh air. I had no intention of walking with her, however. I would simply do as I had always done and meander alone throughout the grounds, making it as far as the trees perhaps and disappearing for a while into the shelter of the woods.

After breakfast, I fetched my coat from the cloakroom – a threadbare thing really, that barely lent enough warmth – and returned to the hall and the front door, having to pull with both hands to open it. As soon as the door yielded, a blast of cold air hit me, causing me to momentarily reconsider my intent, but then as I inhaled and my lungs filled with the lightness and thinness of the winter morning, I realised just how much I had been craving something fresh. Stepping outside with renewed vigour, I shut the door, pushed my gloved hands into my pockets and, with my head down, began to walk, quickly veering off the gravel pathway and onto the grass. I should like to record that the lawns surrounding Mears House were well tended, green and lush, but the truth is they were as neglected as the house; as neglected as I myself. Not words of self-pity, I assure you, just the plain truth.

Walking with Josie indeed! What a notion! Then again,

perhaps I should attempt to ask Father a second time if she could accompany me to London. Surely I needed a maid, if only for the sake of appearance. If Josie could not come, I would be entirely at the mercy of Constance. What would she be like, I wondered, this mystery woman? Kind and pretty or intolerant of my naivety? Would we walk together, arm in arm through the busy and vibrant streets, or would I have to shuffle behind her like a poor relation while she marched ahead with all the confidence of familiarity?

Cease being so negative, Rosamund, she will act like a lady, as must you.

I may have had my misgivings but still I could not help but giggle with excitement, wrapping my arms around me as I continued to walk onwards.

Finally, I reached the trees, grateful indeed for their shelter as the wind had now picked up and was beginning to cause my chest to ache again. Instead of grass beneath my scuffed boots, now I could hear the crunch of crisp dead leaves vying with the squelch of mud. It is quiet in the woods, peaceful. As in the attic, I felt I had entered a different place where only I existed. Myself and… nature. Yes, that was it, only natural things.

Pushing my hair from my eyes, I raised my head. The house was in sight, distant but no less vast because of that. It was far too big for the four of us that inhabited it. Josie's numerous brothers and sisters could have had a room each, not just a bed!

My bedroom was at the rear, and therefore north facing, as was the lone attic window. Sometimes I would go to the rear of the house and stand there, to do what I was doing now – examine it. I fancied the windows were like eyes, so many of them, staring back at me – the house not made of bricks and mortar but something more sentient.

I gasped.

Who was that at the window of one of the reception rooms, not the one I usually occupied, but a different one? Whoever it was had raised their hands to the glass.

It was Josie of course; she must have noticed me, just as I had noticed her.

Was she waving? If so, why was she doing so with both hands? The action seemed rather desperate.

Tentatively, I raised my hand and started to wave back. The moment I did that, her waving abruptly stopped. I shook my head in confusion before briefly closing my eyes, and when I opened them, the figure had gone. Vanished. I blinked and blinked, but there was to be no reappearance. I resolved to ask Josie later what she meant by it; whether she was indeed distressed or simply playing an odd sort of game.

The cold defeating me, I decided to retreat back to Mears House. The last thing I wanted was to risk a relapse of my illness. When Father returned home, I wanted to be fit and well to greet him, and encourage him to take me away from here. There would be no more mention of finances, and no more concern on my part about the subject either. As Father had said, it was his responsibility, not mine.

Re-entering the house, I made my way to the drawing room, there to pass the afternoon and doze intermittently. Whenever I awoke the fire was always blazing, although there was no sign of Josie tending to it. Still, I felt happy enough, the warmth succeeding in making the room almost cosy. As night fell, I realised how hungry I had become. Rising, I made my way to the kitchen, looking out for Josie but not encountering her. Venturing past Father's study, I saw the door was firmly shut, whilst other doors remained either slightly ajar or fully open. I tutted. During winter, doors should always remain closed in Mears House in order to prevent what little warmth there was from escaping. I have instructed Josie on this point several times, so why did she refuse to listen? If I saw her in the kitchen, I would have to tell her yet again.

The kitchen door was shut at least. I stood before it, wondering whether to knock. Quickly, I shook my head. Why should I? This was my house. *Out of courtesy, Rosamund, common courtesy.* Grudgingly I had to agree with my better self. Courtesy should be extended to include everyone, even the likes of Miss Tiggs.

Determined to stifle the butterflies in my stomach – they always started to flutter when I was in this part of the house – I knocked on the door.

"Enter," a voice from within commanded. How imperious she sounded and how ill at ease I felt as a consequence. *But I am the mistress of this house!*

I clutched the door handle, turned it and strode in, my head held high and my back straight. And there she was, by the fire, barely lifting her head to glance my way, a mug of something in her hands, ale I would wager, for it seemed to be her favourite tipple. For a moment I felt like screaming at her: *where is my dinner?*

"Miss Tiggs," my voice was impressively calm, "I should like something to eat."

"You hungry?"

"Yes, yes. Of course I am. It is dinnertime. Past dinnertime, in fact. Why has no one called for me?"

"Why'd ya think?"

From the way she was slurring her words it was clear she was drunk, hence why she was babbling and why there was no dinner available. Could I really blame her, though? I rather think I envied her. Alcohol seemed to blur the edges, thus making the solitariness of Mears House perhaps easier to bear.

"I should like something to eat," I repeated. "Nothing elaborate, just some bread will do, some cheese and some ham if we have it."

Rather than rise from her chair, she nodded towards the larder. "In there," she muttered.

"Am I to fetch it myself?" I said, incredulous.

"You 'ave before now."

She was right, I had. In fact, just lately it was becoming more and more common, as was finding her in this state, slumped by the fire, having supped too well if not wisely, her hands forever clinging to that mug. I supposed I could have argued the point with this excuse for a housekeeper, but I decided against it. She was old, well into her sixties, her body as doughy as her face. Let her sit, let her sup, I was perfectly capable, and at least I could rest assured that the hands which touched my food – my own – were clean. Sometimes the grime beneath her fingernails made me shudder.

Having filled a plate, I took a seat at a small dining table a few feet from the fire.

"You 'aving it 'ere?" she said, observing me.

"Yes, I will not be long."

"Up to you, I s'pose," she muttered, shifting her weight and groaning.

"It would be nice to have a dog, would it not?"

I do not even now know what made me say such a thing, but suddenly I had a yearning for such a creature to inhabit this house – a companion that would have raised its head when I walked in; indeed would have left the solace of the fireside because its need to be petted and fussed by me outweighed everything.

"Your father won't countenance a dog," was all Miss Tiggs said in response. "And neither will I, not 'ere, in the kitchen. Filthy things they are."

Filthy? And yet the smell that emitted from Miss Tiggs was often eye-watering!

As I ate I tried again to make conversation.

"I am to go to London, you know. Father said so."

"Oh?'

"Yes, I am to get an entire new wardrobe of clothes, because I am to be seen, by society, I mean. I am to be presented."

A snort escaped her, followed by a short sharp cough.

"Well, I am looking forward to it," I said, munching on cheese that tasted sour.

"When's he back?"

He? "Mr Howard, you mean?"

"Of course, Mr Howard!"

"Presently," I said, seething at her lack of respect.

"So, you're going soon?"

"Apparently so."

"Good," she muttered, her head nodding. "About time."

I could not help but agree. "I may take Josie with me."

She looked at me then. "Oh, you might, might you?"

"Yes," I said, haughty again. "I think I shall."

"If you can find her."

"Where is she?" I asked.

"You tell me."

Goodness, what I had to put with in this house! It was insufferable.

I took another bite of my meal. If the cheese was sour, the bread was worse, hard at the edges, and the ham was bland, in need of a pickle or a chutney to give it substance. But there were no such fancies in the larder, only the basics.

In response, I saw fit to point out the obvious. "Without Josie, without a dog, without me, you shall be all alone in this house, Miss Tiggs. Does that… concern you?"

Again she looked at me; those hard little eyes of hers – like raisins – so screwed up I could barely see them. She had finished her ale I noticed, her thick tongue darting out to lick the last remnants of it from her lips. "Alone?" she replied. "Alone!"

How the bulk of her body shook as she bellowed with laughter.

Chapter Five

LONDON fulfilled every expectation.

Father returned a few days after my strange conversation with Miss Tiggs, and announced that we were to leave the following morning. He then locked himself in his study, leaving me free to pack the few belongings that I might require. I was to be away for two nights apparently and we were to occupy rooms in Arthur's townhouse.

Immediately I went in search of Josie, whose help I wanted with the packing, running down the corridors, as I was wont to do, but this time for the best of reasons – the most exciting. She was nowhere to be seen on the ground floor and so I changed direction, heading towards the staircase and taking the steps two at a time in order to begin my search of the bedrooms. Because the majority of rooms lay empty at Mears House did not mean that they could forego cleaning. Dust is a perennial problem here, it gathers and it collects; it covers the bedsteads, the cupboards and the wardrobes, cloaking every last hint of colour.

"Josie! Josie!" I called. "Where are you?"

At last I located her, for she was, as I suspected, in one of the bedrooms, a feather duster in hand. She turned as I burst into the room, no look of startled surprise on her face; rather it appeared as if she was expecting me. What a contrast she was to previous maids, who would quake with fear on realising they had not answered a first call. I am not a tyrant, you understand, but servants are *supposed* to be at your beck and call; one should not be required to go in search of them.

"Ah, there you are," I admonished. "I have been looking all over."

She simply smiled at me.

"I am to go to London!" My next words exploded from me such was my excitement, my *disbelief* that such a thing could finally be happening.

"London, miss?"

"Yes, indeed. I am to be bought new clothing, meet new people."

"What kind of people, miss?"

I stumbled at this – what a strange question!

"Erm… well… Father's friends I should imagine; society people. One of Father's friends has a daughter. Her name is Constance. I shall be meeting with her."

"London," she said again, but her amusement had faded, instead she looked perplexed. Or was that sorrow on her face? It was hard to tell.

I drew closer. "Josie? Are you quite well?"

"I'll miss you."

Her declaration both surprised and touched me. Had I ever been missed by anyone before? Not that I could remember. "I doubt I shall be gone long." And then I remembered that I had wanted to take her too. "I could ask Father if he would permit you to accompany me. It is only fitting that a lady should travel with her maid."

At this, one hand flew to her chest. "Me, travel to

London? What a notion!"

What a notion... Those were the words I had thought when she had offered to walk with me in the grounds of Mears House. That she should be using them in reference to accompanying me to London, at my behest, seemed an irony.

As I stood there, attempting to understand that she had just turned me down, if not yet the reason for it, she smiled again, but this time it failed to reach her eyes.

"I can't go, miss," she muttered at last. "I... There's so much work to be done here."

Work that could not wait? Indeed, who was there to notice if it was left undone? But for some reason I did not want to argue, not with Josie, not today. When I think back, perhaps the reason I declined to press the matter further with either her or Father was simply that I wanted her to miss me; perhaps I *craved* the novelty that someone should. All I could do was nod my head in agreement.

"But you shall help me pack, surely?"

Yes, she would do that.

And so it came to be that I left Mears House in a horse and carriage, accompanied only by my father, with my suitcase stowed beneath the seat.

The journey was an arduous one – Father alternating his gaze between the passing countryside and me, but never saying a word. Often I declined to meet his eyes, but instead focused on the grass-covered hills that were still wet with morning dew and an abundance of trees, some evergreen, some bearing no leaves at all. There was such a strange mixture of emotions in my chest that day – a tight ball that I had to strive to keep from unravelling lest they swamp me. Strangely, I began to miss Mears House. It was my entire world, all I had ever known.

When at last the countryside gave way to villages and towns I was further astounded. There were houses! So many of them! Not standing alone as Mears House stood alone but side by side or a few feet apart, and so much smaller. In them there would be mothers, fathers, daughters and sons. What would it be like to live in such a way; to be part of something; a family? I could only wonder. The closer we drew to London, the more congested the area became. But it was not only my eyes that were filled with so much new to behold; my nostrils began to flare too, from the smell. Where I lived the air was clean, it was pure – outside at least; it filled your lungs; it rejuvenated you. Here, I feared my lungs might collapse should I inhale too deeply. It was the odour of so many people gathered close together – an animal stench.

About my neck I had a scarf and so I arranged it higher to mask my nose as I leant further forward.

I had imagined the ladies and gentlemen that paraded these streets so often, and the sophistication that being city dwellers – and therefore so much more a part of the modern world – lent them. But it was not only such characters that greeted me. Here was also a lower class of person; the street urchins Mr Dickens was so fond of portraying, scampering this way and that, with clothes that, contrary to what Father had said, made mine appear to be the height of luxury. Businessmen were also in evidence, suited and booted; but rather than grand they seemed weary, as with heads down, they too hurried along. There were women in skirts and aprons, some as gaunt as Josie, others more rotund and rosy-cheeked. They were walking at a more leisurely pace or standing at the street side, selling wares from their baskets –fruit and vegetables, and matches too, boxes and boxes of them. People were gathering around them, poking and prodding at the merchandise, bartering I think it is called, striving to obtain the best price possible. Aside from street vendors, there were shops, a huge variety of them – butchers, bakers and haberdashers, some with their doors open, inviting you in; others that you could enter by appointment only. And there were buses – marvellous things – not pulled along by horses, not all of them, but able to propel themselves, the people inside either sitting or clinging to overhead straps and looking entirely at ease with this mode of transport.

Exciting, repellent, frightening, and enticing – London was all of these to me, and more. It was bursting with life, with the cries and banter of these townsfolk, and part of me wanted to hurl myself from the carriage into the thick of it; ride on one of the buses – although whether that would befit someone of my station I had no clue. The other part wished to return to the comfort and security of Mears House. *Comfort? Security?* That it should suddenly seem to offer both those things was another irony.

I was about to turn towards Father, to ask him *where* in this vast metropolis we were heading, when a figure caught my eye. It was a little boy, a beautiful child with dark hair and eyes and pale skin.

We had come to a temporary halt – the driver cursing whatever obstruction lay in his path and my father practically hanging out of the opposite window to also learn the cause of our delay. There was most definitely a commotion going on, some rowdiness, but my main focus was on this boy, who was standing as still as a statue.

"What the deuce is happening? We shall be late!"

"A street fight, I think, sir. The police are trying to break it up."

"Can you not go around it, for pity's sake?"

"No, sir. Shouldn't be long, sir."

Although I could hear my father and the driver, their voices were muffled, as if distant. The world around this boy seemed to fade too, becoming little more than a series of grey images. Why should he be capturing my attention so, this boy who was standing rigid without uttering a word? His eyes, though, those glorious eyes! He appeared to be about ten years of age, although of course I was no expert at assessing ages. Did his expression hold wonder? I was certain that mine did.

What's your name?

I mouthed the words, feeling suddenly – inexplicably – quite desperate to know.

Eventually, his lips moved to form a smile.

I smiled too. *Hello,* I mouthed again.

He lifted one hand, slowly, tentatively.

I repeated his action, my smile becoming something of a grin. As young as he was, he seemed experienced, as if his life had spanned a thousand years or more.

Your name?

Harry.

As if I had been struck by lightning, I sat back in my seat.

No, he had not opened his mouth. He had not said a word, but still I knew it to be truth. His name was Harry. There it was. There was no doubting the matter.

Father could not have missed my reaction. He stopped berating the driver and resumed alternating his gaze between what lay outside the carriage and myself. Much given to frowning as his usual expression, his countenance was dark, confused, odd to think it, but it was excited too. Those narrow eyes of his – so different to the boy's – glittered.

Because I had shrunk back; because it took me some moments to summon the courage to look outside again, and only when Father was occupied with doing the same, Harry had in that time disappeared, presumably running through the streets from whence he came.

The carriage began to move, the moment of suspension over.

"We are on our way," I said, feeling the need to say something, even if it was to declare the obvious.

Father settled back into his seat, but his breathing was slightly heavier. As for enquiring of him our destination in London, I thought the better of it. I gazed instead at my hands, clasped together in my lap, and held my tongue.

The miles fell away. I was desperate to look outside once again; to take in the grandeur and the absolute headiness of it all, but I also found myself strangely reluctant – Harry had left quite an impression on me. There was something so very different about him, a little sad too, in spite of his smile. How could it be that one so young could have lived a life beyond his years?

Finally the driver came to a halt. Now the streets were largely empty of people, and instead of shops and vendors, there were houses five stories high, their masonry white; their doors black. No land separated them, but rather they joined shoulder to shoulder, to form a graceful curve.

"We have arrived," Father announced.

"This is Arthur's address?"

"It is."

"This is Hammersmith?"

"Yes," he said, clearly surprised. "How did you know?"

"I saw a sign," I lied.

"Did you, now?" His voice was low, thoughtful. "Did you indeed?"

The driver held the carriage door and extended a hand in order to help me alight. Father followed close behind and together we stood on the pavement outside the house I presumed to be Arthur's, whilst the driver turned his attention towards our luggage. I gazed skywards, marvelling at an abode that was not my own and committing to memory the sight of it so that I could sketch it at a later date, adding to my already copious amounts of drawings. Father had begun striding ahead and I was about to follow obediently when I spied something else – a figure at a window on the second floor, waving at me just as Josie had waved at me, as Harry had also. She appeared to be wearing a white dress, a nightgown perhaps, but most notably her fair hair was flowing free rather than restrained.

I raised my hand yet again to return the gesture, pleasantly surprised at having received the latter two greetings in such a short space of time – how friendly the people in London were turning out to be! Full of hope, I eventually stepped forwards and that is when I noticed Father. Once again he had caught me, his narrow eyes as wide as they could possibly be. He said not a word as he continued to hold me in his sight, but as with Harry, I could read his mind well enough.

What do you see?

Chapter Six

"OH, look at you! You are adorable! Father, I shall take Rosamund to the drawing room immediately so that we can get to know each other better."

It had been something of a whirlwind since we had entered the townhouse, the door having been opened to us by a tall man in uniform – a butler, I believe – Arthur had come into the hall to greet us, shaking my father's hand whilst eyeing me closely, then another person had come flying down the stairs – Constance.

Reaching me, she thrust her hands outwards, grabbing at my arms as she studied me, much like her father had studied me and like my own father tended to do. I felt like a specimen in a jar, unnerved by the attention, but also intrigued as to what they found so interesting about someone so inexperienced and drab in comparison to themselves. However, I was guilty of studying them too. This girl that had hold of me was not wearing a white dress, nor did she have fair hair. Whoever had been waving at me at the window, it could not have been her. Constance was a beauty – Constance Athena Lawton to name her in full, such a grand name compared to plain old Rosamund. From the moment I had laid eyes on her, I was in awe. She was not much older than me, a year or two perhaps, and she had hair that was almost raven in colour, creamy skin and the bluest of eyes – Irish colouring she later told me, courtesy of her mother, who was given to illness apparently and spent her days in bed, being tended. Not that Constance seemed at all disturbed or upset by her mother's poor health, she was another like Josie, seemingly content with what she had; with the world around her. Unlike Josie, however, she had a streak in her that was wild, but wild in a way I envied. She was akin to an exotic creature and yet however fascinated I was by her, she was in turn fascinated by me!

Father and Arthur retired, to where I had no clue, but our destination was the drawing room, located at the front of the house and as grand a room as I had ever seen. It was simply vast, and contained within it so much furniture: two sofas, chairs, rugs, tables, a sideboard and a pianoforte upon which stood a golden candelabrum. There were trinkets on every surface – Constance's mother had a penchant for cherubs apparently – and every wall displayed several paintings. There were portraits, of ancestors perhaps, though none of Constance, and landscapes, two of which were much darker than the others, the figures in them barely distinguishable. As I passed by to sit beside Constance on one of the sofas, a sumptuous affair covered in red velvet, I peered closer. The figures in the paintings were somehow entwined with one another; their limbs flailing; their mouths twisted, some with pleasure, others with something that I would liken more to horror. Quickly I turned my head away, having to swallow hard. They were gruesome pictures, so out of place amongst the other, more commonplace ones. How could one possibly want to sit and admire them?

"So," Constance declared, "tell me about yourself. I want to know everything!"

Again I was stunned. What could I tell? Nothing interesting, that was for certain. "I… well… I live in the countryside, in Sussex, just Father and I, plus our housekeeper and a maid. My mother… my mother is dead—"

"Dead? Oh, I am sorry!"

"Thank you," I replied. What else could I say? "The house in which we live is Mears House and…" already I had begun to falter. "I enjoy reading and sketching."

"Do you go to school?"

"I have a governess… Had," I corrected myself. "Do *you* go to school?"

She laughed as if the question amused her. "I used to, of course. A boarding school here in London, but no longer." She straightened her back in a proud gesture. "I am too old for school. I am now a lady, ready to tackle society."

Tackle society? What an unusual way to put it!

"Do you… do you have a suitor?" As soon as the words left my mouth I regretted them. How could I be so bold as to ask such a question?

"A suitor?" There passed a few moments in which I silently berated myself, and then Constance burst again into laughter. "I have several suitors, dear Rosamund, all vying for my hand. Sadly, none of them *do* suit me, so I'm afraid I shall have to disappoint them." Dramatically, she clasped her hands to her chest. "I believe in true love and until I find it I shall refuse to marry."

I leant forward, relieved and surprised that she had answered me so readily but also desperate to know more.

"And what does your Father have to say about it?"

"He says that in great families there are great sacrifices, that life does not revolve around love. But, Rosamund," she leaned forward too, "it does, it actually does."

"But your Father…?"

"You must not worry about him," still she was laughing. "He roars like a lion but underneath is as soft as a kitten. He wants me to be happy, I know it."

"And your mother?"

Only slightly did her eyes darken at the mention of her mother. "Mother is given to illness not opinions."

"And you mean to be different?"

"Oh, I do, Rosamund. I do."

I had not realised that Constance had rung for tea, but clearly she had as there was a knock on the door and a maid entered. Not the girl I had seen at the window, she also had dark hair, although there was evidence of white in it. Although not an old, old woman, she was bird-like, her back stooped and her hands quite wizened.

When she had poured the tea and left, I turned to my new friend – for that is what I truly felt she was. A friend. One with whom I had shared confidences.

And so I shared another.

"On arriving here, I saw a girl at one of the bedroom windows. At first I thought it might be you, but then discovered you have dark hair, whereas this girl was fair and was waving to me. I wondered who she might be."

"A girl with fair hair?" Constance checked, her dainty little nose wrinkling.

"Yes."

"How old?"

"Young, quite young, about your age, I would say."

"And she was waving at you?"

"Yes, and she was dressed in white."

She did not respond straightaway, but when she did, her words were curious.

"Why," she said. "It appears you're quite different too."

* * *

My next few hours, indeed my next two days at the Lawton's townhouse, passed in the blink of an eye. Constance was quite giddy with being charged with the task of outfitting me, declaring that we were going to have 'the time of our lives.'

At our disposal was her family's driver and in their horse and carriage we ventured deep into the streets of London, leaving our fathers busy in whatever activities it was that engaged them, certainly, I presumed, nothing as frivolous as tailoring.

Frivolous? No, it was arduous! I was trussed up like a doll at times; my waist pinched with corsets that stole my breath away, dress after dress being buttoned up, whilst my feet were stuffed into boots that also pinched. Constance adored this rigmarole, it was plain to see she was well used to it, but it was making my head spin, so much so I had to beg for mercy; ask that we take a break, perhaps visit a tearoom, which secretly I had been longing to do, having read about such pastimes. Although immersed in my transformation, she finally acquiesced and took me to one of her favourite haunts apparently; a hotel in London's West End called The Gaiety.

As we made our way there, arm in arm, she informed

me that women were most welcome in tearooms nowadays. "Society is becoming more enlightened," she insisted, happily chattering in my ear. "As it should." Her voice lowered an octave or two. "Rosamund, people are evolving. This is a good time to be alive."

Who was I to disagree? I simply nodded my head and smiled back at her, finding her enthusiasm, her sheer zest for life, quite infectious. When we arrived at the doors of The Gaiety – having passed several more buses en route, which, to Constance's amusement, I stopped to stare at every time – I was sure we were going to be turned away, in spite of the fact that I was wearing grander clothes than I ever had before. I had to remind myself that we were two young ladies and, although unaccompanied, we were welcome in such establishments; we would be waited on hand and foot.

Stepping inside was like stepping into a world within a world. There were those who sauntered – the ladies and gentlemen of course – and those in uniform whose gait was more determined as they dashed to and fro, carrying silver platters upon which stood elaborate silverware. Without further ado we were shown to our table by one of the waiting staff, Constance having to guide me all the way as my eyes were not just ahead of me but darting all over. The magnificence of it! So many round tables but all a discreet distance apart; the starched white tablecloths; the sumptuousness of the cakes and sandwiches spread upon them in tiered platters; the chatter and polite laughter that filled such a beautiful room; the room itself with its beautiful tiled floor, the art-adorned walls, the Corinthian columns, towering green ferns and oval windows. But more impressive than all of those things – something I had been aware of but had taken an amount of time to fully comprehend – was the light.

As we were seated, all I could do was stare upwards at a chandelier centred in the middle of the ceiling.

"What is that?" I whispered, my heart honestly feeling fit to burst.

"Oh, Rosamund, Rosamund, just as buses, trams and indeed the trains that run beneath our streets are powered by electricity, so too is that."

I turned to her. "Trains that run beneath our streets?"

"Remember you enquired about a rumbling noise earlier? You said you felt as if the ground was shaking. It was then that I told you about the underground train."

She was quite right, she had; but there had been so much to take in, clearly *too* much. "The light," I said again, preoccupied with that.

"Most of the big hotels in London have electrical light nowadays, some shops also. Father has also mentioned that it will be coming to individual homes too at some point. Can you imagine? It will revolutionise the way in which we live."

As she spoke I continued to gaze at the chandelier. The light… it was more beautiful than anything I had ever seen; warm and inviting; pure, with the ability to obliterate all shadows. I wished to reach up and touch it; somehow capture it in my hands as well as my heart. It was magic of the most wonderful kind and I was truly awestruck.

"Rosamund…?"

I shook myself out of the trance I had fallen into. "I am sorry, Constance, so sorry."

Again she laughed, such a wonderful sound, like the tinkling of bells. "I cannot scold you for being so enraptured, I was at first too, but…" She shrugged. "Living here, one really does become used to such things. Indeed, should one happen to grace an establishment that relies on the old ways, one can become quite aggrieved!"

Filled with gratitude suddenly, I reached across the table to take her hand in mine. "Thank you, for bringing me here; for being my friend."

"Of course I am your friend. And I shall insist we spend more time together in the future." Gently retrieving her hand, she raised it to her chest, just above her beating heart. "Oh," she breathed. "Here he is."

I turned my head to discover who she could possibly mean. There was a waiter coming towards us; a young man in a black waistcoat, white shirt and black trousers, with a long white apron tucked into his waistband. Was it this man to which she referred?

I panicked – how was one supposed to order in such a place?

Before I could raise any concerns with Constance, the waiter had come to a halt by the side of our table. He was dashing I supposed, with his hair greased back and blue eyes that were rather piercing, but I thought no more of him than that – he was a waiter. *Just a waiter.* But if I was guilty of such lofty thoughts, it seemed Constance was not. To her, he appeared to be something more, her eyes able to compete with, if not outshine, the electrical light.

"May I take your order, ma'am?" It was a formal enough request from the waiter, were it not for the curve of his mouth.

"Of course…" Constance replied, playfulness in her too. "James, is it?"

"It is, ma'am."

My head swung from side to side witnessing this curious exchange. Did they know each other and not just in this setting?

"We shall have high tea," Constance continued, taking it upon herself to order for us both. "Darjeeling, if you please."

Not only did James' smile widen, he winked at Constance. I may be naïve in the ways of society, but surely a waiter would not dare to wink at his customer?

"Very good, ma'am." He took a step backwards and I thought he was going to turn and leave us, but he was not quite done. His voice low, so as only the two of us could hear amid the general chatter, he added, "I have something else for you, Lady Constance; would it be agreeable to bring that to you, too?"

As my mouth fell open, Constance could only purr. "A gift you mean?"

"Of sorts."

"Oh, the intrigue," she teased. "I shall leave instructions as to when and where."

When he had left us alone, I turned to Constance, my eyes begging for an answer.

"As I have told you, Rosamund," was her sole reply, "it's a good time to be alive."

Chapter Seven

I loathed the thought of returning to Mears House, but return I must. I sat in the carriage with Father, whom I had barely seen these past two days, dressed not in the clothes in which I had arrived, but in white linen and bows. This was not the only change about me, however. I had seen things; I had heard things. Through my encounter with Constance I had been immersed, if only for a short while, in an alternative reality far removed from that to which I was accustomed. Constance and James: I was still amazed by their tryst and how daring she was; how different to anything I had expected.

Of course I insisted that she told me all about it when we were out of earshot.

"We are in love," she had declared.

"You and the waiter?"

"James, his name is James and he is from suitable stock; not the elite, no, I shall grant you that, but a decent family nonetheless." As I stared at her open-mouthed, she continued. "Money cannot make you a good person, Rosamund. It does not make one noble. And some of these families," she gestured about her, although we were alone in our carriage, returning to the townhouse, "who parade themselves, who assume station above others; who imagine themselves to be so high and mighty, they have no money. Do you realise that? It's all theatre. Scratch beneath the surface and you shall find some will not have as much spare change in their pocket as James has. James is very much into politics, into a wide range of subjects; he is so clever, so… informed. So much so that he inspires me. Society is changing, Rosamund. The world is changing. The old ways are disappearing and rather than be afraid, we must embrace it." She had hugged herself at this point; had closed her eyes. "Embrace everything, for everything is new and fascinating."

It was hard not to believe her; I *wanted* to believe her; experience it alongside her. But something did not sit right with me.

"Your Father has no idea about you and James, has he?"

"Of course not." She found the idea that he might, amusing rather than terrifying.

"If he discovers—"

"But I have told you, Rosamund, I can manipulate Father. You must not worry."

That also amazed me. If Father knew I was fraternising with someone from a lower class, I could just imagine the consequences that would befall me. Not that I would do such a thing. Not because I was concerned about anybody's station in life, not after what Constance had said. I felt she was right; people did put on such airs and graces. It was simply because I could not picture myself fraternising with anyone. Besides, her observation applied very much to me too. As refined as I might look thanks to my transformation at her hands, I was on my way back home and home was a place I should be ashamed to invite Constance.

Not for her the dusty surfaces of Mears House – the sheer isolation of it, the terrible neglect. When I got home, I would change back into my own clothes and no doubt slip back into my old way of life too. A thought that was now hard to bear.

"Father, when shall we return to London?"

Surely such an investment in my clothing could not be for one occasion? Also I had really only been seen by Constance, not by 'society' as such. As I have mentioned, I barely saw Father and Arthur; I had listened out for them but I never overheard the low whisper of conversation travelling towards me from another room. Where had they gone during the time I was there? What had they been doing?

Father was reading some papers, handwritten notes, with not just words upon them but drawings too, or rather symbols.

"Father," I dared to prompt.

"Soon, Rosamund, soon," he answered; not bothering to glance up he was so engrossed in what he held.

I should have loved more detail, but I was no Constance; I would not press further. What I had learnt was good enough – at some point I was going back, I would see Constance again, I would hear all about her liaison with James. She was bursting to tell someone and had declared how glad she was to have me in her life; a confidante, a position I felt extraordinarily proud to hold. But as much as I looked forward to our next meeting, I also found myself longing to see Josie too – and found it peculiar that this was the case. In a world far lonelier than London, she had become something of an anchor. She was the only factor that made Mears House seem like home rather than a place in which to exist. Not Father certainly, and as for Miss Tiggs… I sighed, longing again for a dog; a faithful companion – someone to stand by me; to look out for me; to love me. No, I had not the boldness of Constance. I could never ask Father to fulfil my yearning in that respect. But I had Josie, and her smile, as bright as Constance's smile, offered relief as well as a degree of solace.

Despite that, my heart plummeted when we turned onto the path that led to Mears House. It was home. And yet I felt home*less*, as if I did not belong anywhere. *Like Harry.*

Harry? How odd that he should spring to mind – the urchin boy. But it seemed the correct comparison to make – Harry had appeared homeless too. I recalled all those I had seen on the streets of London; the colourful and the less colourful, those who were decidedly more grey, who had stared at me as I passed them by; whose faces had expressed so many emotions – bewilderment even, on occasions. Constance had seemed oblivious to them, but then Constance had her mind on other matters!

It was Miss Tiggs that opened the door to us, her rotund figure such a contrast to the Lawtons' butler, and, although she deferred to my Father, who swept past her and on towards his study, those notes still clutched in his hand, she all but sneered at me. Immediately my hackles rose. Such disdain! Such disrespect! I should have liked to take a piece of her sour cheese and shove it down her throat, a thought that amused me – the sheer wickedness of it – Constance and her wild ways had clearly had more of an influence than I had bargained for.

But where was Josie?

Leaving my suitcase at the foot of the stairs, I called out

for her. Father had not yet reached his study but he turned and looked at me, a scowl on his face. I expected him to reprimand me, perhaps for being so loud, but he shook his head, narrowed those eyes and entered his study at last, slamming the door behind him.

Yet again, Josie was nowhere to be found on the ground floor, and so I made my way upstairs. To my surprise, I found her in the corridor that led to the attic.

"I have been calling for you." I deliberately refrained from saying 'again'. "Have you…" I could feel a frown developing, however, "…been into the attic?"

It was not my imagination; her green eyes lit up on seeing me, but their expression was also guarded as if she was suddenly wary. "The attic, miss? No, why ever would I?"

"Then why are you in this corridor?"

"I'm dusting."

Sure enough, in her hand was the feather duster – an almost permanent feature.

She stretched her hand upwards and waved the duster around. "See? There are cobwebs everywhere." When still I did not say a further word, she added, "It's my job, miss, to keep everything clean."

"But you have not been into the attic?" Why I felt the need to check this again was beyond me.

"No need. It's clean enough in there."

"Josie—"

"Your suitcase, where is it?"

"I left it at the foot of the stairs."

"I should fetch it?"

"Yes. Thank you."

"I'll bring it to your bedroom."

"Thank you," I said again as she squeezed past me.

Before I turned to follow her, I stared at the attic door, a longing deep within me to go inside; to hide suddenly – but from what? The urge was so strong that I actually took several steps towards the door, my hand reaching out to touch the handle; to turn it; twist it. A haven. It still represented that to me and was perhaps the only room, apart from the library, that made this house bearable. But clean inside? What could Josie possibly mean by that? It was cluttered; it was dust-ridden.

Clean.

I continued to ponder as I turned and made my way back to my bedroom.

* * *

Life resumed at Mears House. Father returned to London on his own and when he came back, he barely called for me; barely had anything to do with me in fact. He would eat and drink in his study; might even have slept in there, who knew? His bedroom was quite a distance from mine and I had no reason to keep a constant watch on it. I could hear him well enough on occasion, though. There would come a crash, and then a series of curses as he careered down corridors and into the walls and furniture; whatever alcohol he had poured into himself rendering it impossible to walk in a straight line.

Father's drinking was getting worse. Was he unhappy? Agitated? Did he regret the money spent on bedecking me? Would Miss Tiggs leave if he could no longer pay her wage; would Josie? And if so, then what would become of us all?

Such thoughts and more would tumble into my mind, until I fancied I should like a drink too – something to calm my nerves. Father would notice, however, if any of his precious liquor was gone; he would come chasing after me for certain then. And so I did as I always did: filled the endless hours reading and drawing, creating picture after picture – of London and its busy streets; the townhouse; my mother; Constance and her beau James, and… Harry. Often I would draw Harry and those eyes in which I had momentarily drowned. Sometimes, if my legs grew restless, I would leave the sketches in the drawing room, fetch my coat and let myself out for a walk. Soon it would be December, and I wondered if we might have snow. I was always glad to see it, as it dressed everything so prettily, although I was not so glad at night when the rooms became so cold that even my teeth would ache! It was not snowing on this day, however, but damp and grey; a typical winter's day with nothing to relieve the gloom. Once again I thought of the tearoom that Constance and I had visited, with its electric lights. Soon they would light up London in its entirety, so Constance had said. Having begun my walk, I glanced over my shoulder as I hurried towards the woods. Mears House might be quite different if it was lit up. It could be cheerful rather than dour, a vision that would not quite bear fruit.

As I neared the edge of the woods, I shivered. I had returned from London with a new coat, but I was saving it, as I was my new collection of dresses. I was back in my old threadbares and regretted at least not adorning my head with my new hat, and my hands with some velvet gloves. A mist had begun to develop – the 'Sussex Particular' I rather jokingly called it. It was hovering just above the trees as I approached but gradually it descended in a series of wispy tendrils that held me quite enthralled. Continuing to walk, I watched as these tendrils broke from the mass to weave their way in and around so many naked branches, curling like smoke, as a lover might curl his fingers around the wrists of the lady he adored – a possessive gesture, a possessive lover.

My imagination had been ignited – not only because of my books but also due to Constance and James. Was he her lover? Certainly she had hinted as much. Constance who was brave, bold and beautiful – everything I wished to be; who had her father wrapped around her little finger: if only I could do that with *my* father.

If only he loved me.

Realising once again that he did not, that *no one* did, I began to feel quite miserable. There existed someone who liked me well enough; Constance, or at least I fancied she did, but there were times when I longed for more than that. Tears had begun to fill my eyes and soon they would spill onto my cheeks. I was not given to self-pity ordinarily, but on occasion what I lacked overwhelmed me. As I was contemplating this, something odd happened. The tendrils of mist changed. If there had been anything enchanting about them before – the fey quality of their wispiness perhaps – there certainly was not now. They had darkened considerably; were blacker than a rain cloud waiting to burst. *Like fingers pointing at me.*

As well as confusion, I felt colder than ever – as if those tendrils were not in the distance but were in fact swooping towards me; piercing my clothes; my flesh; diving into the heart of me to find there a fragile thing that could so easily be crushed.

With numb hands I began to bat at my sleeves. "What is this? What is happening?" So quickly rational thought deserted me. "Leave me alone! Please. Leave me be!"

But I knew I would not be able to halt them in their approach. They would be as slippery as eels.

"Stop!" My voice was a screech. "Keep away!"

Although my feet felt as if they had taken root, I forced myself to turn; to attempt an escape. It was with deep shock I realised how far into the woods I had roamed; to the very edge of it, and therefore escape back to the house seemed an impossible distance to cover.

Rosamund, you must at least try!

Heeding my own instruction, I began to run, but the path ahead was far from clear – it was strewn with tree stumps and branches. My foot snagging on something, I felt myself topple, certain that as I hit the ground the tendrils would have formed a mass all of their own; that they would fall upon me to either devour or suffocate me.

"Help!" I screamed again, but in complete despair. Who was there to help me? Who was there to even believe me? This was nonsense, pure imagination… or madness. Indeed, it might be that.

"Miss! Miss! You're safe. Take my hand."

More bewildered than ever, I looked up. There, in front of me was Josie, her red hair still tucked beneath her cap; a shawl covering her thin shoulders.

"Josie, what—?"

"Come on, miss. Let me help."

I reached up. Her hand, as it took mine, was so small, but it was warm; that registered straight away, and I was entirely glad of it.

Back on my feet, I fixed my eyes ahead, only ahead,

refusing to glance behind me. Josie, it seemed, did the same. I offered no explanation as to why I had fallen and she offered none as to why she was so deep in the woods. She simply put her arm around my shoulders and, because of the pain in my knee where I had fallen and struck the ground, I leant against her. Together we limped back to the house.

Chapter Eight

THE cut on my knee was worse than I had realised. Once inside Mears House, we hurried to the drawing room. Ordinarily, I supposed we would have gone to the kitchen. Josie had indeed suggested that, for after all, water would be more readily available there, but I had refused. I had no wish to see Miss Tiggs; to witness a face that could not care less that I had hurt myself, or that I had been so frightened. But Josie cared – her expression made that known. Even when she sat me down on the sofa, she would not let me go, her grip on my shoulders remaining firm.

"All is well, Josie," I tried to assure her, "but if you could bring me some rags, it will help to stem the bleeding. Silly me," I muttered. "I am so clumsy."

"You're no such thing," was her response before she left me at last, returning promptly with not just a collection of rags stuffed into the pocket of her apron but a bowl of fresh water, which she held between her hands, as though it were a sacred chalice. She laid it upon the table, having to push aside my sketches to do so. Again I noticed her glance at them, her hand moving one or two in order to gain a closer view.

"Did you tell Miss Tiggs of my accident?" I enquired as she knelt in front of me, lifted my skirt above my knee and gently removed my stocking. I flinched as she had to peel it where skin and wool had melded, but her hand was steady as she worked diligently away. When it was done, the green of her eyes met the dark of mine.

"What *did* happen, miss?"

"What where you doing in the woods?"

She laughed a little and I did too when I realised how absurd we sounded - meeting each other's question with one of our own. At this rate we would accomplish nothing!

Having bandaged my knee, Josie turned to stoke the fire. Even so, there was still such a chill in my bones. As the flames began roaring I decided to answer her question, although in truth I was not entirely sure where to begin.

"I had simply gone for a walk, just to the woods, where I often go."

Josie nodded her head at my words, rising to stand before me.

"Please," I insisted. "Take a seat."

Obliging, she perched on the chair opposite.

I took a deep breath, still with no clue as to how I should explain what had happened. I winced inwardly, unsure if I *wanted* to remember, and then, quite suddenly, as though my lips were as strong-willed as Constance's, words poured from me.

"There was a mist; I could see it clearly hanging over the trees, and then it was somehow *in* the trees, curling around the branches – little wisps, tendrils, as I thought of them." I shook my head. "Or a lover's hand, but one with cruelty in it, because quickly they began to grasp and snatch; darting here and there as if searching. The more I stared, transfixed, the more defined in shape and substance they became. So many tendrils. They grew darker and darker, not like mist at all now, but something else; something abhorrent. They congealed – that is the only description I have – to form something separate, and I knew… I knew that if I continued to stare at them, if I grew even more frightened, they would turn their focus on me rather than the trees."

I had begun to sob – loud wracking sobs that may have had my father come running had he been home to witness this commotion. Thankfully, only Josie and I were in the house, and Miss Tiggs of course, but she could not hear, being far away in the kitchen. Even if she had, she would ignore me and continue to sit by the fireside, supping her beer and warming her over-inflated body, thinking nothing of it.

"I am sorry, so sorry. I do not understand why I am suddenly overcome."

"There, there, miss."

Josie's sweet words only made me cry more and so she stopped, waiting for the outpouring to run its course. When at last it did, she handed me another rag so that I might blow my nose. I apologised again as I wiped my eyes.

"When you…" Josie hesitated, her eyes downcast for a moment, her teeth gnawing at her lip. She took a deep breath before continuing. "How were you feeling when you saw what you did?" She tapped at her chest. "In here, I mean."

"Well…" I tried to remember. "Scared. Of course I was scared. I have never witnessed such a thing before. And sad, definitely sad."

"Why sad, miss?"

"Because…" Was there shame in admitting it? "I felt that no one loved me… my Father…"

"What else?"

"What else?" I queried. Was this not enough? "I felt… I felt… angry."

"Just angry?"

I shook my head, confused by her intent to probe deeper and deeper. And then I realised, it *was* more than anger that I had been feeling; it was rage, it was bewilderment; it was loneliness and it was terror. They were all there within me, even when I was unable to acknowledge them – when I refused to – bubbling below the surface. Extreme emotions, *negative* emotions; they *characterised* me.

There was realisation on Josie's face also.

"That's why you saw what you did, miss," she said before slowly rising to her feet, touching me lightly on the shoulder and seemingly drifting from the room.

I did not call her back; I did not ask that she elaborate. There was no necessity.

I knew what she meant.

* * *

"Rosamund! Rosamund!"

I awoke to my name being used; a whispered sound, but urgent. I had been deep in sleep and I struggled to lift my head, turning towards the voice.

"Father? Is that you?"

There was indeed a figure sitting on a chair in my bedroom; a hazy outline, almost as black as the room itself.

The figure was perfectly still, staring at me.

The sight gave me the impetus required to push myself up into a sitting stance.

"Father?" I said, trying to make sense of what was going on; to remember the events that had led me here.

I had fallen in the woods, hurt my leg, and then later on, had sat for hours by the fireside, Josie bringing me some food from the kitchen, although I was uninterested in it and had pushed it aside. All this had happened yesterday after… after I had seen something. When she had returned with my food, Josie had sat with me again, her presence such a comfort. We did not talk as we had talked earlier; there was simply no need; we understood each other, she and I, although how that could be, I was quite unsure. But there was a new ease between us and I felt happier to know she lived at Mears House too – the house and I both benefited from her presence.

But this presence – the one who had come into my room; who sat and stared at me; who whispered my name – made the house feel dour again; chilled.

With a speed that was preternatural, the figure rose from the chair and arrived by my side, bending over me; forcing me to lie back down.

Was it a dream? Another nightmare? I had so many nightmares; sometimes they plagued me. Little wonder, I supposed – this lonely house, hidden as it was, was a house that *bred* nightmares.

I could bear it no longer. I closed my eyes, screwed them up tight, wishing I could somehow shut off my other senses too.

Whisky – it has such a sour smell.

That alone confirmed the identity of the figure. When

had he returned? Certainly, I had retired to bed later than usual and there had been no sign of him.

How I wished I could scream, for Josie; for some sort of protection. But there was nothing and no one.

"Father?" I tried so hard to disguise the whimper in my voice.

"Like her," he slurred. "You are so like her."

"Who?"

"She taunted me. As do you."

"Father, I am tired. Yesterday I had an accident you see—"

"It shall not happen again."

Despite myself I was curious. "What, Father?"

"I shall make sure of it."

"I am not sure I understand what you mean."

"Arthur says to tread carefully, that you could go the same way. But all is well for Arthur; all is not well for me. Arthur be damned!"

His hand shot out, a blackened thing, to grab me by the shoulder. His grip was tight at first and I flinched, but then it grew looser. This brought only temporary relief, however, as something more alarming began to occur. With his fingers, he stroked the cotton of my nightshift, and his mouth came even closer.

"So like her," he continued to murmur. "So like her."

"Father, please…" I found myself begging yet again. "I really am so very tired. I was trying to tell you that I fell in the woods yesterday and hurt my knee. Josie was very kind, she tended to me, but it is still sore, Father. Father, stop, let me go!"

I slapped his hand away from me and with my legs pushed myself backwards out of the bed, falling to the floor.

"Come here, you little wretch," he called. "You are mine to do with as I wish."

Quickly, I got to my feet, and as I did, Father hurled himself at me.

I had to defend myself; drink had turned him into a beast, the worst I had ever seen him, and although the darkness cloaked his eyes, I could sense well enough the intent in them. Thankfully, I was close to the fireside. I lunged towards it, snatching up the black iron poker and brandishing it in front of me.

"Stay away! I beg you. Just… stay away."

He came to a halt. "You would dare to strike me?" he questioned, such cruel laughter in his voice.

"You would dare to touch me?" I said, determined that he would not.

Again there was a peel of laughter, but I noticed he did not move further. In truth he could have torn that poker from my hand quite effortlessly.

"Father, the whisky; I think it has taken its toll on you tonight."

"Oh? You are now an expert on such matters, are you?"

"I do not wish to fight. I just want to be left alone to sleep."

"What is it about you, Rosamund? What was it about her?"

His words were such a mystery to me.

"Why do you deny it? WHY?"

As he screamed at me, my legs threatened to buckle.

"You would do better to put that poker down."

If there had been any respite from his approach, it was now over. He was advancing on me again and even with a weapon in hand, I felt defenseless.

Tears began to fall from my eyes as I first held up the poker, and then lowered it. I could not hit out. It was not in me to do so. I knew then I was a victim – *his* victim.

"That is better. Much, much better," his voice had taken on a soothing quality that made my skin crawl. "If you would only do as instructed, Rosamund, all will be well."

His breath, oh his breath! I turned my head to the side as the poker dropped from my hand and crashed to the floor; repulsed by it, by him. In me there was only resignation as I succumbed to whatever my fate should be.

Only resignation, Rosamund?

As his hands grabbed my shoulders again, as he dragged me closer to him, I remembered my conversation with Josie. She was quite right. There was not *only* resignation in me, or fear. She had made me realise this. There existed a whole host of emotions, and of these, my rage at least matched his.

I allowed it to rise upwards; indeed I coaxed it to crawl out of whatever recess it lurked in. I allowed it the freedom to conquer all other emotions; to drown them out entirely. I focused not on Father's hands as they began to paw at me, but on my anger. It was a living thing, I was sure of it; a thing apart. It had such energy!

I heard it first – the rattling.

And then he heard it.

Both our heads turned towards the door.

"Josie?" I breathed.

"Who is that?" Father questioned, becoming stockstill.

Still the rattling continued, reminding me of how it did that on occasions when I was in the attic. I had always presumed it was Father coming to find me, but only daring to venture so far. I was safe in the attic, but not safe here, in my bedroom. This time it was clearly not him, but if it were Josie or Miss Tiggs surely they would call out or announce themselves. Next came a banging – a fierce banging, like so many fists pummelling, pummelling – and the door shuddered in its frame as a consequence. Whoever was responsible would come tearing in soon, surely, having torn it off its hinges. Though alarmed, I was grateful for the sudden commotion and for how it had distracted the man grabbing at me. It had caused him to step away from me, his breathing coming in short sharp gasps, his chest heaving.

"What the devil?" he was saying. "What is it? What have you done, Rosamund?"

What had *I* done? Nothing! I had done absolutely nothing.

As abruptly as the rattling had started, it stopped.

I said not a word, and nor did Father. We stood there for an age; mute.

Eventually he turned towards me, making an attempt with shaking hands to straighten his cravat. "We are to return to London."

"When?" was all I could think to ask.

"We shall leave tomorrow."

Having informed me of this, he left my side and returned to the door, reached for the handle and tentatively opened it. As he did so, I flinched and I am certain he must have done the same, myself half expecting more of those tendrils to come pouring through; to grab me as Father had grabbed me, and this time there would be no escape. When nothing of the sort occurred; when all that met us was the darkness of the landing beyond, his sigh of relief was as audible as mine. Before he disappeared out of sight, however, he stopped, once more a hazy distant figure.

"Arthur be damned," he repeated. "It *is* time."

Chapter Nine

TIRED and bewildered I rose early that morning, retrieving my suitcase from my wardrobe and laying it upon the bed. I had not managed to sleep a wink after Father left, too distressed by all that had occurred. Strangely, much as I was looking forward to seeing Constance and hearing all about any further escapades with James, I was dreading it too. As well as Father's actions, his words had stuck in my mind. *It is time*, he had said. Time for what? There had been such an ominous note to his tone, all slurring and signs of drunkenness suddenly gone. As I watched him leave my room, a thought had crossed my mind – should I run to the attic and hide there? I did not know what kept Father from that room, but something did – something that by contrast, welcomed *me*. He was becoming more and more unpredictable. Last night… I shuddered just as the doorframe had, remembering it. What had possessed him? For that is what he had seemed, a man possessed.

The knock on the door gave me cause to yelp.

At once I reminded myself who it was – Josie, come to assist with my morning ablutions.

"Enter," I called, and the door opened. There she stood,

her smile yet again tinged with sorrow.

A part of me longed to rush and throw myself into her arms; glean some comfort, *any* comfort, and she would oblige – as much a friend to me as Constance – but I desisted. Another part of me wanted no one to touch me ever again.

Her gaze moved from me to the suitcase. "You're going back then, miss?"

"Yes," I replied.

"You're not happy about it?"

"I am. I am just… tired. Josie, was it you that tried my door in the night?"

I knew not why I asked. It was not her. I had previously made my mind up on that.

"No," she said, coming fully into the room. "Was anything amiss?"

My bottom lip trembled. Indeed, everything was amiss, but I held my nerve, lest I disintegrated into a blubbing mess. "I really must pack," I said instead.

We passed the next hour doing exactly that until all my new fine clothing was folded and neatly stowed, all apart from my travelling dress, which Josie helped me into before sitting me at my dressing table and brushing my hair until it shone.

"You've such pretty hair," she murmured, almost to herself as much as me, and the compliment – so genuinely delivered – threatened to produce tears yet again.

I must be strong.

"You must be strong."

Her next words – an exact echo of my thoughts – startled me.

I jerked my head away from the brush as I asked what

she had meant.

"In London, be careful," was her steady reply. "I've heard such tales."

Although I was sitting with my back to her, I could see her face well enough in the mirror, and perhaps it was because the mirror's silver was tarnished, that she looked almost as grey and hazy as Father had looked the previous night. But unlike Father, it was not darkness that surrounded her; she appeared to shine, as though illuminated by London's new electric light. I blinked two or three times before asking what tales she referred to. Had she read such stories as I had myself? If so, I was surprised she could read; or, and this was more probable, had she been told these tales?

"Josie?" I prompted.

Her hands left my hair as she sighed. "It's just there are so many people, and some of them, miss, are not who they seem to be."

"My father is one who is not as he seems," I said, in spite of myself. A gentleman? In the eyes of society perhaps, but never again in my eyes.

"There are plenty like him. Their goal is the same."

I was astounded. Josie was a simple country girl, but sometimes you would not think it. "How can you know all this? Have you been to London before, and if so, why have you not spoken of it until now? Has a member of your family been to London?"

She shook her head, those red wisps of hair flicking from side to side.

"I wish I could go with you, that's all."

"You were aghast when that very thing was suggested before now," I reminded her. "You said you had too much work to do here."

"There's much work to be done everywhere."

At this, I grew impatient with her. "You are talking in riddles!"

"Take care, miss, that's all I meant to say. Be who you are. And…"

"Yes, Josie?"

"Remember what you're capable of."

Again, she was talking nonsense… or was she? Indeed, look at what I had achieved just a few short hours previously; I had saved myself in spite of my terror. I had stood there in defiance against my father with a poker in my hands, for goodness sake! Although in actuality, my salvation had been the banging and crashing at the door. Had that been its purpose, to save me? Or was it more akin to what I had witnessed in the woods and was something that wanted only to devour me? Questions, questions! My head was full with them. "All will be well," I heard myself saying. "Do not fuss so."

Although I registered the hurt on Josie's face, she did as I bade her. I was about to leave this cold, tainted room for the splendour of Constance's family home once again; there I would have another bedroom to myself, one with fine sheets on the bed in contrast to those that had worn thin on the rickety frame of mine. How long this time? More than two nights? I had no idea. Would I ever come back to Mears House? I shook my head to rid it of such thoughts. Of course I would. I had to.

Tired of thinking, tired of talking too, I had to go downstairs to the hall in order to be ready the moment that Father wanted to leave.

"If you will bring my case, Josie…"

"Yes, miss. Of course, miss."

I had almost reached the door when Josie caught up with me. My suitcase, however, was not in her hands. Something else was.

"I found it," she offered by way of explanation.

"Where?" I asked, taking the object from her, feeling compelled to. It was a necklace, its green coloured stones resplendent on a fine golden chain. Immediately, I clasped it to my breast, feeling a faint vibration from it, a slight pulsing that instead of causing alarm, only brought comfort. "Where did you find it?" I asked again.

"I was dusting in one of the bedrooms, the smallest one. There was a vase and I knocked it over; it was an accident of course. This was in it."

I did not want to give it back. I wanted to place it around my neck, but if Father saw it, he would ask a dozen questions about it, no doubt. Furthermore, he might rip it from me and trade it – for this was no common trinket; it looked expensive.

"Keep it about you," Josie said, reading my mind for the second time, "but hidden, perhaps in a purse or something." She paused. "Think of it as a…" it seemed she had to search for the right word "… a talisman, that's it."

"A talisman?" I repeated, only half amused. "It shall protect me?"

"It will." In contrast to me, she remained solemn. "Help comes in many different forms."

She was once again implying that I would need help. I let this go, aware that time was racing by and that Father must not be kept waiting. Obeying her instruction, I secreted the necklace in my purse. In the hall, Father was indeed pacing to and fro. He looked wretched, his eyes bloodshot, tremors coursing through him still.

"Come on," he said, avoiding all eye contact.

Miss Tiggs was at the door. She dropped her usual ungainly curtsey to Father as he passed her, but simply glared at me. No matter. I clutched my purse in my hands, my fingers cupping those stones, feeling the warmth of them penetrate both material and skin, continuing upwards towards my torso, banishing any chill that lingered.

I climbed into the carriage and took my seat opposite Father. He took some notes from a leather case beside him and began reading, once more refusing to look at me or indeed speak to me, this lasting the entire journey. I did not care; I welcomed it. I sought no explanation from him. There was nothing he could say that *would* explain.

We were just a few miles from the Lawton household and I was gazing out of the window, half wondering if I should see Harry, that beautiful little urchin boy, when realisation suddenly struck me; the necklace – I had seen it before. It had been draped across a high-collared dress in a photograph that was hidden. It was the very same! I could see it in my mind's eye as clear as a summer's day.

Surreptitiously, I reached into my purse, as if to retrieve a handkerchief, once again touching the stones but briefly this time, not wishing to alert Father; to have him challenge me on what I might be doing. Oh, the thrill of them; the sense of wellbeing I acquired from them – the *protection*.

Clumsy Josie. Clever Josie. She had found Mother's necklace.

Which now raised another question: What had Mother needed protection from?

Or rather whom?

***

This time, when we arrived at the townhouse, there was no mysterious figure at the window waving, and no Constance either, flying down the stairs ready to embrace me. Had she not known I was coming? If she had, I felt certain she would be here.

As the butler ushered us into the hallway, and the maid – the one with the wizened hands – who had brought us tea directed me upstairs towards my bedroom, leaving Father to seek out Arthur, I kept alert for any sign of Constance.

My bedroom at the townhouse was on the first floor and Constance's on the third, not that I had paid a visit to it; I had not, but she had imparted this information on the previous occasion that we had visited. When the maid had finished unpacking my suitcase – so slowly it seemed, fussing and tutting to herself, about what I could not tell you – and left me alone at last, I hurriedly retrieved the necklace. What were these stones, I wondered, which were as green as Josie's eyes? Constance would know. She knew everything.

And so I resolved to find her. Leaving my room, checking that the passage was clear, I returned to the staircase and ascended quietly past the second floor and up to the third where the stairs carried onwards to the servant quarters above.

There were several rooms on this floor, and all doors were closed. Which one was Constance's room? Taking a deep breath; remembering no harm could befall me whilst I had the necklace about my person, I knocked timidly on the first door and called Constance's name. There was no reply. This happened a second and a third time, but at the fourth door I heard movement inside, if not an acknowledgement.

Filled with hope, I gently pushed the door open.

"It is I," I whispered. "Rosamund."

Because the curtains were closed it was dark, but what characterised this room was the smell – sweet and sickly, it made me screw my eyes shut temporarily as an urge to retch came upon me. Quickly, I reprimanded myself. *Think of your friend, Rosamund, not yourself, clearly she is ill.* Stepping further into the room, I noticed movement on the bed. There was someone lying beneath a thick coverlet. There was a fire roaring too, which only served to intensify the awful stench.

"Nell, is that you?"

Nell?

The voice that had asked was low and croaky. If this was Constance, she must be feeling wretched.

If?

Panic seized me. What if it were not? Constance's mother was much given to illness apparently, spending much of her time in her room. What if her bedroom was also on the third floor? How foolish I had been to go exploring. Why had I behaved so recklessly? I should have waited patiently for Constance to come and find me.

In an attempt to rectify my terrible mistake, I began to back from the room, but I was too late. The figure was now squirming on the bed, craning its neck to see me.

"Nell, is it you? Have you got it?"

"I… I am not Nell," I stammered.

I could see the rudiments of a face but nothing further,

the darkness obscuring my vision.

"But have you got it?" The person – a woman, Constance's mother, it had to be – asked again.

"Got what?"

"Did she send you?"

"Nell?"

"Tell me whether you have it!" This time her voice was much higher, and filled with a desperation that made me feel quite desperate too.

"I am sorry," I said, still intent on retreating, my hand on the door ready to close it behind me; to end this escapade.

"Do not go!" the woman commanded. "Come closer."

Although I was desperate to flee, I could not. If she was indeed Constance's mother, she was the Lady of this house and therefore to be obeyed.

As I began to tentatively make my way closer, the door swung shut behind me and I jumped upon hearing it. Nonetheless I continued towards the bed, my only solace knowing that I had my talisman with me. That Josie had even called it so was comfort enough. To know that Mother had owned it, more comfort still.

The woman shuffled and groaned, pushing herself semi-upright.

I noticed a jug of water on the table. "Would you like some?" I said, pointing to it.

The laughter she emitted was harsh. "No. That is not what I want. Who are you?"

"I am Rosamund. I am here with my father, my father being a friend of Mr Lawton's."

"My husband?" she repeated, shuddering, I was certain of it. "What is your father's business with him?"

Before I could answer she was seized by a violent coughing fit, one hand flailing towards me as she managed to utter in between, "My handkerchief, fetch it."

Next to the jug of water was a handkerchief, such a delicate thing, made of lace and so at odds for the purpose for which it was about to be used. When I offered it to her, she grabbed it, our fingers briefly touching and as they did, a series of images flashed through my mind, each and every one of them tortured. It lasted moments, mere moments, but what I saw scarred me. A woman, so like Constance and certainly as beautiful, as exuberant, as full of life and energy, quickly becoming a wretched, weakened thing; a mere shadow of her former self. But why? Because she was terrified, that was why.

"Madam…" I uttered, wanting now only to embrace this stinking, sweating creature before me who was filling such a delicate handkerchief with blood – for the visions had prompted such an extent of sympathy. Instead I watched as she threw the handkerchief aside; as she beckoned for the water she had only recently refused.

After taking a few laboured sips, she sank back against her pillow.

"I need it you see," she said. "This cough…"

"Are you referring to your medicine?" I asked, wondering where it was and whether I could administer that too.

"It… It helps… With everything."

"Where is it?" I looked about me, searching for a bottle of some sort.

"Need more… Nell… but he, he controls it… controls me."

He? Who did she mean?

"Mr Lawton?" I queried.

She nodded, a brief gesture. "Mad," she said. "Worse… Evil."

"Evil?" My eyes felt as if they would burst from my head. Was she implying Arthur was evil?

"Shall I… open the curtains?" I was desperate to have some light in this room, an open window too, to let some of the stench out. I was sure that if I continued breathing it in I would become as sick as her.

When she did not answer, I took it upon myself to prise the curtains apart, but as I made my way towards them, she cried out 'NO!' My blood curdled to hear such a terrible sound. I swung round to look at her, half in fear, half in surprise.

"It hurts, damn you!" Spittle flew from her mouth. "The light hurts."

Sobbing now, she appeared to collapse in on herself.

I continued to stand there, frozen with indecision. What was I to do? Go to her or call someone?

"Madam…" How like Josie I sounded. "If you will tell me where to find Nell… Or Constance, I can fetch Constance."

"Constance is lost."

"Lost?" I shook my head. "If she is not at home, then perhaps she is out, taking tea?"

"She is lost," again she insisted. "*I* am lost."

I had been uneasy until now, but when Constance's mother began keening and to rock to and fro, I was horrified. If someone should hear her – Nell, or worse, Arthur – and found me here, upsetting her, I would be in trouble beyond imagining.

"Madam, please, I apologise for coming here, I should

not have done so."

I reached out to her again, meaning only to offer comfort, but, as had previously happened, the moment our hands touched, visions filled my mind. I had no power to stop them or withdraw my hands for she had brought hers over mine, both now clutching at me as desperately as if she were drowning and I her only saviour.

Rather than look into her reddened eyes, I shut my own and the images became even clearer. A young woman waiting anxiously at the window for her beau to appear and gasping with delight when she saw him; such a dapper young gentleman, clad head to toe in finery. It was this house he was visiting – not Arthur's then, as I had presumed, but belonging to this woman in the bed in front of me. A charmer, yes, he was certainly that, and handsome too in a slightly austere way. This girl, this woman – Helena was her name – was very much in love with Arthur. Another image: an argument, not between Helena and Arthur but between Helena and an older woman. Her mother? A wedding, such a joyful occasion ordinarily, but there was sadness on Helena's face and no mother in attendance. There were hardly any people at all. This house again, Arthur now the master of it. What had happened to Helena's mother? Or to her father, of whom I have seen no sign? Now she is alone in her bedroom, holding a picture of her mother in her hands as I have done so often myself. She is weeping, and she is confused. *The accident, Mother, the fall... were you pushed? Did Arthur push you?* One hand falls to her belly, her rounded belly – she is with child. A daughter will soon be born – Constance. Helena despairs. *Trapped. Both of us are trapped, in my house, MY house, not his. Do not be fooled, little one. Do not be taken in as I was.*

Having seen more than I could bear, I snatched my hand back, the sheer force of my action taking us both by surprise.

The woman – Helena – was staring at me.

"Who are you?" she croaked at last. "*What* are you?"

"I have told you that my name is Rosamund. I am your daughter's friend, nothing more. I… I need to continue looking for her."

This time I did back away. Resolutely. Nothing she could say, no command she could issue, would stop me. I reached the door, grabbed the handle and yanked at it.

"I must find her," I said again, an attempt at least to explain my swift departure.

"And I have told you," she returned, just as I closed the door, "Constance is lost."

Chapter Ten

"CONSTANCE! Thank the Lord! There you are."

Having fled from Helena Lawton's room, reeling from what had transpired there and how my imagination had run amok, filling my head with such nonsense about a woman of whom I knew nothing, I had dashed the length of the corridor, descended several flights of steps, and somehow found my way back to my room, praying all the while that I would not meet a soul en route, not even my friend.

Safe in my bedroom, I began to pace up and down, feeling both terrified and mystified. Finally, I sank onto my bed and fell into a deep and mercifully dreamless sleep, my fevered brain as much in need of respite as my body. When I awoke it was to find not the pitch black of night but the bright sunlight of morning. Nearby sat a person – not Father this time, and again I was extremely grateful. It was Constance.

Rubbing at my eyes, marvelling that I had slept for so long, I sat up, my arms immediately reaching out for her. Readily she entered my embrace.

She smelt so sweet, so clean, such a contrast to her mother.

"You are not lost, as I had feared," I murmured. "You are not lost."

Clearly confused by my words, she pulled away slightly.

"Why should I be lost?" she asked, her eyes even brighter than before; her skin so flawless – she was perfect, this girl in front of me. To think of any harm coming to her…

Panic set in, though I tried to stem its flow.

"Soon after I arrived I searched for you, but you were nowhere to be found. I… I…" Should I tell her who I had found instead and what she had said? I was about to, remembering that we were confidantes, but then I stopped myself – what could I say? That I stumbled in upon your mother; that she is not only ill, she is a ruined thing; that I touched her hand, and when I did, it was as if I were a part of her? It would sound like nonsense. It *was* nonsense, my mind clearly overwrought due to recent events.

"I am so glad you are safe," I said, hugging her again.

How she humoured me that day, rushing to tell me all that had happened since our last meeting, and all that was planned for us during this one. Much of her chatter centred around James, as I knew it would, although she had only managed to rendezvous with him on one occasion since our visit to the tearoom, when she had been able to give her carriage driver, who doubled as her chaperone, the slip.

"He has become my shadow," she said, wrinkling her nose as she referred to the latter. "He believes himself to be so clever, but guess what?"

"What?" I loved how enthusiastic she was.

"I am wilier! I managed to lose him in the crowds and that is when I met with James."

It was such a daring thing to do, so… improper. My

face must have betrayed my thoughts for she laughed uproariously.

"Oh Rosamund," she declared. "Dear, innocent Rosamund. A woman must take the reins of her life as if it is a tune; she must conduct it."

"Even though society demands something different?"

"It is *men* who say otherwise, but not all; not James; he is enlightened, a radical. That is how he describes himself. I want to be radical too."

Whereas all *I* wanted was to be normal.

"Constance, I worry for you. Your father…"

"Worrywart! You are not to, especially about him."

Her smile became coquettish as she sprung to her feet, a movement that caused her to stagger slightly.

"Constance," I enquired, "are you quite well?"

"I…I'm quite well, thank you," she replied, brushing yet another of my concerns aside. "I am going to call for the maid, she can help you to dress. Now listen here, be as quick as you can, for we have another exciting day ahead."

"Have we?" I asked, excitement beginning to grow in me too, outweighing everything else I was feeling. "What are we to do?"

"Take in more of London life, of course," she answered, heading for the door. "Oh, and pay a visit to a certain tearoom."

As her laughter again filled the air, I tried to smile also.

* * *

We had endless funds at our disposal, or at least according to Constance we did. She insisted that my father had sanctioned such extravagant spending – the commissioning of yet more dresses, more gloves, more hats. As for Constance's father, she had declared him 'the richest man in the world', something I could not help but wonder at. Indeed, if my strange visions had any accuracy, the house in which they lived had not originally belonged to him but to her mother, therefore wasn't it *Helena's* riches that Constance alluded to? But now Helena was a prisoner at the townhouse, a very sick one. Just what was her illness exactly? Did Arthur have independent funds?

How could I begin to ask my friend these kinds of questions? Even to hint at them would surely dent her happiness in some way; it would steal the shine from her. What a thing to be responsible for! *Enjoy the day, Rosamund, stop thinking!*

I strove to do just that. With the carriage driver – a burly man in a long coat and a tall hat – keeping a respectable distance, we joined others in parading the busy thoroughfare, Regent Street being the name of it, and it was apparently the very hub of fashion. This was not difficult to believe as it was filled from end to end with gentlemen and ladies' outfitters, but in amongst them were also jewellery shops and perfumers, as well as one or two bakeries selling a range of delicious cakes and biscuits that you could take home with you in fancy boxes, each of them adorned with a festive ribbon. It had been a bright morning but during the afternoon the light was quick to fade. No matter in a city such as this; gas lamps came on swiftly, joined by the yellow glow of electrical light from a few of the more luxurious shops and hotels. It was breathtaking, all quite breathtaking. I felt giddy with delight.

The roads were crammed with black carriages such as the one the Lawton family owned and on the streets people jostled past, their faces red with cold and excitement. Soon it would be Christmas. An event I was not much given to, for why would I be? It was barely acknowledged at Mears House, Father sometimes being at home for the occasion, but in more recent years, not. Even should he be home, there would be little time spent with me – joyful time that is, rather than time spent interrogating. I shook my head at such a thought. Had there ever been such a thing as joyful time between us? Not that I could recall. And so Christmas Day had always been just like any other – one on which I passed the time reading or drawing, paying no heed to it. But here – in London – the atmosphere fizzed with anticipation.

Having walked the length of Regent Street, we came to a large open thoroughfare named Piccadilly Circus, escaping the crowds momentarily by taking a quiet, mainly residential, side road, before turning left and arriving at a garden square. There, another vision stopped me in my tracks.

"It is a tree," I breathed.

"Correct," Constance replied. "A Christmas tree."

A thing of splendour, it stood as tall as any of London's townhouses and was festooned with ribbons – red and green and gold in colour.

A Christmas tree – I repeated the words to myself. I had never seen such a thing, only having read of its history in one of the broadsheets that Father occasionally brought home, which included a description of the tree that Prince Albert had installed at Windsor Castle; and yet here one stood, before my eyes, even more magical than electrical light.

I could not say a word. I could barely breathe. But I could listen, and so I did, to the sweet voices of a huddled group who stood at the foot of the tree with pamphlets in their hands, from which they sang – "carols", Constance informed me, as I had not heard them before either, their voices swooping from note to note.

"What is this place?" I asked at last.

"This is Berkeley Square," she answered, "one of London's finest. And see over there, the fountain, how pretty it is?"

It was indeed, with its sparkling beads of water, but I could not bear to avert my gaze for too long from the tree. "May we go a little closer?"

"Of course!" she replied, taking my arm and practically pulling me along.

We stood close to the singers, who by now had begun another carol, one that referenced a 'good king' with an unusual name, Wenceslas, perhaps? I could almost reach out and touch the tree, we were so close, but I was a little afraid that if I did it might ruin the magic; might make it disappear. *What do you see?* Such wonders! Such magic! How could I have not known that this existed?

There and then I decided: I never wanted to return to Mears House, ever, despite Josie being there.

"We must go for tea soon," Constance said, giving me a moment to contemplate the prospect of detaching myself from such a marvellous sight.

"Yes, yes, of course," I returned, doing my utmost to commit every detail to memory lest the worst happened and I should never see its like again.

"Before that, though, I…I'll get us some roasted chestnuts."

Her voice sounded slightly odd, a little slurred as Father's was sometimes slurred, so I turned my head slightly to look at her. "Roasted chestnuts?"

She looked perfectly fine, if anything she was more beautiful than ever.

"There is a seller, just over there," she said, "by the fountain. I shall buy us some. You really must try them; it is quite the thing to do at this time of year. Although not too many, I cannot have you spoiling your appetite for later. Stay here, won't you?"

"Yes, yes, of course I will."

Left to my own devices, time seemed to stand still as I gazed about me, listened, and breathed in the smells that wafted on the air – smells quite unknown to me – the roasted chestnuts perhaps, earthy and pungent. When someone began tugging at my sleeve, I was surprised. Who would do such a thing? I looked down, it was Harry, I was sure of it – an urchin boy with a beautiful face and worldly eyes.

"Harry?" I said, to which he nodded. "Oh my," I exclaimed. "It is you!" I had wondered if I should see him again but had doubted it, London being such a huge place. "How are you? Are you well?"

When he declined to answer, I nodded towards the tree. "Is it not wonderful? I can barely believe my eyes. Living in London you must have seen a Christmas tree before, but this is my first time. I know, it is hard to believe, but I assure you, it is so. I just… It truly is wonderful. Harry, Harry, talk to me, why will you not speak?"

Still he refused. He simply continued to stare at me, but his face was beginning to change; it was becoming more shadowed. What with? Concern? He let go of my coat and pointed at my purse instead. I was confused at first and then I remembered, my necklace was in there, but how could he know?

Now, not just pointing, he began to jab at my purse, the action becoming decidedly more frenzied. A little afraid, I tried to seek Constance in the distance. There she was, by the fountain as she had said, in a queue for the roasted chestnuts. It looked as if she would be some time yet. What did this boy want – to steal the necklace from me? I had read of pickpockets, London was notorious for them. Was he one? Was such beauty, such innocence, deceiving?

"You cannot have it, Harry," I said sternly. "It is my necklace."

He shook his head. Wildly, he shook his head.

In the background the carol singers had started yet another song, one more sombre than the last: *Silent night, Holy night.* My unease was growing. No one knew what was in my pocket. Not even my friend, not yet.

Constance had instructed me to stay on the spot, but I began to back away from Harry. He followed me, matching me step for step, his eyes round, pleading almost. I picked up pace, determined to escape him, my hand covering my purse protectively. I could not lose the necklace; I had so little of my mother's, which made it all the more precious. I turned from Harry, hoping yet again to sight Constance, but failing miserably. Where was she? Where was I? I could not see the outline of the square anymore; all I could see were people, so many of them and more than before; far more. I was certain of it.

And some are just shadows.

The more I stared, the more I realised how true that

statement was. And yet we had been lucky with the weather, it was a clear night with no mist to obscure the wonders we had seen. The people milled to and fro, the shadows too, but not all of them. Some had come to a standstill, were turning their heads towards me, their eyes widening with something akin to recognition. Why that should be so, I did not know. They were all strangers to me, every last one of them. One broke away from a group that were standing together, a man, his age quite indeterminable, but if I were to guess, I should say around thirty or so. He was a grizzled man with a long beard, his hat at an angle as if someone had accidently knocked it; his clothes not the clothes of a gentleman. Although his outline was hazy, his eyes were not; they reminded me of someone else's eyes – someone much closer to home; Father's! I did not know the word back then to describe the look in them, but I know it well enough now – malevolence – that was what they contained.

Like Harry, he did not need to open his mouth to speak. *Who are you? What are you?* Vividly, such words imprinted themselves on my mind.

Helena Lawton had asked the same thing. *I am normal*, I wanted again to say it, to scream it. *And you are not. You are far from normal.*

Harry had resumed tugging at my sleeve.

Although I could barely tear my gaze from this man advancing towards me, I felt I must. What Harry had to say was important.

He started jabbing at my purse again. Without questioning further, I reached in to retrieve the necklace – a talisman, a barrier – an heirloom.

Protection.

That was the message Harry wanted to impart – a timely reminder.

The man was now almost upon me. Although a shadow, he was darker than nightfall; darker than any of the corridors in Mears House.

I held up the necklace and thrust it out before me, as if a shield, but it was all too much.

I began to sway on my feet.

Had it worked, had it stopped him?

That was all I could think as my body crumpled to the ground.

Chapter Eleven

"BUT, Father, I do not think she is well enough."

"She has to be, everything is set for tonight."

"She cannot be moved. Not yet."

"It has all been so carefully planned."

"What has?"

"She is to be presented."

"Presented where? Father, what is it you are trying to say?"

There was a silence and I found myself relishing it, drifting backwards, seeking solace somewhere deep in the back of my mind. It did not last long, however. The man was speaking again, not the female, and his voice was troubled.

"If… if she is not to be presented… when so much effort… It would be a disaster. There may be repercussions."

"Is it something I can help you with, Father?"

I wanted to shake my head at this, to shout *No!* Although why I wanted to do so quite so passionately, I could not fathom. Moreover, it would have been impossible. My head felt rigid, as though it were caught in a vice, and my mouth was woolly.

"You… You are not the same as Rosamund,

Constance."

So it was Constance that was talking, although her voice sounded different, having a distant quality, as if she was at one end of a tunnel and I at the other. The man she was conversing with was Arthur.

"We are not so different," she contradicted.

"Do you have any idea why she fainted?"

"None at all. I was queuing to buy some roasted chestnuts, I heard a commotion, looked over my shoulder and she was on the ground. Although… there was something… For a moment I thought I saw…"

When she faltered, Arthur prompted. "You were saying?"

"Oh nothing, nothing. A ruffian, I thought I saw a ruffian close to her, but in the blink of an eye he was gone. Perhaps I imagined it."

"London is full of ruffians."

"It is, Father, it can be. Do you think we should ask the doctor to visit? Her skin seems to be even more devoid of colour."

"We have everything she needs here. She will recover soon, but sadly not soon enough. Damn this accident! Why did you not keep a closer watch?"

"Father," Constance's voice held such indignation. "I was steps away!"

"But how can someone just faint?"

"It was cold, there were lots of people. All this is new to her – the city, the crowds, the sheer noise and excitement. Clearly she was overcome. I could not have foreseen it and I don't suppose she could have either. Father, wait! I think she may be stirring."

There was indeed the sound of someone moaning – was

it me? Again, I seemed so detached from the situation – a spectator rather than a part of it.

Someone was by my side. They had taken my hand and proceeded to stroke it. The touch was light, reassuring. It must be Constance; his touch – Arthur's – would not engender such feelings, not after what his wife had said.

Mad… worse, evil.

Arthur, Father too, that man in the crowds… The latter in particular I could not bring myself to think of, not just now, I was not strong enough. I felt weak, longing for another touch, that of Josie's hand, or that of the mother I had never known. The necklace, where was my necklace…

Constance was speaking again.

"Should her father be here to see to her?"

"I have told you, he is otherwise engaged."

"He is drunk, you mean."

She was so bold! Evidently, her father thought so too.

"You are a fine one to talk regarding vices," he growled.

"Me?" The innocence in her voice was far from convincing. "What tales has the driver been telling you now?"

"You think you are so clever."

"If I am, I take after you, surely?"

"Constance—"

"You are afraid of him, aren't you?"

Afraid of whom? Were they still talking about my father?

"I am curious. What hold does Mr Howard have over you?"

"You ask too many questions."

"Like Mother? What a relief it must be for you then, that now she asks for one thing and one thing only."

"CONSTANCE!"

Arthur's raised voice startled me, almost bringing me fully back to consciousness, but before it did, I found myself slipping again. Even so, part of me silently pleaded with Constance: *do not goad him. Please, do not.*

Constance was her father's girl, she had told me herself on several occasions; she could wrap him around her little finger. But did she know him; truly know him, the way that her mother knew him? Did she realise what he was capable of – destruction in other words, of the human spirit. And was my father capable of that too? *My* spirit?

To my surprise, I sensed no cowering from Constance at Arthur's roar, rather she laughed, that lovely tinkling sound. If she *was* afraid of her father, she did not allow it to show and my heart swelled with love for her because of it. How brave she was, how plucky – everything I aspired to be. This was a woman who would change the world in a trice if she could; who would break free of all convention; who would bend the rules without hesitation to suit her own wishes.

But then a niggling remembrance – what did Arthur mean when Constance accused Father of being a drunk? He had said 'You are a fine one to talk regarding vices.' I remembered her staggering briefly, the morning she had come to fetch me for our outing, and then when we were out… *Dig deep, Rosamund, try and remember more…* In the queue for the roasted chestnuts, she had taken something from her purse, something secreted as my necklace had been secreted – a bottle it looked like – and, unscrewing the top, had popped a few drops of something onto her tongue. Although captivated by the Christmas tree I had wondered at it – was it a tincture of some sort, to treat the onset of a cold perhaps? Although she had not been snuffling or blowing her nose beforehand. Readily, I had dismissed it. It would not be anything harmful, not if she was taking it in public; she would not be so brazen.

But this was the thing with Constance – she believed she could do anything without consequence, not just bend the rules but live beyond them too.

"Father," she had long since stopped stroking my hand and I think had risen to meet her father eye to eye. "*I* want to be the one to be presented."

"I have told you, Constance, no."

"You have said that she is different, implying that I am not. Father, I *am* different. I want to be a part of what you are a part of." When still he made no reply, she continued. "I am not like Mother; I am not weak. And… and… I'm not afraid. Father, please, just listen to me. I think I know what you mean when you say that she is different. She has told me, you see, what she saw when she first came here; a woman at the window waving at her. A woman that does not *live* here."

What was it Constance was trying to say? The woman I had seen; who could she be if she did not live at the Lawton townhouse? A visitor, perhaps?

"Constance, the work the society carries out is highly valuable. We are at the very start of it; we are pioneers. If we do it correctly, our names will live on in history. But… there are dangers involved. Real dangers. I do not want you exposed to them."

But it was acceptable to expose *me*? My father had readily sanctioned that?

Again, I moaned, but this time no one came to my aid.

"Father, sometimes I can see too. I glimpse something,

just like I have told you, you know, such as the ruffian, and then the next minute it is gone. The things I see are just… I don't know how to describe them. Shadows, I suppose. Lately, it has been happening more and more."

Shadows?

"This is because of that substance you insist on taking," Arthur replied; "that your mother crams down her throat too."

What substance?

"I am curious, that is all, merely curious. Father, I *am* like you. I need to know everything there is to know in this world and if there is a world beyond, then why not learn about that one also? Present me tonight. Let me help in Rosamund's stead."

I could still sense his hesitance and prayed for him to refuse his daughter's request, I wanted neither of us exposed to whatever work it was they were involved with. She might not be afraid, but I certainly was.

Her final words, however, wore him down.

"You have admitted yourself that after all the trouble that has been gone to, if no one is presented, there may be repercussions. I rather think Mr Howard will ensure that is so. Surely then, it would be better to take a chance on me than to risk that?"

Oh Constance!

In that moment, my heart broke for her.

Chapter Twelve

I do not know how long I lay in that bed, whether it was for hours or days, but my mind refused to clear. Liquid that was both sweet and spicy had been delivered to my lips on several occasions. I had tried to fight it off, but to no avail. The hands that administered it – wizened hands – were stronger.

What medicine was this? Where was Constance? Crucially, what had happened to my necklace? Had she retrieved it when I had fallen? Was it once more safely ensconced somewhere, waiting to be found yet again?

And who was it that kept creeping into my room at night? For that was what they were doing – creeping, furtive in their actions, to stand over me. Was it Father? If so, he did not touch me; he came nowhere near. Only the person administering the medicine came close to me – was that Nell, the person who tended to Helena also?

Shadows – they also came creeping in. I would refuse to look at them, but they would find their way into my dreams regardless.

How that man troubled me, the one I had seen in Berkeley Square who had noticed me staring; whose eyes had grown wider, looking somehow lascivious. But he was not present in my dreams, nor were any of the other shadows I had seen whilst on the streets of London. They were, however, just as mysterious. They seemed to writhe in front of me, some of them reaching out as if they were begging for help, but others… Those others wanted no such thing. I have often mentioned that I could be beset by nightmares, but it was never more so than when I was at the townhouse. They were relentless, the medicine I was taking perhaps responsible for plunging me back down into subterranean depths again and again. But then I heard screaming and that pulled me upwards, all the way upwards.

There was such horror in it, such disbelief. *What have you done? You monster!*

Was that Constance shouting? No, the voice was different, yet I still recognised it.

"Be quiet, woman! I have told you, shut your mouth!"

Harsh words, but she obviously refused to obey.

"I knew that you would not stop at me; that you would destroy her too. For God's sake, when is enough enough?"

"It is my work!"

"It is your greed!"

"I am warning you—"

"You had plenty. You took it all from me, but no more, do you hear? No more! I will be subdued no longer. Your soul is damned. You have played with fire and it has burnt you." There was a sudden keening and that too was familiar to me. "My poor Constance! Oh, my darling girl! What have you done, Arthur? What have you done?"

Before Arthur could answer, there was a further shriek. "What is he doing here? No! No! I do not want him here! Get him out of my house, for he has darkened it further.

He has led you as once you led me – all the way into Hell. You are weak, Arthur, you are so damned weak. Mark my words; the devil will destroy you just as you have destroyed your own family. What you toy with you do not understand, for that is what you do; you *toy* with it, thinking you know so much when you do not. It is referred to as the unknown for a good reason; we are not *meant* to know! At first, so much is promised, but never is it delivered. Evil is able to bide its time; it is a patient thing, but at the moment it chooses, it will pounce; it will destroy you and I shall be glad of it. You deserve an eternity of suffering for what you have done."

Where was all this commotion coming from? In my bedroom or just outside it?

I will be subdued no longer.

Constance's mother – for that was whom this voice belonged to – was clearly no longer that pitiful thing lying in bed, begging a complete stranger for yet more medication. She was on her feet, and she was screaming, yelling and demanding. For her to do that, something catastrophic must have occurred.

I had to emulate her, force myself from the stupor I was in; no longer exist amongst the shadows, but return to the living, who were just as frightening.

"Constance," I was shocked at how weak I sounded. "Constance, are you there?" How I hoped she was; how I prayed. Having managed to sit upright, I swung my legs over the side of the bed. I pushed them further, unsure whether I could support my own weight. With my feet on the rug, I staggered forwards, my actions reminding me of something I had seen as a child in one of the fields close to Mears House – a foal, just born, rising to its feet, minutes old; legs splaying outwards, threatening to buckle, and trembling, but how determined that foal had been, gradually gaining momentum. I was just as determined. If anything had happened to Constance; if she was in danger… *Constance is lost.* What did that mean? What could it possibly mean?

"Control your wife."

This was Father's voice and immediately Arthur responded.

"Go back to bed, Helena! Do not lecture on what you know nothing about."

The closer I drew to the source of their voices, the more I realised how tense the atmosphere was; as taut as copper wiring. They were not on the landing but in a room just opposite, and that door was open. Was it another bedroom? I was not sure, but I crept through the dimness, towards candlelight that flickered.

Three figures were in the room. As expected it was a bedroom but not Constance's, or Helena's; theirs' were on the third floor. A guest bedroom perhaps, Father's even? Continuing to peer through the door opening, I could see Arthur and Helena facing each other, both shaking but with very different emotions – Helena with anger, Arthur with a combination of that and fear. And there was Father, standing there, glaring at them.

"What happened—"

"What happened was an accident," Arthur was emphatic. "Do you think I would have hurt her, deliberately hurt her? She was my daughter!"

Was?

"You are a monster," Helena repeated, her voice giving way to sobs. "Oh, dear God, what is to become of us now?" Quickly she gathered herself. "You *are* a monster, Arthur, but one driven purely by greed. He, however…" She jabbed a finger at my father, "is driven entirely by something else. Insanity."

To my increasing horror, Helena ran forward and threw herself at my father, her hands held before her, seemingly ready to claw him to pieces.

"Helena!" Arthur was screaming, but once more she refused to obey him. Constance had said she was not like her mother, but it seemed her mother was not as feeble as she had believed. This woman was attacking my father. My heart raced as I witnessed it; the blood rushing through my veins. Arthur had lunged forwards too but was seemingly finding it difficult to grab hold of his wife as her hands were flailing wildly.

"Helena, you must stop!" he continued. Besides desperation, there was worry in his voice; genuine worry, I was sure of it. But still she screamed as she scratched at my father who had to raise his hands to shield his face.

But then the scene changed abruptly. Father reached out and there was a snap, as loud as I imagined a gunshot to be. There followed a brief silence then a thud.

Helena Lawton's body hit the ground, jerking like one of the creatures from my nightmares before becoming still, her head lying at an unnatural angle.

Hurriedly, I stepped back not wanting to bear witness to any more heinous acts, but then sensed movement at my side. Was it Nell, the butler or another servant, come to see what all the drama was about? I felt angry. What had taken them so long? If only they had come sooner. They may have been able to save her!

It was not them. It was Constance. Her beautiful raven

hair was no longer smooth and shiny, secured neatly with ribbons, but ragged around her head, as if she had been pulling at it in a frenzied manner, trying to tear it from her scalp. Her mouth was wide open and her eyes... Was it blood surrounding them, as if she had been trying to tear them out too? It was a terrible sight, yet strangely I was relieved to see her.

"Constance!" I said, reaching for her; trying to pull her close, to comfort her. Had she seen what I had – her mother murdered, by none other than my father?

All I grasped was thin air as Constance faded clean away.

My subsequent screams rivalled any that Helena had been capable of.

* * *

"She is coming round; she is awake."

Were the voices referring to me? Had I fainted again? That smell that assaulted me – sweet but sickly, the oddest perfume – what was it?

I opened my eyes but there was only darkness. If my head had hurt before, it hurt even more so now. What had happened to cause this? For a moment all was blank.

And then a light flickered, one candle followed by several others. I counted them as they were lit, including the one in front of me; there were thirteen in total.

I was in a room, and I was far from alone – there were men, so many of them. I continued counting, perhaps desperate to keep my mind occupied and try to make sense of what was happening; twelve men, plus me – thirteen again.

We were sitting around a table and I was upright, not by my own efforts; I was restrained it seemed by leather cuffs.

"All is well," one of the men assured me. "We mean you no harm."

"That is right," another man said, again a stranger, "we only seek your help."

"Rosamund, listen to my colleagues. And cooperate."

My head swung towards the man who had last spoken. It was Father, and beside him was Arthur, who was sitting with his head bent and his hands clasped together.

Quickly, I tried to calculate where I was – as far as I could tell it was a wood panelled room with some artwork on the walls. There was also a sideboard and a rather ostentatious mantelpiece, two candelabras set at each end. A drawing room then, but at the townhouse or another address? "Where am I?" I was forced to ask.

"At a private residence," another stranger answered.

"The Lawton house?"

"Not there," the same man replied. "Please relax, we will explain what we can."

I baulked at that. "What you can? What can you *not* explain?"

The man who was doing the majority of talking glanced at my father, there was an irritation in him, but it was mild compared to that which emanated from Father.

"Rosamund," he hissed. "Quieten down."

"Another like Constance," someone else said, I did not catch who.

"Wilful," another agreed.

"More Laudanum perhaps?"

Laudanum? What was that?

"No." It was a young man with fair hair speaking this time; someone vaguely familiar. "Drugs should not be permitted. They…" briefly he faltered, "…skew the results. If we influence the subject with laudanum, then how can we expect our society to be taken seriously?"

A general murmur ensued, filled with the comments of those who agreed and disagreed. 'Drugs are useful; they open the doors of the mind. It has been demonstrated' and 'yes, we must strive for accreditation not against it.'

"Please, gentlemen," the young man seemed to have grown bolder, "no laudanum and no…" here he took a deep breath, "other devices either." Before Father could respond, the young man's eyes were back on me. There was a gentleness to him that was missing in every one of the others, and, dare I even think it – as he himself clearly contributed to the terrible circumstances in which I found myself – a kindness? He attempted a smile. "If Rosamund's ability is genuine, as Mr Howard insists that it is, then surely there is no need."

"It *is* genuine," Father hissed again, and I found myself thankful that he was not standing close to this young man with a poker in his hand, for unlike me he would use it. My head reeling, my senses on fire, I begged for yet more information.

"Who are you? What do you want with me? What is this ability to which you refer? I do no understand. I do not!"

Another man spoke, one that was sitting directly opposite me at the round table, the wavering candlelight first revealing his face then concealing it by turn.

"We are the founder members of the *Society of the Rose*

Cross, a magical organisation devoted to the study and practice of the occult, metaphysics and paranormal activity. We draw upon many influences not least Kabbalah, Astrology, Tarot, Geomancy and Alchemy. Sitting amongst us today, you will find doctors, gentlemen and scholars. There is great interest amongst our peers in the spiritual world, but sadly, many treat it without the deference it deserves. Séances, table tipping and mediumship are all considered parlour games. In contrast, our society treats the subject with the utmost respect. We seek to learn from it, and in learning, evolve. Making contact with the spiritual world is an area we focus on. Our aim is to *prove* its existence, something we believe you may be able to help us with."

"Me?" I gasped, trying to make sense of all this man was saying. Some of the words he had used – Geomancy, Alchemy, and Tarot – he may as well have been speaking in a foreign tongue. "How could I possibly help you to prove that?"

"Because you can see."

Again I baulked, struggling against my restraints.

What do you see?

All the times my father had said that to me during my lifetime; it went back years, to when I was but a small child. Running; I was always running away from him, always trying to escape. How I wanted to escape now; to flee from this room and its strange occupants. But I could not. All that it was in my power to do was answer the man as I have always answered Father. "All I see is what you can see too."

My father jumped to his feet, a sudden action accompanied by the banging of his fist on the table, making me flinch and several others around him, I noticed.

"You *can* see, Rosamund! Your ability is genuine, the pictures, all those pictures…" He looked at the men instead of me. "You are right, laudanum can dull the senses, rather than enliven them, I accept that, but this other drug, this new drug, it is different; it prevents lying; the doctors amongst you can pay testament to that. And this child, oh how she will lie. She is adept at it; she is cunning; she will deny all that she is capable of, time and time again. Her mother was the same. If only I had had the drug then…" Anguish caused him to clench his fists. "I urge you all to agree that we use it on Rosamund, here, tonight, in this room. Laudanum has not yielded the results I wanted. It will be easy enough to send someone in a carriage to fetch it. Gentlemen, please, are you not tired of waiting? I know that I am."

The man who had introduced the society to me stood too. "We will do no such thing! Stephen is right, if it is found that drugs have been used in our research, it will devalue everything we do. It will tarnish our reputation, perhaps irrevocably. Now sit, William, and allow me to continue." When Father refused to do so, the man's glare tightened. "You will sit, or you will take your leave."

"If I do, that will break the chain," Father retorted.

"So be it."

There followed several moments of harsh silence with Father still standing and the man continuing to glare at him. I wanted Father to carry on with his rebellion; to break the chain, whatever the chain was, then perhaps I could go free too, but gradually he succumbed, lowering himself into the chair beside Arthur.

Satisfied, the man also sat before addressing me once

more. "My name is Andrew Griffin; Arthur Lawton you have previously met and of course, there is your father. Allow me to introduce the other members of the society to you; there is David Woodbridge, Sir Samuel McPherson, Alan Mathers, Stephen Davis…" On and on the list went, all the way up to twelve.

"And you, Rosamund Howard, are our thirteenth guest; our most esteemed guest, a guest who has the power of sight, and who I am hoping will enable us to see too."

Violently I shook my head. "Please. I only wish to go home." To Mears House; to Josie – to run into her arms; to take refuge in the attic; to hold my mother's picture against my breast; to imagine her arms around me too. I was the same as her apparently; did that mean Father thought she could see also?

Perhaps he is right, Rosamund; after all, you have seen Constance, Harry, the man on the street, all those shadows…

No! Imagination! It was pure imagination, or fever!

I had seen other things I had never expected to see either; electrical light; the Christmas tree, bedecked in ribbons; the rosy-cheeked glow of women in long flowing skirts and tall handsome men in suits and top hats – glorious sights, sights to warm the heart, not frighten it or leave it stone cold.

"Rosamund," Andrew Griffin's voice interrupted such thoughts. "We would like you to demonstrate, that is all."

"You are forcing me to demonstrate. You have trussed me up!"

"For your own safety." He turned to his colleagues. "Gentlemen, I believe it may be easier to see in the darkness. Please, one by one, blow out your candles, following my lead. We will go in a clockwise motion."

What was this? I was to be plunged into darkness?

"Let me go!" I shouted. "I cannot see anything. I will not!"

"What do you see, Rosamund?" Griffin uttered despite my protests, the light from his candle dying.

"What do you see, Rosamund?" the man next to him, David Woodbridge, said in turn, before snuffing his candle out too.

"What do you see, Rosamund?" This was McPherson; then it was Mathers; then Davis… the room growing darker and darker, becoming filled with shadows.

"I see nothing!" The shadows were merely that, although… distorted by what remained of the candlelight, they were beginning to loom… to take shape.

"What do you see, Rosamund?"

"Nothing! Nothing!"

"What do you see, Rosamund?"

Soon it would be Father's turn to ask it.

"What do you see, Rosamund?"

The pictures, all those pictures…

What had Father meant by that?

"What do you see, Rosamund?"

There was yet more darkness, yet more shadows. As on the streets of London, the room was crammed with them. I shut my eyes but I knew it to be in vain; as in the bedroom at the townhouse, such shadows could permeate everything.

"What do you see, Rosamund?"

Harry – I would like to see Harry; such a beautiful face he had, and those eyes of his that looked like they had lived a thousand years – or been dead a thousand years? Again, I shook my head at where that thought had led me. *No! No!*

No!

"What do you see, Rosamund?" That was my father's voice, a growl in it.

"Stop it! All of you stop it!"

A voice beside my own began to speak, concern in it; the voice of the young man, Davis? If so, he was easily overruled.

The girl at the window, waving to me; who was she? I had not seen her within the townhouse, and why would she be waving, trying to gain my attention?

The twelfth man to ask me the same question would be Arthur.

Oh, Constance. I saw you. I saw you and yet you were dead…

That firm realisation caused my heart to plummet and my mouth to gape open. But they were not *my* screams that filled the air. Not this time.

They belonged to Arthur.

Chapter Thirteen

"MY daughter, my darling daughter, my wife… What have I done? What have *we* done? Their blood is on my hands. Look! Look at them! Can you see? They are dripping with blood!"

"Light the candles, all of you," someone commanded. "Quickly, light them."

"Arthur! Arthur! What are you doing, man? Calm down!"

"Light the candles, damn it!"

As the commotion continued, I struggled against my cuffs, determined to undo them; to escape, but to no avail. I was held fast, stuck in the midst of pandemonium.

There was light now, the men obeying the command of Griffin, and the shadows receded as those who were really present in the room came into full view.

Arthur Lawton had gone mad. That is what it appeared. He was on his feet and his hands were in front of him, his eyes bulging with horror and his mouth wide open as he continued to scream; to insist there was blood on them.

"Oh dear Lord, we killed them, didn't we, William? You and I."

Men were rushing towards him but he appeared to have

a strength that was inhuman, throwing them from him as though they were rag dolls.

"Arthur!" I was unable to identify who it was beseeching him again. "You need to remain calm!"

More men approached him, warily this time. I needed desperately to escape. I had seen no door ahead of me or to my side and concluding that it must be behind me, I began to push with my feet, making my chair scrape and bump in that direction.

Still Arthur was screaming. "Constance! We killed Constance!"

"Arthur, what happened was not our fault!" It was Griffin insisting this.

"She was an addict," insisted another. "You never divulged that. If we'd known… That is why it must be the correct decision to ban the use of substances with our subjects from hereonin, because contrary to what has been said, they do not dull a person, but they *do* open doorways, which at our stage of development is dangerous."

"What she saw…" Arthur's voice was as pitiable as his wife's had once been.

"Was hallucination," Griffin rushed to answer. "It had to be."

"She gouged at her eyes! To do that, to go to that length—"

"IT WAS MERE HALLUCINATION!" continued Griffin. "We have discussed this!"

Arthur's whimpers matched mine. "What if you are mistaken? My wife said I was evil, that I was damned. Perhaps I am: because of her, because of Constance—"

"Pull yourself together, man!" I recognised that growl as I continued to edge myself backwards. "Listen to Griffin!

What happened to Constance was an accident. You should never have brought her here in the first place; I was astonished when you did – someone that did not have the sight; who merely fancied she did. What were you thinking, man? How could you be so easily duped, and by a chit of a girl too?"

"Constance is dead!" Arthur wailed.

"Yes, she is, but what is now important is that our society cannot be held accountable for it."

"What? Is that *all* that is important to you; to all of you? You… You bastard!"

Arthur lunged at my father, who, as he had done with Helena, immediately held up his hands in order to hold his opponent at arm's length.

"You killed my wife," Arthur twisted his head towards the others, who had rushed to help but now stood aghast at what was being said. "This man killed my wife. It was in my house; *my* house damn it. With his bare hands, he grabbed her neck; he snapped it, just as if it were a twig. He murdered her in cold blood."

"William?" It was Griffin asking, while the others clustered wide-eyed around him. "What he is saying, what he is… *accusing* you of, is there any truth to it?"

Father kept his eyes on Arthur as he answered. "I rather fear this man is every bit as addled as his daughter."

Arthur renewed his attempts to attack my father. "YOU KILLED HER!"

"WHERE IS THE PROOF?" Father returned. "You are deluded, sir!"

"I am the proof," I said, but my voice was lost in what ensued next.

Father suddenly lost his restraining grip on Arthur,

who, seizing his chance, enclosed Father's neck with his hands and began to squeeze, squeeze, squeeze. A part of me egged him on, wishing… hoping… A part of me I refused to indulge further. Whatever he had done, whatever ills he had committed, William Howard was still my father, and I should be lost without him. I would be an orphan.

A group of the other men also joined in the struggle, trying to release Arthur's grip. In their efforts they knocked over a candle, causing the cloth that had covered the table to burst into sudden flames.

"What the deuce…?" someone shouted. "We need water. Quick! Water!"

Smoke filled the air with alarming rapidity, finding its way into my lungs and causing me to cough, choke, and making my eyes stream. Even more panicked, I bucked, still intending to free myself of what bound me and, as I did, the chair tipped backwards. I crashed to the ground, once more hitting my head. Mercifully, I did not lose consciousness; I could not afford to, not if the room was burning.

"Someone help me. I beg you, let me go," I whimpered.

There were so many voices, but the loudest of all was Arthur's. He continued to yell, seemingly taking no note of the fact that the room was alight. "He killed my wife, in front of my very eyes. He is a murderer, a filthy murderer!"

"Arthur! Arthur! We must leave. We will deal with William later. Come, Arthur, please!"

I did not know who said this, but if they were leaving, surely they would not leave without me? I was not oblivious to the flames as Arthur appeared to be; I did not want to suffocate or be incinerated. I could not imagine a worse way to go.

"Help! Help!"

They *were* leaving! There were trampling all over me to escape. Why? How could they do such a thing?

"Father! Arthur! Help!"

It was a hideous sound that next met my ears; a cry filled with unimaginable pain. I could barely bring myself to look but I must – I could not hide or remain ignorant – not anymore.

One of the men was on fire. He was beating at his torso with frenzied hands, doing his utmost to battle the ravages of such a fierce element. It was Arthur, I was sure of it. Another man tried to help him – the young man I think, Stephen Davis, although his fair hair looked blackened. He attempted to beat the flames back with his bare hands, but as Arthur went careering into the wall, Davis had to admit defeat, although I could sense his anguish in doing so; his sheer disbelief. He stood there, his hands if not burnt, at least badly scorched, and I cried out once again. "Help! Help!"

My voice had become a mere croak, dying in my throat as I would surely die in this room if no one came to my aid. I could feel the heat of the fire searing my face; it was creeping closer, just like the shadows would creep, but soon it would do so much more than that; it would charge towards me, unrestrained, unstoppable, the strongest element of all. Unable to move, I began to sob. Yet again, I was defenceless.

"Help! Help!" I called one last time before shutting my eyes and resigning myself to such a hideous fate.

"Be calm, I have you."

My eyes snapped open.

"What? Who is this?"

"It's Stephen. I have you, Rosamund; we will escape this."

"Where… where is Arthur…?"

There was a moment of silence but it spoke volumes.

"Arthur is lost," he said at last.

As the other members of his family had been lost – all of them gone.

"I have to turn you onto your side, to untie you, I mean."

"Yes. Yes." I replied. "Please hurry."

"I will. We shall get you out, I promise. I am sorry… I just… I am so sorry."

He worked as quickly as he could to release me, enabling one of my hands to become free, followed by the other. I attempted to climb to my feet but my legs would not comply. Stephen must have noticed my difficulty for he put his arms around me and lifted me as though I were a child instead of a girl of sixteen, and together we began to make our way to the door, with the flames not only behind us, but leaping higher and higher on either side. How soon before the entire house burned?

Just as we reached the door, a figure shot forward.

"Unhand her!"

"Father?" I managed.

"I said, let her go! She is my daughter!"

Although the man holding me protested, he set me down. Father, however, was in no mood for remonstration – not this time. With both hands he gave Stephen a great shove and the young man fell backwards, into the flames.

"FATHER, NO! WHAT ARE YOU DOING?"

In no mood for explaining either, he grabbed my hand, his touch so unlike Stephen's; there was no gentleness in it at all as he dragged me forwards. I did my utmost to stop him, the one hand I had free holding onto the doorframe; digging my heels into the floor; but this time I *was* a child, and my strength was no match for his.

"We cannot leave Stephen in there," I shouted as he continued to drag me down the hallway and out of the house, where quite a crowd had gathered, huddled in clusters as if watching live theatre. "Father, we cannot, he will perish!"

Just as Arthur had perished, as Helena had said he would, in the flames of Hell.

"FATHER!"

In spite of my protestations, he merely increased the distance between us and the crowds. I recognised some of the men who had been in the room. They were coughing and spluttering, and some had also noticed us. They were pointing towards Father, and calling out to him, trying to catch his attention. He simply lowered his head and bustled us both along, into what quickly became a warren of streets.

At last I recognised where we were; the crescent with its graceful curve.

"Why are we here?" I asked, my bewilderment increasing at once again seeing the Lawton family home. When he refused to answer, I cried out, attracting the attention of a passerby. "We cannot go back inside there, Father, we cannot."

"Be quiet, Rosamund!"

"Then tell me why."

"There is something I need to retrieve, that is why. Damn them," he seethed as we continued towards the house, "with their rules and their regulations, their *rigidity*.

It is I that holds the key to it all. It is me that has you. Enough questions! Gather your things, Rosamund, and quickly. I will see to it that a carriage is waiting for us when you come downstairs. I warn you, do not dally. We have to leave London and soon."

He rapped on the door and the butler appeared, a scowl on his face at the sight of us, his commitment to his profession perhaps forcing him to hold his tongue. As we entered the hallway, Father issued instructions for transport to be hailed. Whilst he did, I looked about me. What a grand hallway this was in Helena's family home, which had been given over to her husband; stolen from her through marriage. An evil man, but he had loved his daughter at least; Constance had been right about that, the loss of her sending him mad, quite mad. Would he burn forever? I wondered. Would all of us burn in the end?

In the hallway, the gaslight flickered just as the candles had done at that other townhouse, casting shadow upon shadow. As I began to walk towards the staircase; as I stared at their ill-defined forms; they slowly began to move.

Chapter Fourteen

I was awake as I continued to climb the staircase. I knew that. This at least was not a dream. Even so, it appeared that dreams and reality had merged to produce a new version of reality; as though the barriers that had previously divided the two had come tumbling down, allowing so many and so much through.

This house where until today had lived an esteemed London family, was not empty; far from it, it was *full* of people: the fair-haired girl who had waved at me when I first came here but one of them. Like the streets outside, it was teeming; some figures passing blithely by me, passing *through* me even; others stopping to stare at the girl amongst them; curious about her; stretching a hand towards her.

I did not shrink back as I had done in Berkeley Square, or scream or faint – I think my senses had grown numb after all I had experienced in recent days. It was as if I had become unable to react; as though I was now a shadow too. What had happened to Stephen when Father pushed him backwards? What if he had…? No, I must not think that. Better to remain numb.

I did not stop at the crest of the first flight of stairs; I continued on to the second floor and then the third – the floor where I knew Helena's bedroom to be; compelled to go there and not questioning that compulsion, not yet. It was already dark outside but the corridor was darker still with no living person, no Nell, scurrying along the landing. Why would she be? Who was there now here to tend to?

Reaching Helena's room, I pushed open the door and the smell that assaulted me was the same as ever, sweet but sickly. Rather than the darkness, I focused on one thing and one thing only – that smell – closing my eyes and breathing it in, despite how repellent it was. Was this the smell of laudanum, the drug the society had referred to? If so, Helena had been an addict, though perhaps not at first; perhaps initially she had had an illness for which it had proved useful – indeed she had hacked blood up right in front of me, so that could be true. But still she had become addicted to whatever had dulled the pain; dulled her mind – *or opened doors.* Constance had had the same smell about her sometimes. It was only now, standing there, that I fully realised it, remembering how she too had staggered on occasion; how sometimes her words had been a little slurred, or her eyes perhaps over bright. *Drugs open the doors of the mind.* Constance had mentioned that she thought she had seen a ruffian close to me when I had fainted. Was that proof that he was real, or that her drug use had done exactly that: opened her mind? That same drug – laudanum – had been administered to me as I lay in bed on the first floor – I was now certain of it – not as a means to ease my pain but as an attempt to make me more pliable. If so, it was not the only drug that could do that, Father had said there was another; one that was more effective; that prevented lying...

Is that why we had had to return here, so that Father could retrieve it?

As I was about to turn and leave the room – coming here having confirmed my suspicions about the nature of laudanum at least – a movement caught my eye. The bed – previously empty, was empty no more! Although all was silent in the room, I could hear the rush of blood – my own – as it coursed through my veins. *No! No! I do not want this.* Helena Lawton was dead. She should remain that way.

I hurriedly made to leave the room.

Constance is lost. I am lost.

Those were the words Helena had used, and – as if she had indeed had the gift of prophecy – she had been correct. A woman full of fun and enthusiasm, who had given birth to another similar to her, but was then lost to the darkness that her husband had plunged her into. But if it were Helena on this bed, she had *become* the darkness.

That thought was reinforced by something more she had said – *the light hurts.*

How could something as wonderful as the light hurt?

I was about to run down to my room, throw my belongings into the suitcase and go and meet Father, but I suddenly could not bring myself to do it. Not until there *was* light. Not daylight, not electrical light, but the only light there was at my disposal – gaslight. Seized with the desire to illuminate this dark, dark house, I rushed to the table with the candle, beside which would be kept a box of matches and wax tapers. I grabbed them, dragging the match head along the striking surface and watched as it burst into flame. There was nothing threatening about it this time; instead it was something beautiful; something valiant – *the strongest element of all*, that is what I had thought just an hour or two earlier; to be used for good, *only* for good; in this case for the purpose of cleansing. I then lit the taper and, making my way to the centre of the room, inserted it through the hole in the bottom of the globe in the ceiling gaslight. Tilting the chain, there was a popping sound as the gas ignited.

Watching it, I heard a roar in my head; a desperate protest.

Immediately I turned back towards the bed. "The light will not hurt you. Not anymore. There is no need to be afraid."

I took the matches and tapers with me as I left the room. The figure in the bed had, miraculously, quietened at my words; had, I think, *listened*.

In the hallway, I lit yet more lamps before rushing back down the stairs to my room, aware that I had to act quickly; that Father was waiting. All the while I addressed the shadows.

"You must not be afraid. Please. You need the light. The light will help."

Who was I reassuring? I wondered. Them or simply myself? I had no time to contemplate; the words *felt* right, that was all that mattered. I had to get to my room… via the one in which Helena was felled.

That room needed the light most of all.

My breathing was a harsh sound in my ears as I moved towards it. What would I encounter in there? Not just shadows but something more substantial; perhaps Constance herself, just as I had seen her in the corridor – her eyes, oh her eyes! Or it might be Helena again, not in bed this time, but standing with her head lolling.

Hold fast. Do not allow your imagination to take over.

Because some of it *was* imagination, I was sure of it. *Maybe all of it?*

I shook my head. No. Not all. *Do what you came here to do and light the lamp.*

My hands shaking violently now, I moved to the exact spot where Father had slain Helena, and, as I did, a terrible coldness seized me; it was worse than any winter chill; akin to the cold I had felt in the woods of Mears House that day, when I had fallen and Josie had appeared to take care of me.

What Father and Arthur had done with the body I had no idea, or how long the interval had been between the time I had blacked out and when I had been taken to that room where the society had gathered. However long it was, it was time enough for them to remove it. But what had they done with Helena? Was she lying in a ditch somewhere? Or at the bottom of that great river that snaked its way through London – the Thames, no doubt the resting place of many a wronged soul?

I corrected myself; even if her body lay there, it did not imply her soul did.

Light the lamp, Rosamund.

I did, leaving it to blaze behind me as I left the scene of the murder and entered my own room, where I lit another, this time for more practical reasons, so that I could see to pack. As I did, as the shadows became less and less, I noticed something: something glittering.

It was my necklace! Lying there on the floor in front of me!

Squatting, I snatched it up – terrified it might disappear

if I did not act with haste.

I was certain it had not lain there before. I would have sworn to it. It was in so blatant, so obvious a position, that it would have been impossible to miss.

The sound of laughter caused me to gasp – *tinkling* laughter.

"Constance?" I whispered, my head whipping from left to right. "Was it you? Did you keep it safe for me?"

And return it from the dead, my necklace and my protection.

"Rosamund! Where are you? Hurry! Our coach is waiting."

On hearing Father rather than Constance, I straightened up and did as before; placed the necklace in my purse. One day, though – and I promised myself this – I would wear it for all to see – my mother's necklace, and her gift to me.

"Rosamund!"

"I am coming, Father."

Throwing whatever I could into my suitcase, I forced it shut and retraced my footsteps. At the top of the stairs I came to a halt, turning to look behind me.

I saw nothing but light.

"Be at peace, Helena," I whispered. "And, Constance, my dear friend, rest well."

* * *

There is not much that I remember about the carriage ride home. Father sat opposite me, his breathing heavy as he sipped, sipped, sipped from a flask – the smell not as pungent as laudanum perhaps, but it was as sickly, and to combat it, I did my utmost to breathe only shallowly. Clutched in his hands was a carpetbag, what it contained the reason we had gone back to the house to fetch, no doubt. I glanced at him only briefly, trying to come to terms with what I now knew him to be – a murderer. Not only was I at his mercy, I was his descendant. His blood was my blood. If there was darkness in him would it follow that darkness existed in me too?

As we continued to travel over rough roads for what would be hours and hours, I had to remind myself that I was also a part of Mother. And although I had no living memory of her, because of the necklace I felt her presence near and she was good – wholly good. There was so much good in this world… and so much bad. And perhaps, just perhaps, there was a world within us all.

The dawn was breaking as at last we entered the grounds of Mears House. Father was sleeping, albeit fitfully, his body twitching occasionally, causing him to groan.

As the house came into view, I could not resist leaning forward. There it stood, the house in which I had been raised; the mausoleum, with nothing festive to brighten it, not even at Christmas. Inside were Miss Tiggs and Josie. Would they be surprised at our return, or were they expecting us? I would soon find out.

The driver brought the carriage to a halt, another jolt that this time succeeded in awakening Father.

"What is it? Have we arrived? Are we here?"

Rather than answer, I opened the carriage door, the driver helping me to step down. As Father alighted he missed a step and the driver hastened to help him too. Rather than accept, Father brushed his hands away, determined to right himself by his own efforts. Throughout he kept a tight hold on the carpetbag. *What is it you have in there?* Again I could not help but wonder.

Whilst he paid the driver, I turned to the house and once more took it all in; how many windows it had; how many eyes. Above it were only clouds and sky, the early morning colours not glorious but leaden. There were no birds, I noticed. There very seldom were. But not everything stayed away, not by far.

As the driver departed, and Father began to approach the house, I knew I had gained some sort of reprieve. He would need to sleep properly, not the fitful kind you snatched whilst journeying, but deep sleep, the kind that rejuvenated you. Whatever he planned now, he would want to do it properly, not on the back of exhaustion.

As we entered, Miss Tiggs was in her usual position on the inside of the door, although there was no sign of Josie. I hurried towards the staircase and began to climb, making my way not to the attic, but to my room, there to dig the necklace from my purse and hug it to me as I lay on the bed and prayed for sleep to find me too.

For in the coming hours, I would need all the strength I possessed.

Chapter Fifteen

"ROSAMUND, darling."

Darling? Who was calling me that? I cannot recall any person having used that term of endearment towards me, perhaps not even Constance.

"That's it, easy now," the voice continued. "It's me, Josie."

Josie? Had she dispensed with 'miss' completely?

It had been during the morning that I had fallen asleep, and I was so tired that I had foregone the drawing of the curtains. In spite of that, no daylight pervaded, instead the room had about it a hazy quality.

As I sat up I rubbed at my eyes. After a moment, panic set in.

"Don't worry about your necklace," Josie said, the smile upon her face soft rather than dazzling. "It's quite safe."

"How did you know…?" I began, but my voice soon trailed off.

Josie was sitting close to me, still with her red hair captured beneath her cap, but for those rogue wisps that tended to frame her face – heart-shaped I noticed it was, although for some reason that fact had evaded me until now. She was still pale; still with those glassy green eyes –

the shine far more natural than that which had been in Constance's eyes. It seemed to reflect a quality from deep within and I found myself envying it. She appeared just as she always had, but there was also something new and different about her; something I could not quite identify.

"The stones in your necklace," she said, "do you know what they are?"

I shook my head. I had been meaning to ask Constance but had now missed the opportunity.

"Tourmaline. And Harry was right when he said what he did; they'll protect you. They will lend courage when you need it most."

"Josie," this time I refused to allow my voice to fail me. "How could you possibly know about the stones?"

She laughed. "Perhaps there's more to me than meets the eye."

I pondered on this before continuing. "And how do you know about Harry?"

"Because we are connected, Rosamund. All of us. That's how."

Instead of pondering further, it struck me quite suddenly what was different about Josie. Not only was she employing terms of endearment, her entire demeanour had changed. Gone was the simple country girl who would spend her life curtseying to others; she now had, if anything, an air of superiority about her. I leant forward but did not dare to touch her, my suspicion preventing me from doing so. "Who are you?" I whispered, not just experiencing bewilderment but many other emotions besides.

A bang at the door followed by the turn of the handle, caused us both to stare at it, instead of at each other.

Beads of sweat broke out on my forehead. "Is that Father?"

"No," Josie replied, her gaze still on the door. "But it will be soon."

"Who is it, then?" I asked, puzzled.

She turned back to me, taking my hand in hers and gripping it tight. "What you did at the townhouse, it was the right thing to do. You knew that, in spite of what Mrs Lawton had said. No one had to tell you. You drew upon instinct."

Was she referring to the gas lamps and the urge that overcame me to light them? But once again, how could she know this? "Is this another dream?"

She inclined her head a little. "It is perhaps a half dream."

I could not help but become a little angry at the vagueness of her replies, and as I did, the rattling at the door increased.

Rather than be alarmed by it, she smiled again. "See the power you have, Rosamund; *natural* power. Use it wisely."

I could not continue to sit. I snatched my hand from hers, leapt to my feet and began to pace as Father would pace. When I abruptly realised my actions were his, I came to a halt and turned to her, tears beginning to fall. I lifted my hand to touch them and it came away wet. How could this be a dream when tears felt real enough?

"I am afraid," I admitted.

"And where do you go when you're afraid?"

"The attic."

"The attic is safe?"

"Yes, yes it is."

Josie stood too. "How do you know it's safe?"

"Because… because…"

"Instinct tells you so?"

"Yes." It was another admission. "Instinct tells me so."

She reached out and once more held my hand. Her touch was gentle, extraordinarily so; a touch that only she was capable of.

"Trust in your instinct. Always."

I hung my head and allowed more tears to come – a wave that threatened to become tidal. The rattling had ceased completely now; there was no more banging, only the sound of my sobbing. "Josie, Josie," I wailed, as her arms encircled me, "I am so frightened. I am. What is he going to do with me?"

"There, darling, there. Let the tears wash away your grief."

Grief? Yes, that was *exactly* the emotion that I was feeling. Grief at what I had lost, and what I had never had.

A ray of light pierced the gloom. As I stood there with Josie's arms around me, sobbing into her shoulder, it caused me to open my eyes; to marvel at how bright it was; how daring, to venture into a dream as bleak as this.

Still I cried, continuing to relish the comfort of close contact. I cried for me, and I cried for Constance, I cried for Helena too, who had been weak and pitiful, but who had rallied at the end in defence of her daughter, and been killed as a consequence.

By Father.

"Oh, Josie," I whimpered. Did I have the strength in me to face the man that had sired me? Should I simply run from this room, not to the attic, but towards the woods in an effort to escape? But there was something waiting in the woods, I had seen it. Something within the house also, rattling the door…

There was no further comfort to be had and so I pushed Josie away.

"No. I cannot do this. Something is happening here that I do not understand. I just… I want to be normal. I do not want this… any of it. Do you hear?"

When Josie failed to reply, I turned from her and faced the wall; I brought my hands up to my head and tugged at my hair. This dream, this nightmare, it was not populated with twisted creatures and writhing limbs as it usually was; it was just Josie and I, and yet still it was terrifying. I opened my mouth to scream, and scream I did, albeit silently. It was a purge nonetheless – allowing what was in me; what had been contained for so long – at least a degree of freedom.

Spent, I turned back to face this shimmering creature.

"You are not real, are you?"

Again she inclined her head. "I *am* real. But there's only some who can see me."

"A ghost?" I whispered.

"If you want to call me that. If it helps you to understand."

"I understand nothing!"

Her smile grew wider. "You are such a plucky little thing," she declared.

Plucky?

"I am weak," I insisted.

"You are strong, and you are strong because you are beginning to see."

What do you see?

"Miss Tiggs…" I said at last.

"Miss Tiggs died two years ago."

What? "But she has been here forever. I… I have seen her, talked with her, in the kitchen; sometimes at the front door, when she was bidding us, or rather Father, farewell."

"Has your father acknowledged her lately?"

I thought about it and then shook my head. No, I believe he had not.

"She never liked you, did she?" Josie said.

"I never liked her!"

"I don't think anyone did much. She could be selfish."

Could? "But I have seen her!" I reiterated. "A few hours ago I saw her. And as little as a week or two ago, I was sitting in the kitchen conversing with her whilst I ate supper."

She was silent, forcing me to speak again. "I conversed with a ghost?"

Slowly, she nodded.

"Just as I am doing now?"

There was another nod, and so I had to face the truth of the matter.

"It is only Father and I in this house." How solemn my voice was when I spoke these words. "And there has been for a long time. The governess…"

"Your Father wouldn't – *couldn't* – pay the fees."

"He has other matters that require his finances, what little remains of them."

Josie was quiet, allowing me to come to terms with it all.

It was just he and I in this big old crumbling house, set deep within the Sussex countryside, miles from anywhere, from anyone… except ghosts.

"I see what I want to see," I said.

"You construct your world."

And I had; I had retained Miss Tiggs in my version of reality, pretending that she still served me my meals when it was I that had been doing so, month upon month. What a thought to ponder on; what a notion indeed.

"But soon I will see things I *do not* want to see."

"That's when you need to draw on instinct, Rosamund, and act upon it."

"Be plucky?"

"That's right. You are equipped to deal with this. And there is more armour coming, I promise."

"Armour? As if I were a soldier, going into war?"

"There are always battles to be fought. This is just one of them."

Instead of questioning further, I yawned, and as I did, Josie and the room in front of me waivered, flickered from side to side, before becoming complete again.

"I believe I am waking up," I said.

"You are."

"Will I ever see you again?" The thought that I would not was untenable. Josie was but two or three years older than myself; no more than a girl just as I was a girl, and yet she was a mother too, or at least all I imagined a mother to be.

Perhaps sensing another swell of emotion within me, she stepped forward and put her hands upon my shoulders, fixing those tourmaline eyes upon me.

"Not in this lifetime," she replied and there was sorrow in her as well, so deep that I felt compelled to reach out and return at least a degree of comfort.

"We *will* meet again, Josie, perhaps not here, but somewhere." There was a pause before I added, "I know it to be true."

"How?" she asked.

"Because instinct tells me."

There it was! That radiant smile! Oh, how it captured me. How it enlivened me. It resurrected hope when hope had been buried for so long.

I yawned again. I awoke.

I *truly* awoke.

Josie was gone. All that I found myself clutching was the necklace, its stones twinkling.

I smiled to see it and then my smile faded.

There was another bang at the door – and this time it was real.

Chapter Sixteen

THERE was no escape, no one to help me, not now. I had to face him. Pit my wits against his. It was a battle and the only armour I had: a necklace that glittered.

As I secured it around my wrist, the cuff of my sleeve amply covering it, I thought of making safe harbour for myself also. The attic. Perhaps I could open the door, dodge beneath his arm, and run. He would not follow me there. *Why?*

"Rosamund!"

Father's voice almost deafened me as the door burst open. Upon sight of me, he stopped, and, for a moment, we simply stood there, as if he was bracing himself as much as I; as if there was a glimmer of fear in him too. Seeing this, my back straightened, an almost involuntary movement. Perhaps it was this that caused him to lunge across the room; to grab me by the arm; to haul me out of the bedroom and down the corridor – that spark of defiance.

Whatever had caught alight in me, however, rapidly dimmed as we continued past the corridor that led to the attic. I looked longingly at it; it was so close and yet so far.

At the top of the stairs, I dug in my heels. "Let me go." With my free hand I batted at him.

In return, he exchanged my wrist for my neck and

slammed me against the wall.

"Do not issue commands at me, do you hear?"

Briefly, my eyes left his and I glanced behind him, to where there was a window. It was not yet full dark, but soon it would be, in another hour, maybe less. Out here in the countryside darkness arrived so completely. And within it, I would be trapped with a drunk and a murderer.

If I was really capable of constructing my world, as Josie had suggested, I would have done so now; I would have peopled it with a thousand Josies; a thousand Constances; I would have filled the house with them, wall to wall. And they would have come to my aid. But there was no Josie and no Constance. There was not a single soul that I could see. Not even the doughy outline of Miss Tiggs.

At last Father released his grip on my neck, the skin continuing to burn from his touch, and I began to splutter as my breath also found release. And then we were off again, downstairs, while I held onto the balustrade handrail with one hand lest I should trip.

As the kitchen had been Miss Tiggs' domain, the study had always been Father's lair. That was our destination and in it I knew I would be trapped further. As he shoved at the door, not with his hand, but with his foot, kicking it wide open, he pushed me through, throwing me finally into the chair, which squeaked loudly in protest. I looked about me, astounded at what I saw. There were pictures piled upon his desk, all of them drawn by myself. I had, of course, lost count of how many I had created over the years – with so little else to do at Mears House it must have numbered in the thousands. I thought many of them had been disposed of, but plenty had obviously been kept by Father, not just a few, but scores of them, dating back years.

"Father?"

"Look!" he ordered, pointing at them. His face was no longer ashen; it was bright red, from alcohol no doubt as well as from the efforts he had recently expended.

"These are my drawings." What else was I to say?

"Look!" he screamed again, grabbing at my chin and pulling me closer.

"I *am* looking!" I squealed.

Mears House was a perennial subject; the only subject I could think to draw sometimes, but there were a number of portraits too, of me, Miss Tiggs, the maid before Josie, a governess or two… and someone else.

"Who is this?" he said, pointing.

"I… I do not know."

He was not content with that reply. "Who is it?"

"I… I…"

I had sketched in the woman's hair, but because I had used a light hand, it was neither dark nor fair. The eyes were dark, though, and the face heart-shaped.

"I do not know," I repeated, although there were many likenesses of her.

"Rosamund," he barked, turning my face towards him so that I had no option but to stare into those narrow eyes of his. "That is your mother. How do you explain it?"

My mother? A nervous laugh escaped me. And then I remembered, I confessed.

"I have a photograph of Mother! I found it in the library, tucked between books."

He looked shocked, utterly shocked.

"She left something of herself behind?"

"Yes, yes she did. That explains the likeness."

He let go of my face and straightened, one hand reaching up to scratch at the stubble on his jaw. "I thought I had rid this house of every single item relating to her."

Not her photograph, or her necklace, or me. Am I not also to do with her?

A shadow crossed his face and I tensed; my rebellious thoughts – *triumphant* thoughts – quickly concealed.

"Where is this photograph?"

I was loathe to tell him.

"Rosamund!"

"In the attic," I answered at last, a hint of rebellion remaining. He hated the attic; it was safe there.

His reaction, however, surprised me. He simply laughed and shook his head. "It matters not where it is, only *when* you found it."

"When?"

"Indeed. Tell me."

"It was… It must have been… three years ago."

"Three years ago? You are sure?"

Time was often a blur at Mears House, but that day had been a momentous day; unforgettable. "Yes, Father. I am certain."

There was no more laughter. He grabbed at one of the portraits, then another, and another, until he had a fistful of them, thrusting them into my face. "These are portraits of your mother; the same likeness; the same shading, and they were completed well before you reached thirteen years of age; when you were nine; when you were ten; when you were eleven and twelve. You had no idea of your mother's appearance back then; you could not possibly remember her, but still you were drawing her. It is proof I tell you, proof!"

"Father, not all of them are alike. See? There are differences." It was true, there were, albeit slight. As for there being a likeness to my mother, yes, indeed there was, but that could merely be coincidence, my father also being guilty of seeing what *he* wanted to see.

"What was the colour of your mother's hair?"

I shook my head, bit hard upon my lip. How would I know? The photograph was black and white.

"I asked the colour of your mother's hair?"

"I… erm… red," I replied finally, having to pick a colour, any colour.

"That is correct, red! And her eye colour?"

I swallowed hard, knowing I had to answer. "Green."

"Yes!" He said, punching at the air.

"It is because of Josie," I said. "I picked those answers because of her."

"Josie? I have heard you mention her; calling out for her even on occasion. Who is she? Come on, tell me!"

"I… I do not know." A ghost or a spirit perhaps, but not someone frightening, for who could be afraid of Josie? She was goodness itself; a woman who – in the absence of a mother – had been the closest thing.

"Is this her?"

Having let the portraits fall to the desk, he now held several sketches of Mears House – the exterior views.

Again he grabbed me, the back of my neck this time, forcing me to look at what I had, by my own hand, sketched.

"I do not understand…" I began.

"Look at the windows and the figures depicted at them."

Figures? They were just windows, the eyes of the house.

"Is one of them Josie?"
One of them?
"Who are the others, Rosamund?"

Were there figures at the windows? It was shading, was it not? Mere shading?

I continued to stare at the sketches; I had no choice; remembering how, in the drawing room, Josie had stopped to stare at them too; how I had seen her at the window one day whilst out walking, and she had been waving… If it was indeed her. It might have been someone else.

It might well have been someone else.

Shading. Shadows. Figures.

There were so many of them, in every drawing and in every window, staring back at me. Clearly, these were drawn by my hand, but my eyes had refused to see, at least back then; but not now. *You have awoken remember?*

My father took a step backwards. Oh the look of him!

"You *can* see," he whispered.

Still biting my lip, I could feel the tang of blood.

"And if you can see, you can also summon."

Chapter Seventeen

I believed that I knew fear. I *did* know fear. But not like this. Never like this.

Summon? Summon what?

"Ghosts?" I whispered. Is that what he meant?

His voice was so derisory. "Rosamund, there is so much more to this than ghosts."

I began to rise from my chair, determined that I should flee this time. Outside, the night had taken hold; a cold night, a winter's night, frost in the air that would nip mercilessly at my toes and my fingers; but better that than the darkness that had now blossomed inside this house; that had consumed Father so completely. I could avoid the woods by heading down the gravel path, or… I could run to the attic.

"Sit!" he commanded, noticing how bold I was becoming.

I hesitated to obey, my mind attempting to calculate the lesser of two evils.

Evil.

It was not an exaggeration; every cell in my body acknowledged it. Evil was resident in Mears House this night and it wished to invite more in.

You are equipped to deal with this.

That is what Josie had told me. Should I continue to sit there rather than take my chances and run? Should I trust her? Believe in her?

The decision was made for me. Father walked over to the door and, pulling a key from the pocket of his jacket, locked it.

"Father, what are you doing?" I said, aghast at this new development.

"Making sure," was his sole reply.

Sinking into the chair, I screwed my eyes shut as if by that very act I could shut him out too; as if that alone would protect me. My hands rested in my lap, clenched tight, my nails digging into my palms, deeper and deeper; the silence and the tension both thicker than any fog that London could conjure.

Having barred my exit, Father moved to his desk. There was a definite mocking aspect to his leisurely gait; he had no need to hurry: I was a fly entangled in his web.

All I was able to do was anticipate his every move, and hope that eventually he would see sense.

"Father," I urged, trying to hasten the latter. "You believe I can see extraordinary things, but you are mistaken. I cannot. I am an ordinary girl. I want nothing more than to live an ordinary life. Whatever you are planning, I want no part in it."

He did not so much as even glance my way as he bent to pick up the carpetbag he had clutched to himself all the way from London.

I tried again. "We could be happy here, you and I. We could perhaps freshen the house; make it brighter somehow; a better place to live in. We could employ a maidservant; a local girl perhaps; one that is looking for an escape from her own circumstances, because… because it is overcrowded. I do not expect she will demand a vast sum. There may be plenty of girls that would be thankful for such a position. In the past this was a fine house and we could make it so again. Please, Father, listen to me."

Rummaging in the bag, he paused. "We could freshen the house, could we? We could employ more servants? What with, Rosamund? What with?"

I shook my head. "What do you mean?"

"Money, you stupid girl! There is none available. It went a long time ago, on you and your dresses; on having to keep up appearances, it being essential for London; from a certain class so much is expected." His expression was nothing less than bitter. "No, no, no. Every last penny is gone. We are in debt up to our necks. But do not fret," he reached for the decanter on his desk, poured some whisky into a tumbler and downed it in a single quaff, before repeating the action, the alcohol as ever giving him ballast. "I have a plan. There is really no need to fret about any of it."

"What plan?" Again I was bold enough to ask.

"You shall learn soon enough," he said, finally retrieving what he was looking for and holding it up for both of us to see – a brown bottle, filled with liquid.

My heart sunk to see it. "Laudanum?" I asked.

Taking the time to down yet another shot of whisky, he eventually answered me. "You know it is not." He handled the phial more lovingly than I have ever seen him handle anything. "It is Scopolamine and early trials have proved very promising. This is a truth drug, because you, daughter of mine, lie not only to me but also to yourself. All those to whom it is administered find it impossible to deceive.

When this resides in one's system, there is no imagination; there is no power to think or to reason. I shall ask the question and I shall receive the truth."

"You cannot force me to take it." There was a distinct quaver in my voice.

"But I can."

"I shall refuse to swallow it."

"Oh, you will swallow it, Rosamund, you will."

"I can see!" There! It was out, I had admitted to it. Would he leave me be now?

Yet another shot of whisky was poured. "Rosamund, there is something specific I wish you to see and when you do, I want no lies at that point; no denials. I need you to describe it exactly; to commune with it, via me."

"Commune?" The very word was enough to send shivers dancing along my spine. "I do not understand."

How calm he was; how sure of himself. "But you will, soon you will."

"Let me go please."

"Tell me, where would you go?"

I could not sit still any longer. Whilst his hand was halfway to his mouth, the tumbler refreshed yet again, I upped and ran to the door; pulling at it; banging on it; kicking it so hard I thought the bones in my toes might snap. It moved not an inch.

My father roared with laughter.

"If it's Constance you would run to, she is no more – she is dead. As for Josie, I do not think ghosts will offer much assistance. There is no one that cares about you; no one to come looking for you should you happen to disappear."

I swung around. "What happened to Constance, tell

me!"

"It is of no matter now."

"Tell me! I demand to know."

How narrow his eyes were; like a fox, as cunning. "How many times must I remind you? You are in no position to demand anything!"

"Tell me," I continued. I felt I could not take another breath if I remained ignorant of the facts. The ghost of her – the apparition – the blood that had surrounded those once beautiful eyes – yet again it caused my own eyes to water. "Tell me and I will take your drug, willingly, with no force required. Please, Father."

"She was an addict," was his languid reply.

"Yes, yes, I now know that to be true."

"And predisposed to fancy."

"We all have an imagination, Father."

"We do. And hers was vivid."

I had to ask it. "Could she see?"

His laughter was so cruel. "Nonsense is what she saw; nothing but the result of an addled mind."

"And yet you would use a drug on me?"

"A different drug, remember?"

I nodded at his tumbler. "Different to yours as well?"

I was such a source of amusement to him that he continued to laugh.

"Did you kill her?" I whispered.

"Oh, Rosamund! Rosamund! I should have liked to; she was an impertinent madam, so certain of her charms, she thought she could blind anyone with them."

"She was beautiful," I declared.

"But spoilt. That fool, Arthur, guilty as charged."

I disagreed. "Constance was clever; she was determined,

and she was to be an integral part of the changing world."

"Quite enamoured of her, were you not?"

"She was my friend, *truly* my friend. What did she see that caused her to gouge at her own eyes?" That is how Arthur had described her actions, and I knew it to be true.

"She believed she saw a ghost," again Father's voice was full of derision. "Oh, how excited the society became; she could do it, she could see beyond the veil! A ghost, a glorious ghost, smiling at her, with hands held out beseechingly. But then she panicked and started to babble. *I do not want to see these visions. I must shut them out.* She raised her hands and tore at her eyes so that she could not. Arthur bolted forward to stop her, but she pushed him aside. Before it could be prevented, she ran from the room, along the corridor, and pulled open the front door. Arthur shouted after her as did some of the others, including that fool Stephen, but still she would not stop. *This is wrong. It is all wrong.* Her voice was so shrill. I had followed Arthur the length of the corridor, curious as to why she had reneged; to discover what had now terrified her; but I had the good sense to hold him back at the door; to slam it shut before anyone could realise which house she had appeared from."

"How did she die?" I asked, my voice reduced to a whisper again as I envisaged Constance's bewilderment all too well.

"She ran straight into the path of an oncoming carriage." He paused. "It was a sorry end," he added but without sentiment; without any evidence of emotion at all.

"And you shut the door on her?"

"I did, to protect the society."

"A society you are still a member of?"

He shook his head. "Not after this night. Who knows whether in the future it may develop, but it is not for me. I have outgrown it. In truth, it was never for me."

Selecting another tumbler that stood next to the decanter, he began to pour the liquid from the brown phial, after which he returned his attention to me.

"You will keep to your part of the bargain? You will take it willingly?"

I would, what choice did I have?

He advanced towards me, holding out the glass.

"Sip it now," he said. "There is no urgency. We have all the time in the world. In fact, I rather think the world is ours for the taking."

As I sipped at the bitter liquid, which burned my throat, I had yet one more question.

"Why have you outgrown the society?"

He leant forward, his breath in my face; one hand reaching up to stroke my shoulder in a manner that made me grit my teeth. "Because, Rosamund darling…" how he dragged that last word out; how he injected it not with love and kindness but with a scathing disgust, "…I want more than ghosts. And I always have."

Chapter Eighteen

MY mouth was extraordinarily dry. Never before had I tasted whisky, but suddenly I was desperate for it; for any liquor that would reduce this wretched condition I was currently afflicted with. Aside from that, my vision blurred slightly, and I felt nauseous – as nauseous as the laudanum had made me feel.

Would this succeed? Would I speak only the truth whilst under the influence of this drug? Time would soon tell.

It was not just the Scopolamine in Father's carpetbag, it contained his notes as well, and these he studied patiently whilst I was sitting back in the chair, waiting for the drug to do its work. He held various papers in his hand, studying them, and at times tracing his fingers over the symbols etched upon them. All the while he was muttering to himself; the only sound to break the silence.

Or was it as silent as I believed it to be?

This was not a house given to groans and creaks. At times, when I lay awake in bed at night, I would wish for some kind of life, but it never came; just silence… and shadows. Yes, there were plenty of shadows, from as far back as I could recall, and they were silent things, too.

Why was this? Because they wished to terrify me, even though I acknowledged them only in dreams, appearing as twisted, fearsome things, hence making me shun them further? Or was it because – like me – they were frightened also? They knew I would deny them. For years I was guilty of exactly that; at least my conscious self was, but not my sub-conscious, the latter guiding my hand. Only some shadows had stepped forward, Josie and Miss Tiggs; the others had all waited so patiently.

Until now.

From outside Father's study, in the corridor, there came a scraping sound, then a shuffling. Was it Josie who had returned to help me, or others, growing bolder at last; the past residents of the house of whom I so far knew nothing? There had been so many shadows in the townhouse too; in London itself. It seemed as if the whole world was filled with the dead as well as the living, clinging to whatever existence they could.

As Father gathered my drawings into a rough bundle and pushed them aside; as he placed his notes upon the table and remained bent over them, still studying them, and muttering, the nausea I felt threatened to overwhelm me.

"Father, I feel sick."

"Be quiet, Rosamund! Allow me to focus."

A moment later, he banged his fist upon the table.

"What is the matter?" I asked, my heart banging too.

"Some of this is hard to decipher." He said it more to himself than me.

"Is it Latin?"

He did not answer, but scraped his chair back, stalked over to one of the bookcases and selected a book. He thumbed through it, discarded it onto the floor and then selected another, doing this over and over again; the frown on his face growing deeper.

The noises from the corridor continued, but Father appeared oblivious to them.

"Damn it!" He said after a while, flinging the latest book from him to join the others in a pile at his feet. "I do not need books. I do not need Latin. I do not need *them*!"

"Who?" I asked. "The society?" Was it them he was referring to, his esteemed colleagues, pooling their resources in their relentless pursuit? Father had always appeared to me to be an educated man, but in truth I knew nothing of his education, not having talked of such things. Perhaps he was not as clever as we both believed.

Kicking aside whatever books lay in his path en route to where I sat, he grabbed the arms of my chair as he lowered his face to mine. "All I need is *you*."

I shrank back from him. He must have noticed, but he said nothing. He was consumed only with himself and his dark desires.

As he straightened, he reached for the chain of the ceiling gas lamp.

"What are you doing?" I asked, panic momentarily pushing aside any preoccupation with nausea.

"We need the darkness, so you can see."

"But I cannot see anything!"

"Do not lie. You must not lie."

"How can I lie when you have drugged me to prevent it? I am being truthful. I cannot see anything. Not in here. Please, Father, we need the light."

All too speedily it was extinguished.

There was a moment of quiet and then suddenly he

began to speak, not in English, but in a foreign tongue. He knew something of Latin after all, it seemed.

"What are you saying? What are you doing?"

Receiving no answer I continued listening. The same words were being used continually, over and over. It was a chant, I realised, a summons. An icy dread prickled my skin and I shut my eyes to yet more darkness, my head spinning now as the drug increased its hold on me; the bile rising in my throat.

"I shall be sick, Father. I shall!"

He stopped reciting and hope flared within me.

"Father, I need a receptacle of sorts."

There was only silence – even those outside the door had fallen quiet as if they were as tense as I myself was; listening in, deciding whether to flee rather than witness what was being invited here. Father began again, his voice more urgent this time and punctuated only by the taking of more whisky. He always drank, and often to excess, but his drinking now appeared as frenzied as his words.

"Voco... deus magnus... abundantia... divitiae... Clauneck... Clauneck... Clauneck..."

Able to pick up on that last word in particular, I asked what it meant.

"Not what, *who*," Father answered.

"Then, who?"

"He is a demon; one who is capable of bestowing great wealth upon his loyal followers. I need to reveal him; I need him to understand that I will bend the knee; that I will serve him with the utmost respect; that I will do his will, in return for riches."

I listened with disbelief. "So it is true," I breathed. "You have become a mad man."

"This is not madness, this is truth! Tell me, is he listening? Does he show his face?"

"If he does, I will refuse to look upon him."

"You will refuse nothing, not if you know what is good for you."

The threat in his voice was all too obvious. He was my father, but he was also a mad man, a murderer and now a demon-worshipper. Was it possible he would murder me if I continued to antagonise him, again with his bare hands?

"Tell me what you see."

Just darkness. Utter darkness. Oh this nausea! I had to keep swallowing and taking a deep breath, followed quickly by another.

"What is the matter?" he said, seizing upon my breathing as some kind of gesture.

"As I have told you, I feel ill!"

"NO!" On his feet, his fist once again resounded against the table. "Stop lying to me. You can see something. I know it. The phial, where is the phial…"

"No," I echoed. "I shall not take any more." Also rising to my feet, I was amazed at how weak my legs were, barely able to support me. I had to feel for the desk in front of me and lean against it. "I have told you, I am going to be sick."

No sooner had the words left my mouth than it opened further and bile rushed forth, with such a violent eruption that it fouled the desk, the floor and myself. My stomach was aching as well as my head; convulsing as I stood there clutching at it. "Father," my voice was so weak, "what was that drug? I am so unwell."

When he spoke, my entire body flinched. He was beside me, although I had failed to hear his approach. For a moment I remained hopeful that he would not continue in his pursuits if I was sick; that he would allow me to crawl back to my bedroom to lay upon my bed and attempt to combat the toxicity of what had assaulted my system.

Yet again that hope was dashed as he grabbed my shoulders and swung me around to face his desk; standing at the back of me, one hand holding me against him, the other lifting my head so that I was forced to stare ahead.

"What do you see?"

"There is nothing here."

"Do not lie!"

"I swear, there is nothing, not even shadows."

"Call his name out."

"No... I—"

"Say his name!"

"Clauneck."

"Again!"

"Clauneck."

"Again! Again!"

"Clauneck. Clauneck. Clauneck."

"Does he hear you? Is he there?"

"No, Father. No."

"You need more."

He let his grip loosen as he continued searching for the phial. I turned my head in the direction of the door. If only he had not locked it, I would pick up my skirts, take flight and continue running, past whatever it was that shuffled and scraped – that resided here as well as me – all the way to the top floor, to the attic. And once there, I would push something up against the door, keeping him without and imprisoning myself within.

Father had found what he was searching for and, returning to my side, grabbed my head as he brought the drug upwards. I clamped my mouth shut as he jammed it repeatedly against my lips, the contents spilling onto my chin and drenching me further.

With one hand I managed to restrain him and turn my head enough to speak.

"Drugs open the doors of the mind," quickly I had to force the words out, "that is the opinion of one of your colleagues. I heard him say so."

To my amazement he halted in his endeavours.

"Father, if that is so, then *you* take it. See for yourself that I speak the truth. Demons do not exist. This… Clauneck does not exist. There is nothing there."

As he released me, I fell back against the chair. I could hear him drink – not from the whisky bottle this time but from the phial, desperation now forcing him to heed my words and act upon them.

There were tears in my eyes, from not only fear, or the reek of vomit, but – surprisingly – from sorrow too. That it should come to this between Father and daughter; that a relationship that was devoid of emotion could actually deteriorate further. And the medicine I had told him to drink. What if… What if…

I shook my head, the movement causing more waves of nausea.

I waited to see… As did the entire household, spirit or otherwise.

Father had taken his seat; was murmuring under his breath, those same words. *Voco… deus magnus… abundantia… divitiae… Clauneck … Clauneck … Clauneck.*

I peered as he peered, into the darkness. Still there was nothing, his chant taking on an almost whining quality – *Clauneck, Clauneck …*

Father, how I wanted to say it again; *stop this. There is nothing.*

I was afraid of his reaction when he realised this to be true – that there was indeed nothing – as surely he must. Would the madness flee from him or would it drive itself deeper, thereby putting me at even greater risk?

As it sometimes did at Mears House, time became meaningless. I do not know how long we sat there; it may have been minutes; it may have been hours – and if it was hours, certainly the dark did not lessen; it remained as intense as ever.

Incredibly, I was growing sleepy. I found my eyes closing of their own accord and wondered if I should simply give in to it. It had been in dreams that I had seen Josie last; might she visit again, to offer the support I so desperately needed? But I had seen other things in dreams too – in nightmares. Did I dare to gamble?

Sleep is also a drug; one that was impossible to resist. My head fell forwards. There was darkness, but this time it was grey at the edges, and as soft as a blanket. *Josie? Josie? Where are you?* There was no reply, I called again. *Mother?*

A figure in the distance became apparent – a slight female figure, a curious light surrounding her.

Mother!

I was surprised to realise how easily hope could diminish dread. I began to run, forward this time, not back – and my feet felt light, as though I was not running at all; as if I was gliding, as Josie tended to glide. The closer I drew, the brighter the light became, but it was not painful, as staring at the sun would be painful; it was a light I wished to enfold me; to protect me; to keep me safe, forever.

Mother?

I drew closer, and yet still she remained out of reach. How long until I could touch her? Until I could see her? Gaze upon a face I had only ever seen in a photograph?

You had red hair and green eyes. I never knew that about you, I never realised. It is such beautiful colouring, delicate even. Is it you?

That newfound hope refused to abate.

I want so much to see you!

Someone was calling my name!

Rosamund… Rosamund…

Love as well as light filled my heart – but instead of feeling as if it was going to burst, it simply expanded. I never imagined a heart could be so big!

I was smiling, widely, from ear to ear. I was old and yet I was young, just like Harry, I felt ageless, weightless, as though I belonged.

The figure was reaching out and I reached out too. Soon our fingertips would touch for the first time. No, not for the first time, surely. *How did you die, Mother? When did you die?* Not a word Father had said about her; not one word. Had she held me when I was a baby? Loved me? Comforted me?

The haze was lifting; she was becoming clearer.

This woman. Her hair red when mine was dark; her eyes green when mine were brown. This mother of mine, the necklace still in place, draped around her neck.

"Mother," I whispered, suffused with joy.

But that joy was short-lived.

How wretched she appeared close up; so many lines on

her face and suffering etched into each and every one of them; such sadness and such despair.

No! It was not to be like this! My sense of joy must continue.

No! No! No!

How many times had I cried that recently? Too many, and yet it made no difference. No one heard my cries. Not now, not ever.

But I heard another cry well enough.

Chapter Nineteen

"FATHER, Father, what is the matter? Speak to me! What is it?"

I had woken abruptly and with one hand wiped at my mouth. It felt crusty, ingrained with filth. I looked from left to right, trying to understand what was happening – the reason behind such a commotion.

Father was no longer sitting; I could hear he was on the move and still crying, "No! No! No!"

With my dream pushed aside, if indeed it was a dream, I began to strain my eyes, desperate to pick out something; anything.

Still using the desk for support, I found my way around it, at the same time feeling for the candle that sat upon Father's desk, praying that the matches were close by.

"Rosamund," Father continued and his voice was a shriek. "He is here!"

"There is no one here." My intention was to remain calm and collected, although my hands were shaking hard enough as I continued to search. I found my way to the right side of his desk, for that was where I had last seen the candle. My hands reached out and sure enough, there it was; a small triumph, but one I was supremely grateful for.

As if afraid it might disappear from my grasp, I kept one hand upon it, the other still scrabbling for the matches. Were they on the desk too or in a drawer? If the latter, would there be time to locate them?

"He is here!" Father insisted. "I saw him. Hiding in the shadows."

The one searching hand becoming frantic now, I knocked over a tumbler and liquid splashed onto my hand, the peaty smell temporarily overriding all the others but hardly preferable. Where were the matches? We could not remain in the dark; we simply could not.

Here they were – a box that rattled when I picked it up. Another victory!

I had to work quickly; like Arthur before him Father was spinning out of control. Already I could hear banging and crashing as if he was trying to bat at something.

I was right. When the wick caught alight, it revealed Father close to the window, with his back to it and his head swinging vigorously from left to right.

If he registered the candlelight, he made no acknowledgement of it as if he had not noticed it at all; as if it was the one thing he could not see.

Although afraid, I forced my legs to move; the candle as much a shield as the necklace, which was still in my sleeve; safe. A few steps from him, I held the flickering candle aloft. His chin looked wet, as though it was covered in drool and his eyes were narrow no more, but wide and fit to pop.

I had been fixated on him, but I also needed to be alert to what else lay in the dark corners of the room; to see what had caused not just fear in my father, but terror.

There were shadows certainly, but empty shadows, I

was certain of it; no one or nothing daring to encroach.

I reached out and tried to reassure him. "I can see, Father. You know I can. And there is *nothing* hiding here."

Father slapped at my hands, as well as the air around him. "He is here! He is!"

Again I had to look, wondering if it was I at fault; if my wish had been granted and I was now normal and what ability I had, transferred to Father? An outlandish theory, but was not all of this outlandish? The shadows remained empty.

"Who can you see?" I asked at last.

"Him! Him!" he replied, pointing.

I looked at where he was directing me.

"I cannot—"

"Clauneck!"

Clauneck? "The demon?" I took a deep breath. My throat felt sore from my earlier retching and my head still pounded. "There are no demons. Demons do not exist."

Father tore his eyes from whatever had captured his attention, his lashes casting spidery shadows upon his cheeks. "You are wrong, Rosamund. There are; they do."

As if from a spring, he leapt from me and up to the bookcase. With both hands he began tearing at the tomes that lined the shelves.

"What are you doing?" I pleaded, desperate to understand.

"The answer," he gibbered, as around me so many hard-backed volumes crashed to the floor, their leather spines I imagined crumbling. "It will be in here somewhere."

There on the side table I spied the wax tapers, so took the opportunity to light one from the candle and set about illuminating the room with the ceiling gas lamp; a poor and dull light, but a welcome aid to the candle that I still held.

I drew nearer to Father; narrowly avoiding a book flung my way. "The answer to what?"

He paused, turned to me and once again I raised the candle. "He is not as I thought," he whispered as though now I was his greatest confidante. "He is…"

"Evil, Father?" I finished for him, as he seemed to struggle for words. "Did you think him a benefactor with no price to pay? Did you not expect this? You *wanted* to see him."

"If I served him—"

"Then you would serve the Devil, and no one and nothing is worth that."

"He wants my soul, Rosamund, but he offers me nothing in return. All his promises are false. He is a liar. Another liar, like you, like your mother." He lifted his hands to his hair and began to tug at it. "I am plagued by liars!"

I had to try and stop him. He was so agitated that it seemed he would tear it out if he continued, for tufts were already coming away in his hands. Placing the candle back onto the desk – feeling immediately bereft of it – I raised my hands too.

"Stop this! We can leave this house now if you wish; get away, far away; find safety somewhere. But I must reiterate, there is nothing here."

"LIAR! YOU ARE A LIAR!"

Tears sprang to my eyes that madness had him in its grip so completely. As much as I feared Father, I could not hate him – he was all I had, especially now – and without him I should be lost; another urchin on the street. And they were not safe, the streets; in so many ways they were not. I would be doomed; driven mad as well, surely?

Wiping at my eyes, sniffing loudly, I attempted to remonstrate with him again. This time he threw me from him just as he had thrown the books, sending me crashing against the desk, one of my hands flailing, trying to find purchase of some sort, to break my fall. In doing so, another of my fears was aroused. My hand knocked the candle, sending it flying to the other side of the desk where it teetered on the end and fell onto the floor, the flame not catching alight, trapping me in a burning room again, but snuffing itself out. As it did so, the ceiling gas lamp dimmed further and further, until it was barely even aglow.

"NO!"

Father's scream was spine tingling, as once more darkness reigned. I heard more banging and crashing as he hurled himself from wall to wall. In spite of my concern for him, I had need to protect myself whilst he was in such a dreadful state and so I crawled beneath the desk and curled myself into a tight ball.

Again time had no meaning; it may have been seconds, or it may have stretched into minutes that I hid there. Father would hurt himself severely if he continued; I dreaded to think of the bruises that even now must be blooming upon his skin.

I had not realised that I was crying until droplets of tears splashed upon my hands. Even if there was no demon, this was indeed hell, and I was in the pit of it.

If only I could close my eyes again; if only I could dream, but even in my dreams the respite was only temporary. Mother had not appeared to be at peace. Why?

Father was continuing to shriek; to scream, and instead of hugging my knees to my chest, I put my hands to my ears. Because I did this, it took me a short while to register that he had quietened.

"Father?"

I feared to leave the sanctuary of my hiding place, but as with the attic, how long could I stay there?

There is nothing out there, Rosamund, remember? It is all in Father's mind. The alcohol and the drug, when combined, were proving to be uncompromising.

That thought giving me reason, I began to creep forward, soothing him. "Father, I am here, be calm."

His shuddering form was but a few feet away. I had no desire to touch him but I forced myself. He was stricken, utterly stricken, but more than that, lost – reminding me of Constance; of Helena. Should one condemn such pitifulness, even if that person had brought it upon himself?

I touched his shoulder. He was in a position similar to that which I myself had previously adopted; curled into a ball and hugging his legs to him, like a child; as weak as a child, and certainly as vulnerable.

"Father, we must leave this room," I urged him. "It will be daylight soon, we can fetch help." Although from what quarters help would come, I had no clue; but surely there would be someone we could call upon. Never had I felt so alone. "All will be well, Father. It is the whisky, the drug. I believe that... together they have led you to hallucinate. But the effects cannot linger long; it will be over soon. All this will be over."

"No. No. No." His voice was childlike too.

"Father, let us take leave of this room; we can move to the drawing room, and wait there until morning. Then we can decide on a plan."

"Scared. So scared."

"There is nothing to be afraid of. All this… is in your mind. Let me help you to your feet."

As I began to tug at him, I expected to be slapped or pushed again, but to my surprise he acquiesced. "That is it," I encouraged – able to act the parent, even though he never had. "We are on our feet now. Let us move towards the door. There is really no urgency, we can take one step at a time."

Having reached our destination, I turned to him.

"The key, Father, I need it."

"Yes, yes," he muttered, patting at his pockets. "Here it is; here."

I took it from him, my own hands trembling just as much as his, which at first hampered considerably the task of unlocking the door. Hearing the lock slide back into place, however, was a huge relief. I was about to open the door when I heard a sound coming not from the other side – a shuffling or a scraping – but from behind me.

Rosamund.

I turned to face Father.

"Why are you lingering?" he asked. "Open it!"

"Because you called my name. That is why."

"Me? No. No, I did not. Open the door!"

"But I heard you."

"It was not me." He was equally insistent.

"Then who—"

Rosamund!

There it was again, interrupting me – more assured this time, *amused* even.

"Yes," I answered. "Who are you?"

As something rushed towards me; something that hid no more; that propelled itself forth from the deepest part of the shadows, the umbra, the part where no light exists, and no light*ness*, I did not question further. I grabbed my father's hand, yanked open the door, and as I had done so often in that house; I ran.

Chapter Twenty

I had opened the door. Father had opened the door. Very different doors and for very different reasons, but nonetheless, both allowed access.

As we hurried the length of the corridor, I was most aware of two matters: there was something at our backs; but there were also other things; shades, more shadows. For this was not an empty house; it had never been an empty house; it was teeming with life… or more accurately, past life. And imagination, I was certain that this was at work too. *Imagine good things, Rosamund, only good things.*

Damn this corridor for being so long; this house for being so large – it was as if we could run forever and not reach sanctuary. The attic was where we needed to go.

I still had hold of Father's hand; pulling him; forcing him along – an arrogant, selfish, vain man – a man that had instilled such terror in me; who was so formidable. How easily he had broken. That was proving as much a revelation as to what my eyes could now see, the veil having dropped to the floor in many respects.

The attic – I reminded myself – we must get to it without delay. Whatever was pursuing us – and I had no wish to know what it was – I had caught only a fleeting glimpse, and that had been enough; more than enough – would not follow us into the attic. Of that I was certain.

Father will not go in there either.

Oh, he would! I would see to it.

At last we reached the hallway, a vast space with a tiled floor, which no moonlight dared to penetrate. The stairwell was to our left, a yawning chasm. Who knew what we should encounter upon it? I could not stop and contemplate. There was no time.

"Father, this way!"

I began to turn towards the staircase, but to my surprise I found myself jerked in the opposite direction.

"Father, no!"

He did not respond to me, perhaps he was incapable of speech, but even if that were so, he had certainly recovered enough strength to be the leader rather than the follower, and it was to the door that led out into the open air that he directed me. To the woods…

"No, Father! NO!"

I tried my hardest to redirect him, but to no avail.

We had reached the door and with one deft hand he managed to open it. Immediately we were hit by a blast of icy air as together we plunged into the grip of winter, both ill clothed for the night. Our feet skimmed over gravel then grass as we flew along.

My breath rattling in my throat, my eyes streaming with the cold, my body seized by it, I managed to look upward. Where was the moon? Oh, but to see a glimmer of it, shining down upon me. There was nothing; not even the stars.

The woods, that was exactly where we were heading, Father intent on it but mistaken in his reckoning. Those tendrils, those wisps; what if they came for me again? We would find ourselves surrounded on all sides; at their mercy.

What were they?

Did demons really exist? I found myself questioning my own beliefs. Did they not dwell solely within the pages of books? But what was a book if not a story? What was this life if not something of a story too? The boundaries between fantasy and reality, between *thought* and reality – could they blur, as the boundaries between life and death could blur? I had previously witnessed the latter; I knew it to be possible. On this night *anything* was possible.

We had reached the edge of the woods and, without further hesitation we plunged deep into them, the bare branches of the skeletal trees seemingly welcoming us.

I considered Father's study to be his lair, but this was a lair too. Once more I was trapped; my body, my mind, and my spirit. I began to tug at my father, my free hand attempting to liberate the one that was enclosed in his. Again, it was to no avail.

As we ran over decaying leaves, these once welcoming branches began to turn against us, as deep down I knew they would; whipping at my face and tearing at my hair. If they were doing the same to Father, he gave no sign, so determined he seemed.

"We must stop," I yelled, "or we shall fall."

It was as I spoke these words that Father stumbled; a tree root most likely the cause. His footing lost, he fell, and therefore so did I, nearly landing on top of him.

I had no idea if we had outrun what had previously been at our heels, but now was not the time to investigate – not in the woods, in the dead of night, the very air around us freezing our bones through to the marrow. I had never ventured to the other side of the woods, and to my young mind they went on forever; but there must be an end, and if we could reach it – reach civilisation; other people; *living* people…

On my knees, I reached out both hands, my intent to pull us up. To my surprise, I found myself tumbling further as Father's hands pushed me away.

I fell backwards this time, my ankle beneath me twisting furiously.

I screamed with pain as I rolled onto my side, clutching at the injured leg – not a broken bone, surely? I could still flex my toes. A sprain then? If so, all was not lost.

Rather than watch Father regain his feet, my eyes searched frantically for a stick, one that I could use as a crutch, almost willing one into existence. I believed I knew, even then, that Father was about to abandon me. And this time, it would be for good.

A stick. I had to find one. I had to get out of these woods; not to the far side, but back to Mears House, to the attic. Stay there until… Just stay there.

My hands encircling a gnarled length of wood, I dared to look up.

"Father," I cried. "Please, you cannot leave me."

He had resumed running.

"Father. No!"

Oh, the emotions that ran through my body and my very soul, in endless circles, smashing into one another, over and over – the anger, the bewilderment, the hatred, the terror, the betrayal, and as Josie had said, the grief. It was wrong to allow such emotions; far better to stay calm, but I could not. They engulfed me; we were as one –

inseparable. But they were dangerous; so dangerous. The sheer force of them *attracted* things to me; negative things. They were doing so even now.

With no moon visible, the night was black, but those wisps that I had seen before, as slippery as eels, were blacker; and now they began to weave their way through the branches again, breaking off from the low cloud and becoming something else entirely. My jaw dropped open. I had a stick; I could haul myself up, but fear rather than the cold had rendered me immobile. Still they continued to weave, this way and that; seeking their quarry; taking their time; no need to hurry, just as Father had thought he had no need to hurry, I was not going anywhere. I could not.

There! With sightless eyes they had spied me.

Rather than wisps, they swarmed together to form a cloud of their own; a miasma; and as I watched, a part of me was mesmerised, fascinated even. Was it an ugly thing? Yes, yes it was that, but it was also beguiling. It appeared to want me and only me and that fact alone was seductive for none had wanted me before. What would it feel like to touch it? I let go of the stick and reached out. Would it be cold and hard, razor-edged? Would it shred my hands to ribbons, then my arms, and then my entire body? Or would it be something different; something quite unexpected? A void, but one in which there was at least a semblance of peace; a silence as profound as that to which I was accustomed; and I would exist at the heart of it, just as I had existed at the heart of Mears House - alone.

Tempting, it was so very tempting.

Indeed, after tonight, where else could I exist?

"Very well," I whispered.

I think I may have even smiled as the mass began to

swirl; to concertina; dancing for me; toying with me, knowing that I had succumbed; that it was the master.

Not as ugly now, but really quite beautiful. In its own way…

A scream – so wretched – pierced the trance I had fallen into.

Was it Father?

In the corner of my eye I yet again caught sight of something fleeting, and I tensed. Whatever *that* was, it was not beautiful. It was… obscene.

There was another shriek and even the mass in front of me shrank to hear it.

"Rosamund! Rosamund!"

He was screaming my name, just as he had done so many times before.

"Help me!"

My father. My jailor. The betrayer.

The spell broken, I retrieved the stick and struggled to my feet. The mass was no longer leisurely in its nature, but now had grown as frenzied as my father; angry perhaps at having had its carefully orchestrated performance interrupted. It was not beautiful and it had never been so. It was a liar. Another one. And I was not.

Not now.

My father's cries – his begging and his pleading – were terrible to hear. I had to reach him, convinced that whatever had him in its grip – *him*, I reminded myself, and not me; the thing that he had dared to summon – was now tearing him apart, growing teeth and claws that could rip into flesh and bone as if they were paper-thin.

But there was something that had me in its sights – still; that barred my way; that might not hesitate to do the same.

I could not help him. Why should I? He had never been generous to me. I could turn; flee again, as best I could. The attic – all I needed was to reach it.

I did turn, I began to hobble away, but that cry that filled the air; that 'please', drawn out with such terror… *But he is your father!*

Could I do it? Could I save him? And in doing so, would I save myself?

Harry came to mind and the message he had imparted about the necklace in Berkeley Square. *Protection.* Josie too, when I had stated – as if I had known – that soon I would see things I did not wish to see. Acknowledging this, she had counselled, '*That's when you need to draw on instinct, and act upon it.*'

Although my hand was shaking; although the night seemed darker than before; I reached into my sleeve and retrieved the necklace. I had to drop the stick to do so, for I needed both hands to drape it around my neck. It was armour, to be hidden no more. With the necklace finally in place, I turned back to face the mass, ignoring the pain in my ankle; my head that continued to ache, and the fear that wanted to cow me.

You can get tired of fear.

And I was tired. So very tired.

But I was also something else.

As my hand reached up to clutch at the stones about my neck, feeling their warmth penetrate my fingertips on such a cold, cold night, the energy that was at their core, *positive* energy, I realised exactly what – and who – I was.

I was Dickens, the creator of a character I admired; one that was plucky.

I was Josie, who had taught me the magnificence of the spirit world.

I was Constance, brave, tragic Constance; different, as I was different; who embraced both the darkness and the light, as I must now embrace them myself.

I was Mother; a woman who had meant for me to know her, in some guise at least, and who was with me even now, offering what protection she could.

And I was Father, who had taught me perhaps the greatest lesson of all; to deny my fear; to push it back inside me; to contain it.

All valuable lessons when you could no longer run.

Taking a deep breath, I limped forwards.

Instinct told me that whatever lay before me, I was not to nourish it further. I might be connected to some in the non-material world, but to others there was no connection at all, and nor should there be; in spite of how much they might seek it.

I hobbled on, bearing down upon the leaves; listening to their brittle crunch as they disintegrated beneath me.

How dark it was; how loud the screams.

"No more," I said. "No more."

I was so close now. I could have reached out and touched the mass as just minutes before I had wanted to do. It hovered ahead of me but, I noticed, it seemed to do so with uncertainty.

How I smiled to see that. How it bolstered me further.

I continued walking, straight into it.

It was cold inside – colder than a December's night could ever strive to be; a cold to stop your heart; to suck the life from it. And it would. It surely would. Had it not been for the necklace, I would have fallen to the ground, a husk, to rot amongst things that already lay rotten there. But Mother's necklace was warm, and its warmth was as hungry for the cold as the cold had been for yet more cold; as relentless.

In the heart of yet another hell, I saw what ugliness existed – every fear; every terror; every depravity and selfishness; every perversion; every murderous intent and all the anger and injustice which it encouraged; every petty, jealous thought that man had ever entertained, going around and around, endlessly, trying to make sense of itself; to become more substantial; to find something, *someone* to infect, to cling onto. I saw it and I continued walking, emerging the other side.

Knowing what I had just done, and that I had survived, caused all that I had carefully concealed within me to pour forth. I fell to my knees, the pain in my ankle no longer unfelt as great gulping sobs burst from my lungs.

I had done it; I had faced evil, the sum of all my fears, but was I the victor, truly? The things I had seen… what man was capable of… what could dwell so deep, if not within a person's soul then the cavities of his heart…

The darkness is a part of life; just as love is a part of life. You cannot escape it, but you can try and understand it, perhaps better than I.

To whom did that voice belong? Where did it come from?

"Constance?" I longed so desperately to see her. "Where are you?"

She was not anywhere and – miraculously – neither was the mass; it seemed also to have reached its conclusion.

All was quiet; there was no more screaming; no more cries; no one calling for me.

The darkest hour was over. Dawn broke to bring light back into my world once more.

Chapter Twenty-One

IT was not done yet. I still had Father to find, and he had run ahead of me. Why was he so quiet? What state would I find him in? And now, as imagination took over, as a series of visions once more flitted through my mind, he was a bloodied red thing; mere pulp, having been torn apart and ravaged; fed on as a creature feeds upon another in the wild, with nothing remaining to identify that he had ever been human.

Dread filled me. Again, I felt compelled to turn around, put as much distance between us as possible. How much could one person be expected to endure? But to turn my back would be to act as he did, and so I forced myself onwards.

What I saw shocked me even more than what I had imagined.

There was not a mark upon him. The only altered part of him was his hair. Always so dark, it was now white; pure white. I had read that this phenomenon could happen following deep shock but had not believed it to be true. He lay as still as the morning air, and the expression on his face – dare I say it? Dare I even hope it? – it appeared peaceable enough.

I had travelled to Hell and back and I had survived. But in spite of this fact, I was not invincible; I was not immune to all I had experienced that night. As I stood gazing down upon Father's face, his eyes closed forever, I could feel my body stiffening.

I was sixteen years old, soon to become seventeen. I fancied myself on the threshold of womanhood, but in that moment I felt very much the child, as lost as all those that had gone before me, my father especially. Had that which tormented him, the demon that he had called Clauneck, gone? Certainly, there was nothing here that caught my eye; no fleeting glimpse of a body, a creation of some sort, hiding behind a tree, ready to come rushing at me once again. But had I ever really seen him? Or had I merely reacted to Father? In conclusion, was that all this demon was: a creation. Something dredged up from the depths of a greedy man's mind – his mirror image, in other words? And if that was indeed the case, did that make him any the less dangerous? A demon was a demon, no matter where it originated. The wisps, however, I had seen them in their entirety. They had felt real – as real as Josie – attracted to all that was negative in me, whereas she… she was attracted to everything that was joy.

I could ponder it no more. I was spent.

Unsure of what to do with a dead man's body – for certainly I had not the strength required to drag him from his resting place – I embarked upon the journey back towards Mears House, alone. I came upon the edge of the woods soon enough, the mist not above the trees anymore, but covering the ground in thick layers.

For a moment I stood there, as I had done so many times before and looked towards the house with its many windows; its eyes. Yes, there were shadows at them, and there always had been – spirits I decided to call them, rather than ghosts, as it seemed more respectful, somehow – the shades of those who had long gone but who had also left something of themselves behind; their essence. I was not afraid. I had lived with them for years. Once human, they were *only* spirits. There were far worse things, I knew that now: born of the human mind, but never quite a part of it. Soulless, chaotic, desperate entities; as were all things born of negativity.

The mist soaked my boots and the hem of my dress as I drifted rather than limped through it, almost as if I too were a spirit. *One day perhaps, Rosamund, but not now.* When I died, would a part of me remain behind, forever attached to Mears House?

There was so much to think about; so much to discover. And I would face it, the unknown. I would make it my business to know it.

I reached the door to Mears House, still standing wide open, and continued to drift inside. There she was, Miss Tiggs, as sour-faced as ever. I stopped to address her. "You never did take to me, did you?" Her expression did not alter and so I shook my head. "I did not take to you either." There was only acceptance in my words.

As the townhouse had been, the entrance hall was crowded with people toing and froing: ladies, gentlemen, butlers, housekeepers and servants. It had never been this way in my lifetime, but it had been once, and this was proof. I could not make out these figures as tangibly as I could Miss Tiggs, but I could sense them well enough; how busy some were; how others tended to saunter; their happiness; their sadness.

Would I see Josie as I climbed the stairs? Would I see Mother?

On the landing, as I turned toward the corridor that led to another smaller corridor, I could hear the rattling of doors which drew something of a weak smile from me. All the times I had acknowledged the sound of it and attributed it to Josie, Miss Tiggs, Father or Father's friends, it had been none of them, but the others, all along. I fancied they were the closest I had ever known to having an extended family.

Behind me a door shut; a sudden sound that ordinarily would have caused me to jump or at least flinch. Now, however, it appeared normal, albeit *differently* normal.

There it was at last – the hidden staircase that led to the attic. I had caught Josie lingering at the bottom of it once.

I came to a halt in the exact place where she had once stood.

"Josie," I whispered. "Josie."

There was no reply.

If she had ever been there, she was now gone.

If, Rosamund?

Oh, why continue to doubt myself? There was no 'if'.

"You achieved what you set out to do," I said instead. "You equipped me." For the battle at least, the one I had recently fought. How many more battles would I face, however? Was I equipped well enough for them too?

I gently eased open the attic door and entered.

The little window at the back, to which I had often gravitated, allowed the light to penetrate; an extraordinary amount, considering its diminutive size. I had never once been in this room at night; surely there would be no light then; it would be as black as the rest of the house. I could not imagine it somehow. There would *always* be light here.

I needed to find a spot to sleep or risk collapsing where I stood. Already my eyes were closing of their own accord.

At the rear of the attic, the shaft of light pleasant upon my face, I finally settled with my back to the wall; my knees once again hugged to my chest. The door rattled once or twice but I ignored it, succumbing to my body's desire to rest; simply rest.

I do not know how long I was oblivious to all around me, but I awoke to the sound of my name being called.

"Rosamund. Rosamund."

"Mother?" I said, blindly reaching out, but no, it could not be her, and not Josie either. This was a male voice.

I thought fear was done with me. Clearly it was not. It enlivened my senses and pulled me rudely back to consciousness.

"Rosamund?"

"Father?" I said, my eyes snapping open. In death was he more daring?

But it was not Father that crouched down before me; a realisation that brought only mild relief, for it was one of *them*; the society.

"Stephen?" I said, pushing my feet out in front of me, kicking with them, as I tried to escape him. What a maddened thing he looked with his blackened hair; there was black around his eyes too, the whites of them so stark in contrast. A demon. He was a demon. Another. The nightmare continuing... perhaps... perhaps it had only just begun. As I managed to push myself up onto my feet, my mouth fell open to scream as Father had screamed, *savagely*; but not a sound came forth. Instead, only darkness filled my mind, and as I fell, I fell into his arms.

* * *

"My God, Rosamund, what has happened to you? Am I too late? I'm sorry, so sorry. I should have entrusted my instinct; I should have endeavoured to get here sooner."

When I regained my faculties, it was to find myself on the attic floor, cradled in this man's arms. Initially, as I swam my way back to awareness, I felt a sense of relief, of peace even; but then I remembered who it was holding me – the young man, Stephen Davis, a member of the *Society of the Rose Cross*, the group I held responsible for Constance's death, and nearly my own. I began to struggle, my legs kicking out once more, my arms flailing.

"You… you… fiend," I spat. "Get away from me."

"Rosamund, I mean you no harm!"

Managing to put at least a small distance between us, I protested. "You do! All of you do. If you associate with mad men then you must be mad yourself."

"Mad?" he whispered. "Rosamund, where is your father?"

"He… He…" Although there were no windows punctuating the wall, I looked in the direction of the woods. "He is dead," I said finally.

"Dead?" If I could see the colour of Stephen's skin beneath the soot, I knew it would be ashen. "Did you…?"

"NO! It is not I that is the murderer here!"

Sobs began to wrack my body.

"Rosamund…" Stephen crept closer and dared to put his arms around me again. I wanted to kick and punch; I wanted to scream for him to let me go, but I simply had no fight left. Instead I let him hold me, surprised to find that, once again, there was comfort in the circle of his arms. He clung to me and I clung to him, and suddenly it was lighter at the back of the attic – or perhaps it was that I *felt* lighter. Perhaps the two are inextricable.

Eventually I pulled away and looked into his sootrimmed eyes, noticing for the first time that his scorched hands were bandaged.

"You are safe," I whispered.

"So are you," he whispered back.

I remembered now how he had treated me. "You are not one of them?"

"Not now. Rosamund; there is merit in their aim, but not in their methods. There are some that take it too far; that do not know when to stop."

"Like Father."

"And like Arthur."

Fleetingly, defiance returned. "That man sacrificed his own daughter!"

Stephen shook his head. "She came of her own free will."

"But I did not! You tied me to the chair."

"I stood against that," he protested, reaching out and taking one of my hands in his. "Rosamund, hard as it is to believe, there *are* good men in the society, wanting only to understand the material world with which the spiritual appears to be so entwined. They are doctors, surgeons, and they are men of science. I myself am studying medicine. I work at a hospital in London and if you had seen as I have, patients near their hour of death; how they reach out to loved ones from long ago; how they insist they are present in the room; how joyous they become at this realisation, no matter their agony; how all earthly trials are simply…

forgotten, then… we cannot but wonder; try our hardest to make sense of it. That is all I was attempting to do. But men… even the best of men… and so easily the worst… can become…" again he hesitated, "…desperate. I am new to the society, but after Constance, after you, I am finished with it. I want only to live in this world; to help the living as I do. Perhaps it is *only* at the hour of death that we are meant to see."

Not always, I wanted to say, *not for some.*

"Why have you come to Mears House?"

"When I finally emerged from that burning room; when I ventured outside, I expected to find you there. I searched and I searched, but there was so much commotion. Finally I begged your London address from one of my colleagues and made my way there. At the door, I was told that you had left immediately for Mears House. I… I am ashamed that I turned back at that, thinking there was no more I could do and returned home." His eyes as he looked at me were so intense. "I roughly bandaged my hands – the burns are superficial, I assure you – and, exhausted, I fell on my bed and slept; but some hours later I awoke, and I knew… I just knew you were in danger. I had no time to clean myself up as I called for my driver to bring me here. It was unforgiveable that I had allowed myself to even sleep."

"How did you know where to come?"

"I have visited before, on just the one occasion."

Of course! He was the fair-haired man Josie and I had noticed when we had stood together in the drawing room and gazed from the window.

"Rosamund," his grip became tighter. "I am so sorry that I delayed."

"It matters not. You could not have prevented it. Not at the end."

"Prevented what?"

I shook my head as more tears began to fall. "I cannot explain now."

"Of course not. You have been through too much. Rosamund…" how gentle his voice was when he said my name, "…come back with me. To London, I mean."

London? Again?

"There is no need to concern yourself with me," I answered. "I am not alone here."

"What?" How perplexed he looked.

"I am not alone," I repeated, my voice barely above a whisper.

To my surprise, he released my hands and once again hugged me to him. Oh my sobbing, would it ever cease?

"Come with me, Rosamund, please. I will tend to you, I swear it. Our house is similar to the Lawton house; there are plenty of rooms in it. And Constance, what happened to her – how the society tried to shun responsibility for her death – I was against that too. I shall see to it that justice is done, and for her mother too of course; but those most responsible are already dead. Please, please come with me. I cannot leave you here. I cannot."

"I would be a burden to you."

"Far from it. It would be my family's honour to welcome you."

I pulled away and stared just as intently at him. "Why?"

He smiled, his teeth as white as his eyes, accentuated by the blackness of his face. "We can discover all the reasons why in the years to come."

A shiver ran through me when he said that, but it was

quite different to that which I had experienced before; it had an edge to it, but strangely no sharpness.

My instincts told me not to stay at Mears House; that this chapter in my life was over, but to go with him, to trust him – the man that had come racing after me, albeit with only the best of intentions.

I nodded and allowed him to lead me from the attic, along the corridor, down yet more stairs, past the hustle and bustle that only I could sense; the laughter – there was definitely laughter; a tinkling sound; a *bright* sound.

Miss Tiggs was at the entrance as we passed through, as we left the house of my childhood. I chanced a smile but it was not returned. Outside, Stephen's driver was waiting for us, huddled deep in his coat, the loud snores he was emitting disturbing an otherwise quiet morning. We listened for a few seconds and then we looked at each other and laughed, part of me marvelling I was still capable of doing so. Eventually, my laughter subsided as I remembered who lay cold in the woods.

"My father. What are we to do about him?"

Stephen thought for a moment, his brow also furrowing. "I will inform the authorities upon our return to London."

"They may hold me to account," I said, afraid again.

"No, they shall not. I will see to it. You are safe."

For the first time ever.

Stephen prodded the driver, who grumbled his way back into consciousness, clearing his throat in a rather pointed manner before taking up the reins.

Once seated, I looked back at Mears House from the carriage window. What would become of it?

As we drove away, I continued to look back; especially

at the attic, where there were no windows at the front. A thought struck me: Mother had left a photograph for me; she had left a necklace, both of which had been hidden. What if there was something else I had not yet discovered; something that *needed* to be discovered.

There is more armour coming, I promise.

"Rosamund." Stephen interrupted my thoughts. Having noticed me shivering, he was holding up a blanket, gesturing for me to drape it around my shoulders. I did so and he drew me to him, encouraging me to lay my head against his chest, the pair of us caked in filth and not minding one bit. *Safe. Right now, that is all that matters.*

And in that moment, happiness, *true* happiness, began to bloom.

Chapter Twenty-Two

'READER, I married him.'

I had a husband and I had six children – six! Five boys and the youngest – by several years – a girl: Sarah – a final blessing when we had already been blessed so much; a child who could see further than her brothers, which was something we encouraged; something we guided, Stephen and I. And, Reader, I also had a dog – a black Labrador, Jared, who sat with the children and adored them as we did – as faithful a companion as I had always hoped.

It was just before Christmas and all of us were in the drawing room of our townhouse in the Chelsea suburb of London – the Davis family in its entirety. Our eldest, Stephen, named for his father, was almost nineteen, and planning to study medicine, but oh, what a different life he had led compared to me; a comfortable life; privileged. Nonetheless I wished to think that he, along with all our offspring, was sensitive to others; not in the same way that I was sensitive, but in a way that mattered just as much; treating everyone as he would like himself to be treated – with respect and compassion. They all did; they made me very proud.

"Mama," it was my blonde-haired boy, Edward,

speaking. "The tree looks magnificent!"

His brother Paul nudged him. "Look at the gifts beneath it! Which is mine?"

"You will find out tomorrow," our youngest boy, Robert, assured him. "For tomorrow is Christmas Eve!"

Sarah had broken from the fray and gone over to the window. I knew what she was about and who would be there. He always came visiting at this time of year.

"Harry!" she said, her four-year-old chubby fingers pointing.

I went and stood by her side.

"I wish he would come inside," she continued.

I did too. I had beckoned him in on one occasion, but he had shaken his head. His place was outside, on the streets. He was an urchin; a guardian; a child with the eyes of someone who had lived a thousand years, or had been dead for the same amount of time. Guardians came in all shapes and forms; they could even be dogs or cats. Very often that was the case, something I had come to realise through my research at the psychical society; a society I had helped to found that was very different from the one my husband once belonged to; one he now shudders to remember; a society destroyed by its members' role in the death of Constance. Shunned by all in London, their endeavours came to nothing. In contrast our society was held in high regard. *I* was held in high regard. Our goal? Similar to theirs, it was to 'prove' as far as possible, to the sceptical; to those who were quick to damn; to those who clung to the constraints of a religion – a religion that strangely, believed in ghosts, provided they were 'holy' – that the paranormal existed; a world outside the normal – or what we, as humans, perceived normal to be. And this we did via a process of collation; collecting diligently the experiences of those who had encountered the paranormal; people willing to offer their experiences rather than be coerced into it. Of course I have included my own experiences, lately preferring to specialise in another area, one which a number of my colleagues chose not to study: that of the *non*-spirit, of which our understanding is still basic. My father's girl after all? No, for I seek to help them, not use them for my own personal gain.

Sarah was lifting her hand and waving.

"Yes, that is it," I encouraged, "wave to him. He enjoys that."

And it was not only she that lifted her hand, so did the boys. They saw what she was doing and ran over, accompanied by Jared, all of them, even my eldest, as excited by Harry's annual appearance as much as by the appearance of the Christmas tree itself.

"Harry! Harry! Hello!" Their shouting accompanied by Jared's barking amounted to a deafening roar, but Harry's smile became wider to hear it. The boys could not see him, only Sarah and I could, and, I think, Jared, for his eyes never strayed from the spot where Harry stood – but in our house such behaviour was blessedly common.

As Harry began to fade, I shooed the children away from the window, and gradually, one by one, including the dog, they left the room, involved in a game of *hide and go seek*. I resumed my seat by the fire and took up some paper and my pen.

Stephen bent to kiss the top of my head. "Rosamund, must you?"

"There are merely a few notes I wish to jot down and then I shall be done, I promise."

He took the chair opposite me. "You work too hard, you know that?"

"So do you," I countered, for he did, his work as a doctor consuming him sometimes, but he had stuck to the promise he had made at Mears House that day; he was finished with the dead, and tended only to the living. The dead were now *my* work.

Presently, I finished my notes and rose from my chair, crossing over to a bureau in which I kept my writing. The key was secreted in a vase high on a shelf. I retrieved it in order to open the bureau and place my notes in there. We did not hold with secrets, not in this house, but there were some things to which the young did not need access, at least not yet. Let them be children all the while they could!

When I had placed my notes neatly in one of the available drawers, my hand could not help but gravitate to another drawer, pulling at the handle to open it.

All the notes that Mother had written, at last I had found them – the final treasure.

"Darling, are you all right?"

"Yes," I said, my back still to him.

"Would you like some sherry?"

"Perhaps a small glass."

I heard him rise and cross over to the sideboard where the decanter resided. "Dash it," he cursed. "Empty. I shall ring for some more."

This time I swung around. "Why not save old Mrs Lovell's legs and go and fetch it yourself?" Rather like Miss Tiggs, she would be warming herself by the kitchen fire; *unlike* Miss Tiggs, she spoilt us, far too much, and I tried to reciprocate whenever possible.

"You are quite right, I will," Stephen conceded; dear

Stephen, handsome Stephen; my saviour; my equal.

He left the room and as he did so, the lights in the drawing room began to flicker. They often did, as if he took some of the light with him. A curious phenomenon and one I had documented, of course, in spite of the fact that he laughed whenever I told him about it. 'That is just you, Rosamund,' he would say, 'I doubt anyone else would notice a dimming of the lights when I left them.' I understood what he meant, but still…

Alone in the room, I withdrew Mother's notes. I knew them word for word, so had no real need to read them; I just wanted to hold them; to remember her.

We had gone back to the house years later, Stephen and I. I had an urge to see what had become of it since we had closed it up. I had had no more to do with it since, but suddenly, quite suddenly, something nagged at me to return; instinct I suppose you could call it.

The drive was as bumpy as I remembered; the villages, the towns, the countryside had barely changed, but the house *had* changed; it had fallen even more into disrepair – an old house, it had become as much a part of the countryside as the trees that shielded it.

As I alighted from the carriage; as I walked up the gravel path towards the front door; as Stephen heaved his body weight against it; as it finally yielded, I expected to sense at least *something*; the hustle and bustle of before perhaps. But there was nothing. The house was empty, quite empty; no furniture of worth remained and even the shadows seemed to have eschewed it.

"Where would you like to go?" Stephen had asked me.

"To the attic," I replied. "Just the attic, nowhere else."

His eyes were curious but he did not question further.

He chose to trust me, you see, just as I had chosen to trust him all those years before. Implicitly.

In the attic, there was still that familiar shaft of light – my eyes watering somewhat to see it. This room, this sanctuary, why was it so? We began to search, the two of us, pulling covers from furniture, revealing not the twisted limbs I had dreamt of as a child but fine, sturdy pieces that had been allowed to remain, thieves not daring to venture in here either it seemed. We looked in drawers, in boxes and in old leather trunks.

"What are we looking for exactly?" Stephen had asked at one point.

"In truth, I have no idea."

"But we keep searching?"

"We do."

But oh, how frustrating it was proving to be, when time after time our search proved fruitless. My eyes were watering again when I eventually stopped to look around, not just dust the cause, but dismay.

"Perhaps I was wrong," I breathed, as much to myself as to Stephen.

"Darling," his hand was gentle as he laid it not upon my arm but my stomach. "The baby, perhaps we should…"

The baby – our first – was lying deep within me, just as something was lying deep within this room.

An idea formed.

"The floorboards. We need to check beneath the floorboards!"

"All of them?" Stephen had looked aghast at the idea.

"No," I said, trusting myself implicitly too. "I remember once stamping my feet, I thought there was a rat you see, in the corner, and beneath me a board rattled as if loose. Rather than unsettle it further, I moved away from it. Oh Stephen, if only I had unsettled it further! It was a sign I think, another sign."

"Where is this board?"

"There, where the light shines."

Where it had *always* shone; where I had sat when I was young; where I had slept and where I had cried. The exact light that had been in Mother's photograph; a light she had created – clean, as Josie had said – pure. That was where the notes were waiting for me.

Now I hugged them to me once more as tears erupted from my eyes.

My darling mother, how she had tried to help me; to let me know what I could not possibly have known as a child: that what I saw, what I sensed, what I had denied for so long because I was confused and frightened by it, was an inheritance from her. She described it not as a curse but a gift, but she warned me that there were some who would seek to exploit it, as my Father had sought to exploit it. There was darkness in mankind, she said, and because of the gift, I would be able to see it, and be vulnerable to it. And of that darkness were born other things darker still; that lingered in the dumping grounds, as I tended to call them, on the edge of our senses, but always waiting to break through; to be given a purpose; to feed and to multiply.

Oh, how I knew this to be true; how I fought every day to remain in the light. Mother, however, had succumbed, but not because she was weak. She was not.

When we had left the decay of Mears House, I knew I would never return; I would let the land have it; the trees creeping ever closer, their bare branches like the lover's hand I had once imagined – possessive. I had found what I needed – more armour in the form of validation; the truth, or *my* truth at least. It had attracted me to the attic but had repelled Father; someone who could not face up to what he was; whose own demons had destroyed him, a host of them, not just Claunek. But more discoveries were yet to come. I could not forget the dream of Mother. When I had seen her in the distance, she had been a dazzling figure. When I drew closer, she had looked wretched.

She was a good woman. If she were dead, she would have been at peace.

If she were…

Like a woman possessed, I began my search for her, Stephen my ally as always. And we found her – we found my mother! Or rather a semblance of her.

She was in an asylum, in London itself, and had been since I was two years old. An old lady now: if her hair had once been red, it was now white; if her eyes had once been green, they were now as grey as her complexion. Stephen found us access to the hospital, one no better to my mind than the Bedlam Dickens had written about, a hospital that had long since been torn down. As I walked to her cell-like room I could hear the screams and cries of the inmates. They belonged not just to the living.

But Mother did not scream or cry, she was mute, quite mute, and although I introduced myself to her; although I tried to cling to her wrinkled hands and kissed her cheek a dozen times, she gave no response at all.

Locked-in Syndrome is what she suffered from, possibly caused by a stroke. A distressing diagnosis, it was not new to me as I had read about it previously in a book, fiction of course – Alexandre Dumas's *Count of Monte Cristo*, in which the character afflicted was depicted as 'a corpse with living eyes'. She was not expected to recover from her catatonic state and in that, the medical profession was correct, as she did not. She died four years later, on the eve that Sarah was born, and I liked to think at least something of her lived on in this child of mine, which was perhaps why I spoiled her so at times, trying to make up for what Mother endured.

As father had tried to bargain with the devil, Mother had bargained too, not with the dark but with the light, an even more formidable force. She could not prevent me from being born but she would make sure that the marriage produced no other issue, or rather pawns for Father to take advantage of. And me she tried to help in whichever way she could, through the photograph, the necklace, and her copious notes. *Remember me. I did exist. You are not alone. You are **never** alone.*

She had sent me Josie, I am certain of it; a woman so like her, who was there when I needed her most; who showed me what a mother's love could be; who taught me so well.

Anna Sarah Clermont was my mother's name and she had loved me; she had poured all her love into her words, until nothing was left inside and she had become a mere husk. Father had had no choice but to get her committed, because he was not a murderer, not then at least, that was to come as he deteriorated further; as he succumbed. The asylum, as grim as it was, had also provided her with sanctuary. There may have been indignities visited upon her, but the wall of light she had built would have offered further sanctuary still. Often I consoled myself with that thought.

Alone still in the drawing room, as Stephen had not yet returned, I wandered back to the window and looked out.

There are things one should never see. And there are things one should never be: intolerant, selfish, vain and greedy, but at times, we are; it is human nature, only natural. For as long as we maintain some semblance of balance, we can walk the line well enough. When we fall, however, the danger is that we fall into the abyss.

Harry is no longer out there; he has now gone; but there are others. Sarah cannot see them yet; she can only see what is good. But Father opened my eyes a long time ago to what else exists.

Waiting for my glass of sherry, I clutched at my necklace, feeling the warmth of the stones flood through me, and their staunch protection. I could feel Josie too, and Mother, as well as the lingering presence of my husband, my children and my dog, though they were in other parts of the house. I could feel Constance, and I marvelled at how happy she was, caught up in the throes of yet another journey. We were, as Josie had said, connected. Together, we stood against what waited in the shadows, although I lifted a hand, and I acknowledged it. I had only pity for it, you see; this thing that knows not where it belongs, only that it cries out; that it is hungry; that it is insatiable. It cannot harm me, however; not when such light surrounds me.

And that is the thing; the light is there if you look for it. It is there in abundance.

This is a good time to be alive.

Constance said that to me, and I agree, wholeheartedly. I have walked through Hell and I have emerged, to find that life is *surprisingly* good.

And that is why *I* write, not to alarm or to instill dread or fear into others, but to dispel ignorance, for ignorance is our greatest foe. If we remain in it, we remain lost.

The door opened and Stephen entered, brandishing the sherry.

"Sorry I took so long, darling, the damned bottle was hiding at the back of the cupboard. We had the devil's own job trying to find it, Mrs Lovell and I."

I laughed at his words, which were delivered with such innocence.

The devil's own job.

I write to keep the light shining.

The End

Also by the author

Eve: A Christmas Ghost Story (Psychic Surveys Prequel)

What do you do when a whole town is haunted?

In 1899, in the North Yorkshire market town of Thorpe Morton, a tragedy occurred; 59 people died at the market hall whilst celebrating Christmas Eve, many of them children. One hundred years on and the spirits of the deceased are restless still, 'haunting' the community, refusing to let them forget.

In 1999, psychic investigators Theo Lawson and Ness Patterson are called in to help, sensing immediately on arrival how weighed down the town is. Quickly they discover there's no safe haven. The past taints everything.

Hurtling towards the anniversary as well as a new millennium, their aim is to move the spirits on, to cleanse the atmosphere so everyone – the living and the dead – can start again. But the spirits prove resistant and soon Theo and Ness are caught up in battle, fighting against something that knows their deepest fears and can twist them in the most dangerous of ways.

They'll need all their courage to succeed and the help of a little girl too – a spirit who didn't die at the hall, who shouldn't even be there…

Psychic Surveys Book One: The Haunting Of Highdown Hall

"Good morning, Psychic Surveys. How can I help?"

The latest in a long line of psychically-gifted females, Ruby Davis can see through the veil that separates this world and the next, helping grounded souls to move towards the light - or 'home' as Ruby calls it. Not just a job for Ruby, it's a crusade and one she wants to bring to the High Street. Psychic Surveys is born.

Based in Lewes, East Sussex, Ruby and her team of freelance psychics have been kept busy of late. Specialising in domestic cases, their solid reputation is spreading - it's not just the dead that can rest in peace but the living too. All is threatened when Ruby receives a call from the irate new owner of Highdown Hall. Film star Cynthia Hart is still in residence, despite having died in 1958.

Winter deepens and so does the mystery surrounding Cynthia. She insists the devil is blocking her path to the light long after Psychic Surveys have 'disproved' it. Investigating her apparently unblemished background, Ruby is pulled further and further into Cynthia's world and the darkness that now inhabits it. For the first time in her career, Ruby's deepest beliefs are challenged.

Does evil truly exist?

And if so, is it the most relentless force of all?

Psychic Surveys Book Two: Rise to Me

"This isn't a ghost we're dealing with. If only it were that simple…"

Eighteen years ago, when psychic Ruby Davis was a child, her mother – also a psychic – suffered a nervous breakdown. Ruby was never told why. "It won't help you to know," the only answer ever given. Fast forward to the present and Ruby is earning a living from her gift, running a high street consultancy – Psychic Surveys – specialising in domestic spiritual clearance.

Boasting a strong track record, business is booming. Dealing with spirits has become routine but there is more to the paranormal than even Ruby can imagine. Someone – something – stalks her, terrifying but also strangely familiar. Hiding in the shadows, it is fast becoming bolder and the only way to fight it is for the past to be revealed – no matter what the danger.

When you can see the light, you can see the darkness too.

And sometimes the darkness can see you.

Psychic Surveys Book Three: 44 Gilmore Street

"We all have to face our demons at some point."

Psychic Surveys – specialists in domestic spiritual clearance – have never been busier. Although exhausted, Ruby is pleased. Her track record as well as her down-to-earth, no-nonsense approach inspires faith in the haunted, who willingly call on her high street consultancy when the supernatural takes hold.

But that's all about to change.

Two cases prove trying: 44 Gilmore Street, home to a particularly violent spirit, and the reincarnation case of Elisha Grey. When Gilmore Street attracts press attention, matters quickly deteriorate. Dubbed the 'New Enfield', the 'Ghost of Gilmore Street' inflames public imagination, but as Ruby and the team fail repeatedly to evict the entity, faith in them wavers.

Dealing with negative press, the strangeness surrounding Elisha, and a spirit that's becoming increasingly territorial, Ruby's at breaking point. So much is pushing her towards the abyss, not least her own past. It seems some demons just won't let go…

Psychic Surveys Book Four: Old Cross Cottage

It's not wise to linger at the crossroads…

In a quiet Dorset Village, Old Cross Cottage has stood for centuries, overlooking the place where four roads meet. Marred by tragedy, it's had a series of residents, none of whom have stayed for long. Pink and pretty, with a thatched roof, it should be an ideal retreat, but as new owners Rachel and Mark Bell discover, it's anything but.

Ruby Davis hasn't quite told her partner the truth. She's promised Cash a holiday in the country but she's also promised the Bells that she'll investigate the unrest that haunts this ancient dwelling. Hoping to combine work and pleasure, she soon realises this is a far more complex case than she had ever imagined.

As events take a sinister turn, lives are in jeopardy. If the terrible secrets of Old Cross Cottage are ever to be unearthed, an entire village must dig up its past.

Psychic Surveys Book Five: Descension

"This is what we're dealing with here, the institutionalised…"

Brookbridge housing estate has long been a source of work for Psychic Surveys. Formerly the site of a notorious mental hospital, Ruby and her team have had to deal with spirits manifesting in people's homes, still trapped in the cold grey walls of the asylum they once inhabited. There've been plenty of traumatic cases but never a mass case - until now.

The last remaining hospital block is due to be pulled down, a building teeming with spirits of the most resistant kind, the institutionalised. With the help of a newfound friend, as well as Cash and her colleagues, Ruby attempts to tackle this mammoth task. At the same time her private life is demanding attention, unravelling in ways she could never imagine.

About to delve deep into madness, will she ever find her way back?

Blakemort:
A Psychic Surveys Companion Novel
(Book One)

"That house, that damned house. Will it ever stop haunting me?"

After her parents' divorce, five-year old Corinna Greer moves into Blakemort with her mother and brother. Set on the edge of the village of Whitesmith, the only thing attractive about it is the rent. A 'sensitive', Corinna is aware from the start that something is wrong with the house. Very wrong.

Christmas is coming but at Blakemort that's not something to get excited about. A house that sits and broods, that calculates and considers, it's then that it lashes out - the attacks endured over five years becoming worse. There are also the spirits, some willing residents, others not. Amongst them a boy, a beautiful, spiteful boy...

Who are they? What do they want? And is Corinna right when she suspects it's not just the dead the house traps but the living too?

Thirteen:
A Psychic Surveys Companion Novel
(Book Two)

Don't leave me alone in the dark…

In 1977, Minch Point Lighthouse on Skye's most westerly tip was suddenly abandoned by the keeper and his family – no reason ever found. In the decade that followed, it became a haunt for teenagers on the hunt for thrills. Playing Thirteen Ghost Stories, they'd light thirteen candles, blowing one out after every story told until only the darkness remained.

In 1987, following her success working on a case with Sussex Police, twenty-five year old psychic, Ness Patterson, is asked to investigate recent happenings at the lighthouse. Local teen, Ally Dunn, has suffered a breakdown following time spent there and is refusing to speak to anyone. Arriving at her destination on a stormy night, Ness gets a terrifying insight into what the girl experienced.

The case growing ever more sinister, Ness realises: some games should never be played.

This Haunted World Book One: The Venetian

Welcome to the asylum…

2015

Their troubled past behind them, married couple, Rob and Louise, visit Venice for the first time together, looking forward to a relaxing weekend. Not just a romantic destination, it's also the 'most haunted city in the world' and soon, Louise finds herself the focus of an entity she can't quite get to grips with – a 'veiled lady' who stalks her.

1938

After marrying young Venetian doctor, Enrico Sanuto, Charlotte moves from England to Venice, full of hope for the future. Home though is not in the city; it's on Poveglia, in the Venetian lagoon, where she is set to work in an asylum, tending to those that society shuns. As the true horror of her surroundings reveals itself, hope turns to dust.

From the labyrinthine alleys of Venice to the twisting, turning corridors of Poveglia, their fates intertwine. Vengeance only waits for so long…

This Haunted World Book Two: The Eleventh Floor

A snowstorm, a highway, a lonely hotel…

Devastated by the deaths of her parents and disillusioned with life, Caroline Daynes is in America trying to connect with their memory. Travelling to her mother's hometown of Williamsfield in Pennsylvania, she is caught in a snowstorm and forced to stop at The Egress hotel – somewhere she'd planned to visit as her parents honeymooned there.

From the moment she sets foot inside the lobby and meets the surly receptionist, she realises this is a hotel like no other. Charming and unique, it seems lost in time with a whole cast of compelling characters sheltering behind closed doors.

As the storm deepens, so does the mystery of The Egress. Who are these people she's stranded with and what secrets do they hide? In a situation that's becoming increasingly nightmarish, is it possible to find solace?

Jessa*mine*
The Jessamine series Book One

"The dead of night, Jess, I wish they'd leave me alone."

Jessamin Wade's husband is dead - a death she feels wholly responsible for. As a way of coping with her grief, she keeps him 'alive' in her imagination - talking to him every day, laughing with him, remembering the good times they had together. She thinks she will 'hear' him better if she goes somewhere quieter, away from the hustle and bustle of her hometown, Brighton. Her destination is Glenelk in the Highlands of Scotland, a region her grandfather hailed from and the subject of a much-loved painting from her childhood.

Arriving in the village late at night, it is a bleak and forbidding place. However, the house she is renting - Skye Croft - is warm and welcoming. Quickly she meets the locals. Her landlord, Fionnlagh Maccaillin, is an ex-army man with obvious and not so obvious injuries. Maggie, who runs the village shop, is also an enigma, startling her with her strange 'insights'. But it is Stan she instantly connects with. Maccaillin's grandfather and a frail, old man, he is grief-stricken from the recent loss of his beloved Beth.

All four are caught in the past. All four are unable to let go. Their lives entwining in mysterious ways, can they help each other to move on or will they always belong to the ghosts that haunt them?

Comraich
The Jessamine Series Book Two

"The dead of night, Jess, I wish they'd leave me alone."

Comraich – Gaelic for *Sanctuary* – that's what this ancient fortress of a house in the Highlands of Scotland has offered its generations, a haven from the world beyond.

The nesting instinct kicking in, a pregnant Jessamin decides that Comraich, which she shares with her partner Fionnlagh Maccaillin, needs refreshing. Getting to work in one of the spare bedrooms she makes a startling discovery, one that pulls her into a world of the intense and disturbing passions of others that have been here before.

Jessamin has to decide.

Will delving deeper into Comraich's history bring hope and peace to this troubled house or return her to a darkness she's only recently left behind?

www.shanistruthers.com

Printed in Great Britain
by Amazon